Morristown Centennial Library
Regulations
(802) 888-3853
www.centenniallibrary.org
centenniallib2@yahoo.com

Unless a shorter time is indicated, books and magazines may be borrowed for four weeks, audio books on tape and CD may be borrowed for three weeks, and videos and DVDs may be borrowed for one week. All library materials may be renewed once for the same time period.

A fine of five cents a day every day open will be charged on all overdue library books and audio books. A fine of one dollar a day every day open will be charged for overdue library videos and DVDs.

No library material is to be lent out of the household of the borrower.

All damage to library materials beyond reasonable wear and all losses shall be made good by the borrower.

Library Hours

Sunday & Monday	Closed
Tuesday	9:30am – 7 pm
Wednesday	9:30am – 7pm
Thursday	10am – 5:30pm
Friday	10am – 5:30pm
Saturday	9am – 2pm

DIRTY LOVE

ALSO BY ANDRE DUBUS III

———

Townie

The Garden of Last Days

House of Sand and Fog

Bluesman

The Cage Keeper and Other Stories

DIRTY LOVE

ANDRE DUBUS III

W. W. Norton & Company

New York London

For information about permission to reproduce
selections from this book,
write to Permissions, W. W. Norton & Company, Inc.,
500 Fifth Avenue, New York, NY 10110

For information about special discounts for bulk
purchases, please contact W. W. Norton Special Sales
at specialsales@wwnorton.com or 800-233-4830

Manufacturing by Courier Westford
Book design by Barbara M. Bachman
Production manager: Anna Oler

LIBRARY OF CONGRESS CATALOGING-IN-PUBLICATION DATA
Dubus, Andre, 1959–
Dirty love / Andre Dubus III. — First Edition.
pages cm
ISBN 978-0-393-06465-0 (hardcover)
1. Man-woman relationships—Fiction.
2. Life change events—Fiction.
I. Title.
PS3554.U2652D57 2013
813'.54—dc23
2013017214

W. W. Norton & Company, Inc.
500 Fifth Avenue, New York, N.Y. 10110
www.wwnorton.com

W. W. Norton & Company Ltd.
Castle House, 75/76 Wells Street, London W1T 3QT

1 2 3 4 5 6 7 8 9 0

for Fontaine

CONTENTS

———

DIRTY LOVE

LISTEN CAREFULLY

AS OUR OPTIONS HAVE CHANGED

———

A<small>T FIRST THERE IS ONLY THE COFFEE TABLE IN FRONT OF HIM,</small> a swath of sunlight across its glass surface. There's the neat stack of women's magazines, the TV remote lying perfectly parallel beside them. There is the oak floor and yellow wall, the tiled kitchen and granite countertop, the closed bedroom his mother left hours ago because it is almost noon on a Saturday in July and he is waking once again in the garage apartment he built for her. There is no dust, no empty cans or glasses, though his mouth is salt and ash and a familiar ache grips his head. He closes his eyes, but there's the video again. The picture is color and high-resolution. It is a bright spring day in a park in New Hampshire, and there are patches of snow on the ground. Mark Welch has not seen this in a while. The first weeks it came daily, but then, as things have become what they have, he's stopped seeing it so often and its power has faded. Still, he'd rather not see it now and he'd only made himself watch it twice, both times on the Sony flat-screen in the living room of the main house, his heart kicking like a hanged man's feet.

The sun is shining through pine trees onto a clearing of vacant picnic tables and an empty fire pit, its cinderblock walls scorched black. Just beyond it is a two-door coupe, a white import, its trunk closed and facing the camera. The doors are closed, too, and now the lens slowly moves in as if the one filming does not wish to startle. There, in the front seat, a man behind the wheel talks in profile to a woman. He is bald from his own hand, the way so many men are now, choosing to shave away thinning hair so as to appear younger, still virile, though the effect is coldly narcissistic. He is talking and smiling at the woman. Her hair is long and tied back in a ponytail, and now the camera zooms too quickly so there is only the reflection of pine branches in the import's rear window. The frame of the image shifts slightly, pulls back, and the woman is visible again, her small curved nose, her left eye, how it turns down at the corner when she laughs, the way she does now with the bald man behind the wheel. This was one of the first things Mark had noticed about her, and he had seen it in the movie theater in that silly romance they went to that first time, how when she'd laughed he'd half turned in the flickering glow and watched her face; there were other things he'd noticed before that: there was her voice, tentative but somehow decisive too, the sound of one who consistently willed herself through fear or embarrassment. There was her thick, straight hair falling down her back like a girl's and not the thirty-one-year-old showing him condominiums along Pickering Wharf in her navy business skirt and white blouse, those runner's legs leading to maternal hips. And it was the way she smiled at him in the realtor's office, as if she'd been waiting for him for years and now that he'd finally come she was shy about it.

But in the video, in that front seat of that two-door under the sun-mottled pines in the park, there are gray streaks in her hair that has thinned over the years. There are small bags under her eyes that turn down as she laughs. There are lines at the corners of her lips.

And what about those other changes? Though to the man behind the wheel, there are none for he has only known her a few months, maybe a year, so even though he has probably visited her flat belly and seen the stretch marks—light purple and in a vertical pattern—between her navel and pubic hair, they can mean nothing to him, not like they do to Mark. No, he used to kiss them with gratitude, a sign not just of the births of their daughter and son, grown now, but of her body's aging alongside his, a measure of their two and a half decades together.

In the video all this is covered by her nylon jogging suit because they've both just run side by side in that park in New Hampshire, the bald man behind the wheel and Laura. He and she have run together in the woods and now the man passes her a water bottle and she drinks. In seconds, she will lower the bottle. She will smile at the bald man behind the wheel and he will lean toward her, then sink out of sight. In seconds he will sit up and place Laura's running shoes on the rear dash, then Laura will lift her hips to make things easier for him, and soon there will be only Laura sitting behind the wheel of this two-door import, her head back, her hand gripping the dash as the bald man does to her what he does, and Mark Welch, the husband of Laura Welch, who twenty-four years ago was Laura Murphy, he now stands in his mother's garage apartment, his temples pulsing, and he walks through her dim bedroom into the bathroom.

He uses the toilet, splashes his face with cold water three times. He squeezes his eyes shut, and there are the smells of toothpaste and chamomile and cotton. In the darkness he sees the reflection in the swimming pool from last night. He'd been sitting at the round table near the diving board sipping Bacardi with a splash of Coke, his second or his fourth. He'd been watching his wife through the kitchen window, watched her rinse her plate or glass from hours earlier, watched her load them into the dishwasher. When Mary Ann and Kevin were small, when the house was full of their friends and various cousins, that machine would be filled and emptied twice a day, but Mary Ann is in business school down in Cambridge and

Kevin has dropped out of Pratt to design his own video games in a cramped apartment in Brooklyn, so now, while her cuckolded husband lives with his mother in the attached garage, only Laura Welch inhabits the house and it will take her a full week to fill the machine with what she's used and left dirty.

Maybe she knew he was out there beside the pool alone after midnight. But probably she did not for just before she flicked off the kitchen's overhead light she studied her reflection in the window. It was the look a mechanic gives a car engine she knows very well, checking the trouble areas first, then those—thanks to good design and her own hard work—that are still reliable; it was the look of a woman who knows there are probably fewer miles ahead of her than there are behind her, but right now the ride is fairly smooth and there are places along the way to look forward to, places where she will not have to be alone, and for this she's grateful.

Then there was nothing, only a black window and the yellow glow of the exterior light, its still reflection on the pool's surface. Mark stared at it and sipped, stared and sipped. It has not been a smooth ride for *him*, has it? No, it has not. But there's a distance now, a distance from everything. Work and all its endless tasks, his mother and her constant caring for him up there in that apartment he built her—cooking for him, pouring him a drink, making his bed on the couch, trying to get him to talk about Laura and the eviction and divorce his mother insists he must demand. There's the distance from his own body. He'd never kept it as fit as Laura had hers, but he had not neglected it either. He didn't smoke, didn't eat badly, had always drunk moderately, getting drunk only two or three times a year. He occasionally lifted weights in his basement, or jogged for half an hour around his neighborhood, and in the summer he'd swim laps in his pool till he was tired and he would climb out and sit in the sun beside his solitary, sunning wife.

But now his body feels like some dumb beast he merely exists inside, and every now and then it lets him know it needs him to do something: To eat. To piss or shit. To move or just lie down and rest.

He does not remember climbing the exterior stairs to his mother's apartment and couch last night. He does not remember how long he sat near the pool in the dark or when he left the bar where he'd been earlier. But he remembers the woman's face. Not Laura's at the kitchen sink but the one in the parking lot. She wasn't much older than Mary Ann, probably thirty or thirty-one. They'd been talking at the bar under all the noise, the loud mindless chatter, the blaring sound system—ghetto rap that made Mark feel like some white relic from a forgotten time—the drunken laughter of young men in tight T-shirts showing off their gym muscles, tans, and tattoos. It was a place for people his kids' ages, and Mark felt conspicuous in his Tommy Bahama silk shirt, his slightly gelled hair combed back, the silver glint of his Movado wristwatch, a gift from his company after delivering the Infinity Systems project two weeks early. In the bar mirror behind the top-shelf vodkas, under the amber light of the lamps hanging from a tin ceiling, he did not appear unattractive to himself. Or, to be more precise, he did not appear unattractive to a woman he almost hoped might be looking. At fifty-six, like his very own Laura, his hair had thinned and there was more of his upper forehead visible now, but there was only a scattering of gray at the temples, and his face, while lined around the mouth and under the eyes, the skin more loose under the chin, was still the face he'd had all his adult life, his blue eyes deep-set, his chin not square but not weak either, his teeth small but fairly straight and still in his head.

A drunk woman was talking to him. She had too much makeup on in some places and not enough in others. Her eyes—blue or green or brown—seemed unadorned above cheeks caked with some sort of blush that was supposed to hide acne scars, though Mark could still see them, and he felt immediately sorry for her till he took in the rest of her—her braless breasts behind a bright green sleeveless tube top, her tanned belly, the faded denim skirt riding too high above smooth legs and small feet in high heels, her nails painted an almost fluorescent orange. What he felt then was something other than pity, though now, as he leaves his mother's bathroom to make coffee in her galley kitchen, he does not remember what that was only that he was surprised the woman was talking to him and he began talking back. It was about music. He had to lean closer to hear her.

"I ate wrap."

"You ate a wrap?"

"No." Her voice had been warm and moist in his ear and he could feel it in his groin, a stirring where for months nothing had stirred.

"No, I hate *rap*!"

He nodded in agreement. He was drawn to her: her hatred for this music; her warm, wet voice in his ear; her smell—fruity perfume, cigarette smoke, and coconut oil. Then they were outside in the rear parking lot leaning against her car smoking menthol cigarettes. He wasn't sure why he said yes when she'd offered him one, but he smoked it like a cigar, inhaling only to his jawbone before blowing out the smoke and watching it rise in the light of the neon beer signs in the bar's windows a floor above them. And he watched her profile as she talked on and on about something he only vaguely remembers now staring at his mother's coffeemaker. But then the woman was no longer talking and they were kissing hard up against her car, a ten-year-old Chevy sedan. They were kissing and her tongue was in his mouth. He remembers how soft her lips were, how she tasted like menthol and beer. He remembers his erection pressing against his pants against her tanned belly above that faded denim skirt, and there's the feeling, though far away, as if it's floating ten feet above him, that something precious has been irrevocably ruined, and it is not he who should be held accountable. No, not at all: it is Laura, his very own Laura who sleeps alone in their king-size bed, who eats alone at their kitchen's peninsula, who watches TV alone on the sectional sofa in their living room, and does she still watch those same shows? The crime dramas where so often a family's life appears ordered and comfortably predictable and then one early morning a man or woman is soon watching her own nest burn?

Almost always, however, it is the husband who does it. This is Laura's view, too. It's his fault. Even for this. Eleven weeks and four days ago, she is filmed spreading her legs for another man's tongue after having just exercised and so she must have still been sweating quite a bit and yet the bald man did it anyway and she said, well *screamed* really. "It's because of *you*! All you do is *criticize* me! I'm never good enough no matter what I fucking *do*! You *made* me do it!"

"I made you do it." He was still breathing hard, one hand resting on the kitchen's tiled peninsula. At his fingertips was a pool of water and bits of broken glass. Behind him three chairs lay in various pieces on the floor, the heavy birch table on its side, one of its legs gone. Above him, the light fixture was swinging slowly back and forth, its glass face undamaged, the bulbs inside unbroken, though it was hanging by its wires and there was a gouge in the ceiling where the chair he'd swung over his head had scraped the sheetrock before hitting the light, then the floor. This was a detail he would not notice for hours, but he would remember her screaming face and how the light, swinging slowly overhead like that, made her appear as if she were on a night train heading somewhere away from here, away from him, her contorted, raging face so lovely in its betrayal.

She had called ninety minutes earlier. The sun was low in the trees behind their house, and Mark let the phone ring until the machine picked up. His fingers were steady as he turned up the volume and listened.

Hey, it's me. I had a late showing and now I'm off to the gym. There's leftover lasagna in the fridge. Be home soon.

Mark played the message back three times. What struck him were four things. One, she referred to herself only as *me*, as if no one else could be calling him, as if she were rightfully the only other *me* in his life. Two, she ended her message with no subject: *Be Home Soon.* By using no *I* or *will*, she was removing herself from whatever would precede her returning home, which meant that when she called she was heading to be with Frank Harrison Jr., for that was the bald man's name, and maybe she was even sitting in his white two-door import—a 2009 Audi TT coupe—about to unzip his pants. Or, maybe they were driving to that Marriott on the highway two towns over, the one Mark had seen in the second video, Laura and Harrison holding hands as they walked in, then—forty-three minutes later—walked out, their arms around each other's waists. Maybe Frank Harrison Jr. was driving with one hand on her knee while she called her husband, and what did he feel when she advised Mark on what there was to eat? Did he *hear* that? That people cooked for each other over here? Ate with one another? Did he hear the word *home*?

Three, her voice. It was high in her chest, the way it had sounded both times she'd walked into the living room, her pregnant belly stretching the cotton of her nightgown, and said, "Honey, I think it's coming." Both times it had happened like that, late at night, her walking in to announce to him in front of the television that he needed to help her go do something momentous. Four, her choice of words: *There's leftover lasagna in the fridge. Be home soon.* Work with me, honey. Sit down and eat and believe I'm in Pilates class at the gym. Help me do this thing I must do.

Thirty minutes after dark her Civic pulled into the driveway, the security light switching on as if this were any other night. Maybe that night, a cold Wednesday in March, she and Frank Harrison Jr. had driven to the Marriott down the highway, and afterward, in the hotel bathroom, she'd had to sit on the toilet and let the bald man's semen drain from her, for she was fifty-five years old and birth control was no longer an issue and so there would have been no need for a condom. There were diseases to think about, but would she consider this? Mark didn't think so.

He had stood at the darkened living room window and watched her rise up out of the Civic, slinging her gym bag over her left shoulder, her pocketbook over her right. Her keys were clutched in her fingers. There had been a few moments, an hour or two after staring at those videos, when he'd considered changing the locks, barring

her from this house they'd shared and maintained since their early
thirties. She would try the front door, then the rear, maybe a panic
rising in her before she climbed the side stairs of the garage to his
mother's apartment. But Mark couldn't have that. Not then at least.
He would not have his mother involved in this in any way. There was
something else too; to kick her out would be to send her into the arms
of Frank Harrison Jr.

So he'd left the locks as they were, and he'd stood in the center of
the darkened living room and listened to her walk into the kitchen
and set her gym bag and pocketbook down. There was the clank of her
keys beside them, then a quiet stillness, something missing. Usually,
after a long day at the realty office or out showing properties, then a
strenuous workout at the gym, after she'd stepped inside and relieved
herself of whatever she was carrying, there would come an exhalation
of air from her, a sigh—part exhaustion, part relief. But that night she
seemed to be standing in the bright kitchen holding her breath.

Maybe she could sense him out there, the TV remote in his hand,
the DVD cued just to where he wanted it. He could feel his heart
beating in his tongue, and he wished he'd been in the kitchen when
she walked in. That's where he'd usually be, waiting for her as eager
and ignorant as a half-blind dog, dinner on the stove or in the oven
because he got home before she did. No, that wasn't quite true. Many
nights he would wait for her to cook, and he'd be in the living room
on the sectional, his work computer open on his lap, CNN on the
television, slickly packaged semi-intellectuals speaking earnestly into
the camera. She'd walk in and he'd glance up at her over the rim of
his glasses, pucker his lips for a kiss which she'd lean down and give
him, just a brush of lips really. So it was the dark quiet living room
that had probably stopped her. "Mark? *Honey?*"

Honey. How nice.

"In here." His voice had felt old and unused. When he leaned to
switch on the lamp the room tilted a moment before righting itself,
Laura walking in. She was in her nylon running suit and white Nikes

with the pink stripes. Her hair was pulled back in a loose ponytail, and it looked like she'd applied fresh blush to her cheeks. Her eyes appeared a bit sunken, though, those slight bags beneath them that never went away.

"Did you fall asleep?"

The word *no* was in his throat, but it wouldn't come out, and Mark, like the athlete he'd been in high school, the fast and reckless wide receiver, the diving shortstop, aimed the remote under his arm at the TV behind him and watched her face as the image lit up the screen. At first, there was nothing. She was simply watching her silent husband turn on the TV behind him, his back to it. She was watching and waiting to see just what was happening before her. Then there was the gray light of the television on her face and it took only a few seconds; it was as if she'd been burned; her eyes widened and her lower lip twitched and she turned and stepped quickly toward the kitchen.

Mark's movement was a thing he would never remember, only the feel of her arms and ribs and belly as he picked her up and pulled her back and swung her around to watch the show. There were her kicking feet, and there were her screams—fear there, and desperation, and hatred. Yes, hatred. Her hair had fallen to each side of her face and she was looking only at the floor so her husband had no choice but to place his palm against her forehead and pull back till she saw it, Frank Harrison Jr. and her in the white Audi coupe, his profile sinking out of sight, but she twisted away, his always fit and physically strong wife, and she was shrieking, "I can't believe you! I can't fucking *believe* you!"

Then she was past him in the kitchen and what could he do but follow? What could he do but race ahead of her and block the doorway? What could he do but flip the table into the air? What could he do but stomp off its closest leg and start swinging chairs over his head down to the tiled floor, six of those tiles still cracked now eleven weeks and four days later, the three chairs still splintered and left in the garage, the three-legged table upside down in the corner of the kitchen so Laura had to eat at the peninsula, or maybe off her lap in the living room while she watched shows of families being devastated by one of their own.

MARK DOES NOT MAKE COFFEE. He has taken two Motrin for his Bacardi headache, and he needs something cold and sweet to drink. A Coke. He has none left, but there may be some in the fridge of the main house. He peers out the side window overlooking the pool. Normally on a July Saturday afternoon, Laura would be lying in her bikini on a chaise longue on the concrete soaking in the rays that by September left her darker than any of their friends. Mark would sometimes warn her about the weakened ozone layer, the increased likelihood of skin cancer, but she would half smile at him behind her sunglasses and say, "You worry too much, Mark."

It's true. He does. He always has. But what's a senior project manager to do if not to anticipate threats and opportunities, to manage risk, to deliver the finished project on time?

The poolside is empty, the sun too bright off the concrete pad. Mark steps to his mother's hall closet, the one she has cleared out for him, and he undresses, then pulls on shorts and a shirt and walks to the front window overlooking the driveway and street. There is only his BMW sedan. Laura's space is empty beside it, which means she's with tall, bald Frank Harrison Jr., a man Mark now knows many things about: he knows that Harrison is fifty-three years old, his fifty-fourth birthday coming in August. He knows that at six foot one he weighs two hundred and eleven pounds and was a wrestler at Boston College, undefeated in his weight class his senior year. Mark knows that Harrison has nagging sciatica for which he sees an acupuncturist every Tuesday afternoon at 4:45 p.m., and that he lives in a three-story white Federalist with his oblivious wife on High Street in Newburyport, that town nine miles east that at one time was an abandoned cluster of tannery mills and shipyards at the mouth of the Merrimack River, but for years now has been so gentrified that tourists travel to its downtown boutiques and restaurants, its coffee shops and pubs and bookstores, its waterfront theater with a view of pleasure boats moored on the water or cruising east under the bridge. It's the town where Frank Harrison Jr. will stroll with his wife of twenty-three years on a Saturday evening, and they will dine either at a lobster place on the marina, or eat Italian or Thai in the square of clothiers and day spas that used to manufacture leather.

Mark knows that Anna Harrison is a narrow-hipped, large-breasted woman with an automatic smile. That she works part-time as a legal secretary in a law office six blocks from their Federalist, and she usually walks there and back, her sandy hair shoulder-length and pinned away from her face, a face Mark would consider still attractive were it not for that smile and her eyes that, glancing up from the sidewalk in front of her, appear to him weary and slightly dumbfounded and a bit frightened too, as if to do anything other than what she does every day might invite catastrophe. Or perhaps he's wrong about that. Maybe she's just constantly thinking of their children who are no longer under her daily care: Frank III, Thomas, and Gayle, the younger two in college—the boy a hockey player at Bates, the girl at the University of Florida at Gainesville, Frank III following his father into the banking business, though not at Providential where Frank Harrison Jr. is a commercial loan officer, a well-groomed fleecer of the public who arrives at work between 8:13 and 8:17 a.m., who parks his white coupe in front of the concrete river wall behind the bank in this upriver town where, just two miles east, there's the gym Laura has been a member of for twelve years. It's where she stretches, lifts light dumbbells, takes classes in yoga and Pilates. It's where she does all this, then goes running after for she never lets anything come between her and running. Even when she was pregnant with Mary Ann and Kevin, she ran into their third trimesters. It's a habit she developed as a withdrawn child growing up in central New Hampshire, a solitary activity that matched her solitary nature.

That's how she'd always explained it to Mark anyway, that she needed time to herself, that she never should have gone into real estate because it's a job that forces her to talk to people, but that's also why, Mark would tell her, she's been so successful at it; prospective buyers can sense just how little she cares whether they like the property or not, that what she really wants to do is be done with this walk-through, pull on her sweats and Nikes, and run away from them all; this is the softest sell possible and so she sells more than most, her lack of charm a quality Mark had come to trust for he always knew where he stood with her. Other women, women like Anna Harrison, seemed to smile on reflex, as if this were something they were taught to do as young girls—be nice, be pretty, nice *is* pretty—and so you never knew if a woman was genuinely pleased with something you'd said or done, or not. But Laura only smiled when she felt like it, her eyes turning down at the corners, so it was a gift to them all when she did, a gift to Frank Harrison Jr. too, who must have charmed her into doing that at the gym, the place he drove his Audi coupe to every Monday, Wednesday, and Friday, pulling out behind the bank between 4:33 and 4:39 each time, driving through town along the river, past the brick post office and the old Whittier Hotel, past the music shop and Pedro Diego's Mexican restaurant and the insurance office above Valhouli's Barbers that has been there since Mark's father was a boy and he would go there for a nickel haircut and years later, when he was husband to Dorothy and father to Claire and young Mark, he'd own two of the abandoned mills near Lafayette Square, one he sold for a profit, the other he lost so much money on he spent fewer and fewer nights at home, going instead to the bars of Railroad Square till he was hardly ever home at all. After a while, only a year or two, it seemed, he was no longer Bill Welch, property owner and entrepreneur, but Welchy, who drank boilermakers with off-duty cops and men from the mills, Welchy who bought dawn breakfasts for old waitresses and young

runaways, Welchy who ran up tabs he couldn't pay and who died on
a moonless night in February in the backseat of a '63 Impala that
belonged to a man who had gone through the dead drunk's pockets
and called the Welches' house at two-fifteen in the morning. Mark
Welch was still a boy then, but he remembers his mother's voice on the
phone in the hallway outside his bedroom. He remembers the crack of
light beneath his door like some unnatural fire he would never escape.
"Are you sure? *William* Welch?" There was some kind of wire being
pulled through her words, one that was about to snap. But then she
said, "Thank you. Thank you very much for calling." And Mark could
hear the phone being set carefully into its cradle. He heard little else.
Only his own heartbeat; for the first time it was no longer in his chest
but in his head, something steady he listened to between his ears even
as the police car pulled in front of the house, even as the front door
opened and closed twice, even as he began to hear the nearly calm
voice of his mother telling Mrs. Steinberg from next door to let them
sleep until they wake up, let the poor children sleep.

But there was no sleeping. There were his mother's words on the
phone from earlier, and there was his father's name, and there was
Mark Welch's heart having moved up to his head where, all these
years later, he'd heard it once again as he watched those videos he'd
paid an investigator from Boston to film, heard it as he walked by
Anna Harrison on the sidewalk, heard it as he followed her husband's
white coupe three cars behind as Frank Harrison Jr. drove past the
car dealerships on River Street, the machine shops and boarded-up
Dairy Queen, past the Exxon station and Dunkin' Donuts, then
across the highway overpass for the turn to the gymnasium on the
hill where he'd met and wooed the apparently restless and unhappy
Laura Murphy Welch.

THE HOUSE IS TOO COOL and smells like itself. Fabric softener from
the laundry room, rust in the pipes, floor varnish where the sun's

been shining through the windowpanes all morning. Laura has the air conditioner on too high and goose bumps rise along Mark's forearms as he opens the fridge. How empty it seems. In the bright space there are five or six containers of strawberry yogurt, a carton of eggs, jars of condiments, raw hamburger meat wrapped in plastic. On the bottom shelf, behind a grapefruit, two cans of Coke lie on their sides like forgotten children. He pulls one out and opens it, its sudden spray surprising him, but not really. He ignores any mess he's made, and drinks long in the open doorway of the fridge.

He belches and tastes last night's rum. He's been drinking too much too often. He knows this. If he were a team member on one of his own projects, Mark would identify himself as a possible risk and he would begin to monitor and control that risk, for if he did not, he could become a threat to the long-term integrity of the project.

But what if the larger project has already been jettisoned completely?

Mark closes the refrigerator door and glances over at the upside-down table in the corner. The broken leg lies in the middle of it between the other three. It is a clean break, the upper part of the leg splintered but still fastened to the tabletop. To fix it, all he has to do is glue and clamp.

He stares at the floor. Six cracked tiles. He still has a box of them in the basement from when he'd hired a crew to lay a new floor five years ago. It would be more work to replace those. He'd have to break them up fully, wouldn't he? Pry the pieces up off the dried mortar bed, scrape the old mortar down to the subfloor, then, on and on. He is tiring just thinking about it. He glances up at the light fixture. It's back where it belongs, Laura having fixed that one herself.

He takes his Coke and walks through the dining room. They'd only used it for holidays, and it seems impossibly small to him now, the table covered with a lacy runner down the center, the silver candelabra there in the middle with its five new ivory candles, their wicks still white and coated with wax. It was a wedding gift, and when did

Laura apply that wallpaper border along the tops of the walls? It's one continuous illustration of cows grazing in a field, and it had taken her all afternoon, a Sunday not so long ago because the kids were gone and Mark would walk through the room now and then and ask her if she needed any help. She was in shorts and a dark top, her long hair pulled back. She was standing on their stepladder, the adhesive roller in one hand, the other on the border she was slowly rolling against the wall, her reading glasses at the tip of her nose. She'd said, "No, honey. Thanks," and kept working. Mark stared at her long runner's legs, a varicose vein behind her left knee. He stared at her ass and her hips and straight back, and he watched the twitch of the smaller muscles in her forearm as she smoothed the cows along. All these years and she was the only woman he'd slept with, a fact he gave himself no extra credit for, for that's what he'd vowed after all, but he'd wanted her then as fiercely as when they'd first begun to make love in their early thirties in that condominium she'd sold him on Pickering Wharf. Later that afternoon, after the border was finished and their dining room looked more colorful but cheerfully antiseptic, like something from the kind of home magazine Laura enjoyed reading, Mark had brought her a bottle of light beer and stood beside her as she pointed out two air bubbles in the corner above the door. They were in shadow and she hoped no one would see it. He could smell her sweat and that deeper woman smell that Laura's sweating gave off, and he pulled her to him and kissed her deeply, her glasses still at the end of her nose. A surprised sound came out of her, and she pulled off her glasses and dropped them on the table and soon they were making love on the carpet, her shorts and underwear around one ankle, the stepladder inches from her lovely head.

Mark drains the Coke and leaves the can on the dining room table. He climbs the front stairs to the second floor. He avoids the kids' rooms and walks down the hallway into the bedroom he no longer considers his. Very little has changed. There is the same coral duvet spread across their king-size bed. Three decorative throw pillows are

stacked in a pyramid on top of where both their heads used to lie, and
he can see she's taken another pillow and put it where his was before
he'd carried it to his mother's next door. On her bedside table is a
magazine, *Runner's World*. A page is marked with a subscription flyer,
and he sees that she's reading an article of advice on running in all
four seasons, something she's been doing for years so why does she
need to read this? And isn't it interesting, he thinks, that she no longer runs alone but with Frank Harrison Jr., that that time she needed
so badly for herself she's given so readily to another?

He closes the magazine and walks to her bureau. It's a dark walnut that matches his smaller one, now empty, on the other side of the
room. The surface of hers is as clear and spare as it always was. There's
the jewelry box sitting on the lace coverlet. There's her antique hair-
brush and comb and hand mirror, though she only uses the large one
against the wall in front of him. In the upper corner of the mirror,
stuck between the glass and the wood frame, are photos of the kids
when they were in middle school. The pictures have been there for
years, and many times Mark has leaned closer to study them, but not
today. Today he notices the mirror is tilted down at a slight angle,
something he'd probably done months ago just before he and Laura
had made love late on a Saturday night or early on a Sunday morning.

Laura preferred being on top, and Mark would sometimes peek
around her shoulder and hair to see their reflection in the mirror, to
see himself penetrating his lovely, athletic wife. Once she'd caught
him doing it and whispered, "That turn you on? Huh? You like a
show?" He hadn't answered, just kissed her deeply, but he liked how
game she was, how she'd always seemed to enjoy their lovemaking as
much as he did. Over the years they'd heard of friends of theirs who
made love rarely, maybe once every two to three months, if that.

This was something Laura would tell him, for husbands did not
offer that kind of information, though one did, Charlie Brandt. It
was a pool party at the Welches'. The yard was crowded with friends
and their kids, some of them grown. One was the Salvuccis' daugh-

ter, a dark-haired university student in a bikini, and it was hard not to linger on her as she walked barefoot and flat-bellied under the sun to one of the coolers for a beer. Charlie had nudged Mark. He'd leaned closer, smelling of gin and hair gel. "I got one just like that."

"Marie know this?"

"You shittin' me? But hey, she's got no leg to stand on, brother. She stopped fucking me soon as she got fat and she's been fat for *ten* years."

Mark had never liked Charlie much. He was an insurance salesman who stood too close to you and talked too loud, mainly about himself. But his wife was Laura's friend from the Salem realtor's office and so he'd become a regular at the Welches' various parties, and now Mark judged him for cheating like that. Charlie kept talking. Mark had turned over the chicken breasts on the grill. He squinted in the smoke and glanced at Marie sitting with Laura and three other women at the umbrella table. She was a heavy Italian woman with a kind and pretty face, and she was laughing at something one of the others had said and Mark felt sorry for her then and told himself that if Laura ever shut him off he'd go to counseling and do whatever it took to get her back, but he wouldn't cheat like Charlie Brandt who was now wandering off in the direction of the Salvuccis' daughter in his Bermuda shorts and flip-flops, his gin and tonic in his hand like a conversation starter.

Mark opened the top drawer of Laura's dresser. Fifteen or twenty pair of panties were rolled up and nestled beside one another, three neat rows of pink and pale blue, beige, white, and even a few red. Did she wear those for Frank Harrison Jr.? He pictured her standing before him as he lay waiting on the Marriott's bed. Did she shuck them off quickly so they could get to it? Or did she make a dance out of it, something she'd never done for her husband?

That's when he'd first felt the cool draft of suspicion blow between his ribs, when she'd done something entirely new. It was a weeknight, and they'd both gone to bed early. He was tired and distracted, thinking of his next project, an alternative search engine whose design they had to deliver in fourteen months. He was the lead

PM and already suspected the scope of this was too large for its pro-jected cost and time required. Laura's lamp was on. She was reading a novel for her monthly book club, this one by a woman writer with an Indian name. Mark lay on his back and began to plan the meeting he would have to run the following morning.

He'd have to bring in all the principals, sit them down in the Mauer Conference Room at the long table that could seat twenty-two. His first few jobs as project manager, he'd sit in a chair at one side or another, his suit jacket off and his tie loosened, just one of the many contributing members of the team. At the time he was a believer in Motivational Theory Y, that all people are naturally driven and all you have to do is treat them with respect, hold the bar high but not unattainably high, and set them loose.

But his first two projects were managerial disasters. They were completed, but they came in weeks late, over budget, and three of his people had quit halfway through. He'd almost lost his job, but Teddy Burns gave him a second chance. He called him early on a Friday morning, Laura and the kids still in bed, and said, "Retraining Day, Mark. Come in in hiking gear, running shoes if you don't have boots. See you at seven."

It was early May. They drove up to the White Mountains, a two-hour ride in Teddy Burns' black Range Rover, Mark's young, fit, and prematurely bald boss behind the wheel. Mark sat beside him in the Nike sweatshirt Laura had bought him the previous Christmas. On his feet were the worn sneakers he reserved for yard work, and he sipped from the insulated mug of dark roast he'd brewed at home, sipping it slowly. He looked out at the weeds alongside the highway, the newly leafed-out trees, and he tried not to feel patronized and insulted by all this.

Teddy Burns was a lanky vegetarian who supervised every proj-ect manager on the East Coast. Before rising to upper management, he'd delivered some of the biggest projects the company had ever contracted: Elco Systems right before they went public; Bascomb's

Internal Review software; and Zebra Inc. right after the Chinese bought every share of its stock. He had a girlfriend he called his partner, an angular blonde attorney who at office parties sipped Pinot Grigio and eyed the roomful of project managers before her as if she were there to make some sinister but necessary decision about them.

While Teddy drove he'd been talking about new software applications on one of the many electronic gadgets he owned, something to do with GPS systems and the world's dwindling supply of water. Mark nodded and sipped. He responded when needed, but he was from a generation of phone booth users, people who grew up with just a few channels on the TV you couldn't get without fiddling with the antenna on top, a generation of people who went out and bought a hardcover book or vinyl album and then had to wait till they got back home to read it or listen to it; they didn't download them from wherever they were, sampling one song or chapter before pressing a button to skip over to another.

"You're a big sister, Mark."

"What?"

"Like right now. You don't give a shit about my new apps, but you're acting like you do."

"I thought we called that being polite."

Teddy Burns was staring at him, one hand on the wheel, his eyes expectant yet scrutinizing. "Polite's one thing. Being a big sister's another." He shifted into the passing lane though there was no one to pass. Mark could feel the effortless acceleration of the Range Rover, his head pulling back slightly against the leather headrest. "Is this when you go after my manhood, Teddy?" He was surprised he'd said it. Teddy Burns could fire him before he even eased up on the gas. He could pull over and tell Mark to find his own way home. But Teddy was smiling and shaking his head.

"I knew it. I knew there was a real PM in you somewhere. Boston wants me to send you packing, but here's what I know: you're playing the role of big sister, but you're really the mean little brother."

"Pardon me?"

"You heard me."

Burns was right. When Mark and his older sister Claire were kids, especially after their father died, Mark had always hated being left out. More than once, whenever she was set to go to a party without him, he'd let all the air from a tire of her Camaro. He'd listen in on her phone calls for anything he could blackmail her with later. If she didn't lend him five or ten bucks, he'd call her fat and ugly, two things she was not, though he suspected Claire secretly thought she was. Every American girl did. "Yeah, well, whatever. I appreciate your giving me another shot, Teddy."

"Not good."

"What's not good?"

"You just established your edge with me and now you're softening it by sucking up. That's Weak Matrix, man."

"How's that Weak Matrix?"

"Because now your people don't know who's in charge—the edgy guy with balls? Or the smoother and compromiser?"

"I wasn't compromising—"

"No, but you were smoothing. That's what you did for the Laity account, and you did it even more with Converse."

"I had to keep them happy, didn't I?"

"Yes and no." Teddy accelerated past a lumbering motor home with California plates. Its driver was silver-haired and tanned, his plump wife beside him, all their putting-up-with-bullshit-like-this forever in their rearview mirrors. Teddy shot past them over a rise into a banking curve. Off to the left was a sloping valley of pines and blue spruce, mountains looming over them like benevolent big sisters.

"Smooth things out with the client, yes. But do not be the smoother and compromiser with your own team. That gives *them* the power. If they can't work out a solution to a task, then you *force* them to."

"What? Put a gun to their heads, Teddy?"

"See, good. Keep that edge. Hold on to it. Look, do you know *why* I am where I am?"

Because you're a self-absorbed prick.

"Do you?"

Mark could feel Teddy Burns staring at him. To the north, snow lay lazily in a ridge between two peaks. "Because you're not a big sister."

"True, but that's not what you were going to say. What did you really want to tell me?"

"That's it."

Teddy slowed for a curve. Mark sipped his coffee, tepid now, bitter. Fuck it. "That you're a self-absorbed prick, that's why."

Teddy Burns started to laugh. He glanced over at Mark and laughed harder. It was high and unrelenting, like the guttural chatter of some exotic monkey, and Mark began to laugh too.

"Stellar, man. That's *stellar*. I *am* a self-absorbed prick, which is why they pay me so fucking well. Your problem is you've subscribed to the wrong motivational theory. That's what big sisters *do*. They believe everyone has their heart in the right place at the right time and all you have to do is point them in the right direction. *Wrong*. People are naturally fucking *lazy*. They'd rather lie around all day eating, fucking, and scratching their balls. That's why pricks are needed, my friend. It's called micromanagement and it works."

He went on from there, gleefully lecturing as he parked the Rover in a dirt lot in a sunlit clearing, continuing to make points as they both began to climb a shaded trail under the pines, and while Mark still didn't much like Teddy Burns, he admired how he could climb and talk without being winded, but more, he admired his insight into him, Mark Welch, who on this mountain hike over ten years ago, began to feel free now to work the way he'd been pulled to for a long while yet was semiconsciously ashamed of himself for; he'd always wanted to sit at the head of the conference table, not alongside the others, and he'd never felt right taking off his jacket and rolling up his sleeves elbow to elbow with his team. Instead, because he was overprepared for each project and knew it, because he had done his goddamned homework, he'd wanted to issue directives, to delegate and wait, to monitor and control risks, to send his people off to do what he damn well told them to and then to complete the project under budget and on time.

Since that morning with Teddy Burns, despite a few, but only a few, backward steps, Mark had become overwhelmingly successful. He had earned himself a reputation as an immensely productive hard-ass, a PM who was consistently given all the important projects because he could be counted on, even before the project commenced, to prepare and to plan, as he was doing that weeknight as he lay beside Laura reading her book, picturing himself in the Mauer conference room the following morning, addressing his new team, already searching for any negative and positive risks, and that's when Laura had sidled over, run her hand across his hip, and began to play with his balls.

At first it was just her fingertips, a light scratching, and at first Mark had barely noticed. He was thinking of Lucas O'Brien, a software engineer they'd hired as a consultant who would have to be given, once again, a written set of tasks and a firm deadline. He held a doctorate from MIT and encouraged others to view him as somewhat absentminded, a genius of course, so he'd be free from the same constraints everyone else was forced to work under. Now Laura's head was under the covers and when she took Mark into her mouth, he made himself forget Lucas O'Brien and the rest. He closed his eyes and lay his hand on her back. He felt grateful for this distraction, grateful he had a loving wife doing this to him now, though she'd never done it quite this way before, cupping his balls as she did what she did with her mouth. And a few moments later, as she straddled him the way she preferred, she'd reached behind and touched them again, twice, these testicles of Mark's she'd barely seemed to notice before. It was like being with someone in the woods who has just read an Audubon guide on trees, then seeing her awakened appreciation for them, the novelty of them.

After, as he lay beside her in the dark, her breaths rising and fall-ing in an easy sleep, he could feel again the touch of her fingertips on his testicles—tentative, then inquisitive, then, as she cupped them in her palm, comparative; she seemed to be *comparing*. And not one against the other either.

Mark's face had flashed with heat. He seemed to be lying more still than he had been just one heartbeat earlier. He turned his head carefully on its pillow and took in what he could see in the darkness: Laura's narrow back to him under the covers, the strap of her night-gown over her bare shoulder, a wisp of hair. Through the curtains came the shadowed glow of the streetlight in front of their sidewalk, yard, and home, all of which felt to him, in this moment of unwanted clarity, suddenly imperiled by some malicious presence he should not be so surprised at only just now discovering. For there were other details to consider: her more frequent trips to the gym, sometimes two on Saturdays—one for weights, she said, the other for Pilates or yoga. Her longer and longer runs. There was the way she'd been greet-ing him at the end of the day. There was still the brush of her lips on his as he sat in front of CNN, but there was also how happy—yes, that was the word—how *happy* she seemed at dinner. Just the two of them sitting side by side at the island or sometimes at the round table they'd used when the kids still lived here. She'd ask him questions about his day and work, and she really seemed to be interested in whatever he told her, her eyes on his as she chewed and sipped and swallowed, her hair down around her lovely, muscular shoulders. She'd ask him follow-up questions, too, even technical ones that should have bored anyone. "*Did* he enter those stats into the program?"

And this revived interest in him made Mark ask *her* questions about her day, questions he actually meant, which told him there'd been a time when he did not really care what she told him, but he forgot about that, enjoying instead his revived wife and her renewed interest in him, the way, after dinner, they washed dishes together side by side, how, if it was warm enough, they'd then go for a walk down their street past their neighbors' homes, half-acre lots like their own, the houses set back away from the street.

They'd walk along in the twilight, chatting about what they saw—a broken bird feeder in front of the Kazarosians', a new satellite dish on the roof of the Doucettes', the screened porch being built onto the back of the Battistinis'. Often, Mark and Laura would talk about Mary Ann and Kevin, and Laura's voice sounded lighter even then, as if she knew she'd done her best with them and now it was up to their children to live their own lives; it was as if she'd finally accepted something in herself Mark hadn't even known she'd been wrestling with; he'd always seen her as a good mother. Loving, attentive, consistent. Hadn't *she*? When had these changes in her begun?

He kept seeing the leaves of fall, candy in a basket. Even though their daughter and son were grown, Laura still left the porch light on every October 31st. She bought wrapped chocolates and left them in a basket next to the railing outside. But last Halloween, she wore a witch's hat and greeted each group of kids herself. She welcomed them warmly, complimenting their costumes every time. Mark had been on the couch in front of the TV. He tried to remember her ever being this way before. In her voice—almost overexuberant—was not simply holiday cheer but joyous relief, like some terminally ill patient who's just been told she's not sick anymore. Then those more frequent workouts, those longer runs, the way she began to really see and listen to him. Gone was that weary, and wary, look she'd had around him for years, that she was bone-tired from all that being a mother and realtor asked her to do, and now she had to be a wife, as well, whatever that meant.

Mark pushes shut Laura's underwear drawer. Outside the front windows are the bright green leaves of their maple trees. His eyes ache just looking at them. She's with Harrison now. Mark knows this. She got up early, the way she always has. She pulled on her running shorts and athletic bra and all the rest. She probably ate a banana and drank half a cup of coffee, and did she bring a change of clothes?

Would she and Harrison drive to the Marriott after their run in the state park? Would they shower, fuck, then shower again?

MARK DRIVES HIS BMW up the highway. His Oakleys help with the glare off the asphalt, though not quite enough. His AC is on and his sunroof is open and he drives just beneath the speed limit. He does not know this until he becomes aware of cars passing him, a driver or passenger glancing at him so briefly he is clearly irrelevant.

He knows where he is going, though he is not sure why he is going there. It's no longer to catch her in a lie because she has stopped lying to him. How beautiful she looked to him then. In the kitchen ten or twelve days ago now. That's when all things began to feel far away. She was clearly out of his reach and grasp, free of his control. His recognition of this truth was at first a dizzying plummet into a black void from which he would never return. But then came that distance, this detachment of the observer, and now he sees the sign for the Marriott rising above the planted maples around its parking lot, then he is taking the exit and is soon pulling slowly past the parked cars, their windshields and chrome blinding under the sun. He does not see Laura's Honda or Harrison's white Audi coupe. So Mark backs into the shade of an ancient pine, his tires touching the curb, and he puts the gear in park, leaves the engine running for the AC, and he waits.

He watches his finger press the button to close the sunroof, though he had no thought about doing so beforehand. There are advantages to this new feeling, a certain lightening of the load. The management of risk is one of his primary tasks as a PM. You must identify it, analyze it, then develop a response to it. You must monitor and control it.

That first night of the detective's DVD, eleven weeks and four days ago, Laura's screaming voice, "You *made* me do it!" There was the breaking of furniture and the smashing of floor tiles, there was the inadvertent damage to a ceiling fixture, and then Laura was running to the front door and Mark was there, blocking it.

"Let me *go!*" She yanked on his shirt collar, she tried pushing him to the side, but she could not move him. She bolted through the laundry room for the back door, but his arms were around her again, around her shoulders and upper arms and breasts. She struggled and then stopped struggling, both of them breathing hard. He dropped his forehead to her hair. Her heart was beating in her back against his chest against his heart.

"Why, Laura? Why did you do this to us?"

She was quiet. Her breathing was already slowing back to normal. "Please let go of me."

He held on. There came the creaking of the stairs behind the door to his mother's apartment. She was maybe one or two steps from opening that door. There was Laura's voice, soft and hard at once. "I don't want to see her."

He let go of his wife. He moved to the door and opened it.

"Is everything all right?" His mother held on to the railing. She'd cleaned off her makeup, and her gray hair was matted on one side. She wore her yellow robe over whatever it was she slept in.

"We're having an argument, Ma. Good night."

He closed the door slowly. He turned toward Laura, but she was in the kitchen stepping over a broken chair, the light on her hair and back all wrong somehow. The stairs began to creak behind him, and Mark followed his wife into the living room. The TV was still on, the screen blue. Laura sat on the couch with her legs drawn up and her arms around them and if he'd ever seen her sit like that, he couldn't remember when. Without looking up at him, she said: "Did you film that yourself?"

"No." He sat on the coffee table. There was the new thought that *he* had misbehaved somehow, one he dismissed instantly.

"Who did it?"

"No one you know."

"You hired someone?"

"Yeah, I did."

"Who?"

"Does it matter?"

She shook her head. She stared at the wall across the room, though she seemed to be seeing something in the air. "Does he *know* us?"

"Why, Laura? Why do you care about that?"

"Do you?"

"What?"

She didn't answer him. She was staring at the air again. Was she seeing Frank Harrison Jr.? His bald head? His— "Are you afraid for *Frank*, Laura? You worried about his wife over in *Newburyport* finding out? Are we talking about *reputations* here? Because—" his voice broke then, something he had no warning of whatsoever, and he would stop what was coming if he could but he couldn't and now he was crying—"because I don't care about *that*, Laura. I just can't believe you *did* this." There was only his crying now, his chin on his chest, his shoulders heaving up and down. Then Laura was there. Not crying herself, but kneeling on the floor beside the couch and the coffee table, holding him, saying, "I'm sorry, honey. I'm so sorry." Then maybe she did cry a bit, though Mark did not know for sure. All he knew was that he was crying into her hair and squeezing her arm as if it were the one rope thrown to him as he hung over some new and unknown abyss and he wasn't letting go. Ever. He would not let go.

But she did. She stood and brought him tissues from the bathroom. She sat straight on the couch across from him. "Mark. I'm sorry." Her voice was raw and naked and he believed her. Her period of contrition had begun. This was a word he had not had in his head for years, not since church when he was a boy, but it came to him then as he wiped his eyes and blew his nose. In the warm light from the lamp, he stared at his beautiful, cheating wife. She was contrite now, and Mark began to feel the cloak of work fall around his shoulders. He began to see this as an opportunity and not a threat, a positive risk that must be managed and monitored and controlled. This was simply a problem to be solved, and he was forcing the most logical solution. They talked calmly for a long while. She promised to break things off with Frank Harrison Jr. She promised never to see him again.

IN FRONT OF THE MARRIOTT a white painter's van drives slowly by the entrance. A man sits in the passenger side smoking a cigarette. He looks in Mark's direction, but he does not see him or even his BMW sedan, its engine running, the air too cool now. Mark watches his hand turn down the controls. He is thirsty. Or his body is. Water is needed. Cold, clear water. He sees himself buying a bottle of it somewhere. He could walk into the lobby of the Marriott for it. Or he could step into the restaurant there. It's a place he and Laura have been to with friends, the Salvuccis and one time the Brandts, Charlie drinking too much and going on about one thing or another. Mark could sit at the bar and order himself a beaded glass of ice water. Maybe his body would order a burger and a cold beer, and he would sit near the front windows where he could see anyone walking into or out of the hotel, though catching her in a lie was no longer the point, was it? No, the project of saving his marriage seems to have failed and he's inherited a new task. This is not unusual. Some projects collapse for any number of reasons: investors withdraw at the last minute; a design flaw is discovered that prevents forward momentum; the contract with the company is cancelled for reasons both opaque and obvious, often a lack of innovative nerve on the part of stockholders in one boardroom or another. But in this case, there's simply been a change of heart. Or, more accurately, a shift from the hiding of the heart to the showing of it, though Mark had to force that exposure, didn't he?

And so this new task, what is it? He is not sure, but he begins to see those cracked tiles again, that splintered table leg, those broken chairs in the garage. There's the urge to repair things, to see some tangible fruit of his labor. He watches himself put the car in gear and pull out of the lot for the highway. He accelerates into the travel lane and is soon leaving other cars behind him. The sun is unrelenting and in the median is tall yellow-green grass the public works department has not cut. Soon it'll be filled with purple loosestrife, that weed that comes just as summer wanes. Its appearance always depressed Laura, for it signaled the end of her days by the pool, but for Mark it meant fall and crisp days and dying leaves that brought bare branches and the kind of clarity that made work easy.

Mark steers into the Home Depot parking lot. Because it is a Saturday in Seabrook, New Hampshire, the lot is two-thirds full. There are the trucks and vans of tradesmen, but there are more SUVs and minivans and sedans like his, the cars of American home-owners who have taken the day to tinker with or improve their most valuable investment. Mark walks away from his car without locking it. This is a town of gun shops and tattoo parlors, of one strip mall after the other selling beach furniture and Bibles, motorcycles and patio bricks, neon towels and American flags and stone statues of black men holding a lantern for your fine stallion, a lawn ornament Mark has seen in front of a mobile home on cinderblocks just past the Walmart and Kentucky Fried Chicken.

If anybody here wants his BMW, they can have it. Today it is just another object among heaps of objects, and as he moves into the shade of the entrance, he has to admire the ad man or woman who chose the word HOME over HOUSE, for who, when things are good, would not want to improve and fortify their very *home*?

He pulls a cart free and pushes it toward the automatic door. It slides open for him and him only. A man ten or fifteen years older than he is smiling at him, an orange apron tied around his small gut, a yellow tape measure clipped to his belt.

"Can I help you find anything today, sir?"

"I'm all set, thanks." Mark pushes the cart past him. He tells him-self to be grateful. Be grateful you don't have to stand there in that corporate apron smiling at every bitch and bastard to walk through that door. Though there's something off about this thought, and he stops at the display of propane grills just to turn and glance back. The greeter is now talking to an obese woman in hospital scrubs, nodding his head and pointing down the length of the store. He laughs at something she or he may have just said and the woman laughs too, and Mark keeps walking. The truth is, he *does* need help finding things—the wood glue for one, the tile section for another. But has he ever asked for help?

You're hard on yourself.

A woman's voice. He hears it as he pushes his empty cart past shelf after shelf of lightbulbs and fluorescent tubes in boxes, floodlights and smoke alarms and radon test kits. Laura's? No, his mother's. Two nights ago as they sat side by side at her small kitchen island eating lobster rolls she'd bought them.

"What do you mean, Ma?"

Mark sipped his beer, a cold Bud Light his mother had cracked open for him before sitting on her stool with a glass of chardonnay.

"An A minus was never good enough for you, honey. Everything had to be perfect."

The last light of the afternoon came through the side kitchen window and lay across their hands and plates and beer and wine. Mark glanced at his mother. She was chewing thoughtfully, her eyes on the lifetime ago in her head, and even though there were those lines etched around her mouth and cheeks, her hair so thin he could see her scalp, he saw her again as a young woman, her drunk husband dead and gone, all those years ahead of her working as a secretary at Leary's Insurance company downtown, coming home each night to cook him and Claire a hot meal they would then share at the mahogany table in the dark dining room that smelled like old drapes.

"But as much as you wanted that A, you would never ask for help." She turned to him. "Remember that?"

"Most men don't, Ma."

"Well that's a shame. It is."

In the corner of her lip was a dot of mayonnaise, her lipstick smeared just above it. She looked her age then, and Mark wanted to reach over and squeeze her shoulder. He kept eating.

He's hungry now. Or his body is. This distant rumble in his gut. Greasy fried chicken would do. Maybe that KFC just past the Walmart. But he sees the small plastic table he'd eat at, a loud family nearby, and the thought depresses him. He's passing racks of C-clamps now, bar clamps, hooks and chains and bungee cords.

Just before the shelves of fasteners and adhesive is a barrel of threaded pipe, gray and an inch and a half wide and four feet long. They are just like the one that lies in the trunk of Mark's car, and he grasps one. It is cool and hard, the sure diameter of it fitting nicely inside his fist.

He sees himself swinging it into the bald head of Frank Harrison Jr., caving it in like a watermelon, the sheet pulled to Laura's shoulders in the Marriot's king-size bed, her mouth hanging open in a silent scream.

But this image seems to come not from his life, but from a movie Mark saw as a boy, and his hand lets go of the pipe and he keeps walking. How exhausted he is. Soon he finds the wood glue, a contractor's grade in a long plastic bottle he drops into his cart. He moves through busy people and their busy sounds and he finds the tile section, its various tools that apparently make any flooring job easier: wet saws and rubber gloves, grout floats and sponges and big plastic buckets. His stomach is an empty cavern. There's a throbbing in his forehead. Is he really going to do this? Take all this home and get on his hands and knees to repair the floor he no longer even treads? And does he even know how? Most of the process seems to be common sense, and there are directions on the side of the mortar bag, but will they be enough?

He begins to lift and drop items into his cart when something buzzes inside his shorts pocket and he nearly slaps at it. He pulls his cell phone free. He squints at it. It is a local number he does not recognize. It could be work, though his new deadline is months away and he is surprised at his disappointment it is not Laura who is calling.

He watches himself press the talk button, "This is Mark Welch."

"Yeah well, this is Lisa Schena."

He stares at the stack of mortar bags. His stomach growls. He feels caught in a test of some kind, one he did not know was coming. "I'm sorry, do I know you?"

"Not yet." Her voice is young, her tone playful. Then he tastes last night's menthol cigarette, his erection pressed against his pants against the drunk woman's bare belly.

"From The Tap?"

"Probably."

"Probably?" He finds himself smiling at this. "You don't know for sure?"

"No, *you* don't know for sure. Tell me about this Lisa."

"She hates rap music—"

"And?"

"And she's—"

"What?"

"She's very—"

"Hungry."

"She is?"

"Yes. You promised her a meal."

"I did?"

"Mark Welch did. This is *you*, isn't it?"

"I think so."

"You don't know?"

"Not lately, no." Mark's breathing seems to pause in his throat. "Not for a long time actually."

"That's too bad, 'cause I kind of like the one I met."

"What'd you like about him?" He presses the phone into his ear. He seems to be holding his breath.

"His eyes. His sad eyes."

Mark knows he is supposed to speak now. He knows this, but he can't quite summon his voice from wherever it is it just went. He looks down into his orange cart and stares at tools and substances of repair.

Behind the Sea Spray Motel on Hampton Beach, white sand is feathered across the asphalt under the sun, and he parks behind a faded VW Bug, its top down. There is still the far-off feeling that he is watching his body do things, but now he is a bit more interested in sitting back to see how things play out. In the trunk of his sedan are the tiling materials and the wood glue, and he tells himself he is just having lunch, that's all, that he is going to eat a meal with this Lisa Schena, then he will drive home and get to work. But he checks his face in the mirror twice and puts an Altoid under his tongue, letting it dissolve slowly as he walks through the heat of the lot.

Ocean Boulevard is thick with slow-moving cars and Jeeps and vans with open doors, its men, women, and kids looking out at the T-shirt and surfboard shops, the video arcades and pizza bars, the fish shacks and vending carts selling fried dough and cotton candy, the sidewalk crowded with sunburned people in their tank tops and baggy shirts and bikini bottoms, many of them ringed with sand and sea salt above dimpled or skinny thighs, rubber flip-flops flopping, Mark stepping into the dim, cool lounge of Carlo's.

It's a place he's never been. Its bar is U-shaped and there's a flat-screen TV hanging above a fish tank built into the wall, five or six gold and black fish drifting listlessly up against the glass. Above them, men play baseball in a bright green field and a song from long ago plays on the sound system, something about rain falling on all our heads, she is sitting at the bar, her back to the wall. A man is leaning close and talking to her. He is sunburned and wears a white beard and a short-sleeved shirt with blue parrots etched all over it. She's blond, her hair clipped, two things Mark did not notice the night before, but there are her bare brown shoulders in another sleeveless top, this one white, and now she sees him and her expression turns from warmly tolerant to genuinely pleased, and he is not sure he is up for any of this, he is not sure why he is here at all, but he feels himself walk between the tables of families and couples eating and talking and being happily together, toward the bar and this Lisa Schena and the man turning to him now.

"Oh hi, hon," she says. "I got us a table by the window."

The man leans back slightly. He takes in Mark Welch as if weighing whether or not he is a true rival for her affections. Lisa Schena is off her stool. With two fingers, she taps the back of the man's hand. "Thank you for the drink. I have a lunch date with my husband."

She moves by the man, and Mark follows her. A black denim skirt hugs her hips and she's wearing leather sandals, and again, there is a stirring where nothing has stirred since there was snow on the ground and his wife, at least in his head, still belonged to him. He disciplines himself to lift his eyes as Lisa Schena leads him through the restaurant to the only available table in the corner near the window. It is small. On it are two dirty plates, a wadded napkin on one, half a Coke sitting in a glass beside an empty breadbasket. Mark glances back at the bar and the man in the blue parrot shirt. His eyes are on the game above, both his hands cupping his glass like he's afraid it too will disappear on him.

"You look different in the light." She's sitting already, smiling up at him. She has less makeup on today, her cheeks only slightly pockmarked. Her eyes are a washed-out blue, like robin's eggs left exposed to the weather by their mother.

"Is that good or bad?" He sits across from her. He can feel the sun's warmth coming through the glass.

"You look younger, but that's not good or bad for me because I don't give a shit."

"I don't either."

"Really?"

"I think so."

She's smiling at him as if she's known him longer than she has. This makes him feel comfortable which then makes him uncomfortable for feeling so comfortable. He's tempted to stand and leave.

"You two snuck in." The waitress is a warm, fleshy face surrounded by gray hair, her hands gathering up the dirty plates, breadbasket, and half-empty glass. "Cocktails?"

"Bloody Mary for me."

"Two," Mark says.

Lisa Schena is still smiling at him, and he can see she's older than he thought, maybe ten years older than his daughter, closer to forty. This is good, but her smile is making him shy and he glances out the tinted window at the beach traffic, the white sand on the other side, the deep blue rim of ocean beyond that.

"You're a mess, aren't you?"

He looks back at her. "Probably. You?"

"Just with what I told you last night."

He nods his head. His face grows warm, and he glances down at her tanned shoulders and upper arms.

"You don't remember shit, do you?"

"I know we kissed."

"Yeah we did, but that was your idea."

"It was?"

"Yes."

"Is that all right?"

"Hey, I called you, didn't I?"

Mark looks back at the bar. The bearded man is gone, and on the TV above the listless fish, a woman is holding a bottle of floor cleaner, smiling earnestly into the camera. It's the brand Laura has always used. He sees himself kneeling on the kitchen floor with a hammer. He'll have to break the tiles completely before he can fix them.

"I was talking about my son."

Words come back to Mark now, Lisa Schena's voice from last night in his head. She was leaning against her Chevy sedan, her ankles and tanned thighs touching one another, that faded denim skirt and the way she crossed one arm under her breasts while she smoked. Wants to live with his fucking father.

"He wants to live with his dad."

"Correct."

A busboy begins to wipe down their table, then set it. He is tall and slight. On the wrist of his left hand are the tattooed initials *A.R.* He disappears just as the waitress sets the Bloody Marys down in front of them, each with a stalk of celery too short for the glass, their ends just barely rising out of the vodka and tomato juice.

"Oh shoot, you don't have menus."

Then two bound menus are on the table between them, but Mark Welch and Lisa Schena leave them where they are. Without a toast they lift their glasses and drink, the vodka going into Mark like a mildly dangerous thought he ignores, and she begins to talk about her son. His name is Adam and he's always been a difficult kid. "Never listened, always had to have time-outs and then I'd have to physically hold him to his little Fisher Price chair because he could never stay still. His father never did anything, and he's just as bad anyway, can't concentrate, can't ever sit in one place unless it's in front of a computer. He can't hold a job now either, and he still has split custody but Adam wants to live with him full-time because there are no rules over there, or at least no boundaries, no expectations or respect for anyone else's space, and I can't tell you how many times I've . . ."

Mark sips and nods and listens. She is clearly a talker. It's what she did the night before too, talked and talked and talked while he smoked her cigarettes and stared at her in the bruised neon from the bar, drunk and trying not to glance too much at the soft swell of her breasts or her tanned belly or that denim skirt he wanted to unzip and pull down over her hips, half-drunk but grateful for what was happening to him, this old blood descending to his groin where its gathering heaviness left him feeling slightly new again, or at least not dead yet. Nearly three months of nothing, not even in the mornings, and if it weren't for his life floating away from him, Laura continuing to do all that she does, he might have begun to worry, he might have begun to think of his prostate and sicknesses that were not uncommon in men his age, but again, this was something happening to a body he merely existed inside and any maintenance beyond breathing and eating and drinking seemed to be someone else's problem, and last night, when that gathering heaviness turned hard, it was as if a crack of daylight and fresh air had entered him somewhere and so he'd stepped toward Lisa Schena against her car and kissed her, something he wants to do now, too. Shut her up with a kiss, though she isn't boring him, not in the least.

She's telling a story about her ex, how she came home one day from work—an animal hospital where she's an assistant to the veterinarian, an old, sweet lesbian named Carol—and found him and Adam playing some kind of video game where men blew each other's heads off. "And they'd been doing it since I'd left that *morning* and it was a *school* day."

Mark shakes his head, then nods in sympathy, his eyes on her washed-out blues. Strange this ability for his face and head to do the right things. In the tinted sunlight from the window, he is looking at her more clearly now. Her short hair is a dazed blond, treated with chemicals so many times over the years it has no definable color at all. Her teeth are stained with coffee and tobacco, and just beneath her slightly pocked left cheek is a pink scar that directs one's attention to her weak chin and upper arms which have no tone and jiggle slightly as she talks, making points with her hands in the air above her still-full drink. She is absolutely nothing like his wife in any way, and is that why he is reaching across the table now and taking her small hand, squeezing it once softly and saying, "We should eat."

"Oh shit, I'm talking way too much."

"No you're not."

"Decided?" The waitress is standing there with her pad and pen.

Lisa Schena looks up at her as if she's just been exposed in some way, a dark splotch spreading across her throat.

"Just a salad with chicken on it for me."

"Dressing?"

"Creamy Italian, please."

"And you, sir?"

"Same." Though he does not like creamy Italian dressing, but food now, as hungry as he was earlier, seems entirely beside the point. "And two more of these, please."

They are alone again. She is smiling at him. "You drank that one pretty fast."

"Hair of the dog."

"Tell me about it. We had to put down three yesterday." She leans to her straw and takes it between her lips and sucks, swallowing twice. Her eyes are on the table but not on the table.

"What's your job when you have to do that?"

"I hold them down in a three-point restraint, then Carol administers the shot. Fun, huh?"

"That must be hard."

"What's hard are their fucking owners. We had to put down a perfectly healthy retriever just because the new wife didn't like dogs."

"You couldn't find it a home?"

"People want puppies. It's like that with kids, too. You know how many teenagers will never get out of foster care till they're grown? Just about all of them. People don't like to pick up where other people left off. People like to buy *new*." She shakes her head and glances out the window, one finger tapping the end of her straw. He wants to lean forward and touch her lightly scarred cheek.

She looks back at him. "Tell me about your ex."

"*My* ex?"

"You don't remember that either?"

Again, this warmth in his face that does not simply come from his body, but him—it seems to come from *him*. "No, I don't."

"And I thought I was drunk."

"We both were."

She points at his left hand, her eyes on his ring finger. "You were telling me why you still wear that, remember? I said, 'You're married, aren't you?' And you said, 'No, not really.' And I asked you why you wear that ring, and you told me."

The vodka is a small grass fire spreading in his chest, and he knows he doesn't care where it goes or what it burns. *Vow*. His own voice in his head, the tissue memory of it leaving his vocal cords from the night before in the neon lot behind The Tap standing close to this woman sitting across from him now. "I told you I'd made a vow."

"Yep. Then you kissed me." Lisa laughs and shakes her head, and it's as if she's told a very old joke and the waitress arrives with their salads and Lisa Schena orders another round, her faded blue eyes on his, a smile in them that is no longer on her lips.

AFTER HER PROMISES TO HIM, that night of the detective's DVD, Laura had gone to bed early and Mark had followed her. Talking seemed to be finished. If she knew he was only five or six feet behind her, she did not acknowledge it, or him, and she moved into their bedroom, then closed the bathroom door behind her and there was the running of the faucet.

In Mark's side pants pocket was her cell phone, her laptop computer still in its case in the front hallway where she sometimes left it for days. He moved across the room and lifted folded laundry off the wingback chair in the corner. It's where Laura put his clean clothes. Always folded, always in that chair. That night there was a pair of jeans, three T-shirts, and two pair of dress socks, matched and balled together. He placed all this in his bureau and he sat in the chair in the corner and he waited.

There came the flushing of the toilet, then again, the running of the faucet. She kept her cotton nightgown on a hook on the inside bathroom door so it wasn't unusual that she would enter the bathroom dressed, then emerge in her nightgown, her clothes under her arm she would drop into the hamper near the closet door. But that night, it was the first time Mark had ever really thought about this transformation. Sitting in the chair in the corner near the window to the street, he saw this as dirt rubbed into the hole she'd put in his chest, for he suspected she did not do this with Frank Harrison Jr. He was almost certain she did not close doors to *him*.

She dropped her sweat suit into the hamper. When she turned toward the bed, her eyes on something far, far from this room, she saw him and jerked slightly.

"I didn't see you."

"Now you do."

"I know, Mark. I do."

She climbed under the covers on her side of the bed. She lay her head on its pillow. She turned her face toward him. "Are you coming to bed?"

"Maybe."

She nodded. She stared at the ceiling. He could feel her cell phone in his pocket, and he knew that when she was asleep he would check its call history—its sent messages and those she'd received.

"Mark?"

He did not answer. Let her lie there in his quiet for a while.

"Mark?"

He crossed one leg over the other. He stared at her. In the lamplight, he could see she'd removed whatever makeup she'd worn earlier, maybe the third touch-up of the day, it occurred to him—the first for work, the second probably right before the gym for Harrison, the third to hide Harrison from her husband. Now it was off, and the bags beneath her eyes were easier to see, as was the loose flesh beneath her chin, the nearly brittle thinness of her hair. It all looked grotesque to him now. For years there'd been her desire for solitude, all those hours she needed to run and be alone. There'd been her sloppiness in

constantly paying the bills late. Her quiet at dinner parties that bor-
dered on rude. There was Mary Ann as a teenager when she and her
mother hardly spoke to one another or else screamed and cried and
he had to step in as if he had two sixteen-year-old daughters and not
one. There was Laura's polite coldness to his mother, the way she'd
never quite embraced taking her in once she turned eighty. There
was Laura's constantly getting his orders wrong at the grocery store;
they'd be hosting a cookout, and he'd tell her to buy eight pounds of
ground beef, but she'd come back with five because she never really
fucking *listened* to him and he'd have to drop everything and drive to
the store himself. There was her bad breath between meals. There
was her nightly television habit of watching banal crime dramas, her
eyes fixed to the screen as unquestioningly as a child's. There was her
mediocre cooking, her preference for frozen vegetables, a lot of salt,
and bland dishes she wasn't ashamed to serve with ketchup. And now
she'd lied and cheated and adulterated. She'd shifted their home off
its very foundation and shoved shards of hot glass into Mark Welch's
blood and brain and heart: and this searing ache was for what? For
her? Look at her; what was he *losing* anyway?

But this was a question that died before he could even fully think
it, for he loved her. He did. He had since that first afternoon twenty-
five years ago when she led him from one empty home to another.

"Mark? Honey, you're not going to do anything foolish, are you?"

"Please don't call me that."

"I'm sorry."

"Are you?"

She stared at him a moment. He had misstepped and knew it, for
in her eyes was a hardening, some sort of decision being made about
him, or them. Or her and Harrison. Or all three. She turned her
back to him. She did not reach over to switch off her lamp.

"Laura?"

"What?"

"You need to take a personal day tomorrow."

"Why?" She kept her back to him. She didn't move.

"Because you're going to write him a letter, and then you're going to show it to me."

Mark recognized the tone of his voice. It was the same he used when ordering a poorly motivated team member to do one thing or another. And so he was ordering his wife—for she was, by definition, a member of his team, wasn't she?—to stay home. He could not have her out of the house and away from him where she could so easily call or meet up with Harrison. He did not even want her in the company of the other women at the realty office—gray-eyed Barb Thompson and her endless supply of cardigan sweaters, the fearful and for-ever dieting Kathy Ann, Lexus-driving Linda Brown—for he knew women instinctively looked after one another, even when one of their own was wrong, and in fact, had just badly hurt another woman. In their feminine presence, quiet Laura may very well begin to cry, then talk. There would be tissues handed to her, consoling hugs given, and soon Mark Welch, her cuckolded husband, would be on the outside of this womb of solidarity, and because he was on the outside, he would necessarily be in the wrong.

"Laura? Did you hear me?"

"Yes." Her voice was thick with the sleep that was already coming, her breathing shallow and steady. This did not surprise him. She had always fallen asleep when she most needed to: when she hadn't sold a property in months; when she and he had had a bad fight over a bill she'd paid late; when her husband was an ineffective PM and feared losing his job and the house. He'd lie in bed, his hands beneath his skull, and he'd picture the foreclosure, watch the humiliation of the moving van backing to their front door. As they lay side by side, he'd told Laura his very real fears, but she'd only nodded her head as if he were recounting a TV football game, and then she was asleep. It's where she went when there was trouble of any kind, to her dream world or to wherever she went in her head when she ran mile after mile down a long road away from what anyone else would call her life.

Mark sat there for quite some time. He was reviewing the difficulty of monitoring her when he also had to be at work. So there would be no work. He was between large projects anyway. He had never called in sick and so now he would. Maybe for days. He took out her cell phone. He was no expert with these things. With his own cell phone, he knew only how to make a call, take a call, and get his messages. He did not want to know how to do anything else. He refused to be one of these men who stared at small screens in their palms. He knew their weekly calendars were in there, as were their emails, as was the news and any other distractions they could find. But to Mark, this constant staring into a small screen was the sure way to miss the big screen, which was the one day and night you had to reach your goals, and if you didn't see big, you would fail to see opportunities and you would fail to see threats.

But he *had* failed, hadn't he? If Laura had not shown a new interest in his testicles, would he have detected what he ultimately did? For days afterward, he told himself he had overreacted, that his wife had tried something new with his body, that's all. Maybe all those other changes he saw in her was simply evidence of her happiness with *him* and the life they'd built. But the following Saturday, as she changed into her Nike sweats for her second trip of the day to the gym, he waved at her from the backyard where he'd been raking wet leaves and twigs. He waited twenty minutes, then drove to the gym, cruising slowly through its massive lot. There were cars and vans and SUVs of all kinds, half of them coated with dried road salt, but no gray Civic belonging to his wife. His heart began to thump in his brain, his hands on the wheel felt tiny and far away. He drove through the lot five or six times, then he drove home and walked straight into the hallway for her laptop computer in its case, but it was not there. Nor was her cell phone.

He stood in the entry to his home for longer than he ever had. There was the oval antique mirror hanging beside the interior door, the wooden pegs beneath it for their keys. There was the coatrack against the wall, a blue sweatshirt of Kevin's hanging there for years, his baseball cap on the hook beside it. It was from his first B-League season when they went deep into the playoffs and Kevin had made a diving stop at short that broke his wrist. There was the pine trunk Mary Ann would sit on to pull off her winter boots or to pull on her roller blades. Laura had painted the trunk on a tarp near the pool, a sage green Mark had not appreciated until it sat in the entryway and looked to him the color of home. There was the smell of wool and old paint and dust in the woven mat under his feet, three pairs of Laura's running shoes in a neat row across from the trunk. And there was the empty place where her laptop should have been but was not. He told himself this was not a bad thing, for it would force him—the head of this family, the manager of the Welch Team—to remain calm. Over the years he had created a Strong Matrix, which meant he was in control, and if he lost that now, he could lose it all, so he would not look at her emails. He would not open her cell phone. Not yet.

And maybe she'd run an errand before heading back to the gym. It was not good that this thought had not come to him already. It showed he wasn't thinking clearly. He drove back to the lot. He waited in his car for nearly an hour. When he returned home, the March sky a darkening blue, Laura's car was in her place in the driveway. Inside the house, water was running in pipes in the walls, and he took the stairs two at a time to their bedroom.

He could hear the shower. He opened the door. There was steam and the smell of soap and there was his wife's nude silhouette behind a rubber curtain.

"Good workout?"

"Oh, you scared me."

"Go back to the gym?"

"Yeah, it was a tough class."

"Why so long? You run an errand?"

"No, just the gym."

He pulled the door closed. He kept his hand on the knob. He

looked down at his yard sneakers, the toes damp and muddy. She was speaking again, her voice like the chirp of a bird who has flown into a black tunnel but does not yet know it.

There was the greedy, grasping need for him to know everything *now*, before she even stepped from the shower naked and cleansed of whatever she'd done. But no, he would stay quiet. He had identified the risk and now he would develop a response to it. He would delegate and subcontract and wait for a full report.

Mark stood. He walked around the foot of their bed and stared down at her. The light was in Laura's face, though her features were soft and in complete repose. It was the look of one newly relieved of a long-held burden, and did she feel relieved just before falling asleep?

Downstairs his heart was a blooming pulse in his head. He moved through the kitchen, the overhead light fixture hanging from a wire and aiming at the windows like the spotlight from a police cruiser. He stepped over the broken chairs on the floor and retrieved Laura's laptop from its case in the hallway.

In the kitchen he filled a glass with ice and poured himself three fingers of Bacardi and a splash of Coke and he carried his drink and his wife's computer and cell phone into the living room. There was the masochistic temptation to watch the DVD again, to see her head lower out of sight in Harrison's Audi TT coupe. But there came a tremor in his hands and fingers and he drank long and deep. He took her cell phone and pressed buttons that beeped until he found a bar for messages, sent and received. There were none in either file. Had she been deleting these for months? Or had she always done this? He opened her laptop and turned it on. The spartan light of the screen was like the parting of a wound.

What he'd expected to find was filth. Lusty bravado. Pornographic descriptions of what they both yearned for once they were together again. What he found first were work emails going back months, brief and routine messages about house keys and For Sale signs and balloon colors for Open Houses. There were a few old emails to and from Mary Ann, all of them upbeat. From Laura: *That's great about your project, honey. When can you come home for a visit?*

Mary Ann: *As soon as I can find the time. You know I always miss you guys! Love, M.A.*

Mark sipped his drink. He felt both calmed by these messages but also aggrieved. *You guys.*

He found no emails to or from Frank Harrison Jr. He typed his name into the email history bar, but nothing came up. Why was he even doing this? The truth was out, so what was he searching for? He wasn't sure, but the phrase *Know thine enemy* slipped between the heartbeats in his head and that's when he aimed the cursor at the general history at the top of the screen and that's when he saw an endless stack of Gmail accounts, one after the other. The tips of his fingers became cold as bone. He aimed at one of the Gmails and opened it, but he needed a user name and a password. He typed in his wife's first name and the rest appeared in the box: *LauraMW*. She'd never been practical or very careful; she was the woman who lay under the sun at noon with no sunblock, the woman who ran at night in dark clothing; so he typed in the code to their debit card. Eight characters were needed. He typed it in twice, one after the other, the email opening instantly. It was difficult not to feel slightly proud of himself for knowing his wife so well, and it was difficult not to judge her harshly for being so careless, though his judgment of her had never felt so justified as it did now, for before him were two long emails between *LauraMW* and *FrankJH*. He drained his drink and he began to read.

THE SUN STILL SHINES over the water and the beach shacks. Many of them are vinyl-sided and reflect whitely at Mark as he walks Lisa Schena to her car. She has parked in the driveway of a friend, and they are moving down the sidewalk through tanned bodies and sunburned bodies, fat ones and scrawny ones, tattoos abounding the way they do now, piercings too, five alone in the left ear of a girl no older than twelve, a burning cigarette between her fingers at her narrow hip. Lisa's hand is small and fits snugly inside his own. He tells himself it is there, in his, because the sidewalk is crowded and loud with voices and laughter and the thumping of arcade machines, the roar of a motorcycle passing in the street, and it'd be rude to leave her untended in all this, but it was *her* hand that reached for his, a touch of skin, then a grasping that shot into his bloodstream and groin.

They may have had two more drinks. He does not remember eating, only listening to Lisa Schena who had given up trying to get him to talk about Laura, for he would not; to bring her to that table would make that table disappear and he did not want it to disappear. He wanted to sit and drink and watch world-weary Lisa Schena talk all day, though now she is quiet, smoking a cigarette as they reach the corner, nickels of flattened gum on the concrete, a trash barrel outside a pizza shop overflowing with tomato-streaked paper plates and empty Coke cans, and she drops her butt onto the sidewalk, then steps on it and leads him into the street through slowing traffic for the other side.

The sun is warm on the back of his neck. He can smell the rot of the ocean, seaweed and dried-out mussels on a rock, gull shit and wet sand and salty surf he only glances at as Lisa steps onto a new sidewalk and he keeps up with her. This one is largely clear of people, so there is no reason any longer to hold her hand, but she isn't letting go and neither is he.

Up ahead are clusters of beach houses along short sandy streets. He can feel her bare forearm brushing his, and it's strange she's being so quiet. He glances down at her and she smiles up at him as if, in his silence, he's been telling a long story and she is simply listening to it. They have to step around a small mound of sand in the asphalt, then they're off Ocean Boulevard, walking down a narrow street, one-story beach houses wedged close together on both sides behind split-rail fences or chain-link. Some have tiny square lawns, others sand or pea stone. Many of them are flying Old Glory off poles in brass holders screwed into their door casings, and it's as if these hard-earned summer places of theirs have to have some visual justification, that a summer home is yet another gleaming possibility in this continuous American Dream and these flags, most of their stars and stripes faded by the sun and salt and wind, are semi-defiant sanctions of approval for this excess, small as they are, built as close together as they are. It's like a cruel joke is being played on these people, though sensing this, Mark feels above no one; in fact, he feels quite at home here, the brunt of a cruel joke himself, and that's what he feels with this Lisa Schena too, at home, when she is nothing like any home he's ever had. She has pocked skin and bad teeth and faded blue eyes and she talks on and on about difficulty and loss, but she does it with a glint in her eye, the black humor of the condemned, like we are all in this together and who, honey, said it would ever go the way it was supposed to anyway? And how nice for him now to maybe give up a little and stop giving such a shit, so he stops there on the cracked asphalt under the sun and watches his hands pull Lisa Schena to him, her eyes startled for only an instant before they soften and he kisses her deeply, her lips pliant, her mouth opening without hesitation, her menthol tongue there like the answer to a question he does not even know he's been asking. His erection is as immediate as when he was a boy. In the darkness of his closed eyes, things seem to tilt a bit and he knows he's half-drunk but he doesn't care. Her tongue darts in and out of his mouth like a nurse tending to many patients at once and there is the guttural humming of an air-conditioning unit, the needy cry of a gull overhead, the sounds of a television in an open window somewhere, baseball again, the Red Sox, and he was a good athlete in high school, fast enough to play in college though he did not for he knew he was not good enough to play beyond that so what was the point? It wasn't practical. It wasn't the logical thing to do, and he is so tired of logic, so tired of managing every last detail of each and every day, and how sweet to let go of the wheel and let someone else drive, to let Lisa Schena pull away first, her eyes not so washed out this close up, but thin, as if they're blue ice and every year of her life has melted away one more layer yet she has no sadness about this because she's tougher than he is, taking his hand now, leading him wordlessly down the street and around the corner where a small boy sits on a Big Wheel staring up at them, a dried purple ring around his mouth, his mother sunning herself on a chaise lounge just feet away on her coarse yellow lawn. Her thighs are oiled and dark, and oblivion never felt as good as it does now, Lisa Schena letting go of his hand and turning down a driveway where her Chevy sedan sits behind a motorcycle under a blue tarp weighted on the ground with bricks. She's climbing three pressure-treated steps of a small porch. Her face turns to him, "My friend's a cop. He's working a double."

Against the house, a dead potted plant sits on the railing and she pulls from it a single key and unlocks the door. She pushes the key back into the dirt, then they're both inside. The kitchen is small and neat, the floor linoleum. She is at the open fridge pulling out two cans of beer and handing him one. Busch. Beaded and cold. She is smiling, taking his hand again. "He has a deck up top. C'mon."

Her hips in black denim, her ugly hair, her hand in his, small and warm. They pass through the living room of a man—a mismatched couch and recliner, a massive flat-screen television, a glass-topped coffee table littered with newspapers and DVD cases and two Xbox controls beside a full ashtray. The house smells like cigarette smoke and window cleaner and just as Mark takes the carpeted steps behind Lisa, her hand letting go, he sees a framed photograph of a man with a crew cut and trimmed mustache, his arms around three little kids.

"Is he divorced?" The question comes out of him, though he does not want that word in the air, and his fingers reach up and touch Lisa Schena's moving knee. She laughs and says something about his ex-wife being a bitch.

The cop's room is cold, an air-conditioning unit humming in the window beside the slider. Lisa Schena stands there but does not open it. Nor has she opened her beer, nor has he.

"Decent view, huh?"

Beyond a small deck are the roofs of houses, the street ending at a grassy dune and there, on the other side of it, the ocean, just a square of it, but it is blue-green with no horizon, the pale sky rising above it, Lisa Schena turning to him, the unopened beer in her hand.

"What're we doing, Mark Welch?"

"I don't know." His finger touches her small pink scar. "I don't care either."

"That makes two of us." She takes his can of beer and places it and hers on a cane chair against the wall. She straightens and pulls her white top up over her head. She reaches behind her for her bra strap, her eyes—alert and reckless—on his. It's an act he's watched no one else but his wife perform for over two decades, and when Lisa Schena pulls her bra free he does not look at her breasts for he is afraid he will stop if he does and he does not want to stop. She begins to unbutton his shirt but he steps back and does it himself, quickly, then he's kissing her again, unzipping her black denim skirt, pulling them down her hips as he nudges off his sandals and steps out of his shorts and underwear and stands there naked and erect before a woman he has known less than one full day, a thought he does not think but feels as she glances down at what he has to offer, stepping out of her underwear, her eyes intent and deliberate now, as if this is something she will do whether it is a good thing or not, and as she grasps his hand and leads him to the bed, he takes in her straight back and what it leads to, its beauty a dark surprise to him, and he pictures her holding down a strong, young retriever on a steel table, its futile whining and struggling, the needle nearby, about to be shoved in.

THAT FIRST MORNING after the night he'd made Laura watch the detective's DVD, Mark woke curled on the couch in the living room. Outside it was snowing, light flakes that melted as soon as they hit the ground and street. A car drove by wetly on the asphalt. It was near seven, the Welch house quiet and calm, though it was as if the smell of dried blood was in the air and great devastation of some kind had happened near by.

Then he was standing in his garage watching his mother drive off to her volunteer job as a receptionist at the hospital. He had just carried the last of the broken chairs out there, his mother's headlights coming on as she backed away. There was her old profile, her wool cap on her head, her gloved hands on the wheel, then she was gone and to see his and Laura's cars parked side by side was a whip across his eyes.

He wished he'd never read one word between FrankJH and LauraMW.

You deserve real love, Laura. You know that, don't you? I can give it to you. All I want to do is give it to you.

You do, sweetheart. Oh Frank, you ***do.***

Sweetheart. It was a word she'd never used for Mark, and there were pages of this, and it was very little of what he'd expected; he had hard evidence of a sexual affair, but of all he'd read the night before, there was just one hint of this and it was from his wife:

No one's ever made me feel that before.

Reading their private conversations, Mark had expected to feel more justified in his outrage, more fully equipped to develop a response to the very real threat that was Frank Harrison Jr. But what Mark felt instead was small. Inadequate. An insensitive and domineering brute. A lousy lover. That's the picture his dear Laura had painted of him. That's the shadow-man this Harrison knew. Mark was almost disappointed he'd found little of the lewd, for this was far worse: keeping it unspoken, even between themselves, revealed that they were lovers, that they truly *loved* one another.

He had not expected this.

That's when he saw the four-foot length of steel pipe. It was leaning against insulation in a stud bay beside the door. It had probably been there since he'd built his mother's apartment, since his plumber had installed the second oil burner, and Mark's eyes had to have passed over it for years as he walked into the laundry room from the garage. But that morning was the first time he'd grasped it and lifted it and felt its heft. He wiped a cobweb off it. He looked at how his hand was now smudged gray. He slapped his palm on his pants and carried the pipe into the laundry room and rested it against the wall.

From the kitchen he heard silent Laura open and close a cabinet door. There was the tap of a ceramic mug on the counter, the pouring of coffee. He could smell it. Before the mad mornings when both kids were small and woke very early needing to be cleaned and clothed and fed, Mark and Laura would have coffee together. Whoever got up first would make it, then carry it up, and they would sit against their pillows and headboard and sip and talk quietly, their room filling slowly with light. Sometimes they would talk about the mundane, about duties and tasks ahead of them that day. But usually they didn't. Usually they told one another their dreams or fragments of them from the night before. One morning, snow falling outside, Laura had told him she'd dreamt she was a little girl and she lived in the side pocket of one of his suit coats. A few times a day he would lift her out and hold her in his palm and feed her bits of bread or tiny shredded pieces of meat. He would try to kiss her, but his massive lips scared her so he'd slide her back inside his pocket. Mark had told her the dream meant she knew he was her protector. Laura had smiled but said nothing. She nodded her head and sipped her coffee. He had felt like his wife's friend then, her true companion, and he'd disciplined himself not to ruin it by reaching for her hip or breast.

Letting go of the pipe in the laundry room, he could feel in his throat so many sentences from the night's reading of emails, and he needed to shout them at her now as she poured her coffee in the kitchen, its smell always such a comfort to him, but not then; that morning it was like the sweet fragrance of lilacs just before you see the corpse upon which they lie.

He stepped into the kitchen. Laura stood at the peninsula. Above her, the light fixture still hung sideways from its wires, and she was looking at her husband as if she were trying to remember his name.

Mark's eyes ached. His mouth tasted like iron. He pushed the upside-down table and slid it over the floor into the corner. When it touched the baseboards he felt immensely fatigued.

*Oh, you do, sweetheart. Oh Frank, you **do**.*

She was pouring him a cup now. He hadn't heard her pull it from the cabinet. He hadn't heard the tap of it as he'd heard hers. He wanted to walk her into the living room and sit her on the couch and read her some of her own words about him. He wanted to—what? Humiliate himself? Break down like a boy in front of her again?

No, this was the time for a cooler head. For there are always three major constraints: scope, cost, and time. Enlarge the scope and you will increase the cost and lengthen the time. Tell Laura all he's discovered and the scope would become very large indeed.

He lifted his cup. He sipped. "Thank you."

"I called in sick."

He nodded.

"I'm going to write that letter now."

"Good." This came out sounding more sullen than he'd meant it to, but why shouldn't it?

Because she was beautiful. Because she stood there in their kitchen, the gray light of the morning coming through the window onto her hair and shoulders and throat and sternum, her small hands cupping her coffee like some secret he would never get to. His eyes began to burn: perhaps because she and Harrison had written nothing of their sex together, it's all he saw. He kept seeing his wife's lovely mouth around the erect penis of a man he'd never met. He kept seeing her fucking him, straddling Harrison and reaching back to fondle his balls, these new playthings he seemed to have introduced her to, this bald banker thrusting himself into Mark's wife before she eventually collapsed onto him. Mark imagined their sweaty murmurings, though he could not hear them; all he heard was his own heart tapping in his head like a hammer.

Laura was looking at him as if she were willing herself to; but no words came from her, and she turned with her coffee and walked down through the dining room and back up the stairs.

Mark stood there. He put down his cup. He began to follow her but then stopped. He moved into the living room as tentatively as if he were returning to the scene of a crime. What he needed to do was this: he needed to take that pipe and swing it down onto her laptop, smashing its silver cover and glass screen and plastic keyboard until he got to every adulterous gigabyte leaking out one by one. Then he'd move to the television that had always brought Laura such nightly distraction. He'd bust a cavern into its large staring eye. Next would come the glass knickknacks on the fireplace mantel Mark had never liked but had belonged to Laura's mother, a warm woman who'd birthed a cold and deceitful daughter, and once they were nothing but colored bits of glass on the carpet, he'd aim for their small table of framed wedding photos, their shrine to that joyous August afternoon.

Because they'd met and lived in Salem, they married in a small Catholic church there not far from the water. Mark's mother stood in the front pew in a hopeful yellow dress, a white rose pinned to its lapel, a folded tissue in her hand. Next to her were Claire and her husband Thomas and their three kids who'd come up from Connecticut where Tom worked as an industrial engineer and Claire ran a day care center, his tired-looking but happily married older sister smiling brightly at him. There were Laura's mother and father, still alive, still married after forty-three years, her father handsome and ruddy-faced and looking like a New Hampshire farmer and not the high school principal he'd been for decades and would be until his death six years later. There were aunts and uncles and cousins with polite but distant wives and husbands. There was Laura's maid of honor, her pale, heavy, and kind sister Julie. And there was Mark's best man, Danny O'Neil, who'd flown in from San Francisco where he managed an apartment complex for an absentee owner from Brazil.

He and Mark had played baseball together all through high school, Danny first baseman to Mark's shortstop, a kid who had a vacuum cleaner for a glove and always made Mark look good, as he did then on that August afternoon in the incense- and oak-smelling church, Danny handsome and charming and single, probably gay, though he and Mark had never talked about that because they had never talked about much.

The truth is it was strange that he'd called Danny's mother to get his phone number out west; it'd been years since Mark had seen or spoken to him or even thought much about him. But Mark had no brothers, and the only men he saw regularly were those at work, most of them his underlings, or else the husbands and boyfriends of Laura's friends from the realtor's office, men he drank with and blathered nonsense with back and forth. There were buddies from college, a group of them he'd fallen in with his sophomore year, young men who'd also been high school athletes and now had vague desires to earn a lot of money. But except for his roommate Carlos Munoz from Brooklyn, he'd had no contact with any of them since their commencement under a misty rain, the leaves of the campus trees bursting with life. Those first years of working at bottom-floor company jobs, Carlos had written Mark a few postcards from wherever he was living—Omaha, Dallas, Miami—but Mark had never taken the time to write back: to do so was to let the current pull you backwards when his goal was only to forge ahead, to find his momentum, to begin earning and earning and never falling behind. Some nights, usually just before he was up for a quarterly review, he'd lie awake and hear, as clearly as his own beating heart, his father's name: *Welchy*.

And so there was no one to call on this quiet March morning, no one of his gender to give him counsel. For a brief moment he imagined calling Claire, but his eyes began to fill at even the thought for he could already hear his sister's loving voice and she would immediately begin to mother him. This would leave him feeling weak and not up to the crisis he found himself standing in. She would turn on Laura, too, and he could not have that for he still wanted his wife, he wanted her more than he ever had, especially now, her murderous laptop on the couch in the living room, her having walked away from him without a word, and then he was climbing the carpeted stairs to their bedroom.

From the dimness of the hallway he could hear the shower running, see the blue-gray light of their bedroom he had not slept in. He was unbuttoning his shirt. He was going to undress and step inside the shower with her. She'd be surprised at first, but she'd let him in. There was so much he wanted to say to her. There was so much she was wrong about, all those sentences she'd written to Harrison a razor cutting across Mark's organs. They would wash each other. They would begin to cleanse themselves of this. He saw himself drying her body with a towel, her sternum and small breasts and soft, flat belly with its purple stretch marks, her hips that had expanded for their children, her long runner's legs. Surely she would want to make love to him. Surely she would feel, as he did, that they just had to. Then, before she'd sit down and write that final letter, they could talk. Mark and Laura Welch would lie on their bed together and talk like they used to, or perhaps never had before.

But it was Laura who was talking. And it was on the other side of the bathroom door. For half a heartbeat, Mark thought Frank Harrison Jr. was in there with her, that some time during the night he'd walked right into their house and made himself at home. But the phone cradle on Laura's bedside table was empty and now Mark's ear was pressed to the closed bathroom door.

There was only the muffled sound of falling water in the shower, his heart jerking between his ears. There was his own breathing. A car passing by outside. For a full minute or two, he listened to the falling water and heard only that. Nothing else. He was only hearing things, that's all. Bad things. He just needed more sleep. Maybe after he and Laura—

"A *detective*, I guess. Honey, what're we going to *do*?"

An electric jolt through his limbs, his hands on the doorknob that wouldn't turn, the yanking and yanking. There was his yelling in the air, his wife's name in it like a leaf being swept away in a wind not of his making. There was the sting of his palm slamming the door again and again, then he was kicking it, then he was in the dim hallway and in Mary Ann's room, her white cordless phone in its cradle beside her white bedspread and stuffed white animals beneath the poster of a black rapper whose eyes on Mark seemed to be judging him, weighing whether or not he could do now what truly had to be done, the phone in his hand a gun, the talk button he pressed the trigger, the words coming out of his mouth blanks for there was nothing but the electronic flatline of a dial tone unrolling itself endlessly into the vast emptiness he'd been left in.

And by whom? A liar and a cheat, her contrition the night before not an act but a performance. And so the scope of the problem had just gotten wider and deeper and he had no choice now but to physically force the solution.

ON THE COP'S WALLS are nothing. No posters or photographs. No cheap framed paintings. Just four vacant walls that surround Mark now like mirrors, though something has changed; he no longer feels he is watching himself.

Beside him, Lisa Schena sleeps on her back, her face turned away from him. The sheet is pulled to her upper chest, and he cannot see her breasts but he can still feel them in his hands, so much larger than Laura's, so much fleshy abundance. Her lovemaking had been abundant too, though making love, he knows, is not what they just did. Yet he feels grateful toward her, the way one does toward a doctor who has just prescribed you the right medicine and then gives you a free dose. But what *is* this medicine that has sunk him back into his own body the way a baby is slapped breathing into this life? He doubts it is simply what Lisa Schena has just given to him, her breasts and tongue and spread legs, her fingers squeezing his hips as he entered what felt to him to be dangerous territory, for him, for her, the act itself somehow maligned, but her need was strong and so was his and then her legs locked him into a pleasure he began to give himself to, but again, for a long while it was only his body doing it, not him, and so he lasted longer than perhaps he ever had before, her moans a foreign language in his ear. How strange it was to touch and feel this new body. Places were soft that used to be firm, places went out that used to go in, and she moved in a rhythm that was like learning a dance he'd only seen once and that was long ago.

No one's ever made me feel that before.

A rolled towel slapping at him in rebuke, and he reminded himself to reach down and touch that part of Lisa Schena he had not always taken the time to touch on his wife, and that's when he began to feel himself drift back into his own body and its actions, when he felt the presence of lovely Laura who for all he knew was fucking Frank Harrison as he did what he did with Lisa Schena, her moans suspended, her breath jagged in his ear, her legs straightening as she arched her hips and let out a long exhalation of air, then a whimper, and Mark felt Laura there in the cop's room behind him, her long hair pulled back in a runner's ponytail, her arms crossed under her breasts, stunned that he would do this yet he was doing it, not his body but *him*, this knowledge dropping the weight of his days and nights into his loins where it became broken glass and splintered wood and cracked tiles, all gathering in tiny bits before hurling themselves into world-weary yet warm Lisa Schena.

She's snoring slightly. It feels like a violation of her privacy to hear it. He's sober now, or close to it, and outside the sliding doors the light has faded slightly. There's the gurgling hum of the air-conditioning unit, the room comfortably cold. He thinks of his car back in the parking lot behind the Sea Spray Motel, its wood glue and tiling materials and steel pipe in the trunk. It's not too late to at least repair the kitchen table leg, but he doesn't want to wake this woman, and if he leaves he'll be a prick.

He thinks of pregnancy, diseases. Unlike his own Laura, Lisa Schena is still in her fertile years and he just ejaculated deep into her womb. Also she's known him less than a day, yet she called him and fucked him, and how many other men has she done this to?

He looks back at her short ugly hair, her pocked cheek, her tanned upper chest rising and falling in peaceful, trusting breaths, and he feels like a creep for even beginning to judge her.

I love how you don't judge me.

Another one of Laura's razor-blade gifts for him. But couldn't she see that's who her husband was? A professional judge and jury, a man paid well to control the situation?

THE DETECTIVE WAS a retired state trooper, a heavy-faced Irishman with sad eyes and deep laugh lines around his mouth, and he'd given Mark the name Frank Harrison Jr., told him his job and place of work, the town he lived in, but no street address. So on that snowy morning, Laura most certainly back on the phone with her lover, Mark had pulled off the highway in Newburyport, the four-foot pipe from the garage on the backseat of his BMW.

He stopped at a Mobil station and borrowed their phone book from a young man slumped on a stool behind the counter. There were many Harrisons but only one Frank, and he lived on Olive Street. The boy directed Mark to it. "A half mile into town," he said. "On the left just past the high school." And he looked like a high school kid himself. He wore a Bruins sweatshirt, his left cheek stuffed with a wad of chew so that his directions sounded slightly slurred, and he was taking in the wrinkled button-down shirt Mark had slept in, the fact that he wasn't wearing a coat, his unshaven face, his bloodshot eyes that burned from lack of sleep.

When Mark drove his sedan down Olive Street, it was just after eight on a Wednesday morning. Olive was narrow, the way so many were in this old shipbuilding town, the houses on both sides of him historic landmarks that had been recently restored. Their clapboards and shutters were newly painted, and many of them had granite steps leading to small fir porches, brass street numbers screwed into plaques beside their front doors.

Number 37 was on the right, a shingled two-story whose roof pitched steeply into copper gutters only a banker would own. And there he was stepping out his front door, Frank Harrison Jr. He wore a beige overcoat and a gray suit, his tie a muted blue, his head not bald but balding, and he looked younger than Mark, fitter, taller, these traits fuel for the fire he knew he was setting, his arm reaching back for the pipe. Then he was on the sidewalk facing Harrison and his happy home.

Harrison was just stepping off the last step. A leather briefcase hung by his side, and in his right hand was an insulated coffee cup, the kind Mark himself would fill with dark roast before driving to work. Harrison stopped. His eyes took in Mark and his four-foot pipe the way a man would a natural disaster on the TV news just before changing the channel, this problem obviously someone else's.

"Do you *like* ruining other people's lives, motherfucker?"

Mark noticed Harrison's shoes were slightly scuffed, that his suit pants had a double crease in them from hurried ironing. Just beneath his left cheekbone was a shaving nick.

"I'm talking to you, you piece of shit."

"Who are *you?*"

"You know who I am. Don't give me that. You know who I fucking am." The pipe in Mark's hand felt like an extension of the long bones in his arm, and he stepped forward with it and raised it to his shoulder.

"No, I honestly don't."

There were the sounds of car engines starting, a door or two opening and closing. A woman down the street was calling something to her Tommy, something about his lunch. Mark stepped forward. He was close enough now to swing the pipe and do some damage, but his lower legs seemed to be stuck in three feet of mud, and he felt like a man with his penis out in a family waiting room in a hospital somewhere. Something had changed in Harrison's face too, his pinkish young face, and Mark was on the cusp of knowing his mistake before the banker even opened his mouth.

"You looking for Frank Harrison Jr.?"

"You know I am."

"Well that would be my father, not me. Now get away from my property before I make a call." Frank III walked across his small, damp lawn, his scuffed business shoes slopping through what little snow still clung to the grass. He climbed into his Hyundai and backed out of the driveway, his face not on Mark Welch, it seemed, but on all he knew and would rather not know about his good father. He stopped and stared hard at Mark out his open window, waiting for him to leave before he did.

A flash of movement, a curtain parting in one of Frank III's front windows. It was the face of a young boy. He was four or five years old, and he, too, was staring at Mark and his steel pipe, his eyes deeply curious, his lips parted. A woman's hand pulled him firmly away and the curtain fell closed and then Mark was driving a bit too fast down narrow Olive Street. There was the vague hope that his license plate was obscured from view, though he did not really care either way. Let them come. Let them all come for him for it was clear from the son that the father had done this many times before, and Mark now despised Frank Harrison Jr. more than he could contain.

He drove west along the river, passing house after house, fathers and mothers and children leaving them to climb into cars and minivans for the day's demands, so many of the kids shouldering backpacks they could barely carry. He accelerated onto the chain bridge over the river, its muddy banks spotted with snow, and he kept hearing the indignant voice of Harrison's son, how this had all become a tiresome game and look how easily he had turned in his own father. Maybe some of the men at Harrison's doorstep had been contractually fleeced by him, and that's what the son had seen before, but Mark doubted that. It was the young man's tone—*Well that would be my father, not me*. This moral separation he was nearly spitting out of his mouth, a morality rooted in something far more intimate than a businessman's slippery code of ethics.

Mark slowed beneath the highway overpass, then upshifted onto the ramp, gunning the engine across three lanes. An SUV honked, which was a surprise to him for he had not seen it, nor had he been looking. He kept seeing Laura's pale angular face, those small bags under her eyes as he would tell her that it appears her lover, her sweetheart, her nonjudgmental companion did this kind of thing all the time, that she was just one among many notches in his fucking jockstrap.

And this steel pipe nonsense would have to stop. That was a boy's revenge. If he did physically hurt Frank Harrison Jr., he would merely create a martyr and a patient for his wife to nurse. And there would be law enforcement to deal with, charges that could get him jailed and that could get him sued as well. He could lose his house to the very man who was taking his wife, and he saw Harrison and Laura sharing what was once his: his bed, his kitchen, his pool, Mark's mother's apartment empty of her.

He was driving too fast now, the median strip to his left a brown blur. Then a car horn honked and he was downshifting onto the exit ramp for his town. For a moment, perhaps two and a half heartbeats echoing in his head, he began to see Laura as a victim, one who'd been conned by a professional player. He started to feel his arms go around her, then hers around him as it began to sink into her what she'd truly stumbled into in that gym on the hill. But as he turned down his street, an empty driveway awaited him, one he drove into just enough to back out and drive to the only place she could have gone, Frank Harrison Jr.'s place of work, the Providential Bank on Water Street.

Mark drove slowly through the downtown of his youth. On both sides of him, the brick mill buildings were bustling with businesses, bars and restaurants, a microbrewery and music supply shop, lawyers' offices and a yoga studio and lofts for sale overlooking the river and its brush-covered banks on the other side. Men and women walked along the wet sidewalk, most in winter coats and hats, though he did not see them or think of them at all, his heart crashing in his head, his eyes scanning each parked car for Laura's Civic or Harrison's white Audi TT coupe.

He steered down the asphalt ramp into the lot behind the bank, and when he saw a white vehicle between a Mercedes and a minivan, he knew he would once again grab the four-foot pipe whether it was the logical thing to do or not. But it was a small sedan of some kind, and Mark backed into a space against the concrete river wall, and he waited.

It occurred to him he had not yet called in sick. He pressed his phone to his ear. In seconds Darla was on the other end. Twenty-nine years old, she was warm and competent and wore small wire-rimmed glasses that slightly magnified her brown eyes that were constantly anticipating what everyone around her needed, especially her boss, Mark Welch. She'd been married for two years in her early twenties, had no children, and on her vacations would fly to a European country where Mark suspected she'd find a lover whether she was looking or not, her calves upside-down hearts he disciplined himself not to stare at as she'd leave his office, her skirt or business pants hugging the firm, warm rest of her too.

But now her voice was a bath into which he was lowering his bruised and aching body, and Mark felt so wronged, so deeply and unfairly wronged, that for a brief moment he could not speak at all.

"Mark? This is your phone, isn't it?"

"Darla?"

"You all right?"

Through the windshield he could see the fluorescent lights on in the second-story windows of the bank, a bespectacled man in a suit talking to someone at a desk Mark could not see. "No, I'm not."

"You sick? The flu's going around."

"Yeah."

"You should rest."

"Thank you."

"Should I notify anyone?"

"I'll send emails."

"I'm happy to do that for you."

She was, too. She was *happy* to help him.

"I know you are, Darla. I know you are."

"Go back to bed, Mark."

"Darla?"

"Yes?"

He could feel the words forming in the back of his throat, and he longed to tell her, burned to tell her. He did not really know her, had never even seen her once outside the building they both worked in, but she would listen to him, and if she did not fully listen, at least she would hear him. At least one human ear would receive what he had to tell her.

"Mark? You still there?"

"Yes."

"Go to bed."

He did not remember having said another word, but now he was staring at his cell phone. #1 got him to his messages. #2 called home. #3 called Laura's cell phone. There were numbers for his children and one for his mother. There was a number for the central office and Teddy Burns, who'd been so right about his true nature and so Mark had learned to manage with edge and force, never abusively but through the use of incriminating details he'd simply point out to an underperforming team member, a clear and undeniable record of each and every one of his failures.

All he does is criticize me. Nothing I ever do is good enough for him.

He's a bully, Laura. He doesn't even know what he has.

I love how you don't judge me.

Bully? When he'd first read this hours earlier, the word had bounced off him like a ping-pong ball. How about *normal*? How about a man with average expectations? How about *that*? But now the word seemed to hang in the air of his car like a bad smell, and he started his engine and put it in gear.

He was driving again, this time through the back streets and their small vinyl-sided houses, their short driveways and muddy yards. Then he was crossing Main for the realtor's office. Its spaces were in the rear, and they held every car but Laura's. She was with him. She was certainly with him. He could call her. He could pick up his cell phone and punch in #3, but if she answered, it would be in the presence of her lover, and her husband would immediately appear to him weak and placating. No. Mark would drive back home, a foreign word to him now, a foreign country, but he would drive there and he would wait.

A small pickup truck pulled into the lot. Behind the wheel was a young man with a dark wispy beard. His eyes were scanning for a place to park, and he appeared so confident he'd find one, his life so completely and utterly under his control, that Mark wanted to roll down his window and say something to him, anything, anything that might better prepare him for the chaos that lay ahead.

MARK ROLLS AS QUIETLY from the bed as he can. The floor is a deep carpet, and he moves barefoot across it to his clothes. He turns his back to sleeping Lisa Schena. He pulls on his underwear. As he steps into his shorts, it is clear *he* is doing it, not his fingers and feet and straightening legs. He glances down at this sleeping woman. Her mouth is a partly open oval, her closed eyes two slits, and it's as if she dreams of something horrible or simply surprising, not what she expected at all. Her forehead and cheeks are sunburned, and Mark imagines her lying on the beach earlier planning to call him. Then all that sun, the drinks, and what they'd both done. What *he* had done and not just Laura, who had taken a burning torch and held its flame to the dry wood of their house, but now he has taken his own torch and held it there too.

Outside the slider, the last of the sun lies brightly over the small pressure-treated deck and its two plastic chairs. The roofs of the houses appear the color of ash, the sky above them a blanched blue.

On the cane chair against the wall are the two unopened cans of beer. He takes one and grips the handle of the sliding door and begins to pull.

"Lovin' and leavin' me?" Lisa Schena smiles and yawns and stretches one arm behind her head, her knuckles tapping the headboard.

"Not me." He smiles too, though it feels forced. "I'll be out here."

There is the comforting slide of the heavy door in its oiled track, then Mark is sitting with his foot on the rail, the beer cool and surprisingly good. He watches a gull glide silently on air currents not far overhead, and he feels he *is* that bird, alone and floating, a scavenger of the used-up and discarded.

Then Lisa is out there too, sitting in the chair beside him. She rests her feet on the rail next to his. She taps two menthol cigarettes from her pack and offers him one. He takes it and smokes it the way he did the night before when he'd stood with her under the neon light listening to her go on and on.

There's a crack-hiss as she opens her beer can, the muted thump of arcade machines out on the strip, the sucking, pounding surf.

"You're being quiet," she says. "Having regrets?"

"No." He looks at her. Her hair is flattened in the back and there's a smudge of eyeliner beneath her right eye.

"Me neither."

But he does have regrets, or knows he will soon, the way a man who's just broken a bone knows the nerveless shock of the sudden and new is only temporary. Now he misses his wife, the familiarity of her, the constancy of her, though he hasn't felt that for months.

"I had my tubes tied by the way, so no worries there."

"That's good."

"You all right?"

He nods at her. He smiles. He sips from the cop's can of Busch. "Was he your boyfriend?"

"Who?"

"The guy who lives here."

"Maybe."

"You don't know?"

She inhales on her cigarette, and Mark thinks of his wife's spotless lungs, her nearly viceless body. Lisa Schena blows the smoke straight out her mouth. She raises the beer to her lips. "Maybe it's none of your business."

Mark nods. He lets the coldness of what she just said hang in the air between them. It is a technique he uses at work as well, asking questions that lead to the near admission of a flaw or lack of judgment, and then he will just sit there quietly, letting the truth ripple back in the other's face like pond water on a mossy rock.

"Is he *still* your boyfriend?"

"You're a prick, aren't you, Mark?"

He nods his head and smiles. Maybe she's right. Why not admit it? Who better to admit it to than Lisa Schena, who drinks too much and sleeps around and helps kill animals to support herself and her fucked-up son?

"That's right, I get paid very well to be one, too."

"Are you working now?"

"No."

"Then knock it the fuck off." Her cigarette is only half-smoked, but she flicks it over the railing down to the sandy yard below. She turns to him. "Are you *judging* me?"

"You tell me. Would he be all right with this?"

"*I'm* all right with it. Or I was till now. I think you need to leave."

"Do I?" He begins to smile, the act as dangerous and unavoidable as what they'd both just done. He thinks of his semen having dripped out of her onto the cop's sheets. "You just cheated on him, didn't you?"

"Fuck *you*." A flame flares up behind his left eye, the back of her knuckles sliding away like a snake's head, and he is on his feet, the plastic chair sailing out away from them, the clatter of it on the neighbor's roof before falling though Mark's eyes are not on it but on Lisa Schena's, her wrist locked between his squeezing fingers.

"What gives you the right to *do* that, *huh?* **What?**"

"Let go of me." Laura's words, not this woman's, but they come from her mouth like some memorized lines from a script written before any of them were born. And her eyes have changed. What before appeared streetwise now looks lost and scared, alone and used to being alone, all in a nearly colorless blue.

For a half-breath of air, he must admit that he needs to see this, that he is still here and capable of being seen. But now a whimper of fear comes from her, the same sound she'd made earlier, and he lets go as quickly as if he'd touched something poisonous.

"Leave." She lowers her wrist and begins to rub it. He wants to apologize, to tell her he's never touched a woman like that before, even his lying, cheating wife. But no words seem to be forming.

"I said *leave.*" There is no fear in her voice, only outrage, and Mark is pulling open the slider and stepping into the coldness of the cop's room. The scent of their sex lingers in the air as he stoops for his sandals, and Lisa Schena's voice is in the room, her half-shadowed form filling the doorframe. "You're a loser, Mark. That's all I *pick*. It's all I ever *fucking* find. Just one more man who never grew up and is a fucking bully and a coward and a piece of *shit*."

There are more words, more of Lisa Schena's endless sentences, but Mark is down the stairs now, pausing in the cop's TV room just long enough to strap on his sandals and hurry through the small, neat kitchen and out the door, its frame slapping the railing so hard the dead potted plant falls to the ground below, a soft thump that sounds to Mark like the making of a bruise.

HE TAKES THE LONG WAY HOME. It's a road that hugs the ocean for a mile or two before cutting west for small towns of Cape and ranch houses, double-wide mobile homes with white picket fences between their driveways and patches of green lawns. In one, a shirtless man stands under the dying sun before a gas grill, barbecue smoke rising into his face though he holds his ground and doesn't move, squinting into the heat as he flips cooking meat with a spatula. Then he's gone and Mark passes the Beachside Motel, the beach three miles away. He passes a clapboard restaurant, its front deck festooned with red, white, and blue bunting from the Fourth last week, a holiday he celebrated by sitting near the pool at the umbrella table with his mother. Every Fourth of July for years, ever since the kids were little, he and Laura would host a daylong pool party. Five or six families would spend their entire holiday with them—the Brandts and Salvuccis, the Battastinis and Doucettes from next door, Claire and Tom and their kids before they moved to Connecticut. Rock and roll would be blasting on the boom box, ten to fifteen children splashing in the water, inflatable floaties around their arms, most of the mothers sitting at the shallow end with their feet in. Some would be sipping a drink or cup of wine, and they'd all be talking and laughing with one another, Laura visiting with them briefly before she hurried into the kitchen for more chips and dip, cold drinks for the kids, hamburger patties or marinated chicken from the fridge for Mark, who spent so much of his time at the smoking gas grill, cooking flesh and chatting with whoever happened to wander over. He'd sip a beer or a Bacardi and Coke, and he'd take in all this happy chaos he looked forward to each year.

Once the kids became teenagers they started drifting off to their own parties, and so the Fourth became a party for adults. The drinking got harder and started sooner, and there was less swimming and more smoking around the umbrella table, more dirty jokes. One year Charlie Brandt drank too much and called his wife a cow, and she threw a bowl of French onion dip at him that grazed his shoulder before falling into the pool. Mark had to walk him inside the house to lie on the couch and sleep it off.

When the sun was down, Mark would build a fire in the pit a few yards from the diving board, and his married friends would pull their chairs around it and he'd put something quieter on the boom box and he'd sit in one of the chaise lounges, Laura joining him there, her back against his chest, his arms around her just under her breasts, and he'd lie back and listen to their friends chat and laugh or go quiet now and then as they stared into the flames and listened to a tenor saxophone floating a note through them that was both joyful and melancholy, which is how he felt then, his wife's head against his shoulder, the smell of her hair and skin, its baby oil and chlorine and dried sweat, her breath rising and falling beneath his palm, and he'd feel so tender toward her it scared him, the way holding his children as babies had scared him, that he'd been entrusted with these precious responsibilities and there were so many ways for them to get hurt or worse, and then—as he kissed Laura's hair or cheek, one of their friends telling a story or joke—he'd want to apologize to her. He'd want to tell her he was sorry for always being on her case—about meals and bills, about what she watched on TV, about how little money she actually made, about how she took too long on her runs, about what a bitch she was around his mother, what a baby she'd always been with Mary Ann, letting their daughter take charge too soon, because Laura was too damn quiet and meek and if she wasn't fucking up in some way then she was running by herself or sleeping too soon too deeply when they all needed her, goddamnit; her family had *needs*.

None of this would be fully in Mark's head, but holding his wife close on the chaise in the firelight among friends, he could feel all those moments leading to this one like the lingering echo of gunshots.

Once, a little drunk, he'd kissed Laura's jawbone and whispered in her ear, "I'm sorry." But Bobby Batastini had just told a story and everyone was laughing, Laura too, her stomach muscles bunching under Mark's fingers. She had not heard him, and he wasn't going to say it again.

But why not?

Mark drives slowly through a town square. It's nothing more than two banks, a gas station convenience store, a strip mall, and a

Chinese restaurant. He's rolled down his windows and opened his sunroof, and the wind coming in is warm and smells of asphalt and chicken wings and gasoline. A sadness has opened up in him that surprises him.

A fucking bully and a coward and a piece of shit!

He upshifts past a narrow green. In the center stands an eight-foot slab of granite, the names of dead young men etched into it. World War II, Korea, Vietnam. Beside this is a shorter slab, the grass around its base newly placed sod; Iraq and Afghanistan. He accelerates down the road, warm air slapping at the side of his face, and there's the gut-twisting thought that he's a dodger of important moments, that he may, in fact, *be* a coward.

Laura, a Saturday morning in the fall. They'd both slept late. Mary Ann was away at college, and from downstairs came the smell of slightly burned pancakes, Kevin and one of his buddies eating them in front of ESPN. Outside their bedroom windows, the maple leaves were such a bright orange it was as if the tree was on fire and Mark could not stop looking at it.

Laura put her hand on his chest under the covers. "Hey, let's do something today. Just you and me. I won't even go to the gym."

But they were building Mark's mother's apartment then, and the builder had given Mark a punch list of things to do. Door hardware to pick up, handicapped rails for the bathroom, drawer and cabinet pulls for the kitchen. These were tasks he enjoyed doing, and he knew, lying there beside Laura, he could have included her in them too, that they could go somewhere for breakfast, then drive to the Home Depot together, maybe even go for a walk together after that. But lately he'd seen a confused and tender hunger in her, as if she needed something from him she used to think only he could give, but now she was on the cusp of knowing she might be able to get it from somewhere else, too, and that's why she'd looked so vulnerable that fall Saturday morning in their bed, her eyes soft, her lower lip tentative; she was asking Mark to stop her.

But her face, her voice, her hand on his chest, simply made him tired. They were all asking him to drop one project for another, and he did not drop projects. He saw each and every one to completion, and then he began another.

"I can't today, honey. I've got that punch list." And when he climbed out of bed, her hand sliding from his chest, he sensed he'd just enlarged the scope of a project he was not even aware of, one whose costs he would ultimately have to cover.

Mark passes an auto body shop. He passes a boat supply business and pizza joint, then he's driving onto the bridge over the Merrimack River. The sun is low to the west, and there are dozens of motorboats cutting through the currents. On the bow of one, two young women in bikinis lie back on their elbows on towels, and he feels again Lisa Schena's legs around his hips. *Are you judging me?*

He had been. How could he say he had not?

Up ahead is the turnoff for downtown, and he takes it, stopping briefly beneath the overpass to let three teenage boys cross in front of him. They wear low shorts and loose T-shirts, one in a Red Sox cap and untied basketball shoes, and all of them have earplugs in one ear, the wires running into their shorts pocket, each of them hearing different music in their heads while also talking about whatever it is they are.

There is the feeling he is a man not of these times, one who has been left behind long ago and should have been. Then he is driving along High Street. On both sides are the large Federalists built before this country was a country. Some have ornate painted fences set into stone walls, others deep lawns cut down the center with a walkway. Frank Harrison Jr.'s is poured concrete stamped to look like English cobblestone. It's pretentious, and Mark eases up on the gas. He sees two cars in the driveway. One of them is Harrison's white coupe and the other is his wife's white SUV, both of them matching the white clapboards and white flower boxes overflowing with small red flowers of some kind.

Then all of this is in Mark's rearview mirror, and in his head is only a light pulsing, the kind he gets when he knows he has forgotten to complete an important task and can't quite remember what it is. The last of the sun is in his eyes. He flips down the visor, glimpses on the sidewalk an old man. He's in a scally cap and a yellow shirt, his shoulders and chest and belly sagging, a metal cane at his side, and he just stands there, staring down at the concrete as if it is telling him something.

WHEN MARK RETURNED from Harrison's bank and the realtor's office's parking lot, Laura's car was in the driveway and whatever snow there'd been had melted, the asphalt wet and black. Entering his own house, it was as if he were willingly stepping onto a ship whose lower holds were filling with icy seawater, its bow beginning to shift skyward.

Laura stood in the kitchen, waiting for him. She wore her blue Nike running suit, and her hair was tied back, and she had one hand on the edge of the sink as if to balance herself.

"Where did you go, Laura, and don't tell me it was the fucking gym."

"I can't do it."

"What? You can't do what?"

"We talked about it, and I—"

"*Who?* You and fucking *Harrison?*"

"If you yell at me again, I'll leave."

Mark's heart was kicking at the inside of his skull. In the shadows of the kitchen, his wife stood straight and poised, her chin raised, and she appeared to him terrified yet resolute. This did something to him. The earth seemed to have more gravity, his feet in iron boots as he pulled a stool toward him and sat.

"We love each other."

He stared at her, at her straight jaw, the bags beneath her eyes she hadn't tried to minimize with makeup, at her closed lips, at her long throat and arms, at her hand on the edge of the sink in the sunlight coming through the window, a tremor in her fingers. It was as if his grief were a hurricane and this was its eye, and he wanted it to never end, this calm, this quiet. Just the two of them in this space that would soon be swept away.

"Why are you shaking, Laura? Are you *afraid* of me?"

She said nothing. She kept her eyes on his. She blinked. "You treat me like I work for you, Mark. You always have. Well I don't work for you, all right?"

"You really think that?"

She shrugged. "I blame myself more than I blame you."

"That's not fair, Laura." He had to say it, he had to take a stand, but he did not believe his own words and they seemed to fall to the floor between them.

"At first I needed it, I guess. I was drifting really. Even though I had a job and my running, I was—"

"What?"

"Just what I said." She crossed her arms. She leaned back against the counter. She seemed to be waiting for something now.

"I went to his son's house, Laura. While you were with him in your little rendezvous, I was at his fucking son's house."

"Mark."

"You think he'll leave his *wife* for you? He fucks around all the time, Laura. You're just the latest hole for him."

"You're wrong."

"Am I? Talk to his son. He told me all about it. Talk to his fucking *son.*"

She was moving now, past him and through the kitchen and out the front door, the eye disintegrating too soon, too soon, and Mark's feet were light again, his legs the ones he had as a kid, for he was in their driveway slapping both hands on the hood of her car, Laura's Honda pulling fast away from him, bouncing into the street, then jerking forward and speeding up. "You're going to write that fucking letter!" He was running alongside it, Laura's face so peculiar, so still even as his fist was punching the glass that separated them, and he was yelling directives at her that she *would*—goddamnit!—follow.

But it was Mark Welch doing the following. For nine days, he called in sick. For nine days, and a weekend in between, he was the man living behind the wheel of his sedan, his heart a sick companion lodged between his ears, like having a one-way conversation with one who answered in tubercular coughs. He was the man driving three cars behind Harrison's as he drove to his acupuncturist and the gym. He was the man following him to the state park in New Hampshire to run with Laura Welch, her husband having rented a small blue Yaris for that, to sit in the pines in it and watch his wife kiss Harrison, a big handsome man in an expensive running suit, black and shiny, his bald head shiny too. Then they would stretch on the ground together side by side, they'd chat and laugh, and Mark could see through the trees Laura's face. It was more relaxed and contented than he could ever remember, and so he was the man who had tried to break into Harrison's coupe while he was running with Mark's wife. He was the man who let all the air out of his rear tires, then regretted it immediately for that meant Harrison would have to sit with Laura in her Civic while they waited for Triple A, though Mark had not waited for that, for in the blue shadows of dusk, his wife's windows had fogged up, most likely from the heat of their running but maybe the other, too, a thought then an image then a feeling he felt himself push away from, like pushing back from a poker table when your downfall is imminent, standing and walking away, the non-feeling deepening then, this existing inside a body that did what it did. Like following Anna Harrison from her law office to the sandwich shop where she ate alone at a small table in the corner with a book, the same kind of literary-looking paperbacks Laura read for her book group. Mark was the man sipping coffee on the other side of the shop, the place loud with well-dressed workers and young mothers and their young kids, so much normal and happy noise that Anna Harrison, her sandy hair pinned back too tightly so that she appeared compromised in some way, did not notice. Nor did she notice him follow her out, or hang back ten or fifteen paces, the man in a coat and tie for that is what his hands dressed him in those mornings, they'd shaved his face as well, and splashed aftershave onto his cheeks, that sweet-smelling burn in his skin that seemed to reach him long after. The question was: Does he tell her? Does he tell her that her husband and his wife—what? Such an old and predictable story, ageless really, like some virus that affects some marriages and not others. And that's how she appeared to him, too. She was the woman who had accepted this sickness she lived with, a woman who took her pleasures where she could—a good novel, a hot cup of minestrone soup, a freshly baked roll and cold glass of water on a clean napkin. And if he did tell her, perhaps that would be it for her and she would be ready for what is sick to finally die, and then Frank Harrison Jr. would be living in an apartment somewhere and who would be sharing it with him but Laura Murphy Welch?

Mark had followed her the most. As she left the realty office for the gym, as she left the gym for a run with Harrison in the state park, as she left the state park for the Marriott. Three times that first week, she left work at noon to have lunch with Harrison at the Panera two blocks from his bank. They took window seats, brazenly happy together, each leaning forward as the other spoke, nodding their heads, sometimes laughing, one or the other reaching over to touch a hand or arm, his wife's face looking as it had only twice before that he could remember—after the agony of giving birth to their daughter and son, the skin of her face smoother somehow, a light in her eyes that could only come from deep relief and a hard-earned joy.

Sitting in his small rented Yaris, Mark had felt small himself, a grasping failure of a man. How could he deny what he was seeing? Wasn't it time to let her go? But to allow the question into his head and heart was to allow a black tumor to take residence there where it would grow. But the only thing growing was this distance between himself and the world he supposedly lived in. He'd become a man things happened to, and he found himself groping for the tools of his work: Risk response and its plans for contingency and mitigation. The monitoring and controlling of the results of those plans. Staring out the driver's window of his parked rental car across Water Street into the Panera booth, his wife and lover settled there so comfortably, the only contingency plan he could consider was this: He would not leave her, he would not kick his wife from her home, for then she would create one with Harrison. Mark would move into his mother's apartment. He would stop telling Laura she could no longer see him. He would stop telling her to write a letter telling him goodbye. He would pull back and throw his hands up and let what was coming come. Let his wife's mistake take care of itself. For in Harrison's lean and shaven profile—the way he leaned forward at all times, the way his ears lay flat as a wolf's against his bald head—Mark sensed the predator his son's choice of words had revealed. Her husband would let her keep a place of refuge she would need later, and in the meantime, he would take the high road. He would be her "bully" husband who had chosen to move into his mother's apartment until his wife came around, until Laura Murphy Welch came back from the woods one day scratched and bloody and looking for the man who had loved her all along.

MARK STEERS SLOWLY down his street. It is late afternoon, one of his neighbors is grilling burgers, the charred smell of it in the air. In the driveway are his mother's Buick and Laura's Honda, his space vacant between them, and he pulls between the two cars and thinks of his father before he became Welchy, a big man who walked in the door at the end of the day laughing loudly, swooping Claire and Mark up into his stubbled kisses that smelled like Vitalis and cigar smoke, popcorn and whiskey, his eyes taking in his children as if they were his only cure. Then he was gone and Mark was fourteen, scooping a grounder into his glove and gunning it to Danny O'Neil, the smack of the leather, the runner two strides late, the sun low behind the field so that they were all in a warmly shadowed light that seemed etched from someplace golden and far away where somebody good was in charge and they didn't have to worry about anything, just play.

For so many years he has worried, but not now. Strangely, not now. Between his legs is the lingering warmth of what he'd emptied into Lisa Schena, and he wants to call her and apologize. If she'll let him, he may even want to see her again, he is not sure. He is not sure of much, but he knows something has tipped and shifted, and something else has let go and something else is now coming.

He rises out of his sedan. He leaves the sunroof open and the windows down. If it rains tonight, then it fucking rains. He unlocks his trunk and takes the plastic tub and places into it the glue and mortar bag and various tools he's going to have to learn to use. When he slams the hood, Laura is there, her profile in the kitchen window, her hair and face and torso silhouetted against the rear window to their backyard, the maple trees in the late afternoon light. She's talking on the phone. Maybe to Harrison. Maybe to one of their children, whom they never seem to see much of anymore, something that probably won't change and there's little to be done about it. Laura is only in shadow. Her long hair hangs down her straight back, and she is young again and there is the dull stab of remorse, not for what he's done today, but for something he never did but vowed he would for this quiet woman who was nothing like those he'd dated before, no biting wit or even very much charm, no seeming desire to rise up some glimmering corporate tower. She didn't have one's generous curves or another's dark eyes promising pleasures both sensual and intellectual. But there was something so accepting about this woman who had sold him his condo that he was soon inviting her into it, the sun low over the water, Mark distracted by the gold in her hair, her deep green eyes, her high cheekbones and straight clavicle, and he liked how she wanted to hear about *him*, his job and his boyhood, but not like she was interrogating him or sizing him up. There was a calm to her, a passivity he could only do one thing with—to take it in his two hands and begin to shape, then manage her as he saw fit.

Mark's cheeks burn. He squats and lifts the tub and carries it to his front door. He has not approached it since there was snow on the ground. He climbs the three concrete steps. His heart thumps softly in his chest, and he has to lift his leg and rest the tub on his thigh to grasp the brass knob that won't turn. He is only vaguely surprised by this. His keys are in his pants pocket but he will have to put down the tub to get them. He reaches over it and knocks on his own door. His mother is surely in her kitchen cooking herself something, leaving a plate for her son. Or she might be out by the pool nursing a glass of white wine over a magazine, one eye out for Laura. Maybe the three of them could go out there together, all three adults, no hard feelings. They could sit by the water till the sun is down and through the trees come the soft lights of their neighbors. His mother would politely excuse herself, and Mark and Laura Welch would talk. He would tell her things. He would apologize. Maybe she would too, though he no longer needed that, and they would talk not about what had happened, only what had to happen next. They'd speak quietly. Calmly. Maybe they would reach over and touch. Maybe they would even kiss. Maybe Laura would stand and walk away as she had every right to do. Or she would softly squeeze his fingers and lead him back into their house and up to their room and into their bed and they would make love, no matter what each of them had done earlier or with whom, and it would be different this time. He would pay more attention, and he would let her do whatever she wanted, then and later, every day and every night and week and month she chose to stay with him, which she might not, this woman whose footsteps he now heard through the door, this woman he could hear moving through their entryway, his heart in his head once again for he did not know if he was even up for any of this, this change from change, the door swinging inward as he straightened, his wife's face lovely and surprised and waiting.

MARLA

——

SOMETIMES AFTER DRESSING FOR WORK, MARLA WOULD STAND at the kitchen sink with the last of her coffee and feel as if her small apartment and everything in it were props for a movie she wasn't even in, as if she were working for all this for somebody else. She was twenty-nine years old and had been a teller at Providential Bank for eight years. She owned a Honda two-door, and her bedroom closet was full of large tasteful outfits with shoes to match. In her carpeted living room was a high-definition TV and DVD player enclosed in an oak cabinet with glass doors, the bottom shelves filled with workout discs she never used beneath musicals from the forties she watched once or twice a month. Alone again on a Saturday night, she'd curl up on the couch with a bowl of buttered popcorn and watch two movies back to back. She'd listen to the orchestra's manly horns and womanly strings and watch men who could sing and dance their leading ladies into a swoon under the stars over a glittering sea, and Marla would pull her cat Edna into her lap and stroke her head till she purred, and she'd try to pretend she wasn't miserable, even with all she had.

On Thursday nights she'd go out with her friends from the bank, usually to Pedro Diego's downtown because they had nine kinds of margaritas and they kept the place lit up in an aquamarine light. It made the tiled cocktail tables, the huge cacti in the corners, and the straw sombreros hanging on the wall all seem to be in an underwater tequila dream, and when she was a little drunk she always felt prettier, or maybe just more hopeful, or reckless, which occurred to her once might be the same thing. She'd borrow one or two cigarettes from Lisa's pack of Marlboros and she'd suck her peach margarita through the straw, laugh at Nancy's nasty jokes, listen to Nancy bitch about their supervisor, Dorothy, who was fifty-six years old and seemed to have married the bank twenty-five years earlier. But there was a sadness in Dorothy's eyes, even when she was briskly handing you a memo making your job more tedious. If you looked past the hard lines of her face, her short, unstylish hair, you could see how dark and sad her eyes really were. Not pissed off the way the other girls saw her, but melancholy. *Lonely*, Marla was sure.

Nancy's husband Carl was a computer salesman with a square, handsome face, blue eyes with nothing behind them, and the beginnings of a gut he didn't bother working off anymore. He and Nancy had two teenage sons and lived in a five-bedroom on Whittier Lake north of town. Three or four times a year they would host a party for their favorite coworkers from his job and hers, and their place would be full of casually dressed husbands and wives, boyfriends and girlfriends, all sipping drinks, chatting and laughing and munching cheese sticks and buttery stuffed mushrooms, appetizers Marla was careful not to touch. Instead, she'd grab a carrot to chew on while she sipped from a glass of white wine. Soon many of the women would get around to talking about their young children, and something seemed to come into the air between them that wasn't there just a few moments before; the light in their eyes became more genuine somehow, and they nodded their heads not out of habit or good manners, but because they really did know what the other was talking about. The air would be heavy with it. And often it left

Marla feeling so excluded she'd refill her wineglass and walk out onto the deck.

She'd lean against the railing and look at the lawn sloping down to the stands of pines and birches at the water's edge. There was a dock there and a boathouse Carl had built himself a few years earlier. Not long after he'd driven the last nail, Nancy had confessed to the girls at Pedro's that she and her husband made love there while the boys slept up in the house.

"We just had to," she'd said, then shook her head and laughed. "But I got two splinters in my butt and I made Carl pull them out with his teeth!"

Nancy had a small, lined face that was pretty even when she wore her glasses, and sometimes when she laughed they'd slip halfway down her nose, which made Lisa and Cheryl laugh even harder at this picture of Carl's face buried in their friend's rear. Marla had laughed too, though she didn't think it was that funny; it was like being careless with a precious gift, talking that way—not about the boathouse or the marriage itself, but the lovemaking, what men and women who loved each other did when they were alone.

"You shouldn't joke, Nancy."

"Oh, lighten up, Marla," Lisa said, coughing now, knocking a cigarette loose from her pack.

"Why shouldn't I joke?" Nancy's eyes were still bright and glistening with mischief.

"I don't know—because it's special, isn't it?" Marla's cheeks and throat felt hot and she wished she'd kept quiet. Her friends were giving her a look they seemed to give her more and more, their mouths smiling but their eyes still and careful. Cheryl, with her streaked hair and tiny waist she got from six mornings a week at the gym, nodded her head and said, "She's right, Nancy; you're a slut."

"I didn't *say* that."

They'd all laughed, even Marla, but the rest of the night she felt that familiar drift away from her friends. She sipped her margarita and listened to them talk, and once again she began to feel sorry for herself; she was twenty-five years old at the time and still had never slept with a man—not just because she believed it was special, but because no boy or man had ever stopped to take much of an interest unless it was to be cruel; in middle school other kids teased her and called her Marla Marmalade, and in high school at parties she willed herself to go to, she was almost completely ignored. Once in a crowded house, a drunk boy had wedged her against the hall wall and pressed his hands into her breasts under her sweater. Junior year, a tall boy with thick glasses would sit with her at lunch sometimes and talk about how bad the food was or how "oblivious" the band teacher was to "reality." But nothing ever happened, and Marla was never sure why he'd ever sat with her at all. For a while in her early twenties she would drink too much at parties and would sometimes end up with a man who drank too much too. There would be groping and fondling, and once she took a man into her mouth who gripped her hair like he wanted to yank it. But she never opened her legs, was never so drunk she completely lost that part of herself that still believed there was a man out there who would love her.

She started drinking more moderately and began to view her virginity as a gift she was keeping for herself to open with a man special enough to know it was a gift. She knew this was an outdated notion and sometimes wondered if she really believed it; if she were as attractive as her friends, would she think this way? And for a few years now, it had begun to feel less like a gift and more like a burden; she was turning into one of those rare women who had completely missed the train everyone else had gotten on. She began to be convinced something might be truly wrong with her, that she had a defect everyone could see but her.

Except for her weight, she did not consider herself all that unattractive; she had thick brown hair she never had to color, and it had natural waves in it her hairdresser said he'd kill for. Her eyes were small and set a little too deeply into her round face, but she had high cheekbones, a straight nose, and a symmetrical mouth full of fairly white teeth. Since high school she'd tried to lose the extra thirty-five pounds that seemed to gather mainly in her hips and thighs, but exercising felt to her like punishment for a crime she couldn't remember having committed, and when she starved herself she felt as if she was living in a cruel and sadistic world and at three or four in the morning she'd be in her kitchen standing in the light of the refrigerator eating cheese or dipping French bread into a jar of mayonnaise. But still, she wasn't that heavy, certainly no more than some of the wives and girlfriends she saw with men around town, some of the women so big you could see their thighs rub together when they walked.

Over the years, Nancy had suggested it was her personality that needed some attention, that Marla was too *honest*. The first time she said this was on a Monday morning before the bank opened its doors. Nancy had come in wearing a black rayon blouse that made her breasts look small and pointy, which then made her look somehow more middle-aged and inappropriately sexy. When she asked Marla if she liked it Marla had told her the truth. "Not really."

"Thanks a lot."

"You asked me what I thought."

"That doesn't give you license to say what you really think, you know. *Jesus*." Nancy set her cashbox loudly on the counter.

Marla's face got hot and she stared at her keyboard.

"I mean, that's just not how people make conversation, and, I'm sorry, but that's why you never get asked out—you always say what you really think."

Marla's eyes began to fill and she had to reach for one of the tissues the bank left out for its customers. It was the start of another workweek and all she'd done over the weekend was call her parents down in Florida, gone grocery shopping, mopped her kitchen floor, and watched rented movies with Edna. She began to dab at the corners of her eyes, then heard Nancy let out a breath, felt her hand on her shoulder. "I'm sorry, I didn't mean to hurt your feelings."

"I know."

"It's just—you need to go with the flow more, okay? Make a little small talk."

But no matter how much Nancy had suggested this over the years, Marla was not convinced; if a man was impressed with small talk, how big could he really be? When she was a girl, her own father only spoke when he had something to say, his feet up on the plaid hassock in front of the TV, and it'd be one or two words, a question whose answer he only seemed to half listen to. She'd feel invisible and say, "Daddy, you're not *listening*." But by the time she was out of high school and going to the business college in Boston, she had long since stopped waiting for him to respond more than he did. She'd sit on the couch next to his recliner at the end of a long afternoon of classes and he might reach over and pinch her knee. "Having fun? Learning anything?"

"I'm learning things." That the world was a marketplace of numbers, nothing but numbers: debit columns and profit margins, mergers, acquisitions, charts, graphs, codes, leveraged buyouts, and bankruptcies; that she always did well on exams and ate lunch alone; that she began to see her mother as a woman, a truly unhappy one, who had always worried about money and could hardly let a day pass without mentioning how poorly the boxboard company had treated her husband. Marla began to notice how old her mother seemed to be getting, that after so many years working the switchboard at St. Mary's Hospital she spoke to everyone with a slightly impatient edge, as if she still had the headset on and was getting ready to press a button and send whatever you were saying along to somebody else. Soon Marla became friends with another woman who ate alone too, a sweet big-nosed girl who worked part-time at a bank downtown. She said they were looking for somebody reliable to work a window, and just two days after their graduation, she introduced Marla to Dorothy, who never smiled but took her on anyway. Then Marla's friend got married to Frank Harrison III, the son of one of the loan officers, and at the reception Marla had gotten tipsy with her new workmates. She'd danced with Nancy's husband Carl, who had pressed his sweaty cheek to hers; she felt included and welcome, and the whole room seemed to be lit with the light of open doorways; Marla began to believe that her childhood was something she'd endured, and now that she was in the adult world things would get easier, better.

AT THE BANK, her tasks were repetitive and her days soon became predictable, yet there was a real comfort in dressing well and having people trust you to store their money with precision and honesty; sometimes Marla would see one of her customers on the street and get an almost shy but respectful wave, the kind she'd once given to her own gynecologist, the kind you give to the one you trust with the knowledge of what you have.

Marla began to hope for more, too; a real boyfriend, the loving company of someone other than her old cat, Edna. And Nancy was right. Over the years Marla had had conversations with men at house parties and bank barbecues, but she never could seem to keep things going; she could only talk about work, about interest rates and the convenience of online banking, her computer screen hurting her eyes at the end of the day. There was really little else she knew much about. Soon enough even the homeliest of men would smile politely, then drift away with their plate of food to either talk with somebody else, or just stand alone at the bar or buffet table. Marla would stay where she was and try to pretend she didn't care. She knew she was dull company, and she also knew if she were slim and pretty, but just as dull, they wouldn't drift away at all. Sometimes Nancy or one of the other girls would whisper to Marla to follow, to keep the conversation going no matter what. But Marla refused; if someone wasn't interested in her, then he wasn't interested in her.

Nancy suggested she look in the personal ads or log into an online dating service. But the idea left Marla feeling more desper-

ate than she believed she truly was, and she resented these prods
from her friends. All of them had come from big loud families, and
Nancy already had her own, but what they didn't understand, Marla
thought, was that she'd always been alone; she had no brother or sister. Until now there'd only been one real friend, the last two years
of middle school—Hannah. She had a round face, stringy hair, and
always smelled like mustard and clothes starch. She lived next door
and for two years they spent nearly every afternoon playing board
games, reading Judy Blume books side by side on the bed, watching
TV and eating cereal out of the box, washing it down with Coke or
Pepsi, getting giddy and laughing so hard Marla could see a forked
vein in Hannah's forehead. Then it was high school, and Hannah's
face was no longer round; she had breasts and a waist and slim legs
she showed off in tight jeans; she grew her hair long, and if Marla saw
her at all it was as she climbed into a boy's car and roared off down
the street.

Then, in the late spring of her eighth year at the bank, Dennis
Munson started coming to her window. He was big, with a beard
and a hard-looking belly, the rest of him thick and solid like he'd
done something athletic at one time. Marla didn't notice him much
at first. But after a while it seemed he always waited for her window
when another was open, and when he stepped up she felt something
flutter just under her ribs. She was drawn to him: his size and quiet
sweetness, his neat and legible deposit slips, the tentative way he'd
push them over to her, his thirty thousand dollars in savings. Marla
thought a balance like that showed maturity, the kind of person who
planned ahead. He had a high voice for a man, but it was melodious,
too, the way he would say, "How are you today?," each word pulled
smoothly into the next, like a lyric she'd never heard before.

On a Friday in May, twenty minutes before the bank locked its
doors, he deposited his payroll check with her, took his weekend
spending money—one hundred and twenty-five dollars—and stood

there looking at her, blinking fast, like he had something in his eyes.
"Do you have plans after work?"

Marla's blood seemed to pause in her veins; was he asking what
she thought he was? "Not really."

"Want to get a bite to eat with me?" His eyes stopped blinking
and big Dennis Munson was looking right at her—just her face, but
Marla felt as if he was seeing every bit of her, and it was all okay
with him.

"All right."

"I'll meet you out front after you close?"

Marla nodded and tried to smile. Her mouth was dry and she
couldn't look at him and she didn't want to say anything more. She
picked up a stack of deposit slips and tapped them on the counter. She
turned to her keyboard and pressed the space bar three times. When
she looked back up, he was on his way out the door, his tweed-covered
back looking so broad. Soon Nancy's face was inches from Marla's,
her voice a shrill whisper: "Make him take you someplace *nice*."

And it was nice, a small Italian restaurant on the other side of
town. Dennis owned a Nissan, and he opened the passenger door for
her, the inside clean and smelling like vanilla air freshener. Stuck to
the dustless dashboard was a small notepad and pencil and his neat
penmanship:

3 sectors?
Frequency reuse pattern of 7?

Marla asked him about it, and when she did her voice sounded
just right to her, not flat or nervous or overeager to please, and she
enjoyed listening to what Dennis told her as he drove through town.

"I'm a radio-frequency engineer. I get my best thoughts on the
highway."

"Maybe driving fast makes your brain go faster." Marla meant this as a real possibility, but big Dennis laughed and she did too, and she liked how warm his smile was after the laugh was over.

At the restaurant he pulled her chair out for her, a gesture Marla had only seen in Gene Kelly movies. He asked if she'd like a glass of wine and Marla nodded, trying to think if she wanted white or red, but before she said anything Dennis waved the waiter over and ordered a bottle of Chianti. The busboy brought over a basket of glistening garlic bread. Marla was going to abstain, but Dennis cut a section off for her and placed it on her bread plate before serving himself.

They were quiet at first, studying the menus, chewing garlic bread, sipping their wine. Marla was hungry, and if alone would've ordered lasagna or veal parmigiana. But with Big Dennis Munson she settled on a plate of antipasto.

"That's all?"

"Yes, I'm not that hungry."

"You sure?" He looked concerned, his lips pursed behind his whiskers, and Marla knew why she was so relaxed; she felt appreciated and cared for, had ever since she'd first noticed him waiting for her window, and now tonight the way he held his car door open for her, how he'd laughed at her accidental joke.

"Well," she said, "could we share something? Lasagna or something?"

"Sure we could."

They finished the garlic bread, then spilt the antipasto and a platter of lasagna and sausages. The waiter brought them each a clean plate, but Dennis waved him away and pushed the lasagna to the middle of the small table, and they ate it slowly, one bite at a time, till their forks touched and Marla's face and throat flushed.

He'd been telling her about his job scouting locations for cellular towers, about his three brothers, two of whom were engineers, too. How his company transferred him here six months ago, and how much he liked these old New England mill towns, the mountains to the north, the beach to the east. And even though he didn't ask her many questions about herself, Marla felt privileged to hear some of his life. They each ordered a tapioca pudding for dessert, and she was grateful when he dropped her at her car in the bank parking lot and took her hand in both of his, said in his high voice, "I had a nice time with you. Can we do it again sometime?"

"Yes, I'd like that." Marla's face felt puffy to her, too warm from the wine, and she hoped she didn't look fat as he stood there taking her in, her hand lost in his. He leaned forward and kissed her on the upper cheek. His whiskers were surprisingly soft.

They dated for five weeks, ate at nearly all the restaurants in town, went to six movies—most of them action films Dennis had heard were quite good—and started seeing each other during the day as well. One Saturday in early June they held hands and strolled along the new boardwalk along the river. The sun was bright and Marla smelled the drying mud of the riverbanks, the hot pretzels of the vendor in the shade of his own umbrella. There was a young family there, a boy and girl with their mother and father, the woman slim and pretty, her bare legs lean and hard-looking. Marla was aware of her own legs being twice as large and not muscular at all. She was wearing baggy khaki shorts that went almost to her knees; before Dennis picked her up she'd changed out of them twice, but it was too hot for sweatpants or even a long skirt, and she knew those shorts were exactly what she would wear if she were going out today alone. But when Dennis picked her up he smiled at her as warmly as he always did, as if he really appreciated her, *admired* her even; he wore shorts too, and Marla saw how thick and pale and hairy his legs were. Now they were past the pretzel vendor and the family, walking under the sun along the river. She could smell Dennis's cologne—too per-fumey, she thought—but she had begun to match that smell up with him and was growing to like it, the same way she was growing to like nearly everything about him: his bushy beard and big hands, the careful way he held her when they kissed longer and longer after each date, the way he seemed to listen to whatever he had to say—her sto-ries from work usually, describing impatient customers or Dorothy's constant demand for efficiency, for their cashbox and keyboard totals to be perfect to the penny every shift. And Dennis would listen completely, walking slowly beside her, nodding his head, his eyes on the ground in front of them.

At Pedro's the girls teased her gently about being smitten, and Lisa squeezed a lime into her drink and asked if the eagle had landed yet.

"What?"

"You know, the *eagle*. Has he landed in your nest?"

Everyone laughed and Marla's face got hot, and she was relieved when Nancy seemed to rescue her with a joke about a priest and nine nuns. As she did, Marla held her margarita and looked around the table at her best friends in the cool blue light of Pedro's: Lisa and her dark sassy eyes; Cheryl and her streaked hair, square jaw, and tanning-booth tan; Nancy with her wire-rimmed glasses and pretty lined face holding back a laugh as she described nuns riding bicycles with no seats. Marla felt more a part of them than ever. She kept hearing the words *eagle* and *nest*, and something warm seemed to stir and loosen inside her, the same feeling she got whenever she and Dennis touched. She'd been wondering why he never tried to do more than that; he seemed to like her body and did not shy away from pressing his hands into the flesh above her hips as they kissed. Maybe he didn't know she wanted to. Maybe he needed some encouragement.

The next day after lunch, Friday, she walked to the pharmacy in Railroad Square, found the aisle with enemas, vaginal creams, and douches, then the small box of colorful condoms. She was drawn to one with the nude silhouette of a man and woman facing each other, *Maximum Protection* printed where their lower bodies should be. She walked straight to the counter. The cashier was a woman much older than she was, who narrowed her eyes through bifocals at the price on the box, nothing else. Soon the condoms were in a bag in Marla's hand, and as she stepped out onto the sunlit sidewalk she felt part of the bigger picture somehow, more of a citizen of the world she lived in.

That night Dennis had wanted to see a cop thriller, but Marla insisted they see instead a movie about an angel who falls in love with a mortal on earth and is willing to give up his wings to have her. When the movie ended, her mascara was smeared and she was leaning her cheek against Dennis's shoulder. They were sitting at the wall end of a row and didn't have to stand right away when the lights came up. She held his hand in both of hers, and she imagined him as a big bearded angel shucking his wings and all his powers to sit with her in the dark of a movie theater, to make love with her in his bedroom. She kissed his neck and whispered: "I think we should go to your house."

"Right, I should finally give you a tour."

"I don't mean that."

He turned in his seat and looked at her, his brown eyes alert above the tangle of his beard. "Are you sure?"

She nodded and he smiled at her. Shyly, she thought.

It was a quiet drive back to his neighborhood of two-story ranch houses and square lawns beneath evenly spaced streetlights. He unlocked his front door and the dark house smelled like vacuumed carpet and something vaguely fruity, bananas in the kitchen. There was only the light from the steps outside. Dennis took her sweater, then kissed her, his mouth open, his arms pulling her to him.

He led her upstairs. Then she was in his room, and she was grateful he left on only the hall light. As he sat on the bed and began to untie his shoes, she reached into her pocketbook for the box of condoms. Her fingers were trembling. She didn't know if he could see what she had, and she didn't want to call attention to it yet, so she made her way through the partial darkness and placed it on his bedside table. If he noticed it, he didn't show it. The room was too dark to see much, but she undressed quickly and slid beneath the covers, which felt a bit gritty and smelled like his cologne. Then he was beside her. She could feel the entire length of his body, its fleshy warmth. He began to touch her knee and kiss her gently, tentatively.

His leg was over hers, his knee resting where no one else had ever been. She could feel his hardness, and her eyes filled up. She wanted to tell him how much this meant to her, but as he began to kiss her neck and shoulder, then the beginning of her breast, she was afraid if he knew the truth he would think something must be wrong with her and everything that was happening would stop. She let him kiss her nipple, then pulled him to her and kissed his lips; he was careful not to rest his great weight on her, and she felt the pressure of him against her down there, the way she began to open up and take him in, the stretch and slight burn. Dennis stopped.

"I don't have anything."

Marla could feel her heart beating in her arm as she reached for the condom box. Dennis sat up and she listened as he opened it, then unwrapped a package, the quiet of him rolling it onto himself. Was that it? Did he roll it on? She felt cold and covered her breasts with her arms, again grateful for the dark, grateful when he positioned himself over her, grateful for his warmth, for his slow careful push into her, as if he'd known all along anyway, and it was gentle and sweet and hurt all the way to feeling good.

FOR THREE WEEKS she slept at his house every night, living out of her suitcase, garment bag, and cosmetics case. Sometimes she didn't have all she needed and would get up in the near dark an hour early, kiss sleeping Dennis on the cheek, and drive to her apartment to get ready for work. At the bank and then at Pedro's she disciplined herself to tell her friends nothing; over the years she'd seen how tell-ing too much could backfire, especially with Lisa, who would fall in love with a man on Tuesday only to be talked out of it by Cheryl and Nancy on Thursday. Maybe if she hadn't shined a light on some-thing so private, Marla had always thought, then it would have had a chance to grow into something special. And even though a part of her couldn't wait to tell her friends the news, she felt sure the telling would cheapen it, or maybe jinx it somehow, so she sipped her margarita and let them talk about work and their families, about vacation time and bad TV, and even though they had no idea she wasn't the same Marla anymore, she sat back and felt the privileged comfort of the initiated.

EARLY ONE MORNING in July, a Wednesday when it was drizzling outside and Marla was dressing to leave for her apartment and work, Dennis opened his eyes and said, "Wait."

Marla sat beside him on the mattress. The room was dim and she could smell the warm cotton sheets they'd slept in, made love in. He put his hand on her knee. "I have a big closet, you know."

"Yeah?"

"Big bedroom, big living room." He yawned and stretched his arms over his head. "Plenty of room, really."

"Dennis."

He squeezed her knee and looked right at her, his brown eyes swollen with sleep, but bright and hopeful. "You want to?"

"You mean, move in?"

"Yes."

Marla smiled and nodded. Her eyes filled up and she wiped at them, and she and Dennis both started to laugh.

At the bank that morning, Marla performed her duties cheerfully. When Dorothy unlocked the vault for them to get their cashboxes, Marla was the first one in. While she set up her drawer and got her monitor running, she hummed an old tune she felt sure was a love song. She could hear the loan officers talking in the outer offices, Cheryl and Lisa opening their cashboxes and tapping their keyboards; she could smell the lemon wood polish the cleaners had used on the counter early this morning, Nancy's coffee as she passed behind Marla and said, "Morning."

"Morning, Nance." Marla glanced over at her friend, watched as she set down her World's Greatest Mom coffee mug, cashbox, and pocketbook, her glasses already at the end of her lovely nose. Part of her wanted to tell her the news and part of her didn't. She knew Nancy would want to hear the particulars, and Marla didn't want to talk about them yet; she was still feeling them, the way she seemed to see everything as if for the first or last time: all the spots and stains in the lobby carpet, the thin cracks in the plaster ceiling way above the security lamps, the cobweb in the far corner there too, the false green of the plastic potted plant near the door, all the ink smudges on her computer monitor, the creak of the stool beneath her. Somehow, what she and Dennis were planning to do made this building and everything that happened in it seem smaller and less important.

Dorothy walked across the lobby with the key ring in her hand; she wore a gold cardigan sweater that didn't quite match the rust of her slacks and, from the back, with her short hair and flat shoes, made her look more like a man than a woman. Marla watched her unlock the doors, and she felt a surge of tenderness for her that she'd never quite had before, the guilty gratitude of the last swimmer in the life-boat watching one left behind in the water.

That night Marla and Dennis made love twice, once on the sofa in the flickering light of the TV, and again in his bed before sleep. When he finished the second time they were both quiet awhile, Dennis breathing hard, Marla's hands holding his soft, sweaty back. They both seemed to be in the presence of something other than themselves, this silence that pulled Marla to fill it with something significant and true.

"I love you, Dennis."

He took a breath and let out half of it. "Mmm, me too." He kissed her forehead, pulled out of her, and went to the bathroom.

Marla heard the pull of the shower curtain, the running water. She reached for a couple of tissues and patted herself between her legs. Me too, he'd said. Too shy to say *I*, she thought. Right? Too shy.

The next night at Pedro's Marla waited till their second round of margaritas before she told her friends her plan to move in with Dennis. The place was louder and more crowded than usual. A group of businessmen in ties and crisp white shirts were up at the bar laughing and toasting with their drinks. A lot of the tables were full, and even the music on the stereo seemed louder, Spanish guitars and men singing high and fast. Marla and her friends were at their regular table in the corner. Lisa had been talking about this new lawyer she was seeing, Richard, a triathlete who'd told her last night she had to quit smoking if she wanted to stay in his life.

"Is that how he *put* it?" Nancy asked.

"Yeah," Lisa said. "Just before he rolled off of me."

"What?" Nancy and Cheryl looked at each other, their lips parted, their eyes full of the dark joy Marla saw in them whenever they got on the subject of men's shortcomings. This didn't feel like the best time to bring up her and Dennis, but when else would she?

Cheryl leaned forward. "He was *inside* you when he said this?"

Lisa nodded and pulled out a cigarette she'd have to smoke on the sidewalk.

"He's a prick, Lisa," Nancy said. "You know that, right? Don't get caught up in how handsome he is and how much money he makes; a prick's a prick." Nancy wasn't smiling anymore. She looked down at her margarita and stirred it with her straw. Marla thought of Carl, his empty eyes, then Dennis, the way he'd invited her so sweetly to live with him, his big hand on her knee.

The music was too loud on the stereo. Marla leaned forward and half shouted: *"Dennis asked me to live with him."*

"He did?" Nancy looked at her as if for the first time all night. "When?"

"Yesterday morning."

"Uh-oh," Cheryl said.

Marla turned to her. "Why do you say that?"

"I don't know, it's kind of early in the relationship, isn't it?"

"What's that got to do with it?" Lisa said, looking hard now. "I've met guys on Friday and moved in on Sunday."

"Yeah, like you should be Marla's role model, too."

"Are you going to do it?" Nancy's fingertips were on Marla's arm and she was smiling.

Marla nodded.

"Good for you," Lisa said.

"I don't know." Cheryl reached for a corn chip, then dropped it back into the basket. "What's the rush? I mean, are you thinking of marrying him?"

"Maybe." Marla sucked hard on her straw and was surprised there was so much liquid left in her glass. She was beginning to feel hemmed in, and she wasn't sure why she'd told her friends when she knew all along at least one of them would end up talking about it in this way, like the decision wasn't entirely hers.

Nancy gently squeezed her arm. "How did he ask you?"

"In bed."

"Yeah," Cheryl said. "That's where he wants to keep you, too."

"How do you know that?" Lisa said. "Maybe he loves her and wants to spend more time with her."

"Then he should buy her a ring."

"What if I'm not ready for a ring, though, Cheryl?"

Cheryl shrugged. "Look, I just don't think they should get a wife for free."

"But she's not going to be his wife." Lisa raised the unlit cigarette to her lips.

Cheryl leaned closer to Marla. "Will you be sleeping together?"

"Yeah."

"Right. Will you be cooking?"

"What's your point, Cheryl?" Lisa lowered her cigarette.

"I know her point," Nancy said. "She's afraid he's going to be getting his milk for free so why buy the cow—?" Nancy seemed to stop talking in mid-sentence. Heat rose in Marla's face, and a foot kicked her under the table and she was sure it was Lisa's aiming for Nancy.

"Excuse me." Marla made her way past the crowded tables in the blue light and smoke of the restaurant she came to every week with her best friends, but she felt like crying, and she wanted to leave early and go to Dennis's house, to be with him right now and not them. She stepped into the bathroom. It was bright, empty, and quiet. She stood there on the hard tiles and she felt as if she were waiting for somebody to come get her, to come get her and take her someplace else.

BECAUSE DENNIS WAS thirty-seven years old and owned all the furniture he needed, there wasn't much room for Marla's, so Dennis suggested they store it in the garage—her double bed and frame with the turned maple posts, the matching bureau and mirror, her deep rose sofa and love seat, her table and chairs, boxes of dishes, pots and pans—he and Marla stacked them neatly in the far corner of the empty bay next to a rolled garden hose and two rakes. It was a Saturday morning and muggy. They'd rented a small U-Haul truck. It took them most of the day to fill it and empty it, both of them dressed in loose sweats, stopping occasionally to drink from a water jug they shared, to kiss briefly, Dennis's whiskers all wet. What Marla did bring inside were her clothes, three plants, Edna's scratching post, and two small museum prints of a willow tree by a Flemish painter whose name she could not pronounce. She hung one above the stair landing, the other on the blank wall above the toilet. The rest of the wall space throughout Dennis's house was taken up with large framed pictures he called "graphics," a lot of gray and red angular lines Marla supposed only an engineer could appreciate. In the living room was a floor-to-ceiling bookshelf, and most of it was filled with paperback espionage novels, science fiction, and a few mysteries. The sofa and recliner were oversized brown naugahyde. Neither they nor

the books ever had a speck of dust on them. Once Marla had asked if
he had a housecleaner. Dennis smiled. "Nope, just me."

At the end of the day after returning the truck, Dennis went off
to buy them a takeout dinner, and Marla drove back to her old apartment to drop her keys off in her ex-landlord's mailbox, check the
closet and cabinets one last time, and get Edna, who was napping in
her cushioned basket in the corner of the kitchen. Marla picked her
up, held her to her chest, and walked through the bare rooms. Her
footsteps had an echo, and it was as if she were leaving not only a place
in her life, but a time too, that her years of solitude were over, that
she was somehow, miraculously, rising to the next step and would no
more be left behind than Edna, purring now against her, rubbing her
ear against Marla's throat.

Marla's father was the only other man she'd ever lived with; after
his workday was through, he would sit in his chair in front of the TV
with the newspaper, a CC and ginger ale, and a smoking Raleigh. She
imagined Dennis might do something similar, sit in that huge brown
recliner and unwind in front of some news show with the paper or
maybe one of his many books, she on the couch with a magazine or
book of her own. She looked forward to this, quiet evenings just the
two of them relaxing together like that, Edna curled up between
them. But most nights when Dennis came home an hour after she
did, he didn't loosen his tie and sit down: he cleaned the house. He'd
take a blue feather duster and wipe down every flat surface there was,
even the tops of the door and window casings, and he did it cheerfully, whistling as he went. He owned a commercial-sized vacuum
cleaner that was louder than any Marla had ever heard. It had tiny
headlights that lit up six inches of carpet in front of it, and Dennis
seemed to keep his attention on that six inches of space as he pushed
the big machine along.

After watching him do this three nights that first week, Marla
said she'd never seen anybody dust or vacuum that often, even her
mother.

"Yeah." He shrugged. "I like it, though; it clears my head. Plus, there's cat hair now."

"I can clean that."

"No, I don't mind." He smiled at her. "It really clears my head."

Marla smiled too, then walked over and hugged him, this big eccentric engineer of hers.

But there seemed to be more to this than just keeping his head clear; he expected her to keep *hers* clear too. Because she got home before he did, she usually cooked, and after they'd eaten Marla was content to let the dishes soak in soapy water for a half hour or so before she got up to clean them. When she lived alone she'd sit on the sofa with Edna awhile first, watch some trashy TV about movie-star gossip, or sometimes something fortifying on PBS. She'd run her fingers through Edna's fur and sit there with her legs drawn up beneath her, nothing pressing to do for the first time all day. But Dennis didn't do that. He insisted they do all the chores before they did anything else. "Business before pleasure, right?"

The first week or two Marla went along with this; she still felt like a guest in his home, and she did not want to be impolite. But once she settled in it was harder to do things his way just because they were his way. One night after a pasta primavera dinner she'd cooked, Marla stood from the table and went right to the living room. "Let's do the dishes later. I'm going to relax."

He didn't answer her. Soon she heard the water running, Dennis rinsing the plates, glasses, and silverware, stacking them in the dishwasher. Marla stayed where she was. She reached for the remote control but wasn't interested in watching anything, simply wanted the TV to cover up his sounds. She was still in her work clothes—a jacket, blouse, and skirt that was a bit too tight in the waist—Edna in her lap. If she were alone she would unsnap it and relax completely, but she didn't want Dennis to see her that way. On the TV was a game show, a heavy woman trying to guess the letters of the mystery word. Dennis came into the room drying his hands on a dish towel he then folded twice. Marla smiled up at him, and he smiled back. "I love your cooking, Marla, but you sure do make a mess."

"I do?"

"Yep."

"Then how about if you cook next time and I'll clean up?"

"There wouldn't be anything to clean." He shrugged and went back inside the kitchen.

The next night Dennis skipped his dusting and vacuuming. Instead, he baked a meatloaf, boiled and mashed some potatoes, and heated up a pan of frozen green peas. While everything cooked, he wiped down the counter and stove, washed, dried, and put away the mixing bowl and boiling pot, even swept and damp-mopped the floor before they sat down to eat. He lit a candle and they shared a bottle of red wine. Over dinner Dennis was cheerful and expansive, talking about one of his colleagues and the gentlemen's bet that they had to come up with an engineering problem the other would not be able to solve. Marla smiled and nodded her head at all the right times, but seeing the clean, bright kitchen behind him, she couldn't help but feel she'd just been beaten at a game she hadn't known she was playing.

After dinner they both loaded the dishwasher, then sat on the couch watching whatever came on television or whatever Dennis switched the channel to: an old black-and-white war movie, a color war movie, music videos, a comedy from the seventies, the actors in polyester bell-bottoms. A strange stillness had opened up inside Marla. Was there a part of Dennis she hadn't seen before? A nasty competitive streak? Dennis went into the clean kitchen and brought out a bowl of Oreo cookies. Marla didn't want any, but sitting away from him watching him eat cookies made her feel worse; she curled her legs up and laid her cheek against his chest. He rested his arm over her side and hip and after a while she began to feel better. What did she expect? For him to be perfect in every way?

In bed, they made love in the dark, and Marla held him tightly. After, curled up together and beginning to doze, Marla felt little of what she had earlier; Dennis was a good man and she was lucky to have him. She reminded herself that living together wasn't supposed to be easy, and she fell asleep with her cheek on his warm, hairy arm.

Two weeks before Labor Day, Nancy left party invitations on Marla's, Lisa's, and Cheryl's keyboards while they were in the vault getting their cashboxes. Nancy took pride in her invitations, usually scrolling the borders with a pattern from one of Carl's computer programs—blooming flowers on a vine, tiny party hats and martini glasses. In the past Marla's invitations had been addressed just to her, but this time, engraved in gold was: *Marla and Dennis*. This phrase lingered for her throughout the day; it reminded her of all the other phrases she'd always heard but never really listened to quite in this way: Nancy and Carl, Cheryl and Danny, Lisa and, lately, Richard. Even her own parents: Helen and Larry. And now Marla and Dennis; by choosing to be with one she had somehow been invited into a whole society of others.

At the party two weeks later, Marla spent the first half hour introducing Dennis to everyone she knew, standing close enough to him that they would know right away he wasn't just a friend. And Dennis was much better with people than she'd ever been: he called them by their first names he didn't forget; he smiled and laughed a lot, a Michelob Light in his big hand. Marla noticed the glances of many of the women she'd seen at these parties for years, quick appraising looks at both of them. Most appeared happy for her, relieved even. One woman, Anna Harrison, her old friend's mother-in-law, kept her eyes on Dennis's belly for a while, looking at Marla again before turning back to conversation. She seemed to be writing them off as the two fat people who'd found each other, and Marla felt bruised by this but only for a moment or two; Dennis was really hitting it off with Carl and some of his friends from the company, talking software and search engine capability. Nancy and Carl had set up a volleyball net in the backyard beyond the pool, croquet too, but by noon it began to rain, and the guests sat in Nancy's plush furniture around the house eating barbecued chicken and potato salad off plates in their laps. After lunch, most of the men descended to the boys' playroom in the basement and began a dart-throwing championship while Carl and Dennis played a video game on the wide-screen.

Soon it was just the women. They sat in Nancy's deep sofa and chairs in the living room. Outside the French doors, rain fell on the pool, empty lawn, and the trees and lake beyond. The room smelled like leftover barbecue sauce, five or six kinds of perfume and skin cream, fresh coffee. On her glass coffee table, Nancy had set out plates and forks and cheesecake right from the bakery box. Some of the women started talking about takeout food and how they hardly ever really cooked or baked anymore.

"Who's got time?" Nancy said, slicing wedges of cheesecake onto plates.

"Exactly," said another.

"Frank does more cooking than I ever do." It was Anna Harrison, the woman whose eyes had lingered on Dennis's belly earlier. Lisa offered that Richard cooked better than she did, and she believed men were really better at it than women anyway. "Look at all the chefs. How many are women?"

"Right," Cheryl said. "But who do you think cooks at home?"

"Good point." Lisa grabbed her cigarette pack and excused herself to go smoke. Marla could hear the rain falling against the windows, the occasional joyful roar of the men downstairs. Nancy offered her a plate of cheesecake, but Marla said no thank you, and not because she didn't want to draw attention to herself or her eating, but because she really felt full, satisfied. Her boyfriend was downstairs with Carl somewhere and she was sitting in this room as it fell into three or four conversations now, and even though she wasn't talking, she didn't feel left out of any of them. She looked past Cheryl and her incandescent blond hair as she leaned forward to give a woman named Bonnie tips on cross training. Marla could see Lisa on the other side of the French doors standing on the deck beneath the eaves out of the rain, her arms crossed, a thin stream of smoke shooting out in front of her: Marla wondered if she would quit for Richard, and even though he was probably right to make her do it, Marla was glad she had someone like Dennis, who, except for the thing about cleaning up, was content to leave her just the way she was.

A while later he and Carl came upstairs for more beer. They both looked happy and flushed. Nancy asked her husband who won and Carl jerked his thumb at Dennis: "I can't even get *close* to this guy."

Some of the women laughed. Marla smiled up at her big bushy-bearded engineer. She could feel the women watching her. She puckered her lips and Dennis leaned over, said hi, and kissed her quickly before he disappeared down the stairs with Carl. Marla raised her cup to her lips.

She felt watched by the whole room, but she kept her eyes only on Nancy, who was smiling with all her teeth, her eyes moist behind her glasses.

DENNIS AND CARL had hit it off so well that Nancy began arranging double dates for the four of them one or two Saturdays a month. They'd go to a restaurant downtown, then maybe a movie, or, once, dancing. At dinner Dennis said he'd rather go to a movie instead, but Nancy wouldn't hear of it, and they drove over to the Marriott in Carl's Mercedes.

The Executive Lounge was dimly lit and full of people, loud DJ rock blaring from gargantuan black speakers. Carl paid the cover charge, then led his wife between dancing couples right to the center of the crowded floor. Marla could see just the top of Nancy's head as she began to move fast to a song Marla had heard her whole life. She'd never really danced before, but the place was so full and loud and dark nobody would really see her anyway. Why not? She pulled on Dennis's big hand, but he wasn't moving. He shook his head at her, then nodded at a small table a cocktail waitress was just finishing clearing. They sat down and Dennis ordered a round of what they'd all been drinking at the restaurant.

A new song began before the old one ended, The Rolling Stones this time; Marla knew most of their music from the radio. She leaned over the table to Dennis and shouted: "I want to dance!"

Dennis shook his head. *"I don't dance."*

"Never?"

He smiled, then shook his head again, then sipped his Michelob.

Marla sat back in her chair. The dance floor was too crowded to see Nancy or Carl, all those well-dressed bodies bobbing and jerking and swaying in the dim light, the music so loud she could feel the bass beat in her wineglass and under her fingertips on the table, too loud for her and Dennis to even talk. She sipped her wine and watched the crowd. She could feel Nancy and Carl out there, and she didn't like it; Marla and Dennis should be there too, the same fun-loving couple who'd been laughing at Nancy and Carl's jokes all night, who'd been swapping stories from work, raising their glasses to toast the good times, Nancy and Carl smiling at them in the candlelight on the other side of the table, smiling at their fun friends: Marla and Dennis.

Marla glanced over at him now. He was watching the DJ up on the small corner stage, studying his microphone and speakers, the electronics of his sound system, it seemed. Always an engineer. It was that part of Dennis that Carl seemed to admire so much, but without Carl treating him with such respect for his engineering skill, without Nancy smiling at both of them for having found each other, Marla sat there feeling a little lonely. But why should she feel this way sitting next to Dennis? She reached over and squeezed his hand. He smiled at her behind his beard, raised his beer to her in a toast. She toasted too, though she felt like an actor backstage rehearsing for the next scene, and she couldn't wait for the music to end and for Nancy and Carl to come back.

AT HOME, AS ONE WEEK pushed into another, little things about Dennis began to bother Marla: the sometimes nasal way he'd call her "Marl"; how at breakfast every morning he'd skip the newspaper headlines and do the crossword puzzle instead; how he cleaned up so often the place never looked lived in; even their lovemaking needed something—it always seemed to stop just as things began to gather all warm and rising for her, and she didn't like how he always took a shower after. It made her feel dirty and like what they'd done was slightly wrong somehow. He stopped wanting to go anywhere except on weekends, preferred instead to watch TV or go to his computer room and play games where the viewer entered a cyberworld armed with a shotgun, machete, and hand grenades. He taught her how to play it too, but sitting in that dark room staring at the simulated colors of bad muscular men bleeding to death from just the click of the mouse on Dennis's desk, from the electronic blast of the shotgun or the swipe of the machete blade, Marla felt the same bruised emptiness that she did after an action movie, and she'd kiss Dennis on the forehead and leave the room while he kept playing.

There was something else too—and she hated herself for this—but it was his weight: watching him walk naked into or out of the bathroom she often looked away, not out of respect for his privacy, but because she honestly did not like to see the way his hairy chest pushed out to the side like a woman's, how his belly hung almost to his penis, which looked somehow boyish and outmatched in the great mass of all that flesh and hair. At first she thought this reflected his size and strength, his very manliness. But that's when she'd allowed herself to think he'd been a wrestler or weight lifter in college, maybe even a football player. Not the sedentary man she now knew him to

be and to always have been. He told her that he spent his childhood
in his room reading and drawing robots and guns and galactic cities
floating in fiery orbits, that college was one long period of book after
book and a lot of hamburgers, pizza, and fries.

She found herself judging him for this, especially at night after
dinner, dessert too, when he'd bring a box of crackers and a jar of peanut butter to the living room with him, or a second helping of dessert,
or a hunk of cheese and bowl of nuts. One night in late November, a
couple of days after a Thanksgiving they'd spent at a restaurant, she
had a cold and sat on the couch wrapped in a blanket, holding a hot
cup of lemon tea. She glanced at the peanut butter crackers on his
plate and said, "Are you really hungry?"

He'd just sat down. He looked over at her, his cheeks flushed.
"Obviously."

Marla didn't know if he was angry or embarrassed, and she felt
mean-spirited and small. For a long minute or two there was nothing
but the sounds of the TV, the forced laughter of the studio audience, slender actors with good skin and shiny hair looking naturally
appealing.

"You shouldn't talk, you know." Dennis bit off half a cracker and
chewed.

"What?"

"You know what I mean."

Marla's face burned. It was as if he'd just overturned the couch
and she was falling to the floor. "You're talking about my *weight?*"

Dennis swallowed and bit into another cracker, his eyes on the
television. There were crumbs in his beard, and she hated him for
it, and they began to blur, and she jumped off the couch and rushed
upstairs to their room. *His* room, really. *His* bed and *his* bureau and
bedside table. On the walls were framed *his* degrees and another boring graphic. On the bureau were his wallet and keys. Where was her
room? She curled up on the bed and cried. She could hear the jingle

of a commercial downstairs, and she wondered how long he'd stay down there without coming up to address what had just happened between them.

And what did happen?

She was mean and then so was he? But it was more than just that; Marla couldn't help but notice that part of her was relieved to see another ugly side of him.

The TV noise stopped and she heard the creak of the carpeted stairs, then the sinking of the bed, the smell of peanut butter and his perfumey cologne.

"Marl?"

"Yeah?" She sniffled, dabbed at her nose with two fingers.

"Do you think I'm too heavy?"

"Do you think I am?"

"No."

"Then why'd you say what you said?"

"To get back at you, I guess."

Marla sat up and blew her nose. He rested his hand on her thigh and she knew they were on their way to patching this up, but something had opened between them and she wasn't sure she wanted it closed. She looked straight ahead at the dark window. "I've always been fat, you know."

"Me too."

Marla wiped her nose. "But I bet you had girlfriends."

"Two or three. Nobody special."

"Well, I didn't." Marla kept her eyes on the black glass of the window, the reflection of the lampshade in it. "You're my first boyfriend."

"I am?"

"Yes."

"Oh." He nodded his head slightly. She wished she hadn't told him but was also glad she did, as if this were some kind of test they could not avoid, though she did not know who was testing whom.

"Are you surprised?"

"No. I mean, yes, of course I am. What's that have to do with anything?"

Marla shrugged. "I'm not the best catch in the world, Dennis."

"Marla—"

"No, really. I'm not pretty, all I know how to do is count other people's money, I—"

"Shh, stop that, Marla. You shouldn't say that." His voice was gentle but distant too, like he was already beginning to believe what she was saying and didn't want to. He pulled his hand from her thigh and stared at the floor again. "You should never say that about yourself."

They sat quietly for a moment, then he stood and took a long, tired breath. "Want me to bring your tea up?"

She shook her head and listened to him walk heavily out of the room and down the stairs.

LATER, IN THE middle of the night, she woke up with him pushing himself inside her and he did it harder and faster than ever before. It hurt a little, but then felt good, and lasted longer too. He finally stopped and let out a moan, said into her ear, breathing hard, "I'm sorry, I was asleep."

"Me too."

He went to the bathroom first and Marla lay there in the dark. She patted the bedside table for the box of tissues, Dennis's seed swimming freely inside her. What if it found what it was heading for? She heard the shower turn on, the jerk of the curtain, Dennis washing himself off.

That night she dreamed she was sitting in a rocking chair on a screened-in porch overlooking deep woods, sunlight coming through in brilliant patches; there was something warm and soft in her lap, a puppy, she thought. She looked down at it and saw a baby—a baby with fine black hair and a sweet pinched face.

The next day was Sunday, and on the way home from the matinee of a spy movie she hadn't wanted to see, she told Dennis her dream. She studied his profile as he drove, the way he nodded slightly, his eyes narrowed as if he were listening to the radio report of news in a distant country. She took a breath. "Think we'll ever have a baby, Denny?"

"Not if I can help it."

Marla felt slapped. She looked out the window at large houses, one with raked piles of leaves, a swing set in the yard. She felt like crying, not because of what he'd said but how he'd said it, his voice adamant and final. Then his big hand was on her knee and she wanted to push it away.

"You know I love you, Marl, but do you know how much kids cost? How much attention they need? It's nothing personal, hon. I just can't be bothered with that."

"*Bothered?* You make it sound like one big nuisance."

"Well, isn't it?"

"Did your mother think so?"

He smiled. "I know she did." Then he chuckled and began to reminisce about him and his brothers always destroying the house, chasing each other from room to room. He seemed to be done with the real conversation, but it had cleared a cold dead path through her head; it was the first time he'd ever told her he loved her, but hearing him talk this way about what she had always viewed as the highest gift God could give, his paw resting too heavily on her thigh, the sickening smell of vanilla air freshener in his car, another Sunday afternoon wasted at a movie where men shot or impaled or blew up each other, she began to suspect she was nothing more than an easy addition to his life, one he could penetrate half-asleep or go out with on the weekend, but that's it—no one to start a family with, nothing like that. Her seatbelt was pushing into her hip, and she began to feel the possibility of an end ahead of them, the way the light of an August afternoon could sometimes cast the shadows of October.

———

THE WEEK BEFORE CHRISTMAS, Dennis invited her to fly to Cleveland to spend the holidays with one of his brothers and his family. He asked her this before work as they were walking to their cars in the cleared driveway Dennis paid a man to plow. The air was cold in Marla's lungs and her breath was a thin cloud in front of her.

"What do you say, Marl?"

She opened her car door and glanced over at him standing at his Nissan, his tie loosely knotted beneath his overcoat, his beard glistening in the harsh sunlight. "I don't think so; I need to visit my parents. It's been a year."

He nodded and looked only mildly disappointed, as if he were imagining the good times ahead of him anyway. "Well, think about it."

He backed out of the driveway first, and at the end of the street waved in his rearview mirror at her before he turned left and she turned right; and she didn't want to think about it. How could she be the woman he was going to bring home to his family? All the smiles and gifts and polite passings of gravy would feel like one big lie, which is what she was beginning to feel like—a liar. Somehow she was becoming the kind of woman she didn't like, somebody who felt one way but smiled it off in a mask of cheerfulness, the kind of woman who got very good at small talk.

As she drove past all the identical ranch houses of their neighborhood, Marla's face still felt swollen from her cold. If it weren't for the Christmas rush, everybody in the world waiting in line to get their money, she'd call in sick and go back to bed. But again, it'd be *his* bed. Her comforter was on it, but that wasn't enough. She missed her old apartment; she missed the bathroom that only had her things in it; she missed Edna curling up with her on the sofa in her living room with her framed prints on the wall—and no illustrations of perfect parallel lines; no dustless bookshelves full of paperback spy novels; no pressure to keep things clean and just where they belong at all times;

and not this lingering feeling that her life was really no better than it
had been before when she was alone, an earlier unhappiness that now
seemed preferable to this one.

Two days before Christmas Marla drove Dennis to the airport.
He hugged and kissed her and told her not to get sunburned in Florida. She watched him hurry toward the gate and lift his suitcase onto
the conveyor belt for the X-ray machine. He waved to her and she
waved back. Her flight left the next day, but for the past week she
hadn't been able to picture herself on it. Whenever she visited her
mother and father she always felt like a teenager again, a time in her
life when she had no friends at all; she couldn't bear feeling that way
now, and just last week at the vault Nancy asked her to spend the
holiday with her and her family if she wasn't going anywhere. Marla
watched Dennis's back get smaller and smaller. Why not? It probably wouldn't cost too much to change the ticket. When she could no
longer see him in the crowd, she began thinking what she'd tell her
mother on the phone, that she had the flu and would have to come see
them sometime after New Year's.

Christmas Eve after dinner, Marla and Nancy sat on throw pillows in front of a gas fire under the lights of the tree. Carl and his
sons, Luke and Kyle, were downstairs playing a new video game called
Blood Conquest, a gift from Carl to his boys that he insisted they open
that night. Nancy and Marla wore sweaters and slippers, and they
sipped eggnog with just the right amount of bourbon in it. On the
stereo Bing Crosby and David Bowie were singing "Peace on Earth."
Nancy sat with her eyes closed listening to the music, her pretty face
tilted slightly. Marla could still smell the glaze from the ham they'd
baked, the homemade rolls. Outside there was very little snow, but
there was a cold wind, and the bare branches of the trees made a
cracking sound as they swayed.

They had stuffing and three pies to make for tomorrow, but Nancy just wanted to sit and rest awhile in front of the tree and its mountain of wrapped presents, four from Marla: slacks and a cashmere jacket for Nancy, a case of vintage red wine for Carl, matching wool sweaters from Ireland for the boys. She was looking forward to giving them their gifts tomorrow morning, though part of her felt like an intruder into this family's Christmas. Dennis didn't even know she wasn't in Florida, and she could still hear her mother's disappointed voice on the phone.

Against the fireplace were two tall boxes wrapped in gold—skis for Kyle and new lacrosse sticks for Luke, Nancy had whispered to her earlier. Now Marla stared at them; they looked to her like over-sized bricks of gold, and she thought about the huge vault she and the girls put their cashboxes into every night before the bank's doors closed, all the stacks of new currency that were absolutely worthless without the real gold in Fort Knox they stood for, or at least used to. She and Dennis planned to give each other presents after their trips, but she didn't have one for him yet. She wondered what he was doing right now at his brother's house, but there was no pull or ache in this wondering, and she knew she did not miss him. She didn't. Her throat began to close up and her face felt too hot. She looked into the gas fire, at the steady, controlled flames beneath the stone logs. A new song began, strings and bells.

"Marla, honey, are you *crying?*"

Marla covered her face.

"What, sweetie. What's the matter?"

Marla shook her head, felt Nancy's hand on her shoulder. "What is it, hon? Tell me."

"I don't think I love Dennis, Nancy. I really don't." She'd said it, so she must mean it, and now it was out, and there was just her heaving shoulders and wet face and running nose beneath her fingers, Nancy handing her a tissue, her friend's soft, motherly voice saying, "That's it, let it out. It's okay, honey. Just let it all out."

———

NANCY LET HER CRY for a while. She patted and rubbed her back.
"Are you sure about this? You both look so happy together every time
we go out."

"That's because we have a good time with you guys." Marla sniffled and blew her nose. "You're fun."

"Yeah, but I see how you both look at each other. There's something real there."

"Then why do I feel so lonely?" Marla began to cry again. "I just
don't feel like *me* anymore."

"Everybody feels like that sometimes, honey."

"You feel lonely with Carl?"

"Yes."

"All the time?"

"No, and I bet you don't either, Marla."

"Most of the time."

"That's just 'cause you're new to all this." Nancy raised her glass
and stared at the lights of the tree. Her face looked tired and sweet
and vaguely superior, and Marla remembered being new at the bank
and not knowing anything. But this was different, and she didn't like
seeing Nancy look that way right now.

"It's been six months, Nancy."

"What's your hurry? It took me a year to get used to living with
Carl. I mean, what do men *do* anyway? They work, eat, drink, and
play games. Sex for them is in the sports-and-recreation category.
You can't live with a man and not be lonely."

"You think so?"

"Absolutely. Besides, once you have kids it all changes anyway.
Everything seems to make more sense then."

"Dennis doesn't want any."

"How do you know that?"

"He said he didn't."

Nancy seemed to take this in a second, then waved her hand in front of her face. "Have you ever met a man who did? Honey, it's not in their nature. They don't even think about it. Just get pregnant and he'll rise to the occasion. It makes them feel more like a man, you know." Nancy laughed. She looked back at the tree and sipped her eggnog.

For a moment Marla had a hard time swallowing. "You're afraid I'll lose him, aren't you?"

"No, I'm afraid you're expecting too much from him and you'll give up too soon. Which wouldn't be fair to Dennis, by the way."

"Is it fair to pretend around him?"

"There are worse things than pretending, Marla."

"Like what?"

"Not trying hard enough." Nancy smiled at her, her eyes patient and loving behind her gold-rimmed glasses. Marla sipped her eggnog, felt the bourbon flash down her throat, like medicine she wasn't sure she needed.

SHE WOKE CHRISTMAS MORNING to the smell of cinnamon rolls and coffee. She could hear Carl's deep voice coming from the kitchen, then Nancy's, high and cheerful. No sound of the boys yet, though even teenagers would probably get out of bed early today. A weak light came through the curtains, and Marla pulled the covers to her chin. Her mouth was dry and her head ached slightly behind her eyes. Her stomach felt queasy too. It was the bourbon eggnogs, staying up late in the kitchen, helping Nancy with stuffing, rolling out pie dough and pinching it into pie plates. The last thing they talked about before bed was Nancy's New Year's Eve party next week, how this one would be formal. Black tie and gowns. Champagne and lobster bisque.

Against the guest room wall was a dressing table and mirror.

Marla had had one like it when she was a child, though she'd never sat at it the way pretty girls probably did, staring gratefully at themselves, doing things with their hair, trying on new shades of blush and eye shadow and lip gloss. If Marla ever used it at all it was for a desk when hers was too cluttered, and she'd prop a textbook against the glass so she wouldn't have to see what she already knew. And that's what Nancy really meant last night, didn't she? That some people have to try even harder at love than others, and she was one of them. She felt old and tired.

From down the hall came the muffled sounds of music, high voices singing in a chorus on Nancy's stereo. It made Marla think of white flowing robes and baby Jesus swaddled on a bed of straw. There was a soft knocking on her door, then Nancy standing there in her robe and no makeup, holding two cups of coffee. Marla smiled at her friend and Nancy smiled back. "Merry Christmas, Marla."

MARLA WORKED the short week between Christmas and New Year's. Business was slow and when customers did come in, they seemed vaguely ashamed of themselves, as if they'd spent too much money over the holidays and all the bank tellers knew it. There were long stretches when Marla killed time counting and recounting her drawer, restacking her deposit and withdrawal slips, walking to the coffee room for water. At night, at home alone on Dennis's Naugahyde couch with Edna, she watched television she didn't really see or listen to; in the kitchen, her dirty dishes from supper sat in the sink. When she finally went to bed it felt too wide and empty, and she missed Dennis's big warm body beside her, but little else. She kept hearing his voice when she'd called him from Nancy's Christmas day after dinner, told him she hadn't gone to Florida, that she'd decided at the last minute she didn't want to put up with flight delays and crowded airports and not enough sleep.

"Oh." He'd sounded hurt. In the background children were

laughing, his niece and nephews, and Nancy's kitchen began to feel small and airless and Marla was sure she must not love Dennis at all; how could she? Lying like that?

Then she lied again and said she had to get off the phone soon to help out with the dishes. "Have a good Christmas, Den. I'll meet you at the airport."

NOW MARLA LAY AWAKE in the dark in Dennis's bed. His smell was in the pillowcase and sheets. She imagined leaving him, renting a U-Haul and moving her things out of the garage, Dennis inside somewhere—doing what? Feeling what? She didn't know, but she would have her own room again, her own kitchen and bathroom, her solitude, her sharing her days and nights with no one but her cat, just herself, just Marla, the way it had always been. She began to cry, and it was as if she were falling backwards into a dark hole, for how could she have forgotten she was a dull, round woman who'd been a dull, round girl, lucky enough now to have found anyone at all? That for all Dennis was not, for all she didn't feel for him, he was better than a lifetime of nobody. She thought of Dorothy and her sad eyes, all that dark melancholy covered with a bitter gloss of indifference, the two of them for decades to come standing side by side at bank outings talking about work, picking at their food and looking out at all the families, acting as if they weren't completely alone when they were. And now Marla cried harder, turning her face into her pillow.

After a while she stopped and blew her nose. She lay there under the comforter with a balled-up tissue in her hand. Edna leapt up onto the bed and Marla stroked her head and listened to her purr. She stared into the darkness of the bedroom at all the shadowed furniture that had become so familiar—his tall masculine bureau, his recliner in the corner—and she felt a little better. His plane came in tomorrow, the last day of the year, and there was the feeling she was being given one more chance, and there was still time to avoid something horrible.

She just needed to work harder at loving Dennis, that's all. What was wrong with that? Maybe he had to work harder at loving her too.

JUST BEFORE NIGHTFALL on New Year's Eve, Marla met Dennis at the airport. The temperature had come up twenty degrees; there were wide slushy puddles on the highway, and the airport's usually shiny floors were tracked with mud and salt. She was only a few minutes late, but his plane had come in on time and he was already downstairs at baggage claim walking toward her, pulling his gray Samsonite on wheels behind him, smiling and waving, a round friendly face behind a bushy beard. She smiled and let him hug her with one arm. He smelled like breath mints, and his perfumey cologne was stronger than ever.

"Oh, I missed you, Marla." He turned her from side to side.

"Me too."

"You did?" There was fear in his eyes, and he was looking right at her, her face hot with the lie she'd just told.

She slapped at his shoulder. "Yes."

"Really?"

"Yes."

That seemed to be enough for him for now, and in the car she drove carefully along the wet roads in the twilight and listened to his holiday, the three-day video game marathon he'd played with his brother, the sledding afternoon with the kids, and all the food: "The food, the food, the food. I even got drunk with my sister-in-law," he laughed. "Peach mimosas. Ever have one?"

"No." So far that was only the second question he'd asked her. She was aware of him taking up all the room in the dark space beside her, and she turned onto the highway ramp and accelerated quickly. Up ahead was a plow in the fast lane scraping slush, its red taillights blinking, Dennis talking about his brother's house, the addition he'd built full of wireless, high-definition hookups. Marla was suddenly hot under her clothes and she rolled her window down a crack and breathed deeply and sat up straight behind the wheel; maybe it was okay to feel far away from all he was saying; maybe she could just stay busy there in her solitude and think her own thoughts.

When she turned off the highway, he finished telling her his video game scores, then stopped talking. There was only the sound of her wet tires on the asphalt. He took a breath and rested his hand on her knee.

"Why are you being so quiet?"

"I'm just listening."

"Oh." His fingers moved up her thigh and squeezed gently. "Can we make love when we get home?"

"Okay."

He began talking about Nancy and Carl's party tonight, how the last time he wore his tuxedo was for his youngest brother's wedding, and he hoped it still fit. Marla planned to wear her only gown, the red one that cinched in beneath her breasts and made her look pregnant. She heard Nancy's voice in her head saying everything made sense then, but now wasn't the time to bring that up, and when they were finally home and undressing in only the light from the bathroom, his suitcase on the carpet, she said nothing as he reached for the condom, then was soon back inside her, and even though it was over too soon, it did feel good. After, instead of getting up and going straight to his shower, Dennis stayed on top of her, resting his weight on his elbows.

"I do love you, Marla."

"I love you, too." Why not say it? It was sweet of him to say it right now, like this, and she swallowed and was about to say she sometimes felt lonely with him. Did he feel that way too? Did he? But he was smiling down at her behind his beard, happy, so happy to have had his say, and he kissed her on the mouth and was out of her and off her and in the bathroom, and she felt the cool air and pulled the bed-spread up and over herself.

SOON THEY WERE DRIVING along the shore of Whittier Lake, just an endless black expanse of melting ice and snow. Dennis sat behind the wheel in his tuxedo and overcoat singing "Auld Lang Syne." Marla had never really heard him sing before. It wasn't the best singing she'd ever heard, but it wasn't bad either. A strand of hair kept coming loose, and she had to push it off her cheek and press it back into place. On the other side of the lake was the twinkle of lights.

Now they slowly passed all the large houses of all the people who could afford to live here, and her heart began to beat faster as Dennis turned down Nancy and Carl's private road. Both sides were lined with tall pine trees, and Marla could see their lighted house ahead, their floodlit driveway. Curled over and around the front door was a wide gold ribbon. Lining the sanded walk were two rows of lit candles in gold bags leading all the way to the plowed yard where a dozen cars were already parked. Dennis pulled up behind a white Audi sports car. Lisa's Prelude was in front of it, but Marla didn't recognize any of the others and she began to feel afraid and didn't know why.

Dennis got out and closed the door. She pulled the rearview mirror toward her and checked her face. It was hard to see in the dim light, though, and Dennis was already waiting for her at the first flaming bag of the sidewalk. She took a breath. The air wouldn't go all the way into her lungs. She opened her door and stood, the ground so soft her high heels sunk into it, and she quickly gathered up the hem of her gown and had to put a hand on Dennis's car hood to make her way around to where he stood in his overcoat and tuxedo, jangling his keys, his eyes on their friends' house. She was fourteen again, making herself go to a party where no one knew her and never would. She had to stop and swallow something in her throat.

"Coming?" Dennis held his arm out for her, a patient smile in his voice. She peered up at him, but he was just a tall, blurry shadow. There was talk and laughter and music coming from inside the house. Above it the stars were in a black sky. That black, black sky.

"You all right?"

All those stars so far apart. None of them close. From far away they just looked it.

"Marl? You okay?"

She swallowed and took a breath. "Yeah. I'm okay." She stepped forward, and he took her hand, and they walked through the gauntlet of low flames. He was saying something to her, asking her another question, and she smiled and nodded just so he'd stop. Inside Nancy's house, a man laughed and laughed. Dennis opened the front door for her, and she could smell wool and cashmere and the cream of lobster bisque. She stepped past him into the warm foyer. There was sweat on her forehead. She heard the door close behind her, felt his big hand on her lower back. Her hair came loose again. She reached up and pressed it firmly back into place, then climbed the stairs one at a time, and she led them to the rest of the couples, to all those smiling, happy couples.

THE BARTENDER

Robert Doucette met his wife-to-be while tending bar at a dance club on Hampton Beach. It was Labor Day weekend, the season almost done, his sunburned customers already beginning to wear sweatshirts and light sweaters. He had spent the summer living in a one-room rental above the bar and he had four thousand saved, enough to get him through until late winter when he was thinking of hopping a bus to the east coast of Florida to work a topless bar called Skinny's. But late this morning while he was lying in bed listening to the beach traffic out on the boulevard, a phrase occurred to him and he thought he might start a poem with it. The words that came were of a woman "with eyes of black hope." He wasn't sure he liked this line; he suspected it sounded mawkish and falsely heroic, but its unexpected arrival left him feeling there might be something within him worth mining for after all.

Then she walked into the club. She wore a white sundress, her long, curly black hair held back in a loose ponytail, her bare shoulders and arms thick for a woman but tanned and hard-looking. She was with two laughing blondes, both thin and inconsequential. They sat at his bar, one of the blondes ordering piña coladas for all three, and the dark one sat quietly watching him, her stillness a force that pulled him closer, though he did not approach her until setting the fresh rum drink on a napkin in front of her. She smiled and looked up at him, and there were the eyes he'd written about just that morning, eyes of black hope, and they seemed not to see him so much as all he might represent. The women only stayed for one drink. In the half hour it took them to finish it, Robert worked the service bar but kept feeling the dark woman's presence behind him like good news in a letter he wasn't opening. When they stood to leave Robert took a chance and wrote his name and cell number on a napkin and set it down in front of her. She glanced at it, then took out a pen of her own, crossed out his number, and wrote hers.

Her name was Althea, and throughout the fall they dated; they went to movies and restaurants in Portsmouth and sometimes Boston. She was a good eater, always finishing the salad and entrée, then ordering a dessert, too. She was quiet, more of a listener than a talker, which at first unnerved Robert. He was used to being around waitresses and barmaids, women who seemed to talk about almost anything as if they were experts. Althea did not present herself as an expert on anything, which left Robert feeling he might not be either. One night driving her home while she sat quietly beside him, he forced himself not to turn on the radio or to tell her another tale from the bar business: of the fellow bartender who had skimmed ten thousand dollars from the register one winter to pay off back child support; of a cocktail waitress who was kidnapped by her boyfriend after her shift and found tied up in a motel room two weeks later—dehydrated and hysterical—her boyfriend having hung himself in front of her; or any of the dozens of bad jokes he knew, tools of the trade which felt, in Althea's presence, like dried mucus on a handkerchief. He'd already told her of his dreary childhood growing up on his family dairy farm inland, and of course he'd told her that he was a poet, that for ten years he'd been working on a book of poems he hoped to one day publish. She nodded knowingly at this piece of information, but even then, remained quiet. So he drove in the silence and fought the urge to ask her a question about herself, for he already knew the essentials: Althea was an upholsterer, working in the basement of a house she rented and shared with the two blondes, bank tellers Robert didn't like because they talked mostly of interest rates and attractive men who owned property and they wore makeup even when they stayed in at night. But Althea wore little makeup. Her mother and father had immigrated from Greece, only to return there to care for ailing relatives now that their girl was a woman with a trade she'd learned on her own. She had a steady line of business from local antiques dealers who trusted her to strip and redress their ancient chairs and settees in floral brocades, classical damasks, and gold and burgundy tapestries. She had no brothers or sisters, which perhaps explained her silence, Robert thought, her feeling there was no one in the room to whom she had to speak.

After two months of dating, she invited him to spend the night in her room, and as they made love, Robert moved carefully, as if he were trying on new clothes he didn't want to spoil in case they had to be returned. Afterward, they lay quietly together in the dark, the faint sounds of a late-night television talk show coming from downstairs. When he had softened completely, he eased off his condom and was trying to lower it discreetly to the floor when she held out a white tissue for him to drop it in. He did, and she took his seed and placed it on her bedside table next to a copy of the New Testament and two Willa Cather novels she'd borrowed from the library. Outside, an October wind blew dead leaves against the house and across the yard. Her room was spare, no rug or carpet on the pine floor, nothing but a dresser, a cane chair, and at the foot of the bed an old trunk that had once belonged to her grandfather in Sparta. One wall held a framed poster of the Wyeth painting of the young woman sitting alone on the grassy hill staring up at a farm house, her hair lifting in the breeze. Robert could see just the shadow of it.

Althea kissed his shoulder. "Robert." It sounded like more of a statement than an inquiry, as if she were assuring herself of who he was.

"Yes?"

"I haven't done this with anyone I wouldn't want to have a baby with."

There was a slight itch in the hair at Robert's temple, but he didn't move to scratch it. He wondered what his heart sounded like beneath her ear.

"That's good."

She lifted her head and smiled at him in the dark. "For you? Or for me?"

"For both of us."

She was quiet now. Robert's cheeks grew warm, and he felt he'd just lied.

"You mean that?"

"Yes."

"Completely yes?"

"Yes, completely."

She kept her head up awhile, looking at him in the dark. Then she rubbed her nose against his and kissed him deeply, opening his mouth with her tongue. They made love again, this time without a condom. The wind picked up outside; it sounded cold to Robert, though here with Althea it was warm, almost hot. A lone leaf scuttled across the window and was gone.

Two days later, a Monday, the weather was warm, the orange and red leaves on the branches and ground like flames giving off heat. Althea carried the frame of a wingback chair from the basement to work on in the sunlit grass of her rented yard, and Robert had no shift later so he sat close by drinking beer and trying to read from an anthology of twentieth-century poems. But he kept watching her instead, the way she sat on her calves with her back straight, a long curved needle between her lips as she pushed a spring into the seat, then began to sew it down, her wild black hair tied back loosely with a purple scarf, and he had to look away because the word that kept tumbling through his head was *bride. My* bride. He said nothing to her, but in the days and weeks that followed, this knowledge began to transform her silence for him; sitting in the car or across the table at a restaurant, it now began to feel comfortable, like she had accepted him for who he was already, without him having to go on and on, the way a home should feel to a child, Robert thought, and he proposed to her the day after Christmas as they lay in bed watching it snow out the window. "I think I should marry you."

She turned and looked at him, her eyes dark and moist.

"I know I should, actually."

Her eyes were filling up now, but she said nothing. Robert took her hand in his. "Will you?" In the shadows of the room Althea's eyes looked black, but she was smiling and she nodded and hugged him tightly, and they were married the first week of January in Portsmouth with their hands on the Bible of a justice of the peace.

They spent their honeymoon making love in an inn on the waterfront, the mussel-shell, freighter-oil scent of the Piscataqua River filling the room. They ate long dinners in restaurants, and though Althea wasn't a drinker, they both drank too much and Robert would lean forward and recite the poems he could remember from William Butler Yeats, John Donne, and his mentor, Robert Frost. In the candlelight, he saw the moisture in his bride's eyes at what Robert could only assume was her perceived good fortune at marrying a man of true romance and high calling. No one had ever looked at him like that and it stirred in him a low, animal calling, a central pull to the dark depth of her quiet womanhood, a nest in which to sink and blossom his own muse.

Within the first month of their marriage she became pregnant, delivering the news to him one morning after an exhausting and lucrative shift whose end he had celebrated with too much bourbon and beer. As he lay in bed, his face feeling like clay, the inside of his mouth so dry it had clearly cracked, Althea came into his room, kissed him firmly on the mouth, then held up the small white tab of the home-test kit, the pregnant end pink. She smiled at him, her dark eyes full of hope, and he sat up and hugged and kissed her, though his head pulsed and he had to close his eyes. Walking to the bathroom, he felt every bit of the floorboards beneath his feet, and it was an effort to lift his head; it was as if the earth's gravity had just doubled.

In the shower he kept thinking of his father: his substantial shoulders stooped and rounded, his mouth always set in a grim line, even on Sunday afternoons when he would finally allow himself to rest *if* it were a day when no heifers or cows were giving birth, none were hurt, all the calves were fed and dry, if there was no equipment to repair or paperwork to catch up on. When all that had to be done was another three-hour milking at the end of the day, then Robert's father would lie on the sofa in the living room with an *Almanac* or *Yankee* magazine, the television tuned to an old movie, maybe a bottle of Miller on the lamp table beside him. When he was a boy, Robert and his mother and younger sister would be there too. On Sundays his mother baked cookies or a cobbler and she'd let them eat a serving in front of the TV with a glass of milk. His father would have some then. He'd sit up on the couch to eat, quietly chewing and watching whatever was on the screen. Sometimes Robert would see him looking at him and his sister, studying them the way he did his holsteins, looking for any defects that might cost him even more farther down the line.

Althea's visit to her doctor confirmed the home test, and Robert willed himself to try to rise to the occasion. He ordered his wife a dozen roses, and she placed them in three separate vases throughout the bedroom of the house they now shared with the two bank tellers until Robert found something better. On one of his nights off, Robert insisted they sit down and come up with a name, starting with a boy's. If they were to have a son, Robert wanted him to have a strong name, the sort a boy couldn't help but live up to, the way a poem must earn its title. He wanted to name him Ajax, Greek for eagle, after the hero in the Trojan Wars. But Althea had balked without a word, as was her way, simply showed him the scouring powder of the same name, then shook her head and pinched his cheek. But Robert was taken with the image of the eagle, his possible son a lone and majestic bird whose natural surroundings would be life's peaks and precipices.

So they settled on a variation of the Old German for eagle, Adler, a name Althea thought was softer, more gentle and reflective, the way she viewed Robert herself.

For a time.

During the months of her pregnancy, they moved to a place of their own, a one-room motel cabin on a salt marsh across the boulevard from Hampton Beach. It had a sleeping loft, a hot plate, sink, refrigerette, and a shower-stall bathroom with a toilet that flushed its contents into pipes whose smell did not seem to make it out of the reeds. Built on short creosote piers, there were five of these cabins alongside one another, each identical to the next. In front of them, across a crushed-shell parking lot, loomed The Whaler Restaurant, Bar & Hotel, a four-story fifty-two-room attraction open only five months out of the year when its manager rented the marsh cabins to its best waiters, waitresses, and bartenders. The hotel's clientele were mainly dentists', bankers', and architects' families from the Midwest and upstate New York, and Robert—with his literary charm and quick reflexes, his ability to light a cigarette for one while serving a drink to another, all while giving the punch line of a joke to a third—was head bartender and worked the restaurant's bar six nights a week. At the end of his shift, after storing the leftover garnish and mixes, after restocking the beer chest and rotating older bottles to the front, after wiping down the speed rack and soaking all the pourers in a hot rinse, Robert served himself a cold draft and a jigger of Maker's Mark bourbon. He drank off a third of the draft, then dropped the full jigger into the mug, the bourbon spreading up and out into the beer like armed reinforcements.

Tonight, a Thursday in mid-August, the main restaurant's lights were off save for the ones over the bar. The kitchen staff was gone. The barback and busboys and wait staff had all gone, too, and the manager had left Robert and Jackie, the head waitress, to lock up. She sat a few stools down from the register inhaling deeply on an unlit cigarette she didn't want to light. She had thick red hair, gold in places from the late mornings and early afternoons when she would lie on a chaise lounge in front of her cabin in a bikini that barely covered her ample breasts, wide hips, and round buttocks. Sometimes, when Althea was reading or washing the dishes, her back turned, Robert would allow himself a peek out the window. Once, he looked just as Jackie was turning over onto her stomach, her breasts swaying, and he imagined his face nestled in the sweaty freckled crevice there. Now Jackie's breasts strained against her white Whaler blouse, the top three buttons undone, her skin a deep pink, and Robert felt a surge of guilt that he felt no real guilt about viewing Jackie in this way, his pregnant wife sleeping in the tiny loft of their cabin behind the hotel.

On days with no sea breeze the cabin filled with the smell of sewage from the marsh, and Althea would usually feel nauseated and they would leave for a walk down the boulevard, which was almost worse with its canned rap and rock blaring from the shops, the sidewalks crowded with sun-beaten tourists, the smells of fried dough and teriyaki steak from the fryolators and grills, the roar of a Harley-Davidson out on the street, a gang of seagulls shrieking from above. Althea would squeeze his hand, holding her protruding belly with the other, and soon Robert and his wife would have to go into a restaurant for a bathroom where she might throw up and Robert would sneak a quick tequila shot or two at the bar while he ordered two Cokes, one to hide the tequila—a fiery friend and confidant in his gut—the other for her. They would sit in a booth or at a small table in the shadows away from the bright street, and she would sip her Coke stoically, staring at the rug or sometimes just at Robert's hand or chest, which left him feeling she was a bit simple, taking her pain in an unquestioning and almost bovine way. He would think of the heifers on his father's dairy farm, the vague indifference in their eyes as his father loaded the breeding gun with thawed bull semen, his entire arm covered with a lubricated plastic sleeve. But other times, the surreptitious tequila shots spreading out in his belly like a purging grass fire, Robert would feel moved at her silent suffering and he would lean over and kiss her clammy hand, this pregnant woman he was beginning to bronze in a maternal cast only.

Because she was quiet, Robert knew some thought her aloof. Often on a Monday night, the slowest night at The Whaler, the waitresses would throw a party at one of the cabins. They'd prop their Bose speakers in open windows and play loud rock while they barbecued hamburgers on one of the tiny front porches. Other off-duty waitstaff would join them with coolers of beer, hard lemonade, and sometimes a blender, ice, and a bottle of rum. Robert and Althea joined them, too. As head bartender, Robert enjoyed his place of leadership, and he would mix up a batch of frozen piña coladas or daiquiris and drink three in twenty minutes while Jackie and two of her best waitresses cackled and howled about getting revenge on bad customers, like the chronic butt-pinching doctor whose béarnaise sauce they spiked with a tablespoon of urine every time he came in. There were other stories to fall into, and while they did, Althea sat quiet and pregnant in a lawn chair in the parking lot apart from the smoke of the cigarettes and barbecue, and Robert would sometimes feel her presence the way some felt the ghosts of disapproving ancestors. Jackie or another woman would become a waitress for her, asking if she wanted another cup of ginger ale, or did she want to put her feet up on something. But Althea would shake her head no, no thank you, and sometimes Robert would finish laughing at the tail end of another story or joke, then go sit next to her awhile, watching his restaurant friends laugh and drink and smoke, flipping hamburgers and bobbing their heads to the music, and he would feel he was missing something sitting there with his expectant wife who was always so quiet, a quality which, when they were alone, he'd actually come to admire. It seemed to him she was waiting for something only she knew about, something transcendent and holy that would be good for all of them. Alone with her, this woman who had chosen him and was carrying his child, Robert felt believed in, felt called once again to great and important things—namely his poetry, becoming a published poet.

But when the Doucettes were not alone, Robert was beginning to feel Althea's abstinent quiet like the penetrating gaze of a chaperone, and he wanted to flee. Once, when he was in The Whaler's walk-in cooler, the door ajar, he heard Jackie and two of the younger waitresses at the coffee machine talking about his wife, using words and phrases like *conceited* and *holier-than-thou*. Robert did not agree: he had never heard Althea utter an ugly word about anyone; she was simply quiet. But as he left the walk-in cooler carrying his bucket of lemons, limes, and oranges, he said nothing in his wife's defense and instead smiled at them, hoping he looked friendly and handsome as he passed. He was immediately ashamed of himself for abandoning Althea like that. His shame soon turned to resentment, though—not at Jackie and the girls, but at his wife for putting him in the position where he would have to defend or fail her on so many subtle fronts.

Now Jackie was switching from her Melon Ball to a Mount Gay on the rocks with a splash of Coke. Robert made himself another boilermaker, set it down on the stool next to Jackie, then joined her there with the register drawer and night deposit bag. She was copying the week's schedule onto a clean sheet of paper, still sucking on the unlit cigarette, and as he sat next to her she reached over and gave his leg a friendly squeeze, leaving her hand there a second or two as Robert sat up and began to count, log, and bag the night's receipts. Her fingers slipped away and he could smell the coconut lotion she used on her skin during the day. He took a long drink off his mug, the shot glass clinking inside it like a badly kept secret.

"My grandfather drank those, Robert. That's an old man's drink."

"It does the job."

"A lot of things do that, honey." She was looking right at him, her bright green eyes mischievous and kind. Robert and Jackie had been locking the place up together all summer. There had always been an easy camaraderie between them, an oiled, lubricated quality that came from coming off the same shift together, from working in close proximity with one another. But the last few weeks it had been harder for Robert to look into her face directly, his eyes sure to betray the fact that he simply wanted to kiss her, to feel her freckled breasts up against him. So now he shook his head, smiled, and looked down at his hands on the bar, hoping this gesture of genuine shyness would endear him to her. It was after two now, the restaurant and hotel so quiet he could hear the surf out on the beach across the boulevard. Some nights, when Jackie finished her work before he did, she'd leave first, blowing him a kiss from the door before she closed it, and after she was gone Robert would turn off all the lights and sit in the dark with his drink and watch the ghostly phosphorescence of the waves breaking on the night sand, white breaking over and over again in the darkness.

Jackie got up and made herself another Mount Gay, then surprised Robert with one, too. "Nobody does shots and beers anymore, Robbie. Get with it."

Robert laughed. She was the only one who called him that. She sat back down and they drank and finished their night work; the bourbon and beer had already opened up the veins in his head, relaxing and widening the possibilities, and now the rum was a tight ball of fire rolling through without an obstacle to stop it. He wanted to see the night surf; he wanted Jackie to see it, too.

"Hey, Jackie, I want to show you something." He hopped off the stool to go hit the light switch behind her, but then he felt her at his back, her confusion about where he was going to take her to show her something when all he'd wanted to do was turn off the lights. And when he turned to tell her Wait right here, what I want to show you is out the window, his hand brushed both her breasts, their cotton-covered give and release, and she giggled, then smiled, her eyes pleasantly alert, and she lifted her chin and there was nothing to do but lean forward and kiss her. Just this, he thought. Only this. But she opened her mouth, her tongue warm and yielding, and soon they were on the gritty carpet that smelled of sand and ketchup and ashes, Jackie lifting her black Whaler skirt up around her waist while Robert fumbled with her mint green panties, leaving them around one of her ankles as he pushed himself inside her. She gripped his buttocks with both hands, her face hot against his, her hair smelling of coconut oil and kitchen smoke. Outside, the surf pounded, then was silent till another wave rolled in, then another, and now Jackie was moaning, and soon, too soon, he could no longer hear the surf, could only feel the next wave as it began to build and gather, then roll itself out of him and into Jackie.

JUST BEFORE DAWN, Robert stood in the dark bathroom and washed his hands and face three times. He considered a cat bath for his genitals, but lately Althea had been getting up several times a night to pee, and he feared her walking in to see him doing that, washing his penis at the sink. He should have done it at the restaurant but had let the self-locking door close before it had occurred to him. And he couldn't take a shower because he never did that right before bed. He dried his face and hands, then climbed up to his place beside his wife. As soon as he stretched out she turned over and lay her leg over his, her arm across his chest, and he tried to breathe normally, wondering if she could feel his heart beating beneath her wrist in a way it shouldn't.

He may have slept, he wasn't sure, but later that morning, the air still, the slight smell of sewage and seaweed in his cabin, Robert's pregnant wife woke from her sleep and straddled him, and Robert tensed with the knowledge that Jackie's dried juices were still on him and now they were inside Althea. For the first time he thought of the virus, something deadly he could have caught and would now be passing on to his wife. His wife and baby. But Jackie was not the type to sleep around, he told himself, and Althea seemed to be enjoying it, moving up and down, her round stomach hard against his, and Robert felt sure she would begin to sense something different somehow, that a deep and womanly part of her would detect the evidence of another woman's depths. But, instead, Althea came softly and then he did too, and last night's indulgence felt for the moment harmless, forgivable, and behind them both.

But that night, as Jackie ordered drinks from him at the service bar, she looked particularly radiant, her eyes brighter and more mischievous than ever. When Robert put three Bombay tonics on her tray, she squeezed a lime wedge directly onto his hand, the juice running down between his knuckles, and five hours later, the bar dark and quiet, they took their time and did it on the restaurant floor, in the kitchen on the prep table, and, finally, in the manager's office, Jackie's bare bottom on the desk blotter, her heels on his shoulders. After she had left, blowing him a kiss from the darkness of the shell parking lot, Robert went to the men's room and washed his hands, face, penis, and balls. It was very late, probably close to sunrise. He poured himself a tall Maker's Mark on the rocks, his third of the night, and sat at one of the tables at the front window feeling what he viewed as a uniquely male mix of pride and remorse; Jackie was unquestionably the most attractive woman on the waitstaff, respected for her earned authority with the other waitresses, known to be an easy date for nobody. And here she was giving herself to him freely, which left Robert feeling an echo of what he felt with his own wife— special, singled out—but it was a bastard echo, one he knew could gratify but not fulfill. Over the years he'd done this with many waitresses and barmaids, sometimes in their apartments, but usually like this, somewhere in the dark of the restaurant or bar or back office after hours, a few drinks in him and them. One, a single woman with two small kids at home, pulled her panties back on and said, "Will you write a poem about me?" And besides their own nameless hunger and the liquor in their veins, he knew that's what got to them, the fact that he professed to write poetry when so many other bartenders tanned themselves at the beach and worked the numbers on big football and basketball games. The fact that they thought he was a poet.

Now Althea's dark faithful eyes came to him and he drained his bourbon and poured himself another, splashing it with Coke to make it go down faster. Tonight the surf was loud enough to hear clearly through the glass, the white froth of the waves easier to see out on the dark beach. Robert began to feel somewhat imperiled, his chest a bit constricted at the real possibility that on a loose and drunken Monday night, Jackie might tell one of her waitresses about the two of them; and he had no doubts the news would then spread throughout The Whaler and its cabins as thoroughly and predictably as the smell of their own sewage on windless days. He had no doubts about its effect on Althea, either; she would leave him with barely a word. Her faith in him would simply vanish, and she would vanish as well, taking his child with her. For one bourbon-floating moment, Robert felt relieved at the prospect, a reprieve from husbandhood and fatherhood and all of their weight. He drank from his adulterated bourbon, his thoughts already tilted on their axis inside him, his relief gone as he feared this to be the true state in which he would find himself if he were ever to lose his wife: off-kilter, foggy-headed, and directionless. He imagined himself alone in his cabin, perhaps ironing his shirt and vest, preparing himself for a shift of high tips he would squirrel away so he could take time off to be alone and do what? Write poems? Really *write* some? Who was he shitting? For without Althea, without her unquestioning belief in him, he wasn't sure he'd really be able to make that leap onto the page, a leap he truthfully hadn't been making too well *before* Althea. For months and months he would not write one line, or even read a poem; he'd work his shifts, spend the day running errands or watching two rented movies on his laptop.

Sometimes a line would come to him and he might write it down on the envelope of a bill he'd end up throwing away. Other bar and waitstaff would talk of the accounting course they were taking up, or the realtor's exam they were studying for; if they turned their attention to Robert he'd smile shyly and say he was working on a book of poems. Then Althea walked into his bar, the woman he'd conjured with words that very day, and he began to actually feel capable.

Some late mornings as he lay in the loft waking slowly, Robert would look down at Althea as she swept the floor or fixed him some eggs or simply stood at the window with a cup of tea, her belly round and full and heavy, and he was certain he felt an ethereal measure of the same thing, his head and heart germinating what he hoped would one day uncoil and spring into a book with his name on it. After breakfast, if Althea had no upholstery work and wasn't driving to the basement shop she still rented from the two blond bank tellers, she'd kiss him on the cheek, then climb back up into the loft with a novel, and Robert would sit at the table with his open notebook, put his pencil to it, and wait. He'd hear a single-engine plane running an advertising flag out over the beach and he would write: *plane.* He'd hear an off-duty waitress laugh in one of the cabins and he'd write: *woman laughing.* He'd try and combine these to see if some poetic alchemy might ensue, a Robert Frost–like rhyming couplet, maybe. But when he did come up with a couplet it sounded more like an old woman's effort at a cheerful greeting card:

> *A plane flies by*
> *A woman laughs high—*
> *The man sits at his table*
> *Wondering if it is stable—*

But nonetheless, he saw these as seeds, and usually, after a half hour or more of recording them, he felt he'd laid some important and necessary groundwork and he'd close the notebook, place it carefully on the shelf beneath the window, then open a beer and climb the short ladder to the loft, feeling virtuous and almost triumphant.

Once Althea had asked to read one of his poems, but Robert had told her the truth: "They're not good enough yet, honey. They're not done." She smiled at him knowingly, a smile that seemed to respect his honesty about his craft, but she knew better—they were already wonderful—and Robert had felt once again the surging hope that she might be right and that he was destined for an exceptional road after all.

But now there was the feeling he was laying booby traps in that road. Robert finished his bourbon, washed out the aftertaste with a quick draft, then placed the mug and glass carefully in the sink, closing and locking the rear door to The Whaler. He could smell the ocean. He turned and stumbled over something in the shell lot and landed on one knee. It was an empty Bacardi bottle that had fallen out of the full dumpster, and he threw it back onto the heap. It was nearly dawn. The air was cool, and the cabins were five black silhouettes against the dark marsh. He looked at his own, the farthest shadow on the south side of the lot. Inside the front-porch window was the dim glow of the table lamp Althea left on for him every night. He imagined her standing in her full cotton nightgown, leaning forward to switch on the light before climbing with surefooted care up to the loft.

He looked at the other cabins: Jackie's was just two over from his. He wondered if she was asleep yet. Did she share the loft with her cabinmate, a dour veterinarian student and waitress named Kimberly? Or did she sleep alone, and there was room for him to crawl up there and sink into her one more time, because after tonight this would be it? It would only be a matter of days before word got out among the waitstaff, and then how long would it be before Althea would hear a comment through an open window or from one of their tiny front porches? And he knew then, standing in the slight sway of a bourbon swoon, the five black cabins standing before him like a line of executioners, he was going to have to leave The Whaler before the season was up, just take Althea, load up the Subaru, and rent a place inland. He'd tell her he didn't want to subject her and the baby to any more raw sewage; he'd say he wanted to get more work done on his poems. The Whaler always had a waiting list for his job, and he'd tell the manager, Danny Sullivan, a round and sober Irishman who never smiled sincerely, that his wife's pregnancy needed some monitoring from her hometown doctor, something like that, and then Robert Doucette would start anew.

He took a deep breath and struck out in the direction of his cabin but then veered slightly north and stepped softly onto Jackie's porch. He cupped his face to the screen door and peered in. The room was all shadows, the loft a pale strip hovering in the darkness. But then there was another shape, lower, on the floor, a cot or small bed, a woman's hair fanned out on the pillow. Robert swayed a moment, then caught himself. He could hear morning birds in the trees beyond the marsh. He had ten, maybe twenty minutes at the most before it was too light to slip back home. *Under cover of darkness.* The phrase rippled through his head. Shakespeare, he thought, and he fancied himself with billowing white sleeves, a long sword, poetry on his tongue. He reached for the door handle, turned it, and was not surprised when the door opened; most of the cabins' doors were swollen from the sea air and would not close all the way without slamming, and then you needed a pry bar to open them in the morning. He stepped inside the cabin, which could have been his own, but the air smelled strongly of pine air freshener and hand lotion, and one of the women, the one in the loft, was sleeping deeply, a slight rasp in her breathing. Robert concluded it had to be Kimberly, as Jackie would not be so deeply asleep yet. She was on her side in the cot, just a few feet in front of him. He recognized her thick hair on the pillow. He would slide in beside her, lift her top leg, and enter her from behind, his hands on her bountiful breasts.

Robert took off his bartender's vest and dropped it to the floor.

He squatted and untied his shoes, stepping out of them and his pants and underwear, walking over the floor in his shirt and socks, his penis already half-hard. He glanced up at the loft and saw Kimberly's hand, her fingers curled in sleep. He leaned over and lifted the cot sheet, and was about to whisper Jackie's name when he saw Kimberly's profile instead, the low cheekbones and perfect nose that because of her cheekbones was not attractive, the same profile he saw every night as he placed drinks on her tray and she scanned her tables, eyes narrowed in worried concentration. Now her face was slack, her lips parted, a dime-sized drool spot on the pillow, and Robert lowered the sheet and stepped back.

The thought came of climbing the loft and placing his penis in Jackie's cupped hand, but outside already seemed less dark than moments before, the high grass of the marsh becoming defined in the soft blue light out the rear window. The morning birds were calling to one another louder now, more frequently, as if they were already into their second cup of coffee, and Robert began to feel the whiskey-dulled punch of remorse in his stomach. He crept back to his clothes and stepped into his underwear but had to hop to get his second foot in, and when he finally stuck it through he was breathing hard and standing three feet past Kimberly's cot. She turned over onto her back and let out a long breath; Robert held his own, his heart pulsing high above his ears. But her eyes were closed, her lips still parted. He had neglected to cover her all the way and her white tank shirt was twisted on her. Poking from the arm hole was half her breast, her dark nipple as solitary and inviting as a chocolate morsel. He glanced back longingly at Jackie's empty hand, then tiptoed to his pants and sat down on the floor before pulling them on, then his shoes too, leaving them untied as he backed out the screen door and slowly pulled it back into place.

It was dawn now, the shell lot salmon-colored. A lone white gull landed on the dumpster and folded its wings in before jumping onto the heap. Robert began to tuck in his shirt, but something was missing, his vest, and he was just about to reach for the door handle one more time when he felt something a few yards south.

Althea.

She stood there looking directly at him, her long white sleeping gown bunched slightly on her belly, the hem raised in the front, showing her thick ankles and bare feet; most of the shells were broken and jagged and nobody walked on them barefoot. Robert let go of the door. His shirttail was hanging out in front and he wanted to tuck it in but knew that motion would surely reveal everything, though *nothing* had really happened inside the cabin. And this is the truth which emboldened him to step off the porch onto the crunch of shells, speaking gently his wife's name: "Thea?"

She didn't say anything, just looked at him with dark, dry eyes.

"Honey?" The air itself seemed to be stretched tight as he walked through it.

When he got close she raised her chin: "Which one?"

"What?" Inside Robert an elevator cable seemed to snap.

"Jackie or Kimberly?"

The descent was terrible.

"Kimberly?"

"No, Thea, honey, what are you talking about? Let's go inside." Robert touched her hip, was hoping to turn her toward home, but she gripped his wrist and looked into his eyes: "Jackie."

The elevator slammed into the pit. Robert shook his head, but Althea was nodding; she dropped his hand and walked quickly over the broken shells toward Jackie's cabin. There was a great silence and time seemed to slow down to nothing, as if he were in a car breaking into speeding pieces on the highway and all he could do was roll with the fragment he was strapped onto; he watched her go, her curly black hair and white sleeping gown and bare feet as she stepped up onto the porch. Now time moved again and he bolted after her, but his foot slid out behind him and he did a near split and had to catch himself with his hands, then his knees, and then he was up. But Althea was already inside, the screen door a slam Robert was late for, stepping into the room just as his wife grabbed Jackie's empty hand and jerked her completely out of the loft onto her back and buttocks, her bare feet slamming the floorboards and wall, Kimberly jumping to her knees in her cot, screaming. Jackie was screaming too, flailing behind her; then Althea screamed, and it was the only one Robert heard now, a long wail followed by a panting whimper. She held Jackie's hair with two hands but no longer to do damage, it seemed; more, it was to hold herself steady. She was bent over, squeezing her knees together, and blood was coming in slow, sure rivulets, moving down her olive calves onto the floor, onto the floor and Robert's black bartender's vest.

IT WAS JACKIE who called the ambulance. Althea kept moaning, her face empty of color, and Kimberly had her lie on the floor and rest her bare feet up on the cot. Robert had just stood there a moment, saying nothing, doing nothing, but then Althea began to cry, covering her eyes with her arm. He knelt down and touched her hair, but she shook her head away from him so violently that he stood again, then ended up sitting on the cot, holding her bloody feet in his lap as Kimberly squatted and did something with a towel beneath his wife. Jackie stood off to the side in nothing but light blue panties and a New England Patriots T-shirt, her hair still ratty from Althea's grip, looking from Robert to his wife on the floor as if this were something she couldn't possibly have invited upon herself.

Robert had wanted to ride in the ambulance, but the EMT shook his head no and closed the doors, his partner already inside there wrapping a blood pressure cuff around Althea's arm. Robert followed in the Subaru, the ambulance in front of him impossibly white, its siren off but its orange and red roof lights blinking and spinning as the van sped down the empty boulevard. And the sun was the same color, sitting on the water, the beach deserted. Robert had to push down on the accelerator to keep up with the ambulance, and he felt he was actually chasing it, that they were fleeing him, whisking his wife off to safety and high ground. He began to feel afraid. The towel Kimberly had wedged beneath Althea was dripping when the EMTs arrived. And when they lifted her onto the gurney her face was yellowish and she didn't look at him or anyone, just closed her eyes tightly against what must be a terrible pain. *Two months early.* And what about the baby? Was the *baby* in pain?

The ambulance left the boulevard and barreled past the wide salt marsh. Robert kept the Subaru two car lengths behind, though they were moving close to fifty. He wondered what the EMT was doing to her behind those white doors. How could you stop the bleeding if it was coming from inside? Robert's face prickled with heat and he felt nauseated, his mouth nothing but a sticky shot glass, his head aching behind his eyes. Over the years he'd sometimes cheated on his girlfriends, but never anyone as loving, trusting, and faithful as his wife. The wind was blowing in against his cheek, the smell of the ocean and the mudflats of the marsh, and for a moment he could feel his heart beating in his ears and he heard nothing else as the wind pushed silently at his face like unrelenting bad news: *What if you lose her? What if you lose your child, too?* He got an image of himself alone in the fall, working at Skinny's in Florida, a youngish man with all his promise gone: squandered and lusted away. If he'd ever had any in the first place.

The ambulance hit its siren once as it pulled into the emergency bay. Robert parked his car nearby. He was shutting his door when they wheeled Althea through the doors, her profile small and anemic. He hurried inside, his head pulsing with no sleep and the leftover Maker's Mark. But there was only an emergency waiting area, a woman at a desk typing something into a computer, her glasses pushed to the tip of her nose. He approached her and was conscious of his bloody white shirt. He wanted to tuck it in, at least, but the thought felt ludicrous.

"Where did they take my wife? I think she's having the baby. Where would they take her?"

The woman glanced up at his shirt, then up at his face as if she weren't sure she heard him correctly.

"Have you preregistered?"

"Excuse me?"

"For the delivery, sir. Are you in our computer?"

He told her no, they were going to do that later. His wife wasn't due to deliver for two more months. "She's bleeding. Where would they take her?"

The woman looked at him over the rim of her glasses.

"I need to see my wife." Robert's voice cracked. His eyes began to fill.

"Of course you do, dear. But first you need to sit down so I can enter her into the system."

Robert sat in the chair facing her desk. His legs felt momentarily useless and he was grateful someone had told him what to do. The woman pressed a few buttons to clear away old work, then sat forward and, looking only at the computer screen to her left, asked him questions about Althea: her full name, her date and place of birth, her next of kin—"Me, her husband." And as he spelled out his name, he began to feel the strength return to his legs and feet. He sat up straighter and perched himself on the edge of the chair. He answered that they had no medical insurance, she could bill him directly. And he gave her the address of The Whaler Hotel—they would either be there or they wouldn't, but at the thought that he and Althea and their son or daughter might *not* be living in The Whaler cabins, Robert forced himself to imagine it was only because they would move, and not because there would be only one returning there instead of three.

Soon enough she let him go, directing him to the maternity ward where a man in a turquoise smock told him his wife was being prepped for surgery. *Why? What's wrong?* But the man just told him to have a seat, then disappeared behind a swinging door. The small waiting area was six cushioned chairs, a table spread out with magazines, and a watercooler and Coke machine. His mouth and throat were dry. There was an evil taste in his mouth. In his right pocket was the cash from last night's tips, and in his left were a few stray coins, enough for a Coke. As the can came clacketing down through the machine, two women in those same turquoise smocks walked quickly and quietly down the hall. Their shoes and hair were covered with blue-green netting. Their white breathing masks were hanging loosely beneath their chins. They pushed through the swinging door, and Robert did not know if they were going in to help with Althea, but their silent and urgent rushing left him feeling queasy and lost, like he was falling backwards away from all this, his mouth dry, his stomach a terrible mistake, his knees liquid. He sat with his unopened Coke, rested his elbows on his thighs, and breathed deeply through his nose. He saw his shoes were still untied and left them that way. He remembered Jackie's heels on his shoulders; he remembered the sound Althea made as she wrenched Jackie off the bunk, a deep sustained cry that could only come from a well of quiet.

He sat there a long while. He felt he should call someone. There had been a friend in college, before he quit over a decade ago: his roommate, a thin, sad-eyed existentialist with whom Robert would often go drinking.

Robert thought of him now and suspected that even if he knew his phone number, he wouldn't want him here; at a local bar or at a dorm party, the existentialist would get morose and sneer at the young men and women dancing or huddling together over a joint in their loose jeans. "We're all going over the falls, man. Drink up, Doucette! God drowned in the first boat!" And Robert *would* drink up, then leave his friend and join the others—women mainly, those with delicate throats and wispy hair which, when they danced too close, would catch on his face if he hadn't shaved—women who smiled at him because he was almost handsome, which meant cute;

and when he told them over the music and through the smoke that he was an English major and wanted to be a poet, their interest would deepen and some of them wanted to drink alone in a corner with him, talk about life and beauty. And so he adopted the sentences of his poetry teacher and he'd tell them that life was a song that had to be sung and *forget* iambic pentameter—too cold. "Life's a burning building; life's a ride through the rapids before we all go over the edge, and we only have so much time to get things down. Like your delicate throat," he'd say to one. "Like your eyes," he'd tell another. "The way they make me think of minks in Russia, a family of minks in the snow." He'd leave with one of them and later, after he'd ejaculated into her, after he'd slept in her room, the dawn's hopeful light piercing the windows, he'd *know* he was a poet; he just hadn't put it all down on paper yet. He'd slip out of her warm bed, sometimes taking one last look at her naked buttocks as she slept, or at that sweet triangle of pubic hair between flaring hipbones, and he'd dress and leave the dorm that smelled of cigarettes and cold pizza boxes and beer soaked into the carpet. He was Rimbaud, Baudelaire, Wilde; he was all the rascal poets he'd been reading. And as Robert left the smells of the dormitory and stepped into the cold New Hampshire air, he was grateful he no longer smelled hay and silage, warm udders and oak-handled shovels and hoes, cow manure and diesel fuel, the smells of a life he thought he'd never escape: in the winter, the twice-daily mud-and-ice trek to the barn to lead six dozen holsteins eight at a time to the milking room; to clean the valves and tubes after; to rake manure and haul corn silage from the silo to the feed bunk; to keep the calves dry and fed in their stalls; to inseminate heifers, then calve them months later, changing the hay they slept in, hauling bales as if he hadn't hauled enough in August, the baler shooting them out at him when he only had a few seconds to hook his fingers into the twine, heaving and tossing the bale into place onto the trailer behind him, the sweat in his eyes, his back a tight cord about to snap. And in the fall they'd have to pack the silo with load after pickup load of the corn they'd planted in the spring, and the vacuum chute was always getting clogged or breaking down, so while his father climbed the ladder with a tool apron, Robert would build a huge mound of corncobs he'd have to load into the silo once it was fixed. There were always things breaking down: the tractor, the picker, the baler, the milkers. One summer the freezer went and hundreds of dollars of bull semen thawed and died. And if all the machinery was running smoothly, a storm would come in and there'd be a roof leak, soaking some of the stock who were too stupid to move, and then they'd get sick or just more dopey than usual, and one might trip on her way to feed and cut a foreleg, and Robert would have to nurse that, clean it and wrap it with gauze. But sometimes an infection would come anyway and the cow would get a fever, and even if she could make it to the milking room the milk itself might be tainted, and Robert's father would have to sell her off for scrap beef: cat and dog food, hotdog filler.

In college, Robert tried putting all of this and more into a poem. And when he finished he felt it was the most honest thing he could possibly have written, the most passionate. How could anyone read it and not know how life at Doucette Dairy was for him? How could they not know all of its tedium? He stayed up till almost dawn typing it and retyping it into the shape he wanted, the right stanza length, the right verse. After a few tries, he found the title too: "Dairy." He slept in his clothes on his bed but woke before his alarm went off, then went to poetry class, handing his professor, a resident poet and Pulitzer Prize nominee, his manuscript. His professor said he would read it that morning and to stop by before lunch.

"It has the authority of lived experience, Robert, but I don't believe there was no joy in any of that work. You've written in the voice of the suffering hero and I don't buy it. Try writing a poem without you in it. Show me the cow's fever without your bitching about having to change the bandage. The farm life's the subject, not your whining about it."

Robert had just stood there, his mouth a dry web. The Pulitzer Prize nominee sat down at his desk and began to read a hardcover book. "Write it again, if you like."

Robert had spent the day in his room lying in bed. He had an afternoon class but didn't go. He read the poem over and over, but kept hearing the poet's last three words, *if you like*. They were completely apathetic. Would he say those same words to someone he thought had talent? The following week he skipped all three poetry classes. At a dorm party he got drunk and next morning at dawn he woke up at the base of a red maple tree planted by the Class of 1945. He was hungover and cold and could see he'd covered himself with leaves the color of bright blood. There was a stone engraving on the ground: *Dedicated to the valiant young men of this university who gave their lives for freedom—1945*. And Robert wished there was a war *he* could go fight, but it wasn't fighting he craved, or danger even. More, it was something to be honored and known for—an ability, an act, anything. The night before he'd told a girl that the poet had praised one of his poems, saying it had the authority of lived experience. She'd had a sweet milky face and thick red hair and she'd looked at him askance, as if he were a real blowhard for repeating praise like that.

He didn't know her name and never saw her again, but in the last ten years her skeptical face would sometimes come back to him, the way it came to him now, along with the question to which she seemed to have the answer: *Was* he? Was he a blowhard?

"Mr. Doucette?"

Robert raised his head. It was the same man from before, his curly hair matted from the surgical cap he now held in his hand.

"It was a placental abruption, but we've stopped the bleeding and your wife will be in recovery soon. Your daughter appears to be healthy as well, though we'll have to monitor her pretty closely."

"Daughter?"

The doctor told Robert he could see his child in the neonatal unit, and his wife would be going to ICU after the recovery room.

He said congratulations and offered his hand. Robert, still sitting, reached out to shake it, then stood quickly and squeezed; the man's hand was small and soft, and Robert was acutely aware that it had just performed two miracles: saved his wife, and delivered their baby. "Thank you, Doctor. Thank you." Robert did not want to let go, but the doctor stopped squeezing and glanced down at Robert's shirt. He said it would be a little while before his family was ready for a visit, and he should feel free to go home and change if he'd like. The doctor let his hand slide out of Robert's, offered his congratulations once more, then disappeared back behind the swinging door.

Robert did not want to leave. He wanted to find the neonatal unit and see his child. His daughter. Be with her. Let her hear his voice. Smell his skin. But what would she smell? Jackie's scent? Coconut oil? Old bourbon and her mother's blood? And later, when he visited Althea, would he want to show up in the same clothes he wore when everything went wrong? No. He would drive home, shower, shave, change his clothes, and buy flowers on the way back.

JACKIE WAS SITTING on the porch step of her cabin when Robert drove over the shell lot and parked alongside the marsh. She was smoking a lighted cigarette this time, and she still wore the baggy Patriots T-shirt she'd slept in—that, and a pair of shorts, Robert noticed, her hair pulled back. She was barefoot, and when Robert turned off the engine she sat up straight, blew smoke, and waited; she was a beautiful woman, her thick red ponytail hanging straight down her back, her thighs and calves hard- and supple-looking, covered with tanned freckles. Robert's cheeks became warm, his throat dry, and he took a long drink off his Coke before he got out of the Subaru and walked over to her.

She was looking up at him, her eyes empty of mischief. Instead, Robert saw fear in them, and something he could not begin to name.

But he must have been smiling because Jackie said, "Everything's okay? The baby? Everything?"

"A girl. We have a little girl." He was conscious of the word *we*, the exclusion of her in that, and, as if to make up for it, he sat on the step next to her, their hips touching.

"You're smoking."

Jackie nodded, took a final drag off the cigarette, and flicked it out into the broken shells of the lot. "How'd she find out?" She was looking at him, her eyes full of sorrow, as if *she* had been betrayed, and he knew then Jackie would never have told anyone.

He shrugged. "She saw me come out of your place. I snuck in to see you, but you were asleep, so I let myself back out again."

The screen door opened behind them and Kimberly said excuse me and didn't wait for Robert to finish scooting over before she stepped between them and off the porch. She was dressed for work, the early lunch crowd, her white blouse and black skirt freshly ironed, her bare legs lean, disciplined, and moral. She walked straight to the Whaler's service door and didn't turn around once.

"She hasn't talked to me all morning." Jackie looked halfway over at Robert, her eyes fixing on his shirt, his bloody shirt. "I feel really bad." Her voice broke and Robert put his arm around her. She seemed to be crying, her shoulders bobbing slightly, though he couldn't be sure because he didn't hear anything. He could smell her hair, the natural oil in it, the linen of her pillowcase. He began to get hard, and he pulled away.

"I should get my vest."

She looked at him, her green eyes shiny and dull. She blinked twice, as if she were trying to focus on what he'd really just said. She sniffled, wiped under each eye with one finger, then stood and led him inside. His vest lay on a towel on her bunk, the top sheet balled in a heap at the foot of the bed.

"I rinsed it in cold water."

"Thank you."

"Why weren't you wearing it?"

Robert picked up the vest, damp and dark. "I was carrying it. Just forgot about it." He didn't like lying to Jackie; he should not lie to at least *somebody*. He could hear the beach traffic out on the boulevard, the clown horn of a motorcycle or truck. The air in the cabin was still and hot, and he smelled the sewage, all of theirs, his and Jackie's and Kimberly's, all the other barbacks and waiters and waitresses, the ones who waited. And Jackie seemed to be waiting too, her face sad but open to spontaneity, her nipples erect beneath her shirt.

"I'm sorry about what happened, Jackie."

"Me too."

Robert moved toward her to give her a hug, he told himself, that's all, but she stepped back and held up her hand. "Don't."

Disappointment and relief twisted inside him. He nodded, thanked her for the vest, then left the cabin and walked back to his own where he showered and changed into khaki pants and an oxford shirt Althea had ironed and hung in their tiny closet under the loft. He was sweating a foul sweat: bourbon and desire and a profound weakness; he was almost certain he would have done it with Jackie one more time, a final time. All the windows were open, but there was no sea breeze at all, just the smell of sewage and salt water from the marsh, the faint scent of garbage from the dumpster on the other side of the lot, rancid fried fish and clams, hot metal and dried soda, and he could not imagine bringing his wife and baby back to this. *If* she would come—there was the way she'd turned her head away from him as she bled on Jackie's floor, her placenta "abrupted."

He wiped his forehead, slipped on his loafers, combed his hair back, then crossed the shell lot. It seemed an entire night and day had passed since he'd closed up, but it was still early, the lunch staff pulling chairs off tables, running the vacuum over the sea green carpet, setting each plate with silverware, cloth napkins, and a Whaler's placemat menu. Kimberly was drinking coffee at the window table with three other waitresses who were taking a cigarette break, and

Robert didn't have to guess at the topic of conversation. Still, he waved to them on his way to the manager's office. One of them, Dotty, a small-hipped woman who owned her own video store a few miles west, asked if his wife was doing all right. Robert nodded and smiled, though he felt as if he were lying again.

His manager, Danny Sullivan, was sitting at his cluttered desk with a clear glass of creamy coffee, smoking a cigarette and studying last night's receipts. He had a thick red mustache and a wide double chin. He wore reading glasses. A small paper clip holder was turned over on the blotter at the edge of the desk, and Robert remembered Jackie's hand bracing herself there. He'd forgotten this was the last place they'd done it. He felt like a house burglar walking by one of his victims in the grocery store. Dan Sullivan glanced up at him, then back at the receipts, the smoke from the cigarette wafting in front of him.

"We're switching over to Sprite on the guns, Bobby. When you lock up tonight, have the barback put all the 7UP canisters outside, all right?"

Sullivan flicked on his adding machine. Robert scanned the desk for any more evidence of last night, but there was none, just the general paper clutter of beer and liquor orders, the only hint a clear semicircle of space at the front edge of the desk where Jackie had rested her ass.

"We had our baby today, Danny."

Sullivan looked up, his eyes suddenly empty of numbers. "Already?"

"Eight weeks early. Everything's okay, though." Robert felt himself smile, and now, telling the news to a man, a father, though twice divorced, Robert felt genuinely happy. "We have a little girl. She'll be in the hospital for a while, I guess."

"Your wife?"

"She's good." Robert's forehead felt like plastic.

Dan Sullivan stood and offered his hand. "Good for you, kid. Sit down." He waved at a sawed-off barstool, its upholstered seat sealed with duct tape. He left the office and was back before Robert had even sat. He was carrying a bottle of Bushmills Irish whiskey and two highball glasses, still steaming from the machine. It was the last thing Robert wanted, his bourbon-dry gut already shrinking back at the news, but when Sullivan poured him three fingers and put the glass in his hand Robert knew he would drink it. His manager raised his own glass, said something in Gaelic, then tapped Robert's, and Robert drank the Bushmills slowly, enough for his insides to acclimate themselves, and when they did things weren't so bad: it was a warm, amber day on the beach and his gut was lolling in the water. His manager must've seen something in Robert's face and poured them each one more, though this one was shorter.

Sullivan raised his glass again. "A girl's the way to go, Bobby." His manager drank down the Bushmills and Robert followed suit, the second glass feeling a bit shy in kick and weight, Robert remembering something about Danny's grown son tending bar here till his father had to fire him for stealing from the register. Sullivan sat back behind his desk and took a deep drag off his cigarette, the numbers back in his eyes again. "I'll get Davey to cover for you till you're all set. Give yourself a couple of days, all right?"

Robert thanked him and left the office. He'd meant to give his notice too, to tell him he was done for the season, but Sullivan's gesture of the Bushmills and toast had thrown him. The aftertaste of the Irish whiskey was a bit coarse in Robert's throat, and he walked to the bar and filled himself a glass of ginger ale from the soda gun. The waitresses were gone from the window. It was set now with napkins and silver and clean water glasses. Devon, one of the bus girls, was setting a table at a corner booth, and it was hard not to stare at her young ass in her black pants, but the word *daughter* was in his head and he made himself look away. Outside and across the boulevard, the beach was already full of people sunbathing, others throwing a Frisbee or football back and forth, still others wading out into the green and white surf. He was exhausted, the glass in his hand heavier than it should be, his legs stiff and unsure. And he felt the toast too, his face and head a wide reckless expanse with no borders, and there was the feeling of being left behind, something important going on someplace else he really should not miss.

Then he was in his car backing over the broken shells, perhaps breaking more himself. Though the windows were rolled down, the inside of the car was hot and he began to sweat beneath his ironed shirt. A screen door slammed back on its jamb and there was Jackie standing on her porch in her sunbathing bikini, holding her folded lounge chair and a glass of something iced. She'd pulled her hair out of its ponytail and now it hung thickly just past her shoulders. He didn't wave or acknowledge her in any way, mainly because the car was moving forward, he told himself, but in the rearview mirror he watched her watch him go, her lovely face looking small and sad with resolve, her breasts as ample and inviting as two peaches on a limb on the other side of a steep gorge.

In Exeter, Robert stopped for coffee and flowers. He parked across from the small gazebo off the main square and stepped up under the awnings of the shops and restaurants that filled the old mill buildings all the way to the river. The air was warmer here than on the beach, no breeze, and his mouth was dry, his shirt sticking to the middle of his back. Down a side street was a florist. He went inside and ordered a dozen long-stemmed roses but then changed his mind; red wasn't the appropriate color for the occasion and, under the circumstances, he didn't want Althea to think he was trying to romance her. He asked the lady behind the counter to make up a fifty-dollar mixed bouquet, then stepped outside to escape the earth-strangled odors of all those green stems in the water. Across the road was a Mexican restaurant, its doors open. In the dark bar two men sat laughing. Robert considered a quick beer, but the Bushmills had worn off, leaving him sleepier than ever, his eyes burning slightly, the terrible all-nighter behind him like a faraway sound. The sight of the two men bruised him in a way he couldn't pinpoint, and when he walked into a newsstand at the corner for a cup of coffee, he saw the humidor of cigars and knew not only was he genuinely afraid of Althea leaving him now, but he was lonesome too, lonesome for at least one male friend to whom he could hand a cigar.

He immediately thought of calling his father. It was almost noon in August; he'd be putting up the hay, driving the baler while a couple of hired hands caught the bales, then stacked them onto the trailer. At this moment he was a grandfather and didn't know it, and as Robert paid for the wrapped flowers he told himself to make the call from the hospital, though he hadn't seen or talked to his mother and father in over four years. What would they have talked about? Robert's tips? The tuition money he still owed them? The poetry he wasn't writing? But now there was something to show, something worth his mother calling his father from the fields to the phone for. But the notion of his baby girl being identified as his father's granddaughter left Robert feeling naked and weak, like the better man would get picked to step in and finish a job with which Robert, of course, could not be trusted. That poet-in-residence had told Robert he should start looking at *other* people instead of expecting everyone to look at him. There was the week of drinking and skipping all his classes, then leaving school, and then his father standing in his bedroom doorway saying, "You're all talk, aren't you, son? Nothing but talk."

Robert thought of Althea's anemic face and dark dry eyes. Jackie in her bikini watching him go.

He drove slowly. The coffee was bitter and too hot and wasn't mixing well with the Bushmills. A band of sweat came out on his forehead and he wiped it off with the back of his arm, then dumped his coffee out the window, the plastic lid falling away. In the rearview mirror he watched it roll and flip onto the yellow divider, then lie flat, seemingly accepting its fate as the tires of a pickup truck just missed it. But Robert didn't feel so lucky; the surge of joy he'd felt earlier when he'd told Sullivan of the birth had now backed up on him and turned into an almost suffocating awareness of his own worthlessness, and as he took the left turn for the hospital, his stomach queasy, it seemed almost inconceivable that in his short marriage to Althea she had, in her quiet way, left him feeling not only worthy, but exceptional, a man not only capable of being a real poet, but a husband and father too.

The hospital sat on a rise surrounded by woods, its windows reflecting the glare of the sun. Robert squinted, his head aching. He parked in the shade of a sugar maple and got out with the flowers. When he swung the door shut it pinched off the head of a daisy and a flower he didn't know. He opened the door to retrieve them, but they were both crushed. He reached inside the bouquet for the flowerless stems but couldn't find them, his fingers feeling thick and clumsy. He left them there, hoping Althea would not see them. Inside the hospital at the information desk he asked an elderly woman for his wife's room number. It was on the second floor, she told him, Room 214. Robert asked about the neonatal unit too, and the woman said it was on the third floor, though this time she smiled at him, an understanding and encouraging smile, one with which she obviously hoped to fortify him. Robert hadn't been looking for or expecting that; it frightened him. He walked quickly to the elevators, remembering the doctor's words earlier, that his daughter *appears* healthy, and Robert's face flushed with shame that this hadn't been the primary word on his mind since he'd first heard it.

In the elevator he pressed the button for the third floor, bypassing his wife's. The neonatal unit's door was locked. Robert had to press an intercom button beside it to announce who he was. He cleared his throat and leaned close to the speaker, his throat dry from the coffee, a bad taste in his mouth. He pressed the button.

"Your name, please." The voice was clear and free of static.

"Robert Doucette."

There was no answer. Robert saw he was holding the wrapped flowers tilted to the floor, their heads lolling on their stems, and he righted them.

"We have infant girl Doucette."

"That's her—I mean that's me. I'm Robert. She's my daughter." And it occurred to Robert their child did not yet have a name. The door buzzed loudly and Robert entered the floor. There was a polished passageway, and in it was one chair next to a sink beneath a fire extinguisher. A dark-haired nurse greeted him and smiled, this one genuinely warm but brief and businesslike. She handed him a yellow gown and said he would have to leave the flowers on the chair and wash his hands at the sink. Robert did as he was told. He dried his hands quickly, put the gown on over his shirt, and was tying its sash at his waist as he followed the nurse into the unit.

At its center was a brightly lit nurses' station with four or five women sitting behind a circular counter writing or reading something or speaking quietly on a phone. One stood and pulled a clear bottle from a cabinet. The nurse led him past a large, dim room whose windows were covered with closed blinds, eight or nine tiny cribs scattered in the shadows, transparent bassinets on wheel stands, really. At each one was some sort of electronic monitor. Some were unplugged and dark, others lit up with green, red, and orange lights. Next to these were metal stands with intravenous bags hanging from their hooks. Two or three babies were crying, their voices high and strained and plasticine, as if their vocal cords were only thin distressed membranes. Robert tried to swallow but his throat was too dry, his heart beating in his palms and fingers. He followed the nurse into another large room, this one a bit brighter, its window blinds pulled up halfway. There were four bassinets, and the nurse stopped at the first one on the right. There was an intravenous stand and an electronic monitor. All of its lights were lit up green and red, its screen and opaque orange showing the graphic rise and roll of a beating heart.

"Here she is."

Robert's eyes filled.

There were so many tubes and wires running into the bassinet

Robert was at first not sure what he was seeing. Then he saw her bare chest in the folds of the linen; it was red and orange really, a network of tiny blue capillaries beneath the skin. She was not much larger than his hand.

Her arms and legs were thin, crooked, and short, and her eyes were closed, her face the size of a small apricot. Her lips were tiny rims of purple, and they were parted, her dark round mouth smaller than a dime. She had no hair and hardly any eyebrows or lashes. On her bare chest and stomach were the monitor wires connected to what looked like small round Band-Aids. Just above the miniscule diaper was the stump of her severed umbilical cord, pink and blue, still bloody at the tip. Around her upper arm was a blood pressure cuff no wider in circumference than a cigar band, and taped to her wrist was the IV tube, which dwarfed it.

Robert wiped at his eyes and nose. "Is she all right?"

"Yes. She just needs a little extra help right now. Would you like to hold her?"

He looked at the nurse: she was smiling, her eyes bright with a certain knowledge she seemed to know Robert did not yet have, one she was happy to give him now. For Robert it was like looking into an angel's loving face while sitting on the toilet, or masturbating, or stealing money, or standing there with a sleepless hungover head and body and freshly washed genitals while your wife recovered from surgery she probably never would have had, this infant deprived of eight precious weeks in her mother's womb, this miniature infant girl, her belly rising and falling in short, almost desperate-looking breaths.

How could he not? A cool sweat came out on his forehead and the back of his neck.

"Here." The nurse stepped closer, reached into the bassinet, and picked the baby up with cupped hands, her head fitting snugly between two of the woman's fingers, the wires and tube reaching only so far. Robert held out both palms. They trembled slightly, and as the nurse slid the child onto his hand he was terrified of dropping

her. The infant turned her head to the right and left, then nudged
her nose and cheek into the soft flesh at the base of his thumb, her
feet barely reaching his other hand. The flowers he'd bought were
five times heavier than this. She began to blur. He sniffled and held
her close to his chest. Her ear was pinkish red and perfectly formed
but as small as if he were seeing it from a hundred feet in the air. The
nurse covered her with a light blanket smaller than a man's handkerchief. His daughter blurred again. The nurse dragged a rocking
chair over and set it beside him. Robert was afraid the tube and wires
wouldn't reach. The nurse began to uncoil some slack from the IV
stand, but Robert shook his head and told her that's okay, he'll stand.
She looked at him briefly, as if she were making sure that was what
he really wanted; there was something like satisfaction in her eyes.
Warmth, too. Wisdom. She turned and took all that to another baby
in another room.

Robert looked down at his daughter, this infinitesimal baby girl
curled under a piece of cloth in his hands. He held her as close to his
chest as he could. He stroked the top of her head with his thumb, her
eyes closed, her mouth a dark oval. He wanted to feed her. Shouldn't
they be feeding her something? There was the tube in her arm, but
was that enough? He would ask the nurse about this on his way to see
Althea. Althea, who had stood barefoot in the shell back lot of The
Whaler, her cotton nightgown fitting tightly over her pregnant belly,
her dark eyes afraid but strong and ready to act, when all fear ever did
for him was scare him away: scare him away from the farm and his
father's joyless toil, from the poet's class, from school, from the piti-
ful jottings in his largely empty notebooks, from his quiet wife who
had loved him so faithfully and unquestioningly he had taken refuge
in the dim chaos of The Whaler and the warmth between Jackie's
thighs. And now this three-pound baby girl in his hands needed a
refuge, a solid nest in which to grow, and Robert felt certain he had
already failed in giving that to her; and he felt the need to place her
back in the bassinet, leave the flowers on the chair in the hallway, and

drive away from there. He would go to the bank and withdraw half their savings, almost four thousand dollars. No, he'd leave Althea and the baby all but a thousand. That would be enough to get him to Florida or the West Coast where he'd soon find a job and a place, where he'd go back to just working his shifts, sleeping with an occasional waitress or barmaid, telling himself he was a poet gathering material the way he'd seen so many waitresses use the story that they were only doing this while they saved for night classes; it was the lie restaurant workers told each other so they wouldn't have to admit the truth, that they'd rather watch life's swimmers go by from the deep warm sand of the beach. That's who he was. That's who Althea married. And she can do better, he thought. She will do better. This one, too.

Robert stepped closer to the bassinet, but when he began to lower her inside a loud beeping went off, and he stopped where he was, holding the baby midair as the nurse came walking swiftly into the room, her face calm and smiling again when Robert had expected a look of alarm, or at least chastisement.

"Her IV's sensitive." The nurse stepped in beside him, so close he could smell her hair, the lingering scent of shampoo and the deeper scent of her scalp, just skin, the skin of a woman working, and he felt strangely calmed. He let her take the baby and nestle her back into the folds of linen, patting the wires back into place, pressing gently on the intravenous tube in his daughter's thin arm. Robert took one step back. He breathed deeply through his nose and a sound came out which surprised him and his eyes filled, and there was a hand on his shoulder. "She's really fine, you know. We didn't have to ventilate her. She's a little trooper." She squeezed his shoulder and let go. "Is she your first?"

Robert nodded but could not look at the nurse, not after what he'd just been planning to do. Instead, he looked down at the baby, at his daughter, the rise and fall of her first breaths, at the way her sleeping face was turned to the side, her lips parted, her clavicle almost visible beneath her skin.

"What are you going to name her?"

"We don't know yet."

And he meant it, not the not knowing, but the *we*; as far as he knew, he and Althea were still a *we*. "Has my wife seen her yet?"

"No, would you like to bring her to her room?"

"Yes." He took a breath. "Yes, I would."

"I'll call down and see if she's awake."

The nurse left and Robert kept his eyes on his daughter for a moment longer, then turned and walked to the window. The sun had disappeared and he could see a cloud bank to the east, the air not as bright or dangerous-looking as it had seemed earlier; it was probably raining on the beach, on The Whaler, the cabins, and the marsh. Jackie had probably jumped up and carried her chaise to the porch, maybe stood there in her wet bikini looking out at the rain. He imagined it coming down on the fields of his father's farm, maybe a downpour. That would stop the baling and send the men into the house, into the kitchen where his mother would serve them coffee or iced tea, probably something sweet she'd baked. Robert had been one of those hands himself: sitting at the table with his shirt sticking to his back and arms, his pants damp and matted with hayseed, his work boots still on because his mother knew they were going right back outside after the rain had passed, the soles heavy with mud and bits of manure and silage, his father sitting in his chair at the table, chewing and staring straight ahead into the rest of the day's chores, barely tolerating this momentary interruption from the work that called him.

From the doorway the nurse said Althea was still asleep and they would ring her when she was ready for the baby. Robert thanked her and looked back outside. Down below in the parking lot was a young family: a man in sandals, shorts, and a T-shirt, and a woman in a sundress holding a little boy with a blue cast on his arm. In his hand was the string to a large red helium balloon floating over their heads. The father opened the rear door for his wife and son, and while the mother lowered the boy into the backseat the father took hold of the balloon with both hands to keep it from popping or drifting away. He stood there a moment and looked past the parking lot to the stand of pines beyond, his face tanned, maybe from outdoor work, Robert thought, landscaping or carpentry or roofing—honest work. The man was smiling in the grey light, holding his young son's balloon. His wife straightened and her husband watched her walk around to the passenger door, his smile deepening. He leaned into the backseat with the balloon, handing it to his son, waiting for him to get hold of the string. Then he kissed him and shut the door gently, clicking it shut with his hip.

Robert's heart was beating fast. He turned from the window, walked to his daughter's bassinet, and touched two fingers to her tiny forehead. She was warm and stirred slightly. He left the room, smiling politely at the nurses at the counter, though his daughter's wasn't there. In the passageway he hung up his gown, picked up Althea's flowers, and carried them close to this chest all the way to the elevators and down to her floor.

Room 214 was directly across from the nurses' station, and Althea's door was closed halfway. Robert slipped in shoulder first; he was relieved to see her asleep, but her face was puffy and still yellowish, her lips dry, almost chapped, her wild black hair matted and tamed-looking. Beneath the sheet and light blanket, her belly was flat.

Robert's face grew warm and he felt queasy again. He sat in the chair near her bed. It was deep and soft, welcoming his body as if it had been made just for him, and he knew he could easily sleep in it, would sleep in it if he weren't careful. He sat forward, looked at his wife's sleeping face, noticed how even her eyes seemed swollen. Her mouth was closed, and she was breathing steadily through her nose, her breasts rising and falling.

Robert's mouth was dry again, his fingers trembling. He was afraid of her waking, but more afraid of not being the first human being she saw when she did. Then he remembered the flowers still in his hand; some of them looked as if they were beginning to droop, and his heart began to pound an insistent echo through his throat. He stood to find a vase. But in the small room there was nothing but the chair in which he sat, Althea's bed, her table and moveable tray, a TV built high into the wall, and the bathroom.

He went in there with the flowers. He thought there might be a water pitcher or a plastic urinal container or something, but there was just the sink, toilet, and mirror. He could put them in a sink full of water, but then she wouldn't be able to see them or know that he had brought them. He plugged the basin and began to fill it with cool water, afraid now the sound would wake Althea; he pulled the door closed and when the sink was half-full he shut off the tap, unwrapped the flowers, and lay them in stem-first. He took a long breath and let it out. He opened the door and saw his wife still asleep. He knew he would not be able to hand her the flowers now when she woke, to use them in the way he'd imagined, but that no longer seemed to matter.

He walked to her bedside and stood there, then sat on the edge of the chair. Althea's bare arm lay at her side on top of the blanket. He reached for it, but then stopped, not wanting to wake her, not wanting to see her eyes yet. He lowered his hand and looked at hers. It was small and he could see the sewing calluses at the tips of her fingers. His own hands looked softer, and he thought of their daughter's, pink and curled into tiny fists. He wanted her here now, but first he had to see how Althea would look at him in all her silence. He would wait for that, truly wait. Soon enough she would open her eyes, and he could only pray that when she did they would be the ones she'd first shown him, the ones he'd received for a poem he never wrote and knew now he probably never would, eyes he did not deserve but hoped to earn—eyes of black hope.

DIRTY LOVE

———

IN HER HEAD IT'S ANGRY, MOST OF THE RAPPING VOICES JUST A few years older than she is, mostly black, one white, all of them boys though she knows they think they're men because they're known and can talk like animals and everybody loves them for it. *She* loves them for it, though she doesn't. Not really. But there's respect there, respect for their rage. She can feel it like a small fist inside her just barely touching another's, then they're gone, all the motherfuckers and nines and dead boys in caskets, a woman singing now, a guitar and piano and the woman is a face and a name on the covers of magazines Devon never reads but sees in the 7-Eleven on her walks home from work. All the store magazines have three-quarters naked women on them, all of them, even the ones about cigars or antique trucks or guns. Always a woman's cleavage and long naked legs, her arched back and ass, her fake smile and too much gloss and eyeliner that some nights makes Devon want to kick them all in the face. Sometimes she buys a Coke. It used to be a pack of Merits, but no more, not for sixty-three days anyway, and not to save her lungs or skin, teeth, and hair. It's so she isn't like him in any way, her piece-of-shit father, Charlie Brandt.

But anyway she's still working, running the duster over the cooling unit under the windows in 419, the British woman singing about running after her boyfriend, chasing him and chasing him but he never stops or even seems to notice. The window has a gray mark on it. Like whoever used this room last threw the remote or something else hard and plastic, his cell phone maybe, or his BlackBerry or iEverything, a screen with his entire life on it he can't stand anymore. Or maybe there was a fly and it was the heel of a shoe, this grayish smudge Devon has to reach up and deal with now, scratching it off with her fingernail. They're still long but she doesn't paint them anymore. Two nights ago, her laptop on her knees in bed in the near-dark, a man in Albania asked her to paint them for him and she nexted him like pulling a trigger but then ended up with two drunk girls in France somewhere. They just looked at her the way girls do, like she's their competition and they already know they don't like her and never will.

Devon scrapes away most of the smudge. Outside, the sky is a bright gray, the August kind that can give you a sunburn when you think you're safe, and she has to squint and now she's pissed that she has to even deal with this window and she presses shuffle on her iEverything till she gets mad music again, a dead boy rapping about slinging and his niggas and his nine. Now everything is lined up, her mood and the music in her head and this always makes her feel like she's moving forward, gliding down a moving sidewalk at the airport, that time she was on one, back when she was little and her mother and father seemed happy, or at least laughed a lot together, her mother still pretty or at least looking like she cared, big but still sexy-big, though Devon never thought about these things, just felt them, like she was lying in a soft bed surrounded by cool, deep pillows and the smell of something sweet was in the air, and that day the three of them were getting on an airplane to Disney World where everything was more real than real could ever be.

A gunshot ratchets through her head, then three more, fast and one after the other. Boys are yelling and running, car wheels squealing, then it's the low rapping voice of a man sitting in a prison cell. All his homies are dead and he's got nothing to do but sit in his cell and miss his little girl, her mother a cheatin' bitch he's gonna cap soon as he's out, and after a while Devon doesn't listen anymore, just hears it, this song from a world she'll never be a part of though she's never really felt part of her own either.

This isn't a window day, but she gets Glass Plus from her cart in the hall and shoots where the mark has left a white shadow and she pulls the rag from her back pocket and wipes it clean. Paula wouldn't even see that smudge, and if she did, she wouldn't fucking do anything about it. She's still on the second floor, and Devon has already done the third and now she's in the second to last room on the fourth. Outside and down in the gravel lot, the waitress shacks look like those toolsheds you buy at Home Depot, but each has a little porch with railings, and Devon can see Jackie in a bikini lying on her back on her chaise lounge, her red hair fanned out around her face and shoulders.

Devon wonders if she feels guilty about what happened, and she can see why the bartender wanted to fuck her but how could Jackie have fucked *him*? Not just because his quiet pregnant wife lived with him two shacks down, but because Robert Doucette was a creep. Friday and Saturday nights, Devon bussing tables with three boys, Doucette would call one of them over to get him some ice even though he had a barback to do that. His bar would be full, tanned men and women sitting and standing, drinking, eating, talking and laughing, the restaurant even busier, every table taken by families staying at the hotel or tourists staying at other hotels, sometimes couples, never anyone sitting alone, the fake jazz the manager liked blaring, the tinkling of silverware on plates, low voices and high voices and obnoxious laughter, and Devon just wanted to put her headphones on and make the whole place the background of her world, just a crowded carpeted bad dream she had to move through that smelled like perfume and shrimp scampi and sweat. But Danny Sullivan didn't allow headphones or iEverythings on the floor (or her nose stud or more than one in each ear), and Devon had to work those nights with her insides never matching her outsides so there was never a sliding forward on a current you made yourself.

Instead, she had to load her bussing tray to bad jokes from sunburned fathers, dead stares from sullen kids, tired smiles from half-drunk mothers who just knew her and her life because they had been young and pretty once before, too, when Devon knew they never had. And Danny only allowed trays, never the rubber tubs from the kitchen which would have been much easier for loading the dirty dishes and glasses, and Devon hated the polyester black pants she had to wear, the white blouse buttoned up past her bra. Sometimes clearing a table she'd glance over the heads and tables out to the street where cars and pickup trucks cruised slowly past, their headlights lighting up whatever car or van was in front of them, and on the other side of the boulevard was the dark beach and the black ocean and she almost pictured herself on a ship to France or Portugal or Italy. Only she didn't. Maybe she used to. But why go there now? She went places every night—France, Spain, Turkey, Belgium, Algeria, once Moldova (wherever that was), Portugal, Luxembourg, Italy. And she was seeing only rooms; behind the head and shoulders of whatever man or woman or boy or girl she'd found, was the room they sat in. Sometimes it'd be morning or afternoon and the light would be coming in, but usually it was rooms with shades pulled to day or night, very little on the walls, a shelf with a TV, a few magazines or a book. In Ireland one time, behind a drunk boy with a beard, a sword hung on the wall over a PS3 station, somebody else playing a soccer game on it behind him; there were couches with blankets thrown over them, empty wooden chairs turned facing nowhere. There were lamps on small tables cluttered with ashtrays or empty glasses or a sweatshirt balled up and hanging off one corner.

In Morocco, a man stroking his penis lay sideways on a mattress, his whiskered cheek propped against his hand, and on the wall behind him hung an oriental carpet the colors of plums and blood. Usually Devon nexted right through the assholes masturbating, but this one was pulling lazily back and forth on his erection like someone would pet a cat. His shirt was off and his skinny torso was covered with black curly hair, and now she knew he could see her, but nothing changed; he kept pulling on himself like he was just passing the time, waiting for her to do something or say something or write or draw on his screen anything that would get him to stop or take more of an interest, but he just stared at his screen in Africa and she stared at hers in her great-uncle's guest room in Hampton, New Hampshire, and they stared and stared while he did what he did and then the chat wheel began to spin again, and she was sitting in front of a man in England her father's age, behind him a brightly lit room and framed photos on a wall that looked like family. He had high thinning hair like her father and fleshy cheeks and he was wearing reading glasses and a loosened red tie and white button-down shirt. Immediately his typed words appeared on her screen.

Hello. Are you alone?

Normally she would next him like a slap in his face, but she typed: *Fuck you. We're all alone.*

Then she nexted him and kept going, but she never really knew what she was looking for, if she was looking for anything, only she knew now that other parts of the world no longer interested her. What was there to find there but houses and buildings with rooms in them that held people like her? She'd seen enough and no longer needed to see more. So the money she was saving was for a car and a room of her own somewhere, a quiet zone of her own, away from everyone, even her kind, lonely great-uncle Francis, and she'd be rounding the corner of the bar for the kitchen, carrying a full tray of used plates and glasses and silverware, when Robert, looking over his shoulder while pouring a drink and shooting a mixer into it from the soda gun, would shout over all the human noise: "Ice, Devon! Thank you, honey." And even then, working away like he was, his eyes would drop to a side view of her ass and she'd want to kill him. She'd push through the swinging doors into the bright kitchen, and she'd see one of the young homies in her head doing it, just walking up to Doucette with a nine and pressing it to his sweaty neck and squeezing the trigger.

Devon pushes the cotton rag into her back pocket and blows once on the glass. The smudge is gone, no sign of it, no sign of Doucette anymore either. The song in her head is a happy one, dance music, a Puerto Rican girl from New York singing high over thumping bass, and because Devon's done with this room it's a good song to keep. She runs her hand over the spread of the perfectly made mattress. She checks the bathroom one last time, the sink, toilet, bath, and mirror, the toilet roll full again, its first square folded into an inviting V so the next customer thinks no dirty fingers have ever been here before.

That's what Doucette made her feel, dirty, his eyes taking her in like he'd already fucked her and wanted just one more cheap go at it again. She was eighteen. Didn't that stop him even a little? But she knew better than that. There were all those men around the world who perked up as soon as they saw her. There were the fathers and husbands in the bar and restaurant, their eyes taking her in like a nasty memo to themselves. There were the boys and men behind steering wheels as she walked down the street, their hungry eyes on her in the side view mirror. And there was her own father and Amanda Salvi, his twenty-three-year-old girlfriend with her tits and flat stomach and big mouth she showed off on her Fuckbook page.

Devon places a Going Green card on the pillow, a wrapped chocolate beneath that. She steps into the hallway and locks the door behind her. Just one more room to go, then she's off till she has to come back to bus at five. She pulls her iEverything from her shorts pocket and checks the time. Three hours to do whatever she wants.

Except shit, it's Friday and she has a tutoring session with Francis for her GED. Not that she wants it, but Francis wants her to get it and he's letting her live with him for free so she kind of has to.

Devon checks her messages. Three texts from her mother. One from Sick. None from her "friends," which is how it is now, and that's fine with her.

Mom: R u working 2night? Thought we'd have dinner 2gether.

Mom: Did u get my text? I miss U, honey.

Mom: Text me please!

Sick: Wuz up D?

Like they're just friends and that's all they ever were. Fucking asshole.

The happy dance song is all wrong now. She runs her finger over the screen till once again there are gunshots echoing through her head, the bass beating between her ears. The man's voice is her own, rapping about all the motherfuckers out there she's gonna cap, her body and cleaning cart gliding down the hallway, nothing and nobody holding her back, especially Sick and her weak father and even weaker mother who still lies to herself and hasn't kicked him out of the house he took a shit in like it was a toilet and never once had been their home.

UP AGAINST THE FENCE, the mixed yarrow have gotten out of hand. They've ranged too freely and shoved everything to the side: the asters droop to the left and right; the day lilies, taller than the asters, look like they're holding their own, but the flat heads of the yarrow—rose and ivory and apricot—surround them like approaching thugs; only the white phlox seems free of them. Three years ago Beth planted them closer to the deck, and they began to bloom again only days ago, clusters of tiny white flowers that from the kitchen window look to Francis like the heads of intelligent beings nodding in assent to something quite reasonable.

If only things had ever been reasonable. Though his life has been, hasn't it? Except for having been a drunk, he has lived it reasonably. He has filled it with reasonable things and people, including his wife Elizabeth, whose death, while unexpected, was reasonable too. But he's begun his ninth decade now, and as his own death draws nearer, something he does not fear, his dreams have become more vivid. In this morning's offering, he is once again nineteen years old on a July afternoon sitting behind the wheel of the captain's jeep just outside Pusan. Captain Hunt has folded down the windshield and is resting his elbows on the hood so that he can better steady his camera, a Retina 35-millimeter Kodak made in Germany. Francis has lingered on that many times over the years, the word *retina*, our lens of witness running directly to the brain. And of course he's had to confront the word *witness* as well.

For weeks it had rained, but then it was July and there came a break in the summer monsoons, and all along the ridge above the ditch, the sun glinted wetly off a stand of Korean pines, their branches gnarled and stingy. Down in the ditch three hundred members of the Bodo League were shoveling dirt out onto one long mound, still moist and dark. They wore the white cotton clothes of farmers and peasants for that's what most of them were. Many years later, Francis would learn they'd been promised good jobs if they joined the Bodo League, that they had no idea of its leftist leanings, of its supposed alliance with the north.

Standing on the ground above the ditch were thirty or forty uniformed police officers. Nearly half of these had pulled their pistols from their holsters. An officer in the center Francis could not see yelled something in Korean and the men in the ditch began to drop their shovels and climb out and stand, breathing hard and sweating, in front of the police. The sun was in their eyes, many of them squinting, and Francis could see boys fourteen, fifteen years old, standing beside men who could be their fathers or uncles or grandfathers. Another shout in Korean, and all three hundred boys and men turned to face the ditch they'd just dug. From where he sat behind the wheel beside Captain Hunt, Francis's heart a high hum in his chest, he could see three shovels leaning against the opposite wall of the ditch, left there with the hopes of returning shortly to work. And before Francis could turn away or shut his eyes, the first policeman stepped forward, raised his side arm, and shot a boy in the back of his neck. There was a spray of blood from the boy's throat, and his body collapsed like an empty sack, Francis throwing up half into his lap, half onto the ground. But with the sound of his own retching came dozens and dozens of pistol reports, the click and rewind of Captain Hunt's Retina, clicking and rewinding, clicking and rewinding, and Francis despised him, but not nearly as much as he despised himself for sitting there wiping his mouth and glancing toward the ditch once again. Fewer than half the men, maybe a hundred, still stood, their shoulders hunched, many of them having soiled themselves. There was more Korean shouting, then the surviving Bodos climbed down into the ditch and began pulling bodies one on top of the other before grabbing shovels, many of which they had to jerk from under the newly dead, then they climbed over the mound of dirt on the opposite side of the ditch and began to shovel it in.

"Fuck it, Brandt. Think of it as a turkey shoot."

These were Captain Hunt's actual words, but in Francis's dreams over the years he does not allow—as Francis did in life—the good captain to just leave it there. Instead Francis engages him in debate. But it is the older Francis doing it, the one who survived the war and went on to college and became a reader and a teacher, a man who for years and years drank too much until he quit though he would never use the term *cold turkey.* He avoided that word whenever he could, and while as a kid he'd enjoyed its stringy, salty meat, he's never eaten it since. In his dreams he convinces Captain Hunt that what they are doing is morally obscene, that they're American soldiers, goddamnit. *Americans.*

But there is no convincing Captain Hunt, no dissuading the other American officers sitting in other Jeeps either, and so in some dreams Francis is the one grabbing his M2 carbine in the backseat. He is the one sprinting toward the ditch and firing at the South Korean police until they all lie dead on the ground, their Bodo captives turning to him, grateful and alive. Or, in other dreams, Francis is aiming his weapon at the SKPs, squeezing the trigger, and nothing happens and he has to fight them by hand and he always loses. More than once he is tossed into the ditch of the dead, and more bodies fall onto him, smothering him, then there are the scrapes of shovels and the taste of cool dirt in his mouth and throat and he tries to open his eyes but he cannot.

For sixty-two years, his dreams have returned him to that day in July under the South Korean sun, and his dream-mind has always made things different for him. But not this morning's. Today he woke from a dream of what precisely happened—no changes, no wish fulfillment. Simply what happened. Which is that young Francis William Brandt was a passive witness to, and therefore an active participant in, a massacre.

Francis clicks on the flames beneath the water kettle. He glances at the wall clock above the microwave. Two twenty-two. Devon should be here soon. On the table he's laid out today's lesson: Language Arts and Writing, Part I. Its focus is on grammar, mechanics, and punctuation, and the national GED website provided a sample letter purposely riddled with errors. It's a letter to a finance company written by a young man just graduated from college and hoping to land his first job. An hour ago Francis wasn't sure he should use it. In the letter, the young man (Jonathan Penn) lists all his academic and extracurricular achievements, including chess and varsity rowing, even volunteering for a hunger relief mission to Africa. Francis wondered about the logic of this kind of letter. Were the GED people in Washington hoping to inspire their high school dropouts to greater things? Or did it occur to them that perhaps most of the young men and women having to take the GED test had already given up on achieving very much? Why rub it in their faces?

Francis thought of writing his own test letter, but it had always pained him to make mistakes, and he could not bring himself to do it. Correcting errors had been one of the primary joys of his teaching all those years. While his colleagues on a Friday afternoon groaned about the stack of essays that needed to be graded over their weekend, Francis looked forward to them. Maybe because he and Beth had never had children of their own. That may have been part of it; except for an occasional dinner party or afternoon of domestic errands, there never seemed to be anything very pressing to get to, and Francis looked forward to sitting in his upholstered chair in the living room, a two-inch stack of student essays on the lamp table beside him, next to that a cup of black coffee. He'd take his sharpened blue pencil between his fingers—never red; too admonishing—and he'd lift the first clipped or folded-together paper off the stack, and it was as if he were about to open a home-made gift from one of the hundred and ten kids he stood in front of five days a week.

His colleagues would scoff at this, Rita Flaherty especially, who was six feet tall and wore heels. She favored purple skirts and purple sweaters and in her forties had let her hair go completely gray. She drank too much wine at night, lost her husband young, swore too much in the teachers' lounge—"Bullshit, Mary, that Ramirez kid would shoot you in your fucking sleep." She called Francis Frank because she thought Francis was too soft for him, a veteran of the Korean War, and at six feet five he was the only teacher or administrator taller than she, something she seemed grateful to him for, so once over a cold lunch at the Formica table in that windowless room, he'd told her what he felt about each essay a student wrote for his class, even the cynical ones, the ones that seemed written with one hand while the other was giving him and this school the finger, that these typed words were essentially gifts from inside them.

"Oh, Frank, *please*. One in three hundred of these kids really gives a shit and you know that's true."

He did not know that, and he told her so. But she waved him off and wiped egg salad from the corner of her mouth and stood to leave, always in a hurry, this tall purple-wearing, foulmouthed woman Francis missed more than any of the others. She retired two years after he did and last he'd heard she was living alone in a retirement community down in Tampa.

The kettle begins to whine, then shriek. Francis switches off the flames beneath it and fills the carafe of teabags, the steam rising into his face and fogging his glasses. Devon will walk in with a diet drink from the 7-Eleven. She left the house this morning wearing black jeans and a sleeveless black T-shirt, red headphones over her ears, that tiny blue stud lodged in her left nostril. Some mornings she also put three or four rings in her right ear and six or seven in her left, but today she'd inserted only one in each, perhaps because she had to work in the restaurant later, Francis didn't know. There was so much he did not know: what it was she listened to all day and night behind those headphones; why she had the tattoo of a butterfly—deep blue and green with red veins in the wings—just above her right ankle; what she did most weeknights in her room, the door closed, as silent in there as if the room were empty; how it was her father, his nephew Charlie Brandt, could have lived fifty-seven years and still be acting like the reckless and selfish little shit he'd always been.

Because his father, Francis's older brother George, had given him everything, that's why, never really made him work for it. Francis pulled off his glasses and began wiping the lenses with the hem of his shirt. His fingers and glasses were a blur, but he didn't care. This morning's visit to Pusan had pulled him backwards and now he could feel his brother as if he were standing behind him in the kitchen. George, gone now—twenty-one years, is that right? *Twenty-one?*—yes, because Francis had just turned sixty. Half the cake his colleagues had feted him with the day before was still wrapped in foil on the table in the teachers' lounge, and Francis had been staring at it as he held the phone pressed to his ear and Beth delivered to him the news. A heart attack at the airport in Cincinnati. George, who'd always worked too long and hard and whose insurance business operated in seven states.

The Depression had shaped George more than it had his younger brother. George had known their father William, for one. In the fall of 1932, the year Francis was born and George turned ten, their father lost his job with two hundred others at Cohen Shoes. He and all the rest knocked on the doors of the other mills in town—Zinger's Hat Factory, Kaplan's Soles, a ladies' comb manufacturing shop down on River Street that years later Francis would work in himself as a twelve-year-old, all the machinery retrofitted to make aluminum rivets that were then trucked up to the Portsmouth and Bath shipyards, building naval destroyers to help destroy Hitler. But those first months of Francis's life, his father and most of the men he knew had little luck anywhere. That winter a soup kitchen operated by the Young Men's Christian Association opened its doors on Water Street every day at noon, and even if it was snowing or too cold out, the Brandts would walk down from Washington Square with other families, Francis bundled up and carried by his mother or father or even George, his brother used to tell him.

They'd reach Essex Street, passing one shuttered mill after another, stepping under the iron trestle of the Boston & Maine Railroad. Less than a year later Francis's father would hop that train in search of work. (Or at least that's the story that was told forever afterward, that he was looking for work, that he did it for his family.) Perhaps, walking to that free meal with other families, their shame was lessened because they were all in the same situation and the families had chatted on their way downtown. Two months later, William Brandt (his friends called him Billy) would have to sell their house and move to his wife's mother's place on Ginty Street, and the four Brandts would share one room, George on a pallet on the floor, their

mother and father in the narrow bed, Francis sleeping in the bottom
bureau drawer lined with blankets. The house eventually became
his, but for most of his eighty-one years, if Francis thought of his
young family's beginnings at all, he did not think of them sharing
that bedroom; he saw his father running alongside a rolling, jolting
freight car, tossing his cardboard suitcase into an open door, then
leaping half-inside, his legs hanging out, his toes hitting one tie after
another before he was able to lean in and pull himself up and into
the darkness.

And at age ten George went to work. He fired the boiler at the
boxboard factory across the river, shoveling coal past its glowing iron
doors. In the fall he picked apples in the wild orchard up on Hilldale
and sold them out of a cart downtown. At twelve, tall for his age, he
got work in the steam room at Cohen's, a job few wanted but took
anyway, steaming leather so it could be stretched for cutting. He did
piecework at Fantini's and ran a sole-stamping machine at Kaplan's,
and once the WPA was in full swing he worked with grown men
pouring concrete sidewalks, laying brick walkways and side streets,
then helping to build three bridges before the war broke out and he
fought in France and Germany and came back in one piece and even
then he'd been sending his army pay back home to their mother, this
dour superstitious woman who'd raised Francis alone, who became
a seamstress downtown and never married again, though Francis
remembers a man, Bernie Donovan, Irish like her.

They'd met in church, this bald man in a black frock coat who
would sit with her in one of the two chairs on the porch. They would
speak quietly, as if they each had intimate knowledge of a close friend
in trouble and they did not wish to be rude. Sometimes he would
laugh, but she would not. Perhaps she smiled. It was the only time
she was truly pretty. She kept her red hair pulled back and up, and she
never wore makeup, her eyebrows thick as a man's, her eyes a glinting
blue, her cheekbones a bit too sharp to be lovely. But it all softened
when she smiled, and though he had no gift for telling a story or

a joke, Francis worked hard to make that happen. Yet if he tried
to impersonate someone—the iceman for one, a tall Italian whose
shoulders dipped to the right even when he wasn't lugging a block of
ice—his mother would shake her head at him with a quiet urgency, as
if what he was doing was being watched by someone powerful who
would surely punish them all.

Francis put his glasses back on. Things are clear again, everything
he sees Beth's. There's the oak rack of spices hanging above the stove,
each of the bottle caps labeled and facing out alphabetically: *Anise,
Basil, Coriander.* There are her reading glasses hanging from their neck
straps from a clip magnet on the side of the fridge, beneath that a
reminder card for an appointment with the dentist that came and
went without her. There is the yellow linen spread on the table. They
bought it at a yard sale in South Carolina from an obese blind woman
who'd told them that the tiny blue flowers etched into the cloth were
hand-sewn and called African blue lilies. That was a good trip, and
Francis was grateful to Beth for making him do it, to just get in the
car and start driving. Why not? They were both retired. Were they
just going to sit in their living room in front of the TV until they
died? And Beth was different when they traveled; it was like watching one of her own flowers get more water, fertilizer, and sun, its
stem straightening, its leaves opening. She'd sit in the passenger seat
beside him, a map or guidebook on her lap, her glasses magnifying
her eyes a bit too much, and she'd tell him the names of small towns
just off the highway: Mooresville, Hickory, Cary, High Point. She'd
read to him all the history she could find, and she'd want to take
any exit that looked promising, though most of them looked good
to her because of their numbers: 37, 13, 9. Or simply the names of
towns, their very sounds. One was Joslin, a soft girl's name, so they
were both expecting to find a central green surrounded by clothing
shops and a bookstore, maybe an ice cream parlor, pub, and café.
Instead they found a stretch of strip malls and gas stations leading
to an industrial park of squat cinderblock buildings surrounded by

a high chain-link fence. At the paved entrance Francis turned their car around and headed back for the highway. Beth had shrugged and said, "They need a new name for that place."

Francis probably agreed, as he so often did with his wife, whether he agreed with her or not, but that detour to Joslin had done something to him, had flushed some black bird of regret from the brush; it was too much like something else.

Back on the highway, Beth switched on the audiobook they'd been listening to, one of those novels set in the royal court of France with all its incest and adultery and bloodletting, and as the actor began to read once again, Francis knew what it was: driving into Joslin only to discover what they had was a bit too much like marrying Elizabeth Harrington only to discover what he had, that despite her work at St. Mary's Hospital nursing the sick and injured, despite her dry wit at the restaurant dinners he would take her to, despite her green eyes that appeared warm and nothing like his mother's, despite those soft-looking lips that smiled at any of his failed attempts to be funny, despite the way her body fit against his as they danced to a song on the jukebox or once a live jazz band at Benny's in Boston, despite how much she seemed to admire his choice not to work for his brother in insurance but to teach instead, despite how tenderly they'd made love that very first time, how after she'd held his cheeks and looked into his eyes, hers welling up while he was still inside her, despite all these signs of only good things to come with Beth as his wife, what he had not seen, or had not allowed himself to see, was how critical she was of everything and everyone but herself.

Last week Devon allowed her mother to visit just long enough to bring her more clothes. Marie stood in his living room taking in Beth's stack of paperbacks beside the sofa, her throw blanket draped over the hassock, a pair of her slippers on the floor beside it. His nephew's wife is so much larger than she's ever been, her sad and lovely features nearly lost in flesh, and she glanced at him with pity for his transparent grief. He could not say he did not feel grief, this dark empty corridor inside him he seemed to be wandering down alone, but what could he do with this other feeling? That after forty-three years of hearing nearly daily of his shortcomings, it was a welcome respite to be left alone? How could he say that since that sudden January evening of last year, what he felt now was a dumbstruck sense of freedom for which, daily, he felt the need to apologize?

DEVON IS PAST the strip walking on the edges of lawns. Across the street is the ocean she doesn't look out at, but right before she left The Whaler she glanced at it because the sun had just broken through the gray and the surf broke on the barrier rocks and she liked how they glistened. She's thirsty and sweating. Her jeans feel sewn against her legs and crotch, and she just wants to take a shower and why did she tell Francis she'd study for that fucking test?

In her head plays something soft. It's that skinny British boy moving his fingers over his piano keys the way Sick would run her hair back away from her face. Devon hits shuffle till it's the band from Las Vegas, the lead singer skinny too, and he always wears vests and string ties like cowboys and his songs are half-mad, half-sad, like he's about to do something he'll always, always regret but he can't stop himself.

Devon leaves it on and crosses the side street to the lot of the 7-Eleven. An open Jeep is parked there, the top down. One boy sits in the passenger seat, two more in the back. They all have their shirts off and they're all looking at her. She takes them in for only a half second, but she can see they're her age, maybe a year or two older. Tanned. Dark tats around their arm muscles to make themselves look badass, the two in the back with an earbud in each ear, sharing an iEverything, the one in the front wearing shades, and she steps up onto the concrete walk in front of the store and grabs the door handle and she knows they're checking out her ass in her black jeans and they may even be calling out to her but she's got her Dr. Dre phones on and that's her excuse for completely ignoring them. It's what she tries to do now, but she catches herself walking into the 7-Eleven just a beat slower than she has to, letting them linger on what she won't ever give them.

The inside air is almost cold and her skin gooses up. She moves down the aisle past bags of chips and cans of dip to the drink cooler in the rear, the Vegas singer in her head suddenly a hard penis she's sucking on, that part of it always a letdown, the rush coming before any of them unzipped their jeans or dropped their cargo shorts and she got down on her knees or lay down on a bed or leaned over in the front seat of a car or once squatted up against a tree while her old boyfriend shoved himself into her mouth and throat and his friend caught it all on his phone and then everything that would happen began to happen.

Devon grabs a Diet 7UP. The can is barely cool, though, so she grabs a Coke instead. She won't eat much later to make up for the calories, and besides she needs the jolt to get through Francis and his "lesson." Such an old word. One that comes from an old man. But because it comes from him, she can't hate it.

A new song comes on now. It's desperate and too fast, the lead singer with his string tie no longer a hard-on to her but a fucking baby crying over how jealous he is. She reaches down and flicks her finger across the screen till she gets one with only instruments. They're ancient, from a CD Sick gave her from a movie about Jesus. The word *Mesopotamia* is in her head. And *Aramaic*. Words from the only class she ever liked from the only teacher she'd ever liked at a school she'd only ever hated. This is music from some land of goats and olive trees, wooden flutes and lambskin drums that beat together like a herd of camels racing or a throng of people pulsing in jeering waves at Jesus forced to carry his cross, the thudding in her chest as her father's Lexus pulls out of the driveway on a Saturday night, Charlie Fucking Brandt behind the wheel, his thinning hair freshly gelled, Devon's pathetic mother standing at the window pretending she doesn't know what she knows, the crying that will come later that Devon will try to block out with her Dr. Dre's, though she'll still feel the vibrations of it in the air of her closed bedroom. Dangerous vibrations. Like she feels now as she reaches the counter and the driver of the Jeep is taking her in. He's bigger than the rest. A faded red tank top over a shelf of chest muscles, blue eyes that ignore her face completely and drop to her breasts, hips, and crotch. Then he's out the door and in his Jeep and she's only looking at the man she buys a drink from every afternoon.

He has gray hair and dark skin, his shoulders narrow, ashy spots under each eye that make him look unhealthy. He never looks at her body, only her face, and he half smiles at her and takes her money without ever trying to talk to the girl wearing headphones. A man in her head cries out a song from some mountaintop rising above a desert plain, and she imagines it's him, the man's dry fingertips touching her palm as he places there one quarter and one dime, and then she's out in the heat again and she's glad to see the Jeep gone. She cracks open her cold Coke and drinks down half of it, swallowing and swallowing, and she sees Jesus down on one knee, that crown of thorns pressing into his forehead, the cross pushing its weight onto his back, and she walks across the lot under the sun, everything matched up again: the heat and this desert music, the smell of something dead coming off the ocean, a crowd judging you, a crowd of people calling you names and wanting only to hurt you.

FRANCIS SITS AT the kitchen table trying not to feel put upon. His grand-niece walked into the house right on time for their lesson, but she was flushed and sweating, the blue stud in her nose a bright contrast to the red headphones over her ears.

"Uncle, do you mind if I take a quick shower first? I *stink*."

"*No, not at all.*" He had practically yelled this for he never knew if she was talking to him through blasting music between her ears or not. She smiled at him and disappeared down the hallway. Moments later he heard her bathroom door close, but that was over forty minutes ago, nearly thirty of it with the water running.

This is not a new situation for him, of course. With the hard cases, it was always a walk along a high wire. Call them to task and then risk having them close themselves off more than they already were; ignore this opportunity to teach Devon something important—about consideration, for example, or someone else's water bill—and abdicate his responsibility to her entirely. But what *was* his responsibility? It wasn't Charlie or Marie who had called him at one in the morning on a Tuesday, but Devon, this young woman he'd known and loved since she was an infant.

"Uncle Francis?" She sounded as if she'd been crying or drinking or both. He was in bed and had been asleep a long while. When the phone rang in the darkness, he thought *Beth. It's Beth*. And he sat up and jerked the receiver from its cradle. He needed to know where she'd gone, and he needed to explain himself.

"Uncle?" A plaintive voice. Then there was Beth lying in her casket in pearls and a light blue dress, and Francis was trying to make out the glowing orange numbers of the alarm clock. He began to see the face that was joined to the voice in his ear, his grand-niece who had her mother's pretty eyes and small mouth, her father's square jaw. Her own chopped bleached hair.

"Devon?"

"Can I come live with you?"

Her voice had sounded so small and it'd carried him back to the child she'd been just a few years before. Diminutive and thin with black hair she liked her mother to braid for her, how after an Italian Sunday dinner Marie had cooked, Devon liked to sit on the lap of her Great-Uncle Francis and he'd read to her from books she'd pull from her shelf. But once, when she was six or seven, it'd been a fairy tale that ended badly for everyone, something Francis hadn't seen coming. "Uncle? Did all the kids really get *eaten*?" And her young voice seemed to come from a part of herself poised to curl up away from the world.

"Devy? What's wrong? Where are you?"

"I can't take it anymore. They're fighting. Everybody's—"

"Who's fighting?"

"My fucking *parents*. Please, Uncle, please—"

There was more to that conversation, but he no longer remembers it. And there was more to Devon's troubles than her mother and father's faltering marriage, something he sensed without Marie's long-winded, worried, and vaguely defensive emails to him either.

Francis sips iced tea, adjusts his glasses, and reads again the sample essay topic from the GED website:

> *What is one important goal you would like to achieve in the next few years? In your essay, identify that one goal and explain how you plan to achieve it. Use your personal observations, experience, and knowledge to support your essay.*

But what if the student has no goals? What then? What if his or her only goal is to get through today? Francis had seen so many kids like that over the years, the ones who openly slept on their forearms on their desks, or those who couldn't sit still and would do anything to make their day more interesting: write *cunt eater* on the board just before class; flick a pen cap at a slow girl across the room; light up a cigarette ten minutes before the bell rang—Jimmy Swansea, the way he sat back and blew smoke out his nostrils and stared at Mr. Brandt staring at him. What Francis had wanted to do was march down the aisle and grab Jimmy's throat and jerk him up from his chair, but Jimmy was six feet and a hundred eighty or ninety pounds, a boy who, like so many of them, was being raised in a neighborhood much like Francis had been raised in too—no fathers, or if they had them, they were bad fathers, drunk or cruel or distant or all three. And mothers who, unlike his own, had given up in some way or another so that these children sitting before him—too thin or too heavy, poor teeth and bad skin, one or two surprisingly fit-looking, like Jimmy Swansea—were to him solitary ghosts just drifting from one demand on them to the next, and on his good days he could usually summon enough compassion for them to at least try to do the right thing.

When Jimmy Swansea lit up his cigarette, the smell of its smoke filling the room, thirty-three young heads turned to him, and Francis knew he'd already lost them for the day anyway.

"Class, anyone who is not smoking a cigarette in this classroom is free to leave now, ten minutes early. If a hall monitor gives you trouble, send him to me. *Go*."

Jimmy smiled as if he were the ringmaster in some dark circus of his own making. He inhaled deeply and blew out smoke and looked around at his classmates pulling on their backpacks and glancing back at him as they shuffled out of the room. Then it was just Jimmy and Mr. Brandt, and Jimmy's expression changed because his circus now had no audience and Mr. Brandt was sitting on a desk across from him. "One day, Jimmy, and it may come sooner than you think, you'll be dead in the ground and that's when you'll know you didn't even begin to live your life."

Jimmy was looking straight into Francis's face. His earlier defiance had been replaced by a blankness, but it was a blankness that seemed to mask deeper fears he tried daily to ignore. He sat up and flicked his ash. Francis ignored it.

"Here's what I know, Jimmy. You're afraid there's no place for you to go but where your parents have gone and the thought of that terrifies you so much you'll do anything to escape the days leading right to where they are."

"Don't talk about my fucking family."

"I don't even know your family, Jim. And I mean no disrespect. But I want you to think about what I just said. You're no clown. In fact, you're a leader, I can see it. But you're running from that role because if you step into it and work hard and become who you can truly be, you may just have to betray where you come from."

Jimmy put the cigarette between his lips. He stood and pushed back his chair and walked out of the room. There was more Francis wanted to say to him: *One more interruption in my class, Jimmy, and I'll break your fucking neck.* But those were the kinds of words Jimmy was looking for, the ones his days and nights served him up anyway. And Francis had never planned to use these other words either; usually they just came without forethought. He'd be sitting across from a difficult kid, looking into a face that always appeared to be so much younger up close, and he could feel the words begin to rise in him from who knows where. He suspected his subconscious was taking in things about these kids every day whether he wanted it to or not, and so he allowed his little speeches to come. Sometimes they brought changes in kids, subtle but good ones. Other times, as with Jimmy Swansea, nothing changed and he wondered if he'd wasted his time. A year after that day with the cigarette, Jimmy dropped out and Francis heard he'd joined the Marines, something that surprised him at first but then did not.

Last winter, Beth gone a year, Francis was driving a bit too fast up the highway. It was a Wednesday, close to midnight, and because he could no longer stand his quiet, empty house he'd pulled on his coat and climbed into his cold car just to drive. He hadn't had a drink since his fifty-third birthday twenty-eight years earlier, but that night he'd wanted one—why not? He no longer had anything left to lose: a family, a job—and he was just on the cusp of deciding to exit the highway in search of a bar or roadhouse when he'd flicked on his radio and his car was filled with madly insistent violins. He had stumbled onto Beethoven's Ninth Symphony just as it had begun, and now the barely contained hysteria of the strings section was pulling him headlong toward someplace wonderful yet horrible, this long, dark corridor inside him, his wife's betrayed spirit hurling itself around his head, then he was pushing down on the accelerator to outrun her and there came the flashing of bright blue lights in his rearview mirror and at first they seemed to be part of the violins, the unrelenting violins, and Francis fumbled for the switch and turned off the radio, the silence a relief and an echoing failure as he pulled over and rolled down his window for the state trooper who shined his bright flashlight into his face.

"License and registration, please." It was just a voice Francis had to squint at, the flashing blue in his mirror a strange respite. The officer pointed his light onto the empty backseat, and Francis handed over what needed to be handed over.

"I thought that was you, Mr. B." The trooper shined his light into his own face. The strap of his hat was pulled slightly into both cheeks, and because he was smiling he looked fleshy when he wasn't, but there, beneath thicker eyebrows, were the same blue-gray eyes that had narrowed up at Francis so many years earlier when he'd told Francis not to talk about his fucking family.

"'Member me?"

"Of course I do. Jimmy, right? How are you?" Francis had offered his hand and Trooper Swansea pulled off his leather glove and squeezed.

"Good, real good. Married, kids, the whole shitstorm. You?"

"Retired, Jimmy. I lost my wife last year—" He stopped himself. He had said it only to explain his speeding, and he felt cheap.

"I'm sorry to hear that, Mr. B."

"Francis."

Jimmy let out a short laugh. "I can't. Isn't that funny? To me, you'll always be Mr. B."

"Was I driving too fast?"

"Yeah, there's black ice. You should take it slow." Jimmy handed Francis his license and registration.

"No ticket?"

"Not tonight." Trooper Swansea flicked off his flashlight. He was just a shadow in the road. "Listen, I know I was a handful as a kid. I want to thank you for not taking any of my shit."

"I had worse, Jimmy."

"Really?"

"No, I'm just lying to make you feel better."

Jimmy laughed softly. He patted the roof of Francis's car. "You take it easy, Mr. Brandt."

"You too, Jim." Francis put the car in gear and pulled carefully back onto the highway. In his rearview mirror the flashing blue lights went dark and there were only the headlights of Trooper Swansea growing smaller and smaller till Francis was alone. He drove a long while, it seemed. He kept the radio off.

Mr. B.

How many times in his adult life had he heard grown men and women call him that? And nearly always with respect and affection. He'd be in the grocery store or walking down the street—even in this beach town he'd retired to—or else at the mall to buy a new belt or socks, and he'd pass a graying man or woman whose eyes would come alive and they'd smile widely and wave as if they were still kids. "Hey, Mr. B.!"

Sometimes they'd keep walking, but more often they'd stop and want to chat. If they were doing well (employed, married, still reasonably healthy), they seemed to want to point all that out to him. If they were not doing well (divorced, unemployed, maybe had gained a lot of weight or smoked and drank too much), they did not stop him at all, or if they did, it was a brief conversation where they deflected his questions with vague generalities, or else they tried to talk about their son or daughter whom Francis had also taught.

Walking away from these run-ins, Francis often felt he'd been awarded a mantle of respect he just did not deserve. There were all those years he'd been hungover in class, his mouth dry, his head being squeezed by a large invisible hand, the sea of adolescents before him a blur of flesh and denim he saw only as his tormentors. Then he'd glimpse a girl looking at him. Her eyes would be focused, her lips parted in some kind of private concentration on whatever it was he was trying to tell them, and he'd take a deep breath and wipe the cool sweat from his forehead, and work harder. The sober years were far better. Even though they did not come until his fifties, he'd felt like an athlete at the top of his game, each day a challenge he seemed to have the tools and desire to overcome. And driving away from Jimmy Swansea that night, Francis no longer wanted a drink. For while he had no work and his wife had left him behind for all time, he did have something to lose, didn't he? The largely unearned and undeserved respect of hundreds of mothers and fathers, of wives and husbands, of troopers and janitors and teachers and lawyers and electricians and bar owners, all of whom had once been children sitting at desks covered with ink graffiti, tubes of buzzing fluorescent light above, the beckoning world outside their windows while Mr. B stood before them trying to teach them something about reading and writing and the truth.

"Can I have some of that?" Devon emerges from the hallway barefoot in a T-shirt, her short shorts nearly covered by it. Her hair is wet and combed back from her face so that she looks both older and younger.

"Of course." Francis starts to stand.

"I'll get it, Uncle." She breezes past him, smelling of shampoo and clean cotton, and he sits back down and takes the printed page from the GED website and folds it in two. No essays on important goals for now.

She sets a glass of ice on the table in front of Beth's place. It's the center chair facing the French door out to the yard, and Devon pours herself tea from the carafe.

"Sugar?" He holds a spoon out toward her.

"No, I'm good."

"I know you are."

She smiles, but her eyes seem to darken as she rests the carafe on the table and sits. She nods at the papers before him. "L.A.?"

"Yeah, but we're going to skip all the rules for now. I just want you to write something."

"What?"

"An essay. It'll be part of the test."

"About what?"

"They'll give you an assigned topic, Devon, so you need practice with that."

"You're giving me a topic?"

He nods at her and smiles. "I am."

"Do I have to write it right now?"

"Yep. You'll have forty-five minutes."

She looks out the window, squints at the sun on the yarrow and asters against the fence. "You know I don't even want to do this."

"You'll thank me later, Devy. At least college will remain an option for you."

"I'll never go to college."

"How do you know?"

"Because I hate school."

"Not when you were little. You used to run up to me with your report cards. Nothing but A's."

She glances at him, her eyes incredulous and resigned, as if she sees just what she thought she would. It makes him feel old.

"Let's just get this over with."

"All right."

"Well? What's my topic?"

He has no idea what to say. But he opens his mouth and begins to speak. "I want you to write about something bad that's happened to you, something you wish did not happen but you ended up learning a lot from it anyway."

She rests her finger on the lip of the glass. "Something bad?"

"Yes."

"What do you mean by bad?" Her chin is low. She's looking at him as if he's just revealed something bad about *himself*, and he can see his mistake. She thinks he's trying to draw her out, to tell him things Marie in her emails has alluded to without any real specifics, mainly the depression Marie fears she's passed on to her daughter.

"I'll leave that to you. Anything from burning a batch of cookies to whatever comes, but make it honest and don't skimp on the details."

"Cookies?" There's a patronizing but mischievous light in her eyes, and he feels them both shift back onto safer ground.

"Brownies then."

"I need my headphones. I can't write without music."

"They won't be allowed during the test, Devon."

"I hate this."

"I know." He pushes toward her a notebook, pencil, and pen. He peers at his watch, and he ignores her bare foot beginning to tap under the table. "Begin . . . *now.*"

SHE WANTS A CIGARETTE. She hasn't for a while, but she does now. Outside the glass doors, Francis waters flowers with a hose. He looks so much older in the sunlight, his shoulders slightly hunched, his eyebrows bushy and white. She stares down at the open notebook. She keeps tapping her heel on the carpet. With no music in her head, there's too much in her head: Trina's Facebook page. The word WHORE under the picture of Devon at a pool party. It might have been at home, it could have been at the Welches', but it was last summer, her in that red bikini, one arm around Davey Price, the other Rick Battastini. They had just lifted her up, and she liked this picture because even with her legs in the air, her body leaning forward, her stomach looked flat and tanned, and all three of them were laughing and two seconds later Davey and Rick tossed her backwards into the pool, but Trina didn't take that picture.

Trina, who'd been her best friend since they were twelve. Half-Italian like her, her breasts were already showing in seventh grade, and by freshman year they were big, her waist small, her hair black and curly while Devon's was long and too straight, her breasts small, her hips like a boy's so she ran faster in track and would've gotten stuck going only to lower classmen jock parties if it weren't for Trina who dated seniors like Bobby Connors. He worked and drove an almost new Sentra and would pick them up down in Lafayette Square. Trina had told her mother she was watching movies at Devon's and Devon had told her mother she was watching movies at Trina's, and Trina would sit up front with Bobby, his black Nike cap sideways on his head, his whiskers shaved into a chin strap like a West Coast rapper. He was big from lifting weights, but his blue eyes looked sweet even when he was trying to look badass.

His best friend Luke McDonough was almost always in the backseat. He had blond hair he gelled into a sideways flow across his forehead, and he was constantly chewing gum, texting someone as she climbed in, smiling at her though his eyes never really seemed to see her. Gangsta rap would be shouting out from Bobby's speakers, and Bobby would be driving before Devon had even buckled up, something she stopped doing once she noticed Trina never did.

It was always about the house parties. They'd cruise from one to the next, sometimes hitting three or four in one night. They'd pass vodka nips around because you could toss them out the window if you got pulled over and vodka didn't stay on your breath like other things did. Some parties were in quiet neighborhoods or culs-de-sac, and they had to keep the noise down for the cops. But the best ones were in houses in the woods or out on Whittier Lake, Luke McDonough's place when his mother and father were away for the night. His father sold computers or something, and his mother worked in a bank and they had a pool and a boathouse with a motorboat in it, though Luke never let anybody take it out, even when he was shit-faced.

That was a bad thing that happened. Maybe one of the first. Devon picks up the pen, then drops it for the pencil. She writes *Luke's boat.* She and Luke sitting on the cushioned seat of the boat in its dark little house that smelled like wood and something decaying in the water. From where they sat, Luke's arm around her shoulders, they could look past the boat's windshield and out the open doorway to the dark water and the tiny lights of houses on the other side of the lake. It was October but warm. The dead leaves in Luke's yard had felt like dried skins under her feet. She'd been drinking hard lemonade with Trina and two other girls since the sun went down, and from the boathouse she could hear the party in the McDonoughs' behind them, thirty or forty kids, most of them upperclassmen and most of them guys, Luke's hand on her breast over her sweater now. In Luke's basement was a playroom with a wide-screen TV and a pool table under a low green light shaped like a fish. There were deep leather couches and chairs and a soft carpet under your feet, and on the TV was *Call of Duty*, soldiers' heads getting blown off in a blood splatter by boys with game controls in their jerking hands. Dubstep thumped from the surround sound and Devon could feel the bass drops in her crotch, but she'd been laughing with Trina and Allie or Ava Something, a blond girl with the tattoo of a black bird at the base of her neck right where her collarbone was, and Devon had kept staring at it, even while she was laughing at something, and then she couldn't look at the bird anymore and she was over by the ping-pong table under a brighter light, this one a rectangle of stained glass like in churches, but it hurt her eyes to stare at it and two boys had been swatting the little white ball back and forth but now three or four guys and girls on each end were playing Beirut, trying to flip one over the net into a Solo cup of Bud Light they would then have to down, and that's when she heard Luke yell over the Dubstep and all the laughing and loud talking and kill shouts from the *CoD* boys, "Watch the table! Watch the fucking table!" But his voice was just noise swept away by the party wind, and anyway he looked too drunk to do much about it. His flow had drooped over one eye, and one collar of his blue polo was up, the other down, and it reminded her of dog ears and maybe she was smiling when he looked over at her propped against the wall, an empty bottle in her hand, because he smiled back. It was the first time he'd ever really looked over at her and seen her. Then he was standing in front of her, his face so close

she saw the shaving rash under his chin and they were talking, trying to talk, but nobody talked. On the other side of the pong table,
seven or ten kids sat all over each other on a long couch and each one
of them was staring at the iEverything in their hands, their faces lit
with a soft white glow. Some of them were texting with one thumb,
and she knew others were updating their Fuckbook pages.

   Rockin' at Luke's. Cum ovah!

   Luke's sucks. Where r u?

   Then Luke had her by the hand and was leading her out through
the sweaty noise past the sliding doors he left open to the yard and
the dead leaves under her feet, the covered pool.

   "I'm drunk, Dev. I'm fuckin' toasted."

   She was talking too but does not remember what she said. She
can still feel, though, the way her face had felt like cooled wax and
she'd probably been smiling at him too hard. He was looking at her
differently now. She was wearing tight jeans and a low-cut sweater
she regretted because she was too warm in it, her hair down when she
wanted it up, and he was taking all this in like he'd just discovered
how to solve a math problem he'd been putting off. Then she was
letting him take her hand and lead her down to the boathouse, and
they'd been sitting in his boat kissing for a while when he took her
fingers and pulled them onto his hard-on still under his pants. It was
the second one she'd ever touched. The first was her cousin Steve's
when she was ten and he was twelve, and he'd stood in her room and
unzipped his shorts and shown it to her like it was a small animal
he'd found outside.

   "Just touch it, Devon. Big deal. Then, you know, you'll know."

   Know what? she'd wanted to ask, but Steve had always been big
and a little scary and all she had to do was put one finger on it to
make him go away, and she was surprised how warm it was, almost
hot. "See?" he'd said. "Now lick it." And Devon had run past him,
jerking open the door to her own room and slamming it behind her.

   But now she was fourteen and Luke wasn't Steve, his tongue sliding around inside her mouth. He tasted like beer and wintergreen gum, and he'd moved his hand to her cheek and Devon liked how gentle it felt against her skin and she concentrated on that instead of her hand over his hard-on, and Trina was always teasing Devon for being a mouth virgin. Everybody gave BJs. You couldn't get pregnant, and it satisfied boys for a while so you didn't have to do anything else, and it made them want to be only with you. Trina said you got more respect if you swallowed. Like running an extra lap after working your ass off just to show you could. Then Luke's zipper was open, and his hard-on was in her hand, and it was stiff and warm and she was surprised by how soft the skin was.

THE FRENCH DOOR OPENS. Francis walks in carrying white flowers. She presses both hands over her notebook, over *Luke's boat*, but he doesn't even look down at the two words she's written. He just closes the door and walks past her at the table like she's not there. She watches him take a glass vase from a cabinet and place it in the kitchen sink and fill it with water.

"I can't write with you standing there."

"People will be in that testing room with you, Devy." He winks at her and pushes the white flowers stem-first into the vase. His glasses hang on a string against his chest, and she can see a sweat stain under the arm of his yellow shirt, and he's every adult who ever stood in her way starting with her father and in this moment she hates him.

Except she doesn't. Her cheeks grow hot, and she feels ashamed. She needs music in her head. Something that will block out the bad or else lead her right to it.

Uncle Francis sets the vase of white flowers in the middle of the table, and she can smell them and his old man smell that makes her sad. As soon as he's gone she writes under *Luke's boat*—

Uncle Francis dying

But that hasn't happened yet, and it better not happen anytime soon. There was Aunt Beth lying in her coffin in that periwinkle dress that was all wrong for her. There were the framed photographs set on small tables around the funeral home, pictures of Aunt Beth and Francis when they were young, and Devon was surprised how pretty she'd been, sexy even, her hair thick and blond, her lips fuller, and there was the way she leaned her cheek into Uncle Francis's shoulder.

Devon writes: *Aunt Beth dying.* Then she crosses it out and writes: *Getting old.* But that hasn't happened yet either, though she feels as if it has; she *has* gotten old. Years and years before she was supposed to. Just tired of it all. Just wanting to be left alone now. Except there's Sick, too. The way he never quite leaves her. She writes:

Sick finding out.

And she remembers his face on the other side of the small window to the right of her front door. The week before, he'd dyed his hair red but in the sunlight it looked purple, his long bangs hanging over half his face like they always did. She could only see his left eye, but it looked bloodshot and puffy, and his narrow shoulders were slumped in his Kurt Cobain T-shirt, no coat though it was cold out, and it was seeing Cobain's face on Sick's chest that made her open the door, that gun Cobain forever sang he never had when he did all along and now he's not on earth anymore.

"How's it coming?" Francis's voice shoots from the doorway between the kitchen and living room. She does not turn her head to look at him.

"I can't fucking do this."

"Yes you can, Devy."

"Do I have to write something bad?"

"I guess not. Write whatever you want, but write something. You have thirty-one more minutes."

She hears the creak of the floorboards under the rug in the living room, the flap of a newspaper page. But what is she going to write about now? Something *good*? What the fuck was good?

Her mom's cooking. Every time.

Sausage lasagna, manicotti, eggplant parmigiana, meatloaf with gravy. The mac and cheese she baked in the oven, then served in a steaming square alongside green peas and pearl onions in a wine butter sauce.

Devon writes:

When I was twelve years old, my mom taught me how to make eggplant parmigiana. She told me the secret was to first bake the breaded slices of eggplant and not to fry them because then it all comes out too oily and the eggplant tastes too much like eggplant which nobody really likes when you think about it.

Devon sips her iced tea. Her heel is tapping again under the table. She reads over what she's just written. She crosses out *when you think about it.* She remembers how sharp the knife was, her mother showing her how to grip the eggplant firmly so it wouldn't slip while you cut it into slices very thin. "An eighth of an inch." Devon did not know what an eighth of an inch looked like, and she was wondering how her mother knew and that's when her father had breezed into the kitchen. It must've been summer because there was the clacking of his golf shoe cleats over the tiles. His hair was combed back, and he must have been leaving and not coming home because his eyes were still clear and when he smiled at them both, he really seemed happy to see them, even his wife. "Ooh, look at this. My favorite girls cooking my favorite dish." He walked around the island and kissed Devon's mother on the cheek and Devon on her forehead, then he was gone and not long after Devon sliced her finger cutting the third eggplant, this one slippery because she hadn't dried it after washing it, even though her mother warned her about that. Her blood looked so bright and wrong on the cutting board, and her mother grabbed it to rinse it off and told her there were Band-Aids in their bedroom's bathroom cabinet, and now Devon writes:

Wrapping my finger in a bandaid while staring at the stack of Penthouse magazines on the back of my father's toilet.

There were so many of them—twenty, twenty-five—and she must've seen them before and known about them, but she had her own bathroom off her own bedroom so why would she?

Devon writes:

Sitting on the closed toilet and ignoring my throbbing finger I wrapped too tightly with a bandaid

Opening my dad's dirty magazine and seeing a hard penis pointing at the hole of a vagina

Feeling sick because the only vagina I'd seen that up close was my own two months before this when I had to use a mirror for my first tampon.

She'd done it herself without asking her mother for any help. She'd felt grown-up and a little scared but strong and ready for whatever would come next. But this magazine of her father's made her feel young and stupid, ugly even, and Devon closed it and put it back on the stack. And was it later in the kitchen, dipping the eggplant slices into the milk and raw egg, then the bread crumbs, that she began to wonder about her mother? Her heavy, beautiful mother who smiled at everyone and treated them as if they were special and deserved kindness just because they were alive? Was it then, the first time Devon had helped her to bake eggplant parmigiana, that she began to feel sorry for her own mother?

"Sixteen minutes, Devy," Uncle Francis calls this out from the living room. Devon stares down at the notebook. She reads what she's written, ending with *my first tampon*. She crosses out the small *t* and makes it a big one. Then she crosses out the whole paragraph because this is bullshit. All of it. The reason why she hates school in the first place. Everything so fucking fake. She can't write about her vagina or her father's magazines. They want her to write about making eggplant parmigiana with her mother so it shows how close they are; they want Devon to write that this is a precious memory for her, one that has helped her to become "the confident person I am today," and she needs to do all this in five paragraphs, her conclusion a neat echo of her introduction, which she does not have. They want her to type it up with no misspellings, all the rules obeyed, every mark of punctuation right where it should be, then they want her to solve math problems and science problems; they want her to memorize important dates from history and be able to point to any country and its capital on a map, all of this and more so that she can *what?* Pretend she walked up onstage in a borrowed gown with a bunch of fucking drunks and hypocrites like Trina? Get a framed piece of paper with her name on it so she can look forward to another four years of sitting in more classrooms on some campus somewhere, memorizing and writing and reading just so she can get another piece of paper with her name on it? And then what? Get some job sitting at a desk in some office in some building in some city where they'll pay her money just so she can use it to have a house of her own on a quiet street like Haven Court with a green lawn her husband will cut on the weekends when he's not sitting in the pool drinking a vodka tonic, thumbing through his iEverything for a half-naked picture of his girlfriend?

Devon writes:

I found out about my father's girlfriend because I used his phone.

She stares at what she's written. She stares out the glass doors to the yard outside, but she doesn't see anything. She hates the quiet. She doesn't know how Francis can live with it. Once he played a classical album on his old record player, but he never turns on the radio or watches TV, and he only seems to use Aunt Beth's computer in the dining room to play solitaire. She'd walked by and seen him doing it, the cards on the screen sitting there in bright, neat stacks.

She no longer wants a cigarette, and she's had it with this. She rips her page from the notebook and balls it up and stands and shoves it into the front pocket of her shorts.

"You all through?" Francis's voice drifts from the living room. She pictures him sitting in his chair, his thick glasses on his nose, the paper fanned out in his lap.

"I can't do it."

"I can't hear you, Devy."

"I can't—" She turns toward the kitchen and the dim doorway of the room where he sits, but she can't walk there. She won't go in there and tell him she's failed him, too. She cups her hand to her mouth. "I have to get ready for work!" And she's down the cool hallway and into her room, locking the door behind her. She digs the balled-up paper from her pocket as if it's a bruising stone, and she stuffs it into the trash basket, burying it beneath wadded tissues she's blown her nose on, stiff and dry under her fingers.

IT'S HIS FAULT, of course. He should have run her through a few sentence diagrams, that's all. Perhaps talked about the lyrical beauty of the rules of punctuation, how just because they were rules did not have to make them constraining. *You can never leave well enough alone.* One of Beth's constant rebukes of him. After a family dinner or an outing with friends, Beth driving during his drinking years, she'd glance over at him and hiss those words. She'd tell him he was too nosy about other people's opinions, that once they'd offered one, he was too pushy about wanting to know why they thought that way. John Brooks, long dead now, that night ending the way so many other nights had ended. Brooks was a corpulent accountant married to Annie Brooks, an RN Beth had befriended years earlier working the beds of St. Mary's. At the restaurant Brooks had gone on and on about welfare cheats, an entire generation of lazy bastards our tax codes make us pay for. "But finally we've got a president doing something about it." Francis sat quietly and buttered his bread. He sipped his gin martini. He lifted three speared olives to his mouth and tried to ignore that Brooks was wearing a navy sports jacket with an anchor insignia on the breast pocket simply because he co-owned a pleasure boat. He tried to ignore that Brooks had gone to Exeter and was most likely pledging a fraternity at Babson the same winter Francis was curled up in a wind-whipped tent just south of Kaesong, the ground under him so frozen it felt like buckled concrete, the howling 155's overhead like some deafening blunder from God himself.

"As far as I'm concerned, they should just take a backhoe to all those neighborhoods."

"With all those freeloaders still inside them, John?"

"You bet."

Beth's thumb had pressed into Francis's thigh, but he ignored it. "Quote me some numbers, John. Lay out for me precisely how many of these poor people are actually *faking* their poverty."

"Most of them, Francis. Look it up."

Annie, her face small and nearly pretty, laughed as if her husband had just told an awkward joke. But Brooks' face was flushed, the skin around his eyes drawn tight, and Beth's thumb was pushing harder into Francis's thigh. There was the pleasant rush of blood to his head. "Let's talk about the rich, John, shall we? Do you know hHow much Exxon paid in taxes last year? Can you tell me? Because I can tell *you*: Zero. Zilch. Not a fucking penny. Now you tell me who's cheating whom."

"No politics, boys. Please," Beth said. "Annie, tell us about the kids."

"What're you saying, Brandt? Cream can no longer rise to the top in this country? Is that what I'm hearing, comrade?"

"Kiss my ass, Brooks. I was fighting communists while you were swilling beer at frat parties."

"All right, that's *enough*. Any more from you two and Ann and I are leaving." Beth's tone was of uncompromising finality, the same one she might use on a man smoking at a patient's bedside, and Francis had stood and dropped his napkin beside his uneaten salad and walked into the men's room and splashed his face with cold water.

Brooks *was* wrong, and he *was* a greedy and ignorant asshole, but this was also a night out with friends, and Francis knew he had to go back to the table and apologize and leave it at that. Which he did. And while John, Annie, and his wife went gamely on about one thing or another, the air thick with a polite stoicism, Francis had gotten quietly drunk.

On the dark ride home there was Beth's prating voice, the headlights of their car lighting up the night ahead of them. Francis had to shut one eye to keep it all from crowding together in his head: tree branches and leaves, the red taillights of other cars, shadowed houses and aluminum mailboxes and a bright gas station Beth had pulled into, slamming the door behind her to pump the gas he was in no shape to. Those were his words, too.

"I'minoshape, Beth."

The following morning he'd woken in sheets damp with sweat. His mouth was a desert sin. It was not a word he used or even thought of very often, but those mornings after drinking far too much yet again, he felt riddled with sin: weak, undisciplined, vaguely malicious, and therefore poisonous to all that is good and constructive.

If Beth was somewhere in the house, he'd make sure he was showered and shaved before she saw him. In the bathroom he'd pull down each eyelid and apply a dropper of Visine. He'd splash cologne on his cheeks and comb his hair back and tuck in his shirt. But his tongue would feel thick and useless, and there'd be the pulsing ache of his head because he'd so dehydrated himself with alcohol there was no longer enough fluid in his skull to float his brain. When he looked in the mirror he saw not Mr. B, the educator, but Francis, the degenerate, Francis, the afflicted.

If Beth had gone to church or was out running errands, it was always a relief. Francis would swallow a handful of aspirin and wash it down with two glasses of cold water. The thought of food left his stomach floating uncomfortably inside him, but it didn't compare to remorse's heavy hands pressing down on his shoulders, and he'd lift the kitchen phone from its cradle while he still had the nerve and Francis would call whomever he had to apologize to that day.

John Brooks was cleaning his boat. At least that's what his wife had told Francis on the phone.

"Annie, I was a drunken fool last night. Can you forgive me?"

"You weren't the only one, Francis. Next time, Beth and I will just do lunch together." She'd laughed, but her words had lingered long after Francis hung up, and he could add them now to all the dozens and dozens of comments like that he'd heard from friends and family over the years. It was like having to carry a huge basket of roiling snakes on his back he somehow ignored every time he sat at a bar or restaurant table and ordered a drink or a beer which always led to more beers which led to more drinks which led to yet more mornings like these.

But the one after the Brookses, Beth had not driven off somewhere; she'd been sitting in the living room reading a book, and when Francis hung up the phone, she said:

"Aren't you tired of making those kinds of calls, Francis?"

"Yes."

"Then maybe you shouldn't drink so much."

"Maybe I shouldn't drink at all."

She'd closed her book and was soon standing barefoot in the doorway. She was wearing a skirt and light blouse. Her hair was just beginning to gray, but it was still long enough she used a barrette to pin it away from her face. She was holding her glasses between two fingers at her side. "Your brother quit. Maybe you should, too."

"I think you're right." Just saying the words did something. It was like being locked in a dark trunk, then the lid slowly opening, the shock of sunlight, cool clean air seeping into his lungs. Beth stepped toward him and hugged him. The smell of her hair and the threshold they both stood on did something more to him and soon they were making love on the sofa and when Francis let go inside her he felt as if his seed was foul and dirty and not worthy of her but that he'd also been given a second chance to cleanse everything about himself and he would. They'd held one another without speaking. Beth's skirt was still up around her hips, and Francis had sensed a return to how it was for them when it began twenty years earlier, that they liked and respected one another, that they had each other's welfare in mind at all times, that they fit together as well as two people possibly could. He would be a new Francis—cleaner, healthier, clear of mind and heart, which would make her a new Beth, though it did not; she was always saying something: Don't slouch. You're tall, don't be ashamed of it. Don't put your dirty clothes in my hamper, you have one of your own, you know. Don't eat so fast, enjoy your damn food, Francis. Don't look around so much when you're driving, for Christ's sake. You never let the engine warm up enough first. I wish you wouldn't leave the trash cans in front of my gardening tools. Can't you put them somewhere else? Your brother's a big blowhard, Francis. All he ever does is talk about himself. And his son Charlie's a little shit. It makes me glad we never had children.

Though the lines of her face lost some of their sharpness when she said that, because for years she had wanted children fiercely and they'd tried everything to get them, including driving to Toronto for experimental surgery on her ovaries. But in the end, her body wanted nothing to do with making a baby, and even though they'd had Francis's sperm checked twice, she seemed to blame him for her barrenness without ever using those words or talking about the subject directly. Then she turned on him in a hundred small ways, each of them minor and not unusual when one human being lived with another, but this was like saying that a typhoon was nothing more than single drops of rain pushed by a little wind.

Francis began to tell himself it was his wife who was making him drink so much. He'd have finished his preparation for the next day's classes and, as a reward, he'd pour himself a bourbon on the rocks with maybe a beer chaser. He'd sip them in his chair in front of the TV, Beth on the couch with one of her paperbacks. But just about every time he sipped and the ice clinked in his glass, he could see her stiffen up and he knew she'd be saying something to him soon, and so he began to do it on the sly. He bought a case of Cokes and poured out half of each can, filling the rest with rye or rum, and he set the can of Coke on the lamp table where Beth could see it.

"Caffeine this late? What're you thinking, Francis?"

But this lasted only a week or two for he must've been slurring his words one night when she picked up the can and smelled it and whisked it out of the room and poured it down the kitchen sink. Then she was standing in the doorway, saying, "Don't you ever pull that kind of shit on me again, Francis. You need help."

Sitting there, drunk yet again in his chair in front of the blabbering television, he knew she was right, that he probably *did* need help, but wasn't it funny that for years nothing changed after that moment? Wasn't it strange that neither of them did anything to get him some help?

To avoid her judgment, each and every day on his slow, careful drive home from the high school, he sipped vodka in a Dunkin' Donuts Styrofoam cup. Three blocks from his house, he'd pull into the 7-Eleven lot and drop his cup and nips into the trash barrel beside the door. He'd walk in and buy breath mints and a bottle of water, and he'd be sipping it when he walked into his house carrying his briefcase, his tie loosened around his neck. Just another day, darling. Just another day working so hard on behalf of so many children.

For years, he and Beth were in the habit of eating their dinner in front of the nightly news, which made things easier. Not having to talk. Not having to look directly at his wife while she said to him whatever she had to say, which most often was a barrage of complaints about the administration at St. Mary's, the absent doctors, the badly trained and lazy LPNs, the pushy families of her patients. She'd talk and sometimes he'd doze off, waking an hour or so later to an empty couch, her paperback open and facedown like a dead bird she'd left behind just for him.

Then for years Beth worked the night shift, and Francis could drink as much as he wanted right there in his own living room. Before bed, he would make his way out to the driveway and fumble with the key to open the trunk of his car. He'd lay the empty bottle or bottles or cans inside there, then get rid of them the next day or the day after that. He'd fall onto his mattress and wake hours later to his scolding alarm clock, his pulsing head, his wife's warm sleeping body curled up away from him.

But after that final call to Annie Brooks, all that madness could be behind him. George had urged him to go to meetings with him, to read the Big Book and to begin the hard spiritual work of the twelve steps, but Francis couldn't do it. Ever since Captain Hunt and the Ditch of the Bodos, a phrase that still shoots through his head as suddenly as pebbles from under a spinning tire, *Ditch of the Bodos*, a phrase he consistently wills to be nothing more than that, no images to follow, though he'll begin to see that stand of pines on the ridge, the flat light of the July sun—ever since that unspeakable afternoon when he'd done nothing but obey the rules and regulations imposed upon him, he would have nothing to do with rules of any kind or the entities that created them. He would not be a member of this cult of steps and meetings his brother George was a member of; Francis would do it on his own, though he did borrow one of their slogans he found helpful: *One Day at a Time*. "Today is Monday. I will not drink on Monday, but on Tuesday I'm going to get stinko." But on Tuesday he'd tell himself he would not drink until Wednesday when he would tell himself just what he did about Monday and Tuesday. And it worked. For three months. But on the half day before Thanksgiving, his fifty-third birthday, Rita Flaherty smuggled a bottle of champagne into the teachers' lounge, and she poured six or seven of them a Dixie cupful and why not? It was his birthday, for Christ's sake. It was Thanksgiving. And it had tasted awfully good going down. It was not unlike Beth, in those last three clearheaded months, offering him her body more willingly and more frequently, her womanly scent rising up to him like a slowly unwrapped gift he'd always deserved but had somehow been denied him.

On the drive home, he stopped at the liquor store in Lafayette Square and bought a six-pack of Miller bottles and a fifth of rye. It was Thanksgiving Eve, his birthday a lifelong prelude to a day bigger and more important, and he'd had to wait in line behind a man who wore painter's coveralls and a wool cap, the cashier glancing at Francis with eyes so neutral and empty of judgment that Francis felt he was easily getting away with something that maybe he never should have been deprived of in the first place.

A dank resentment settled over him. Walking with his beer and whiskey out of the package store into the cold, exhaust-smelling air, he was a man who'd been wronged, a man who had earned in every way his right to just this one, small reward.

These last three months, as if to accentuate the clarity of body and mind he woke to each morning, he'd gotten into the habit of sipping coffee on the eleven-mile ride to the high school. Beth had bought him an insulated thermos, and now Francis sat in his car behind the package store and poured the rest of his morning's coffee out onto the cracked asphalt. His fingers were trembling as he poured rye into his thermos and twisted open a Miller and poured it in too. Then he took a long pull from his thermos—cold hoppy carbonation shot through with a leveling fire—and soon he was parked at the seawall down the boulevard from The Whaler. The other parking spots were empty for it was the off-season and from where he sat he could see just a lip of ocean on the other side of the seawall, but the song on the radio was an old one from an AM station in a holiday mood. He did not know what it was, but it was Big Band and had horns in it and the tempo was upbeat and he was fourteen or fifteen years old and his brother George was dancing with their mother in the small kitchen on Ginty Street. He was wearing his uniform, his collar open, and he was twirling their mother who was laughing, her hair coming loose, her eyes soft with something that never rose there. Then the music became a man talking about used cars and Francis was wiping his eyes so he could fill his thermos back up again and he was walking along the hard sand of low tide till he found a kelp-wrapped plank, its grain open cracks of rot he had to look away from for they were death itself and how long had he been weeping like a boy?

There was a woman before Beth. They'd both had too much to drink, and he'd driven her to her small apartment off Route 1 in Saugus. It was a trailer home really. She lived there with her brother, a merchant marine at sea, the shelf above his sofa weighted with shot glasses from all the bars he'd been in from New York to Naples, Italy, and back. Her name was Patrizia, but everyone called her Triz. Francis had been stateside for only a few weeks. Classes at Suffolk didn't start for another month, and George had insisted that he stay in the guest room of his house. Francis was twenty-one years old, a war veteran, and he couldn't just sit around George's while his wife tended to little Charlie and the new baby. Francis didn't like how George's wife kept looking at him either. It was as if she were trying to measure whether the things he'd seen and done over there had made him somehow dangerous to her kids.

Every night George wanted to drink. He wanted to drink and "only talk about it if you fucking feel like it, Franny," and George would talk about his own war as if he were the only soldier in it. They sat in lawn chairs in the small yard of the house George would later sell at a profit, and as the night grew cool and the mosquitoes became a problem, George came back to Francis about working with him selling insurance. But the idea was cold to Francis, all of it, from having to take orders from George to having to sell policies to people who did not want or need them. It seemed like a racket to Francis, and that's the word he used in the bar in Boston on a Saturday in August talking to an Italian woman everyone called Triz.

She was plump and large-breasted. She wore red lipstick and smoked Pall Malls, and he kept buying her Brandy Alexanders and talked about whatever came up though he seemed to listen to her more, even though all these years later, half-drunk on the beach on his fifty-third birthday, he could not summon one thing she'd told him except, "Your eyes are so sweet." Then, later, "Enough. You're coming with me." In the orange light of a Tiki lamp, they were on her and her brother's couch, Francis's erection in her gripping hands as she pulled him to that warm darkness between her legs, and how could he tell her he'd never done this before?

There were whores in Japan. They lived with their families in alley boxes that smelled like dead fish, and they'd looked like school-girls to him, those black bangs, those cheeks they'd covered with so much rouge they became laughing clowns leading his buddies one at a time to where Triz was leading him now. How *warm* it was. How tight and slippery, a tremor of pleasure as she arched her hips and pulled him in deeper. It had seemed to him she was offering him something so personal and private he must have lied to her in some way to get it. She was looking straight into his face, and he could not bear her eyes for she seemed to be searching for something he knew she would not find and then maybe she'd stop and he lowered his cheek against hers. Her skin had the sweet talcum scent of makeup, her hair stiff with spray. She was making sounds he'd never heard a woman make before—moans of encouragement, but also melan-cholic surrender, not to him but to something inevitable and ageless, as if she were foreseeing their own distant deaths but until then they had this; they had this.

Then it was winter two years later, and Francis was making love with Elizabeth Harrington one month shy of their wedding date. It was her first time, his second. There was no Tiki lamp, no trailer couch or shot glasses above. There was no red lipstick, no sounds coming from Beth, and because it *was* her first time he moved as slowly and as gently as he could, her silence, he assumed, a biting down on her pain and discomfort. They were under a blanket on her bed in the cold-water apartment she shared with another nursing student, a fast-talking girl from the south shore. Outside the window in the slanting afternoon light stood the elevated tracks of the subway train, and Beth held his face in her hands and made him look at her. Her eyes did something to him. There was so much hard will in them—Yes, Francis, I've chosen *you*, I've chosen *you*, I've chosen *you*. Her lips were parted, her chin raised almost in defiance at each of his thrusts, and it was this and the way she held his face and the iron clatter of a train passing full of men and women and children that set everything loose and that good woman Triz had made him withdraw but even his wet shame on her soft pale belly she seemed to think was sweet, and in the Tiki lamp light she smiled up at him as if he'd just brought her flowers, and Francis had closed his eyes against that smile as what was inside him was now pulsing into Elizabeth Harrington, this woman he too had chosen, this woman he had chosen for life.

For *life*, goddamnit. He was walking close to the water. When he leaned down to pick up a smooth stone the sand rose up and smacked his forehead and knees. Where before there'd been resentment, there was now only outrage at the unfairness of how he'd been treated. Though he could not quite pinpoint what had been done to him or by whom, only the empty-chested feeling that he'd been sent something beautiful by someone beautiful and someone else had not done his job and delivered the damn package. Then he was back in his car driving again. He was drunk and knew it, but it wasn't far to his street and what was he doing going home like this?

Fuck it, Brandt.

Triz, her black hair and red lipstick, her brown eyes and that smile as she held him and pulled him to her. So long ago, but was it a door he should have kept open? A door that would have pointed to a road taking him someplace softer? A road that would have led to children? That would have led him to no shame in anything about himself—his eyes "sweet," his seed "sweet"—no shame, no shame, no shame. A nodding off, his eyes opening to see how the sun struck the side of a house, its white trim nearly gold, then the horrible bouncing over curb and lawn and the looming house jolting him into darkness.

FRANCIS STANDS IN Devon's room. He's surprised at how neatly she keeps it. The bed is made, the bedspread tucked cleanly under the pillows at the headboard. The closet door is closed, and the T-shirt and shorts she put on after her shower lie at the foot of the mattress, one folded on top of the other. Her laptop leans against the bedside table in its unzipped case, and there's a tiny wink of blue light there.

He was in the dining room when she left for work. He had wanted to check for any emails, to open the most recent one from Devon's mother, but he was afraid Devon might walk in, and the last thing she needed now was to feel conspired against. It was already a mistake to encourage her to write so personally. She left with a loud "Bye" at the door so he at first thought she was angry till he reached the front windows and saw her walking under the late-day sun in her black-and-white restaurant uniform, those big red headphones over her ears, so perhaps she had the volume turned up and that's why her own was too.

He would not be in here if she had not ripped a sheet from the notebook he held. On the desk is nothing but a layer of dust and the brass lamp Beth bought in a barn in Vermont. Or maybe it was that flea market in Boston. Or one of the mall stores she went to more often in her last years. He walks over to the wastebasket. There, under three or four used tissues, is a wadded piece of notebook paper. He reaches in for it, half squatting to spare his back, both knees aching in response. Against the white tissues the liver spots on the back of his hand stand out, and this makes him feel old and unseemly as he straightens and carefully opens what his grand-niece has so tightly compressed. He lays the page on the desk and smooths it out. His glasses dangle from around his neck, and he lifts them into place and reads:

Luke's boat
Uncle Francis dying

He lowers the page. He looks at her bed and her folded shorts and T-shirt. He continues to read.

Aunt Beth dying Why did Devy cross that out? Because she did not want to write about it? Or because her chilly great-aunt dying was not such a bad thing to her?

Getting old

Sick finding out Illness with a mind of its own? No, there was that name in one of Marie's emails. Sick. Yes, Devon's ex-boyfriend, Sick. Why a name like that?

When I was twelve years old, my mom taught me how to make eggplant parmigiana. She told me the secret was to first bake the breaded slices of eggplant and not to fry them because then it all comes out too oily and the eggplant tastes too much like eggplant which nobody really likes when you think about it.

Wrapping my finger in a bandaid while staring at the stack of Penthouse magazines on the back of my father's toilet. Charlie. With a daughter in your house, for Christ's sake.

The next paragraph is crossed out but easy to read.

*Sitting on the closed toilet and ignoring my throbbing finger I wrapped too
tightly with a bandaid*

*Opening my dad's dirty magazine and seeing a hard penis pointing at the
hole of a vagina*

Francis glances over at the open doorway, his cheeks heating with
the knowledge he has now transgressed. But there are only a few more
lines and despite beginning to feel like some ancient creep, he is also
becoming more informed about the home Devon fled. He notices his
fingers are shaking slightly, and he shrugs it off.

*Feeling sick because the only vagina I'd seen that up close was my own two
months before this when I had to use a mirror for my first tampon.*

I found out about my father's girlfriend because I used his phone.

Francis balls up the notebook sheet as tightly as he can. He pushes
it back down into the wastebasket and covers it up with the tissues.
He's staring at the tiny blue light just beneath the zipper of her
computer case, and he knows she spends her nights in front of that
machine. He's tempted to open it and turn it on, but no, he won't do
that. He won't.

Feeling like a thief, he walks across the carpet of his grand-niece's
room and pulls the door closed behind him. It's been nearly five
months and no word of any kind from his nephew Charlie Brandt.
Of course he would have a mistress, wouldn't he? Of course he would.
Francis sent him several emails to update him on Devy's GED plans,
her solid work ethic, but there's been no response of any kind, only
those from Marie asking Francis to tell Devon to text her or email
her more often, to pass on her love. Such strange times we live in,
entire families separated into their own private cybercells, the same
warm blood pumping through their organs and limbs.

On the kitchen table are the vase of white phlox, Devon's barely
touched glass of iced tea, beside it her pen and pencil.

Luke's boat.

Clearly an honest start. Why didn't she continue? Because it's none of your damn business, Francis, that's why. Still, he wants to know more about her and he wants to know nothing, for what can he truly do? He carries her glass to the sink and dumps it. He sees her holding a mirror between her legs, this poor girl left to her own devices, and Francis plucks the wall phone from its cradle and pushes the buttons that will ring his dead brother's useless son, though it's happy hour on a Friday in August and unlike his father and uncle and perhaps their father before them, that hopper of trains to nowhere, Charlie still swallows down the family's poison and whoever gets hurt gets hurt, including his one and only daughter who jumped overboard and swam to this half-empty old boat she somehow assumed is stable. Should Francis tell her the truth? That until she came, the captain, so free now, so permanently free, had begun to feel it listing and taking on cold water? Should he tell her that he dreads the day she'll leave?

2morrow then? Breakfast?

OK

9?

Noon

NOON?

I'm working. Bye.

Luv U!

The break room is a wall of lockers behind the dishwashing machine, and Devon stands under the fluorescent light with her glass of Diet Coke scrolling through her iEverything the way she used to draw in on a cigarette. She wants one. She's pissed she wants one because she hasn't for a while, but that essay stirred things up and she's been working hard all night to push it back down again. She needs music for that. Mean music. Her Dr. Dre's are on the shelf of her open locker, but she only has three more minutes. She can smell cigarette smoke the way someone on a diet smells melting chocolate. Behind her, the door to the loading dock is propped open and a new dishwasher she doesn't know leans in the doorway, his back to her, smoking. He's older, a bald spot on top of his head, and she almost feels sad for him that he's still doing shit work like this. She's close to asking him for a butt.

Sick: Wuz up D?

She flicks her finger over the screen and scrolls back to the first words she got from him after Trina posted everything.

Sick: Y Devon? Y???

Then he was on her doorstep on a cold morning in his Cobain T-shirt. When she opened the door he stepped back and made a funny sound in his chest, like the last thing he expected was for that door to ever open. He stood there staring at her. His hair hung down over half his face and she wanted to be closer so she could push it back behind his ear.

She didn't know what to say. Her throat felt hot. "Hi."

"Don't say that."

"Fine." She crossed her arms. There were goose bumps there, though she wasn't cold.

He held out to her their butterfly cup. That's what they called it. When they were together they drank vodka and cranberry juice in it, or hot chocolate, or just water. He'd won it for her last summer at the beach, working the mechanical arm in the big glass box and picking it out of a pile of stuffed animals. But it was in a cardboard box, one of the game's "mystery" prizes, and only when she opened it, standing in the sun outside the loud arcade, did she see the butterfly etched into the cup. It was blue and green and its wings were spread in flight as if it was going to take her with it, wherever it was going. Then she was kissing him, and Sick's kiss back was soft and kind, like he wasn't trying to get anything from her. Like this kiss she just gave him was enough.

"Why, D?" He stepped toward her in the doorway and pushed the cup into her hand. He swung his hair away from his face and stared at her. Both eyes were puffy and they didn't look so beautiful anymore, but they were the same cracked blue she'd stared into as she let him be the first, the second, the third, only him. No one else. But how could she tell him she didn't cheat? How could she tell him that what she'd done had meant nothing to her? She was crying, and Sick was walking away. She may have called his name, but she can't remember. There was screaming in her head. *Sick! Sick!* And it was like stepping on a baby bird. It was like plucking a flower and tossing it into a fire. It was like shitting on the pillow of a bed someone had made just for you.

Then she was in a tattoo parlor on a road of auto body shops and gun stores and a thin man with no more empty skin of his own, shirt-less in a black leather vest, was holding her bare right foot in his hand. He'd offered her some Tylenol, but she wanted to feel it. She leaned back on one arm and held the butterfly cup for him to keep glancing up at, and there was the buzzing of the tool, the pricking of her skin against her bone. Her eyes filled and she said to the man, "Put red in there too. I want red."

Sick. Whose parents treated him like he was a nothing and would always be a nothing. Sick. Who brought her small gifts every time he saw her. A pebble. An old nickel. Once a silk scarf he pulled from a trash bag out of the Salvation Army box. Sick. Who made sad, sweet sounds during and after. The way he held her and stroked her hair as lightly and gently as if she too had wings and might one day fly away.

"Break's over, honey. Let's *move*." Danny Sullivan claps his hands twice.

"I know." Devon pushes her iEverything back into her locker and padlocks it. She takes her Diet Coke and walks past him and his smell of cigar smoke and old coffee and she's relieved to hear him yelling at the new dishwasher behind her because that means he's not staring at her ass as she pushes open the swinging doors into the loud, reckless din of people eating too much and drinking too much after lying too long in the sun with too many other people and now they're spending too much money. Devon drains her Diet Coke. She sets her glass onto a tray, then carries it out into this room full of reckless noise she wants only to block out with more noise, the kind she can control with just the flick of her thumb.

IT'S QUIET NOW. The air is cool, and she can smell the dark ocean. She's standing near the front door of The Whaler waiting for Francis to pick her up because he never lets her walk home this late. She pulls out her iEverything. She keeps rereading Sick's message from yesterday: *Wuz up D?* Normally her thumbs would start answering texts before she even started thinking about them. But this was the Sick before he became *her* Sick. This was the quiet boy with dyed hair and skinny jeans who only came alive on his iEverything. Onscreen he was funnier and more relaxed. He knew what to say and when to say it. Then he started sending her links to things he thought she'd like—that funny YouTube of the baby smiling after it burped, an interview with Kurt Cobain when he still loved life or at least tolerated it, color pictures of deep space from the Hubble telescope that scared her because it was all just too big and endless and how could there ever be a God for it?

Sick: Do you need a God?

D: I guess.

Sick: Why?

D: Don't you?

Sick: No.

D: Why not?

Sick: God's just a big babysitter. Don't you want to be FREE?

D: Yes.

Sick: Me too.

Wuz up D? This is his old self from his pre-D life. It's the tone of the boy who doesn't hurt anymore, and so maybe he's just curious about her: Where's she been for five months? What's she been doing? Though she's only ten miles away and everybody knows the answers to those questions. Since April, when Danny Sullivan hired her, Devon's seen people in the Whaler she knows: the Welches (and twice Mark drunk at the bar by himself). She's seen the Battastinis stuffing their faces in the corner booth. In June or July, Luke McDonough's parents, Nancy and Carl, came in. Nancy had smiled up at her and asked where she was going to school in the fall. Devon had always liked Nancy. She was small and pretty and good to people, but could she really not know one thing about her son's senior year and the people in it? Did she really not know all about Dirty Devon Brandt standing in front of her in her restaurant clothes holding an empty tray in her hands? Devon's face was smiling and talking. Words were coming out of her. Words like *travel* and *Gap Year* and *Europe*. A sentence fragment like *saving up for it*. And she kept glancing at Nancy's husband not because he was smiling generically up at her, but because he had Luke's eyes—or Luke had his—and now Devon could see a slight shift in Carl and Nancy's smiles: they were trying not to show how sorry they felt for her, this girl who so young had already given up on climbing to the top of some shining fucking mountain with swimming pools and boathouses and drunk boys killing men in *Call of Duty*. She wanted to tell them it was Luke who'd started everything. She wanted to tell them that their lacrosse-playing son heading to Dartmouth had practically *made* her suck on his penis. But that wasn't true. She'd wanted to. Or at least she'd wanted to get it over with so she wouldn't be a mouth virgin anymore.

Walking away from his parents' polite table, she could feel it again in her mouth. This warm, hard animal that seemed to have a heartbeat of its own, a life that wasn't just Luke's. He'd rested his hand on her back and then her hair. "Squeeze it." She didn't know if he meant with her lips or her fingers but she did both and then he was pushing himself in and out of her mouth, and she had to pull back so she wouldn't choke and the animal that belonged to Luke stiffened even more and spurted Luke's wet moans down her throat she swallowed so she wouldn't gag.

They sat in the boat for a few minutes. Luke kept stroking her hair. He zipped himself up and got out of the boat first and offered her his hand to help her out. On the walk back across the lawn he put his arm around her. He was different. He seemed so calm and peaceful, and it was as if Devon had opened a door inside herself that held a gift she hadn't known she had. Something that had the power to do what she'd just done to Luke McDonough, changed him from being restless and grasping and distracted to this quiet, satisfied boy with his arm around her, this boy who first thing he did when they walked back into the thumping, sweating party was get her a hard lemonade he opened and handed to her, nodding at her lips to drink, the taste in her mouth not terrible but not as good as this. She drank down half the bottle and smiled at him. It was like stepping into the first chapter of a book all about her, and she felt more important somehow. She wanted to know what would happen next.

NOW IT'S AFTER MIDNIGHT and she's sitting against the headboard, her laptop open on her bare legs, her Dr. Dre's on. Devon's heard this song but never really listened to it. Behind her eyes, the famous white rapper is shout-singing over a drum machine and a sad violin about the daughter he never sees but wishes he did. Devon can hear how much he means this. How he really does miss her.

I didn't raise a fucking **whore**! Her father's reddened cheeks and forehead, the Sunday morning light coming through the kitchen window onto the side of his face. It was early, and he hadn't shaved yet and there was a lock of hair sticking up behind his ear. She'd been up all night, and maybe he hadn't slept either, though he was in a V-neck T-shirt and boxer shorts, his legs pale because it was March, and it was funny how Devon seemed to hover slightly above herself and

to the right. Like he was yelling at Devon the body, not Devon the
girl. Then her mother was rushing in from the hallway. She wore
that terry cloth yellow robe, but it was open and Devon could see her
mother's white nightgown, her breasts and belly beneath that. Devon
thought: That's where I came from, that's where I started out.

That's enough, Charlie! Enough!

Then her father was whirling around to yell at her mother, to
blame *her*, and Devon was back in her body yelling at them both.

The young father in her head is too much. His whole life is his
daughter, even though he never sees her because he's too busy writing
songs for people like Devon. She flicks to something else and doesn't
care what it is.

She types in *Chatroul*, and the rest of the word comes up. Not yet,
though. For so long she's stayed away from everybody's Fuckbook
pages, but now she types in Facebook. She stares at the login screen
and tries to remember her username, her password. DDBrandt and
ButterFly. She types in her username but then stops. The last page
she was on was Trina's, but Trina had unfriended her so Devon had
scrolled down her news feed. Party talk. Beach talk. Mall talk. Devon
moved to Trina's wall. Nothing but chatter about Dirty D. About
Skanky Sick C. trying to kill himself.

Which he never did.

He probably has his own Fuckbook page now. Maybe he finally
started a band. Maybe he's got a lead singer and she's cute and skinny
like him. Devon doesn't want to know. That Irish band's in her head
now, the singer's voice high and angry, so tired of all the fighting, so
damn tired of it. She pulls the headphones from her ears and picks up
her iEverything and finds *Wuz up D?*

With one thumb she writes: *I'm not here anymore. Where r u?*

She sends it and tosses it down near the foot of the bed. She exits
the login screen, tapping the red x box much harder than she needs
to. Then she's in the roulette room running her fingers back through
her hair, though she never wears makeup for this. Before sitting on

the bed she put the blue stud back in her nose, and she started to fill every hole in both ears with all the silver she had, but that felt too much like putting on a show for whomever she might meet and she is not putting on a fucking show. Not for anyone. Whoever she meets does not know her. Whoever she meets does not know one little thing about Devon Denise Brandt.

She presses start and the wheel spins to a dark screen in Texas. Then it lights up and a boy is staring at her. His head is shaved, and he's not wearing a shirt, and she's about to next him because she thinks he's going to point his screen down at his hard dick, but he says, "Hey." Like he's known her a long time. Like he just got back into town from a trip far, far away.

She types: *Hey.*

IN THE DARKNESS Francis wakes into an old body, its diminishing state a continual surprise to him. The time glows in digital numbers on the bedside table, but even squinting at it he can no longer read it without his glasses. No matter. For years now his bladder and prostate have made him shuffle to the toilet for a long wait and then just a few drops, but he knows that if he does not follow their commands now there will be no sleep.

In the bathroom he has to steady himself with his hand on the wall. He holds himself over the toilet and closes his eyes and waits. Before shutting out the light hours ago, he'd been reading a book on the history of the duel. A duke in 1700s England had killed over twenty men in defense of his honor, a word we don't seem to use much anymore, and it seemed to Francis that this "gentleman" must surely have been looking for affronts to his honor whenever and wherever he could.

A trip with Beth to the Adirondacks. It was early fall and he must have been retired for he had no memory of gearing up for the school year. Instead, there was a lot of rain. Beth in her blue raincoat with the belt at the waist. The way she hurried past him over the puddles in the gravel lot and into the antique barn. It had smelled like dried flowers and damp sawdust and was filled with artifacts up to the trusses: coats and hats and cane chairs; ornate fire tools and books and framed lithographs of families long gone. There were nautical flags from around the world and old road signs and a glass case of tarnished jewelry the owner sat behind reading a children's book nearly one hundred years old. She was young, which surprised Francis, thirty-five or forty, and she wore glasses and a sweatshirt with a construction logo on the back.

Beth had gotten lost in a stall of glass figurines, and Francis found himself staring at an open walnut case of dueling pistols. They lay side by side in green velvet. When he lifted one out, he was surprised at how heavy it was. Then his wife was standing beside him. He could smell the wet vinyl of her raincoat.

"You'd defend my honor, wouldn't you, sweetheart?"

"To the death," he'd said, aiming the pistol at a photograph of Babe Ruth. Beth leaned her head on his shoulder, and he'd kissed her damp hair.

The tickle of release. A few drops. Then a few more. Not even enough to warrant a flush. Francis rinses his hands and splashes his face. So many moments with Beth like that one. It used to be a memory for both of them, but now it's only his. And when he goes, will it really be gone? Will they all be gone? Some private library burning to the ground? There is a crack of light beneath Devon's door.

It has to be after three in the morning. Maybe she fell asleep with the light on. At first he hears nothing, but then comes the tapping of computer keys followed by a voice, strangely tinny. "C'mon, we been doin' this a long time." A boy's. A young man's. Francis is about to open the door, but there's more tapping, Devy hunting and pecking out sentences, he's sure. This must be some kind of Skype. Beth used to do it with her sister in Virginia, his sister-in-law smiling at them both from her bedroom, chatting about her work saving street cats while her second husband—a quiet and aloof tax attorney—read a book in bed behind her.

It was probably a good thing, this technology, but it seemed to Francis like just one more stripping away of privacy. What was wrong with talking on the phone and *imagining* what your sister looked like and what room she was sitting or standing in? Why did we have to see how large her eyes looked behind her reading glasses? Why did we have to see the covered form of her husband reading in bed?

"C'mon, Sarah, I want to hear your voice."

Sarah. So whoever she's typing to is a stranger and she's lied to him.

Devon types again, and Francis turns away and walks on his toes back down the carpeted hall and into his room, his empty bed, the red glow of time too bright and insistent. After Devon had left for the restaurant, he'd reread Marie's emails to him from last spring. But they were filled with the language of self-help books: *Devon's been "acting out"; Devon's in a "shame spiral"; Devon's been "isolating" herself; what she needs is to feel "validated."* Like a parking ticket. The language of today becoming increasingly mechanical and cold, the machines taking over one word at a time.

Francis lies back in bed. He pulls the sheet up over his chest, but there's the nagging pull he's left a duty unfulfilled. *I want to hear you.* This boy with a southern accent. What else does he want? There's something basely sexual about the whole thing. Devy onscreen for a man she does not know posing as a Sarah. Shouldn't her uncle do something?

He closes his eyes and waits for sleep. He can feel the empty expanse of bed beside him like a silent reproach from his wife. Like he can do better and she fully expects him to do so. The truth is she was rarely wrong in her complaints about him. There were just so many of them.

To the death. Her head on his shoulder, her damp hair against his lips. They must have had thousands of good moments like that one. Surely they must have.

From down the hall comes the muffled click of Devon's bathroom door closing. Did the young man make an exit? Or is he still there? Francis pictures him waiting for her in her machine, his eyes on the wall of Francis and Beth's guest room, this boy they do not know and never invited into their home.

DEVON WIPES HERSELF and flushes. She washes her hands and looks at herself in the mirror to see what Hollis from Texas has been looking at. She looks tired. Her hair isn't short anymore, but it isn't long either, and she wishes tonight it was one or the other. The blue stud in her nose looks like a bug or a mole, and she's surprised he only mentioned it once.

"You have a lot of them?"

What?

"On your nose."

Did he mean more studs to put in that hole? Or more on other parts of her body? But he didn't sound creepy when he asked, just curious.

And she was curious about him. All these months doing this, and that had only happened once. A boy in Denmark. He sat there in a black sweater staring at her through the screen. He had blond hair that stuck up in a cowlick he didn't seem to know about, and he was quiet like her, only typing his questions, not drawing any pictures on the screen or talking right at her. He wrote: *What do you want?*

I don't know.

He read what she wrote to him at the bottom of the screen. He looked back up at her. That night she'd worn all her ear rings, her stud too, and he seemed to be seeing them for the first time. He looked sad. He typed: *People should know what they want.* Then he nexted her and she ended up in a party of drunk Turkish boys and she closed her laptop and felt like crying.

After that she stopped talking or writing much to any of them. Maybe a *Fuck U* if they were jacking off, or that man in England who reminded her of her father. Once she got a fat black girl in Florida and she did write to her, just a few words because she looked so lonely and was only wearing a red bra. Behind her on the wall above her bed was a poster of a rapper who hit his famous girlfriend and people still downloaded his songs.

Don't give them anything. They don't deserve it. None of them deserve it.

Devon had nexted her before she could respond; she didn't want to get sucked into that hole again.

So she just stared at them all. She waited for the talking or the typing or the drawing on the screen to begin, and she'd just stare and say nothing.

Y arnt u talking?

*C'mon, **pleeease?***

U just wanna fuck, don't u? Give me your number.

Ur a cold cunt huh?

A bald man with a kind face drew a heart on the screen with an arrow through it. Another, young and with a chin strap like Bobby Connors, took out his guitar and sang her a song he'd written himself. It wasn't good, but it wasn't bad and Devon had listened to it with her arms crossed and she felt like a bitch when he finished and she still didn't say anything.

"Man, you're *tough*." But he played her two more songs. She liked them but not as much as she liked how much he needed her to say or do something. Nothing was better than watching them all want her to do something for them she would never ever do.

Till now.

It was the way he leaned back and stared at her, like she was the one he'd been looking for though he wasn't desperate about it. He also didn't seem to be playing any games or looking for someone to jerk off in front of. His name was Hollis, and he was twenty-seven years old and lived in a small town near Houston. He said he'd had a girlfriend and they were going to get married, but when he came home in '05 she was pregnant with the baby of one of his best friends.

"You probably think I'm a big loser now, Sarah."

She'd typed: *No I don't.*

"Well. You should."

He spoke softly and had an accent that made Devon think of cinnamon rolls. On his bare right shoulder was a tattoo she couldn't see too well.

Can I see your tat?

At first he didn't say or do anything. Then he leaned forward and turned his shoulder to the screen.

"See it?"

A little.

He grabbed a small lamp with a shade and a bulb burn on it, and there, etched into his shoulder were two crossed swords, a big number 7 sitting on where the blades touched. She typed: *What's it mean?*

He put the lamp back. He read her question, then lit up a cigarette and took a deep hit. "The Garryowen."

What's that?

"Seventh Cavalry."

Horses?

She was trying to be funny. It was like stepping your bare foot into the ocean after a year away because she hadn't tried to be funny in so long. But he wasn't smiling.

"It won't be there for long."

It's a good one though.

"No, ma'am. It's not."

Mam?

"What's your name?"

That old question. Usually she'd just sit there and stare at whoever just asked this. Let their need build up. Let their love and hatred for her show up, too. But tonight she couldn't say nothing. Not to him.

Sarah.

"That's a good name. It's from the Bible, did you know that?"

Maybe.

"Maybe you know that?"

Yeah.

"How come I'm talking and you're not?"

She shrugged. She hoped he wasn't some Christian like a lot of southern people seemed to be, and she felt bad for lying like she just did. He took a short hit of his cigarette and blew the smoke out the side of his mouth as if she was really in his room, sitting there in front of him. A woman's voice broke from behind a wall. She sounded angry.

Who's that?

"Nobody."

Your wife? Her fingers were shaking slightly. Why did she care so much what his fucking answer was?

"You don't want to know, Sarah."

Yes I do.

He drew in on his cigarette and looked away as he blew out the smoke and stubbed the butt in an ashtray Devon couldn't see. She craved a Merit, could feel the kick of heat down into her lungs, the tingling clarity of everything after. He crossed his arms and read her answer. She liked his body. He had shoulder and chest muscles without being all pumped up, a thatch of dark hair on his sternum. She thought of Sick's narrow, pale chest.

"She's my mother."

Why did she feel relieved, almost happy? She didn't know what to write.

"You gonna next me now, Sarah?

She shook her head. She typed: *I lied. My name's not Sarah.*

"Why did you lie?"

Why do live with your mother?

He didn't answer her question, or maybe what he started talking about *was* his answer. He told her about his "stepdaddy" Roger, how he used to take him hunting out at Big Bend when Hollis was only eleven or twelve years old. He told her about how pretty the woods were, the jack pines and live oaks, the sun coming through. How much he loved the smell of gun oil, and he told her more things. How he liked hitting his target but hated killing anything. Always did. Couldn't look at what he'd done. Was both proud and ashamed of what lay in the back of his stepdaddy's pickup, its beautiful antlers sticking out.

He told her other things, and she listened. Couldn't remember the last time she cared so much to listen. Sick maybe. Yeah, it was Sick and how he'd lie beside her after and talk about music. How sometimes he wanted to *be* music. Just notes floating through the universe and into the ears of living things who'd appreciate him.

Hollis talked about the first time he saw his girlfriend Bonnie, or the first time she saw him, how he was in camos coming in from a three-day hunt, a few whiskers on his face, mud caked on his Timberlands, so maybe she started falling in love right then with someone he never really was.

Every few minutes he'd stop and light another cigarette and ask her to please say something, that he wanted to hear her.

"C'mon, *Sarah*, I want to hear your voice."

He said Sarah with an emphasis that wasn't happy but wasn't too pissed off either.

I told you, that's not my name.

"Then tell me what it is."

I have to go to the bathroom.

"You comin' back?"

She nodded at the screen, and now, standing in front of the bathroom mirror, she's so tired her eyes burn and she wants to brush mascara onto her eyelashes, just a little, but she can feel her heart in her chest and hands and she worries that even after all he's told her, or maybe because of it, he's going to next her or already has, and she hurries across the dark hallway and closes her bedroom door and sits on the bed to see him staring back at her from his laptop. He's wearing some kind of black cowboy hat. It has a strap under the chin and it makes him look older, ageless somehow.

"I like your hat."

"I like your voice."

"Where'd you get it?"

"The Garryowen."

"You look good in it."

He takes it off. He tosses it somewhere she can't see.

"I should burn it."

"Why?"

He's staring at her again, like he's trying to see if she really wants to know. But then his eyes seem to narrow with some kind of dawning respect for her. *Respect.* She has to swallow and she wishes she had water or hard lemonade or beer. She says: "You want my number?"

"I want your name."

"I know."

"I feel like we've met before."

"Me too."

He puts an unlit cigarette to his lips. He takes it out. He gives her a sad smile.

"It's Devon."

Slowly he shakes his head. Like her name is something he's always known but from a life he hasn't lived yet and he can't believe that tonight she's sitting right in front of him. "That's perfect."

"Why do you want to burn your hat?"

"Give me your number, Devon. I'm afraid this wheel's gonna start spinning and I'll never find you again."

She types it out for him, her breath high in her chest, her fingers feathers in the air.

"You done talking?"

"No, but I should go to sleep. I'm meeting my mother for breakfast."

"You don't live with her anymore?"

"No." She's about to lie and say she lives alone, but she can't. With this ex-soldier from Texas, his nice shoulders and warm accent and respectful eyes, she just can't. "I'm living with my great-uncle. He's old but he's sweet."

"My mama's old but she's mean." He laughs, and she can see his teeth are yellow, and he has a lot of fillings, and this makes her like him even more.

FRANCIS PULLS INTO the lot of the country club and parks his Buick between a black SUV and a sun-glinting Mercedes sedan. He has only been to this place once and that was for the wedding of a colleague's daughter thirty years ago. It was built not long after the war—George's war—as a refuge for businessmen like his brother, a pretentious two-story red brick compound with fluted columns flanking the front double doors as if what lies inside is something grander than what it is, a mediocre restaurant and two function halls of artificial blue carpet overlooking a patchy golf course. A cell tower looms in the distance.

Charlie said he'd be waiting for him in the bar. "But don't be late, Uncle. I tee off at one." Francis glances at his watch but cannot read it with his sunglasses on. He takes them off and squints in the sunlight and pulls open the oak door to the club. There's the pleasantly new feeling that he's being useful, but then comes a creeping shame for he wonders if that is his primary reason for meeting his nephew for lunch, not to help bridge the barren canyon between him and his daughter, but to give Francis Brandt something more important to do than water yet again his dead wife's flowers or to prepare a lesson for his grand-niece that goes nowhere.

Charlie's sitting at the bar with his back to the room. Fewer than a third of the tables are taken, all by gray-haired retirees eating lunch, and there's no background music playing, the air-conditioning too high. Even in his sports jacket, Francis feels cold.

Charlie hasn't seen him yet. He's hunched over his drink, a martini of some kind. He's wearing rimless glasses, golf cleats, bright salmon shorts, and a navy jacket. It appears he's dyed his hair a darker color, and his eyes are on the rear of the young bartender as she bends forward to place a glass of wine on the waitress's serving tray. She straightens up and sees Francis before Charlie does. "What can I get you, hon?"

"Soda water with lime. Thank you."

"Well if it isn't my dear old Uncle Francis." Charlie seems to stress the word "old" for the pretty bartender's benefit, but he's also smiling as if he's genuinely pleased to see him and he squeezes Francis's hand a bit too hard, slapping his shoulder twice.

"I'm glad we could meet, nephew."

"You sound so serious, Uncle."

There's a forced playfulness in Charlie's voice. He taps the screen of the device beside his martini, his eyes back on the young bartender as she places Francis's soda water on a napkin before him. Francis thanks her, pulls the straw free, and squeezes the lime wedge into his drink. He's aware of being cold while his face feels warm by what his nephew just said.

"Having a daughter *is* serious, Charlie."

"How would you know?"

"Is this how we're going to start?" Francis's voice sounds high to himself. He can feel his own heartbeat in his neck, and he does not like how Charlie is resting both forearms on the bar as if his elderly uncle is a momentary interruption from more important matters, as if the real conversation he's having is on the small screen in front of him or with the young woman working a few feet away. Francis pulls out a stool but doesn't sit. He wishes there was a brass footrail to take the strain off his back, and he leans one elbow on the bar the way he did for years and years.

"*You* wanted to meet, Uncle, I didn't."

"Why not?"

Charlie glances at him and shakes his head. He lifts his martini and drinks. This close, Francis can see the chemical darkness of his thinning hair, a fresh shaving nick on his jaw, the slight tremor in his hand as he sets the glass back down on its napkin.

"Hair of the dog?"

"Maybe."

"I'm not here to judge you, Charlie."

"Bullshit, you're not." Charlie raises one finger to the bartender. He points to his half-empty drink. "You've been judging me my whole fucking life."

"Why do you say that?" Francis feels caught in a lie. He sips his own drink. He watches the bartender pour vodka into a large mixing glass filled with ice, and he wants what's in there. He does.

"C'mon, Uncle, let's change the subject."

"Fine by me."

"Does she hate me?"

"Devon?"

Charlie nods. He's staring at his cocktail napkin, rubbing one corner between his thumb and forefinger.

"No, she doesn't hate you."

"She tell you that?"

"No, but she hasn't *not* told me that."

"Then she fuckin' hates me." Charlie shrugs and drains his martini just as the young bartender places a new one in front of him.

"I'm working with her on her GED preparation."

"Marie told me."

"I asked her to write an essay, and she wrote about you."

Charlie nods as if he's about to hear a story he's heard many times before. "Yeah?"

"She didn't get very far, though."

"Because she's lazy, Uncle. Always has been."

"I don't see that."

"Oh? What do *you* see?"

"I see a girl who keeps her room spotless. Who does her own laundry and folds her clothes. I see a girl who works hard bussing tables and cleaning hotel rooms. That's what I see."

"You go to work with her?"

"No, but I hear good things from the manager."

Only last Saturday night, Francis waiting in his car in the parking lot, Danny Sullivan stood under one of the Whaler's exterior lamps smoking a cigar and talking to a man in a suit. When Devon came out, walking quickly, her head down, her red headphones already on her ears, Danny had glanced at her, then motioned to Francis to roll down his window. *She's doing good, Mr. B. Real good.*

That's nice to hear, Danny. Thank you.

Devon pulled off her headphones the way she always did as she climbed in and sat beside Francis.

You hear that, Devy?

What?

Your boss says you're doing well.

That's nice. Too bad he's such an asshole.

"Is that what she's gonna do her whole life? Be somebody's fucking chambermaid?"

"A strong work ethic transfers to anything, Charlie, you know that."

But did he? His brother, Charlie's father, had built Charlie's business to what it is. And not long before George hired his son and changed his company's name from Brandt Insurance to Brandt & Brandt, George took on a new manager and chief financial officer who over the years since his death have kept Brandt & Brandt a smoothly running and viable business. Charlie sits at a big desk and sells policies and enters claims, but he also has a large staff to do that kind of thing and there's golf to think about, skiing in the winter, afternoon drinks with pretty women who aren't his wife.

"It bothers her that you have a girlfriend, Charlie."

"Excuse me?" His nephew turns fully toward him. He appears both indignant and guilty. "That's nobody's fucking business."

"Does Marie know?"

"That's none of *your* business, Uncle."

"I agree with you, it's not."

"Good." Charlie lifts his martini, pauses, then rests it back on its napkin. "Do you even *know* what Devon did last spring?"

"No, I don't."

"Marie didn't tell you?"

"She only said Devon had shame about it."

"Not enough. Not efuckingnough, I'll tell you that." Charlie checks his screen and stands. He pulls out three tens and drops them on the bar, then drinks as if he's alone. Francis pokes his straw into his soda. He stirs and he waits. It feels wrong that he wants to know. "She could use a call or an email from you, Charlie. That's all I'm here to tell you. That's it."

"Yeah? And what should I say to her, Francis? Making any more *pornos* lately, honey? Still blowin' every boy in fucking town? Look her up on the Internet, Uncle. Go 'head. See for yourself."

Charlie slips his device into his jacket pocket and walks quickly back through the dining room. His calves are tanned and surprisingly fit-looking, his shoulders held back as if he will no longer stand for insults, no sir, he will not. Not one second more.

"You all set, hon?"

The bartender's pulling away Charlie's damp napkin and dry cash. Francis nods, though what he'd like is for her to make him one just the way she did his nephew. Make him one. Then two. And maybe one more.

Pornos.

Little Devy jumping onto his lap, her long brown hair and happy, hungry eyes, how she would settle against his chest and open a new book, how she would wait for him to adjust his glasses, clear his throat, and begin to read. Then they would both be in a story far away from all the busy family noise around them, just the two of them, Francis and his older brother's only granddaughter, this miracle gift Francis had been given, one he fears now he has inexcusably taken for granted and is in danger of losing, if he has not lost her already.

IT'S HOT. Devon can smell her mother sweating on the bench beside her. The sun shines too brightly on the worn shingles of the restaurant and on the tar roofs of the cottages down the hill to the blinding ocean, but there are other people in the courtyard, families as hungry for brunch as Devon's mother is.

After closing her laptop last night, Devon couldn't sleep. She turned out the light and lay back and stared into the darkness until her ceiling became dim and flat above her and she kept seeing Hollis there. It was his resigned laugh, and it was the way he stared at her once he knew she really wanted to know more about him. Then her eyes finally closed and she saw him and Sick sitting beside each other on a couch playing *Call of Duty*, then Sick was on top of her, inside her, and Devon had felt guilty and she kept reaching her hand out for someone to take hold of, and it was Bobby Connors putting his hard-on in her palm and she was running down her street and years later her mother was knocking on her window waking her up, her tanned moon-face peering inside, Uncle Francis gone who knows where.

Her mother is reading the menu to her. It's laminated and colorful, and Devon wishes she would just read it to herself.

"Eggs Benedict, Dev. You *love* that."

Devon wants a cigarette. She holds her iEverything in both hands like a prayer. It's close to one in the afternoon, and nothing has come in, even from Sick. *I'm not here anymore. Where r u?* Though now that feels like a lie. Meeting Hollis—and what's his last name? She needs to know his full name, to try it out on her tongue—she's somehow more here than she has been in so long. But why hasn't he texted her? Or called? He could still be asleep, but what if he isn't for real? What if he spins to a new girl every night, makes her feel special, then never calls? Like catching a fish just for the thrill of reeling it in before you unhook it and let it go. But no, he really did sound scared that the wheel would start spinning and he wouldn't see her again. She'd been tired from work, though, from staying up so late, her eyes burning: did she give him the wrong fucking number?

"*Honey*, are you listening to me?"

"Sorry."

"You look tired. Are you working too hard?" Her mother has her hair up. She's wearing those pretty earrings Devon gave her last Christmas, silver pendants she bought at the Mall with Sick. But her mother has gained so much more weight, and the pendants are pointing down at her tanned flesh like exclamation points. "Don't they look nice?"

"Yeah, they do."

"You getting enough rest?" Her mother's hand is damp on her forearm. Devon wants to pull it away. She likes her mother's dress, though. Big blue flowers on summer cotton across her breasts and belly.

"I sleep."

"What time does Uncle Francis get up?" Her tone is concerned and nosy.

"I don't know, but I think he's doing okay."

"Why do you say that?"

Devon shrugs. "He's always seemed so alone to me anyway."

A few feet over a young father is sitting on a bench, his small son standing between his bare legs, the boy's hands on each knee. The dad keeps squeezing him with his legs and making him laugh.

"How about you, Dev?" Her mother pats her forearm. "Have you made any friends at the restaurant or hotel?"

Paula loading her cleaning cart and bitching about her son. Rayna the bus girl who looks like she does nothing but play Goth games on her computer all day. Danny Sullivan and his wet cigars, his eyes on her.

"Yeah, I guess."

"Brandt?" A man in shorts and sandals peers over his reading glasses and looks around the courtyard, then Devon's following her mother inside over a wooden floor in a sunlit room of families eating and sipping coffee she can smell and wants badly. The man leads them to a table in the corner, a flower garden out the open window.

"Oh, isn't that lovely."

It's a part of her mother Devon hates and loves, her appreciation for everyone and everything that's good. Devon's just sitting down when her iEverything vibrates in her hand. It's as if someone has just grabbed her and hugged her from behind and she flicks at the screen and sees it's Sick, a long text from him, and she feels like crying and hates herself for it.

"Please, honey, you know how I feel about those things."

"All *right*, Mom, *fuck*."

"Devon." Her mother scans the tables around them, and Devon presses the off button. She wishes she had her Dr. Dre's on right now.

"Coffee, ladies?" The waitress is one of those women with a deeply lined face from too much sun and fast winds from the back of a motorcycle or some drunk's speedboat.

"Yes, please," Devon says.

"I'll just have water, thank you."

The waitress leaves. Devon feels bad about snapping at her mother. She picks up her menu. "Get a Bloody Mary or something, Mom. Live a little."

"Your father lives enough for both of us, thank you."

"Then boot his ass out."

"I really don't want to talk about it, Devon. Not today, okay?"

"Fine, just don't expect me to come back with him there."

"I don't want you to." Her mother's eyes are on the flower garden outside, and it's as if she's just reached over and dug her nails into Devon's face. She has no intention of moving back, but she's never considered the option closed and she's surprised by how she has to look away and focus on her menu, though she can't quite make out the words.

"I don't like how he treats you, honey. That's the only reason. You know that, right?"

"Decided yet, ladies?" The waitress sets the water and coffee down. She's just a voice Devon speaks to—eggs, please. No toast. No bacon. No potatoes. Her mother orders fried eggs and sausages, whole wheat toast and chocolate chip pancakes with whipped cream. Devon admires this, her mother not hiding anything about herself, her own fuck you to the world. Devon pours an Equal into her coffee, stirs it, and sips.

"Honey? You know that, right?"

Devon looks directly at her mother. She half smiles and nods, but what she really thinks is this: her mother doesn't want her to come home because she can't stand Devon's judgment of her.

"Good. How's the GED prep coming along?"

"Sucky."

"Why do you say that?"

"You know why."

"College will be different, Dev. It's not like high school at all."

Devon wants to ask her how she knows this; she only went for two years, and she was a day student and now she's working in a realty office. That's all she's ever done. Worked at Salem Realty and met Charlie Brandt at some party and got married and had her and now she just eats while Charlie does whatever the hell he wants.

"Honey, it really isn't."

Devon feels cruel. She looks out the window at tall white flowers. They're like the ones in Francis's backyard, something beautiful and living Aunt Beth left behind. This both cheers Devon up and makes her sad. Her coffee is hot and sweet. She wonders what Sick wrote.

Her mother lowers her voice. "I'm still trying to get that video

removed. I hired a lawyer Laura Welch uses. She says he specializes
in violations of privacy, and he tells me there are so many phony businesses that it's going to be hard to—"

"Mom? Are you *serious?*"

"What? I thought you'd—"

"Well I *don't*, all right? I don't ever want to fucking talk about it
ever again, I've told you that."

"But honey—"

"Mom, *shit.*" Devon stands and snatches up her iEverything. "I'm
going to the bathroom." A muffled buzz is in her ears. She's moving quickly over the squeaking wooden floor, people chewing and
swallowing and sipping and nodding their reasonable heads at one
another. She wants to be somewhere where there's no one. A white,
silent room. No windows. No door. Just music in her head, her fingers on buttons that will bring whatever she wants when she wants it,
which is nothing.

Except that's not true.

She does want that video gone, and she's grateful to her mother
for trying to get rid of it, though she doesn't believe it's possible.
Those little netfilms are forever, and she can't take the thought of
how many people have seen it already, have maybe jacked off to it,
have sat around—if they're Trina and her new fucking friends—and
gloated about it. And Devon hates that her mother had to see it, and
Sick, and if her father actually watched it she's almost glad, though
it's the kind of glad you feel when in a fight you break something you
didn't mean to, that dark echo after.

She locks the bathroom door and sits on the closed toilet. The
room smells like lemon soap and tissue paper. Something cold rolls
deep in her belly before she thinks it: What if Hollis in Texas finds
out? What if she did give him the wrong number and he types in
Devon? Could he be led to *Dirty* Devon? Would he actually see her
and the others? Though hers is the only face he'd see, the only mouth.

Fuck.

She taps her screen on and pulls up Sick's text. *D, y arnt u here any-more? That's not good. Everybody fucks up and guess what? I forgive u. I do. U were always 2 easy, D. Not that way. The other way. Yur like a blank picture in a frame and you let everybody else paint u. But u should paint yourself, D. Yur beautiful.*

Don't looz our cup. All my good memories r in there.

My dreams 2.

Sick

Devon's face is hot. There's not enough air in the room. Her thumbs start punching letters under glass. *U were the only one, Sick. U do know that, right? Please tell me u know that.*

A knocking at the door. A little girl's voice. "'Scuse me?"

Devon stands and flushes the toilet and unlocks the door for a black-haired girl staring up at her. She's wearing a green T-shirt with a turtle on it. She can't be more than five or six, and there's not a grownup anywhere near her.

"It all yours, honey." Devon holds the door for her, then pushes it closed behind her. She waits until she hears the slide of the lock on the other side, then she walks through the full tables back to her mother smiling sadly at her from the corner. Devon feels she's just cursed that little girl. *It's all yours, honey.* Good luck with everything. Let me know how it turns out, boys and blow jobs and feeling you have to do something even if you don't want to, and then you take pride in killing that part of yourself that used to care and you do things with such little feeling about it you're surprised people think you actually did them.

Devon sits and drops her napkin onto her lap. Her mother starts talking about the Welches, about Laura living in the big house while poor Mark has to sleep on the couch in his mother's garage apart-ment. Devon knows the story, and she's surprised her mother's talking about it. Did she forget Mark had his own wife filmed, too?

Devon sips her coffee. She's hungry now, her eyes drifting to the white flowers outside. *I forgive you. I do.* She's going to save that one. She needs to. And she's glad she texted what she did to him. It makes her feel like something bad is falling further behind her and that good things might be coming. And could she have typed the wrong number to Hollis? No. She knows it better than her own name. She sees him smiling at her, pulling off his cavalry hat and tossing it onto what has to be his bed, the one he's probably just waking in right this second, the one he's going sit up in and text her in before he does anything else.

FRANCIS DRIVES DOWN River Street feeling naïve, inept, and exposed. Charlie was right, he *has* been judging him his entire life, this boy who had been given a father, a man who—drunk those early years or not—provided well for his family; Charlie had also been given a warm and doting mother; he'd been given new bicycles and tennis and golf lessons; he'd been given four years at a private high school on acres of wooded green, his graduation gift a shining Camaro, his college education paid for in full, and then he was given a job. How could Francis *not* have judged him? And to see Charlie walk through this world as if he *deserved* all this, well, it made Francis hate him, really. His brother's son or not, he did. Part of him always had.

Except then Charlie had the surprising good sense to marry loving Marie Labadini who bore him Devon Denise, and Charlie wasn't so unattractive anymore. Somehow he had brought joy into their family. Charlie's house became the home they would all gather in for holidays—George and Evelyn, Francis and Beth, and all those loud, animated cousins, aunts, and uncles from Marie's side of the family. Then, as more children came into the world from the Labadini side, Sundays became family dinner days at Charlie's house, and it was something Francis and Beth both looked forward to, all that warm chaos once every week.

Beth would bake dinner rolls or a strawberry rhubarb pie or sometimes toss a salad, and Francis would bring bottles of red and

white. Because his drinking years were behind him, it was now quality over quantity and he made sure he chose expensive wines from
France or the West Coast, handing smiling Marie the bottles in her
kitchen, feeling selfless and virtuous and so very happy to be in his
nephew's house, Devy running up and wrapping her arms around his
legs. "Uncle Franny!"

Making any pornos lately, honey?

Francis shakes his head so hard his sunglasses shift and he has to
push them back into place. He's driving under a hot white sun, his
sports jacket bunched up around his shoulders, though it has always
been his habit to lay his jacket along the back so he won't wrinkle it,
but he barely remembers even driving away from the lot of the country club. Nor does he recognize this neighborhood.

The triple-deckers are still here, their asbestos or asphalt shingles
and small crooked porches, their dirt or cracked concrete driveways.
But on the river side there's a Dairy Queen and BMW dealership, the
sun on red, white, and blue balloons tied to windshield wipers. There's
a package store whose front window is completely covered from the
inside by Xeroxed copies of winning lottery tickets, and on the other
side of the street it seems as if every other three-family home has been
torn down and replaced by an auto parts store, a bodega—its Spanish
neon sign a mystery to Francis—more liquor stores, a check-cashing
shop, a Cambodian restaurant in front of which stands a sandwich
board advertising meals in that language, too.

Ditch of the Bodos. A tilting of what he thinks he knew for what he
obviously does not. A horn barks behind him. In his rearview mirror
is a white sports car, the driver bald and middle-aged, expensive sunglasses across his eyes like an executioner's mask.

It's a relief to speed up, and it's a relief to drive under the trestle of
Railroad Square, for while these brick and granite mill buildings of
his youth are full of restaurants now, microbreweries and art galler-
ies, clothing stores and bank offices, they are still familiar, and seeing

them under the sun, the street always in shadow, he feels the empty passenger seat beside him like a knife under his ribs. How lovely those Sundays had been.

Perhaps another childless woman would have stayed away from a house of young kids and their young mothers and fathers, but at Charlie's, Beth came alive the way she would much later on their car trips, more curious about everything, more grateful for whatever she was given. She'd sit on the living room floor with two or three of Marie's nieces and nephews, playing a board game or teaching them Crazy 8's or helping to pull a sweater onto a Barbie. Or she'd be out in the backyard tossing a ball or pushing a boy or girl in one of Devon's swings, and after dinner, when their exhausted parents were lingering over coffee and dessert or one more glass of wine, she would offer to supervise the whole brood down in the basement playroom.

On the drive home later, gone was her vigilant hunt for flaws or incompetence. Instead, her cheeks would have more color to them, her eyes more light, even her hair seemed thicker, her lips, and while she told Charlie about a game she'd played with one of the kids or the remarkable thing one of them had said, he'd reach over and squeeze her hand or rest his fingers on her knee and he'd be aroused.

It's what he never understood about pornography and prostitution, the easy way so many men could become erect at the prospect of flesh and flesh alone. For him, what happened below his waist was inextricably tied to what happened behind his sternum and between his ears. And it was a rare Sunday afternoon after a family dinner at Charlie and Marie's that Francis and his wife did not go straight home to bed and make love. After, as Beth held him and he held her, there was the clear and unburdened air of acceptance, not so much of one another and their slowly aging bodies, as of their roles in this life as aunt and uncle; it could have been so much worse.

Francis drives through Post Office Square, then east along Merrimack Street. In front of an office supply store an obese woman leans on the handle of her shopping cart smoking a cigarette. The cart is stuffed with bulging plastic trash bags, and Francis looks away. He tells himself to be grateful, but it's turning into a tough afternoon. How is it possible that sitting in the deep nest of those Sundays at Charlie's, he rarely, if ever, imagined them never happening again? How is it he did not anticipate his disciplined wife dying first? How could he not have ever considered, given the nephew he knew, that Charlie and Marie would not last? How could he not have foreseen the day Devy's body would change and she would be too mature to sit on his lap while he read her a story, his gratitude for her love for him bottomless?

Francis is too warm. He turns up the air conditioner and presses buttons to crack his windows. The car ahead is a gold sedan with twin exhaust pipes, the back and front seats filled with young men. Their hair is short and they have brown skin and their stereo system is blaring so loud Francis can feel the thump of bass in his chest. The singer doesn't sing but recites, his voice low and what they used to call negro then black then African-American and now the N-word if you're black yourself, and every other word is an obscenity. Francis resists the old man's urge to condemn them all. On the sidewalk before the boarded-up Woolworth's building, the same one his mother would take him to when he was a child, a girl of no more than twenty holds a young boy's shirt collar while she stares at the small screen in her hand. She moves her thumb along it. She glances up at the passing noise and Francis looks away from her son, for he sees him ten years from now sitting in a classroom lighting a cigarette.

At the intersection the gold sedan swings right and accelerates onto the bridge over the river, its twin pipes belching blue exhaust, and Francis drives straight ahead. His breath is uneven and he's aware of his heart being a muscle, one that simply will not go on and on forever. He's already outlived his brother by ten years and his mother by one. And what about his putative father, Billy Brandt? Did he die old somewhere? Or was he one of the young ones? More than once over the years Francis has imagined his father leaping up into the open doors of a moving freight car only to lose his grip and fall, those spinning iron wheels slicing him in two.

On Francis's right is a shopping plaza, half its store space taken up by a weight-training gym. Another change. No one lifted weights when he was young. Or tattooed themselves so much. Or shaved their heads and pierced holes into their skin. They all look like convicts now, a generation of felons.

That butterfly on Devy's ankle. All those holes in her ears, the blue stud in her nose. He passes a weed lot to his left, the river reflecting the sun beyond, and he shakes his head again for he's glimpsed only one stag film and that was, of all places, at Charlie's bachelor's party over twenty-five years ago.

George and Francis had driven there together in George's Seville. They had taken their wives to dinner first, then dropped them off, and both Brandt brothers were clean and sober so Francis was hoping for perhaps the pleasure of a cigar, a hand or two of poker, a cup of hot coffee and a slice of pie. He did not know any of his nephew's friends, but he knew the club. It was in a granite building on the river on the north side of the trestle in Railroad Square, and when Francis was a boy it had been a factory for buttons and zippers, but sometime in the fifties, not long after he'd returned home, it had become a social club for men.

Francis remembers the night was cold. There were dead leaves scattered over the sidewalk as he and George walked into the club. George handed his cashmere coat to the coat check girl, a ten between his fingers. It was understood this was a gratuity from both of them, and perhaps Francis had been feeling patronized once again as he followed his brother into the main barroom, the party having already arrived at its center, an assault of men cheering and whooping and applauding, cigar and cigarette smoke so thick Francis's eyes began to water. The room was lit only by dim lights from beneath the bar that was empty because the crowd of Charlie's friends, twenty or thirty of them, was gathered around the dance floor, young executives in ties and shirt sleeves holding drinks or bottles of beer or both, and at first Francis thought they were watching the flickering screen behind them, for on this screen a man's erect penis was plunging in and out of a woman, and it was such a private sight that Francis couldn't quite take it in and his eyes moved to the center of the floor where a young man in a dark suit sat in a chair, his pants and underwear around his ankles, a blond woman in shorts and heels kneeling there between his legs, her head bobbing up and down. Three or four feet away Francis's nephew Charlie was hollering louder than the rest, his tie untied and hanging on either side of his unbuttoned shirt. He held a bottle of brandy and turned laughing at a big man to his right, and now George was nowhere Francis could see and he'd seen enough. On his way out he'd turned and looked back once more at that bright flickering screen just as the man began to ejaculate onto the woman's belly, Triz in the Tiki light smiling up at him, the only woman Francis had ever done that to, all of his seed inside his wife for all of these years, and perhaps he'd taken a cab home that night, Francis does not remember, but there was the raw, skinned feel of some important barrier inside him having been kicked down, the sense that we are all ugly and that beauty is a respite and innocence is a lie.

Of course he never assumed Devy to be without any experience, though he'd not let himself think too much about that part of her life. It had been his failing as a teacher, too. So many girls over the years who would sexualize themselves just as soon as their bodies began to change. They wore makeup and low-cut shirts and tight jeans, and Francis saw the new power these girls held over the boys in class. It was like watching a child light a match and see that she was capable of starting a fire all by herself.

Rita Flaherty would take all this in and regularly depart from her lesson plan to talk about birth control and the risk of having a baby when you were still one yourself, the diseases you could catch and perhaps never cure. She would chastise Francis and their other colleagues for not doing the same. "Hell, I've given rubbers to some of these girls. You should too, Frank."

But he hadn't. Even to the boys, though he was happy to give out hallway advice about college or a practical choice of work after school and, once he was sober, he began to take more of an interest in any kid who showed signs he might be a drinker. But when it came to these young people and their sex lives, Francis preferred the natural generational wall between them to stay up, no windows or doors or ladders over to the other side.

Making any more pornos lately, honey? Devon not being able to write. The way she walks with her head down and that music pounding in her head. How she spends so much time alone in her room, and when they eat dinners together at the table, how she eats quickly and makes conversation as if she's pressed some automatic button inside her. How some nights while Francis reads the newspaper in his living room chair, Devy will sit on the couch where Beth used to read, and she'll stare at the screen in her hand or thumb through one of Beth's old *People* magazines, but it's as if some timer is clicking away inside his niece for she's only doing these things to be polite. So why has he felt even closer to her these past five months? Is it because she reminds him of himself when he was only a year or two older? Back from the other side of the world and a plunge into a way men should never be? That distance after? That wanting to be left the hell alone?

And perhaps this is what he should do. Just leave her alone. If she does not want the GED or a shot at college, why should he force her to? Francis passes the fire station on his right, the old folks' home on his left, and his cheeks flush hot for while he does believe she should get that certificate he also knows the joy he's taken in preparing those lessons for her. She's made you useful again, hasn't she, Francis? This young woman he now feels utterly incapable of helping in any way, Devy, who last night called herself Sarah to a boy on the screen.

Francis presses buttons and rolls up his windows. He drives slower. He is in no hurry to get back home. Through the trees the river shines under the sun, though he knows how dirty it is. Everyone knows how dirty it is.

HER MOTHER WANTED to go shopping. She wanted to drive up to the outlet stores in Kittery, buy a blouse or something, maybe get an ice cream at the Ben and Jerry's stand between the endless parking lot and the salt marsh. There are picnic tables under the sun where they'd sat before, but Devon just wanted to go home. She said that, too.

"Home?"

"I mean Uncle Francis's."

Her mother looked hurt, which was funny after what she said at breakfast. But Devon didn't want to be at Francis's either. She was going to wait for her mother to drive away, then she was going to put on her Dr. Dre's and walk to the beach under the sun with her iEverything, find a place for herself between the boulevard and the water where she could stare at her screen and wait.

When Francis's phone rang, she almost didn't answer it, but the caller ID said *The Whaler* and she picked it up and got fucking Danny Sullivan on the other end. "My Sunday help called in sick, Dev. Do me this favor, all right?"

Devon wanted to ask if he'd called Paula, but she knew the answer already; Paula had a kid at home and Devon didn't, and now she's running the vacuum over the carpet in 106, Kurt Cobain screaming in her head, his voice beautiful though he's trying to ruin it to make a point and right now she doesn't want to ruin anything beautiful so she flicks to a new song. She gets that West Coast blonde singing how all she wants to do is have some fun, but that's not right either. Devon stops vacuuming. She leans the handle against her hip and pulls her iEverything from her front pocket and flicks her finger over the glass till she gets something that's not down but not up either. Irish rock and roll, the singer's voice worried but hopeful, which is how she feels, so she turns it up, the guitar humming back and forth behind her eyes, drums like rising thunder. She scans for texts, but there are none, even from Sick, and she pushes her iEverything back into her front pants pocket and keeps vacuuming. Hollis is beginning to feel like only a dream she had, the respectful way he looked at her just a wish she had.

But it feels good to move her body and sweat a little and, unlike Paula, she gets down on her hands and knees and makes sure to reach the dust under the bed. Something big gets sucked into the beater bar. Devon can feel the high vibration of it in the handle, the singer singing how he still hasn't found what he's looking for, and Devon pulls the beater bar out from under the bed and there's something red and made of cotton and she gets her fingers around it and yanks it out, the bar spinning again. A pair of thong underwear. Devon tosses them toward the closed door. She wipes her fingers on her knee and pushes the beater back under the bed and works it back and forth.

That picture of Amanda Salvi. She must've taken it herself because it was a side view to make her waist look smaller, her bare breasts bigger, the side of her ass naked too because she was wearing a thong just like the one Devon was going to throw in the trash. Salvi must've just sent it to her father's phone because it came up as Devon was getting ready to punch in Bobby Connors' number. Her iEverything was in the back of his car, Devon was sure, because she'd had it in her hand nodding off against Luke's chest the night before, streetlights whizzing by outside.

On the radio the DJ was selling concert tickets or cars, and Bobby and Trina were fighting again, Trina bitching about something he said or did. She was always bitching at him. Devon was drunk, her eyes closed, and she wanted music and she'd come to hate Trina's voice, a rusty razor thrown through something good. She was going on about Tracy Fields, how Bobby's been texting her, Trina fucking knows he has. Bobby's voice. One low grunt of denial here and there, the switching of radio stations till he got some hip-hop fuck music, a black woman's street moans as she practically licked the microphone.

"*Bobby*, are you fucking *listening* to me?"

Trina's jealousy was like a fever she could never get rid of, and until Sick, Devon had never understood it. And it was strange leaning into Luke because she hadn't been this close to him in three years, not since that night in his boat. For five or six weeks that fall and early winter, people called them a couple. He texted her every day and she texted him back and on weekends they'd cruise around in Bobby's Sentra with him and Trina. It was the closest Devon had felt to Trina since middle school. Their boyfriends were best friends, and now there was this glue between them and it smelled like Axe and denim and hair gel and cum.

The morning after Luke's party and Luke's boat, Devon had texted Trina before she even got out of bed.

I'm not an MV anymore.

No f-ing way!

Way

U swallow?

Y

U my gurl!

There was the feeling she'd put something important behind her and now she was somebody different: older, wiser, better. But that was like being at the beach and surfing your first wave, then standing there waist-deep in water thinking you were through now; how could she not have thought of all the waves that were coming one after the other without a break? She could have turned around and walked up onto the sand, but once you were in the water, it was hard to get out.

Just two days later, a Sunday afternoon, she was doing algebra homework at the dining room table, the drone of football announcers out in the living room. Her hungover father dozed in front of the TV, and her mother was baking lasagna in the kitchen, and Devon's iEverything had vibrated on the table.

Go for a ride?

I'm doing homework.

Take a break.

A thinning of the blood in her fingers, a shiver across her face.

Ok.

So easy to leave the house. A smile at her mother, some line about Dunkin's and she and her friend needing a coffee for homework.

"But we're *eating* soon."

"I know. I'll be right back."

From behind the wheel of his father's Mercedes, Luke kept glancing at her as he drove. His hair was in a perfect flow across his forehead and he wore a new sweater and chewed wintergreen gum, and she felt bad that all she did was brush on some mascara and pull on a sweatshirt, her hair down around her shoulders. But he couldn't stop looking at her face and smiling at her, smiling at her lips. Smiling at her mouth.

"I keep thinking about, you know—"

"Yeah."

"The other night."

Something like that, Devon can't remember it all, only what his voice sounded like—high in his throat, almost scared—and she knew it was her doing that to him, *her*, this girl he had always ignored.

It was a day with no clouds, the sky so blue it was hard not to believe in something big behind it all. Then Luke was parking his dad's Mercedes in a stretch of woods near the highway. Half the leaves were off the trees, and Devon could see through the trunks and branches all the cars rushing past, everybody in a hurry, even on a Sunday.

There was no kissing. No touching. But there was Luke's face. His eyes dark with a need for her, his throat flushed pink, and when he put his hand on her shoulder, his fingers were trembling and how could she not use this power she'd been given? How could she not lean down and wait for him to unbutton and unzip his jeans, his soft grunts, his hand on her back like he was her patient and she was the only one who could cure him.

That calm in him after. The way he put on the radio and drove them down into Lafayette Square, the shy smile he gave her, his eyes grateful but distant too. At the Dunkin's drive-up window, he ordered them two sweet coffees, and even though hers was too hot she sipped it right away.

When he dropped her off, he didn't even put the car in park. He rested his hand on her knee, said, "That was awesome."

"*You're* awesome." But stepping out of the car and walking back up to her house with her coffee, she knew she didn't mean it.

On weekends he wanted to do more things. They'd be stretched out on a bed in the dark room of some party house, drunk voices on the other side of the door, and she'd let him get a finger inside her and it felt good but wrong too. He moved like a boy running down a field trying to hurl a ball into a net, the ball everything, and all that power she'd held over him seemed to leak out over grass, its center lost, and she'd pull his hand away and unzip his jeans and lower her face and mouth to what she knew would make the boy stop running and running and then she could just walk away and rinse her mouth and leave all the players and spectators with nothing to do because she was the main show, wasn't she?

Except she wasn't the only one who did this. So many girls had learned how to do this. Trina did it to Bobby (before she started doing all of it with him end of freshman year), Tracy Fields, with her thick red hair and crooked eyeteeth, her field hockey calves—she did it just to make boys go away. She did it the way some girls kissed.

Drunk together, Devon and Tracy in a bright kitchen drinking hard lemonade they'd spiked with vodka nips, Eddie Vedder howling through an electric rain out in the living room of so many wasted kids two lamps were already broken and a girl ran out crying and it was like storm clouds you ignore till it's too late. Tracy was saying, "A tongue or a dick in your mouth, what's the fucking difference? It's not even *sex*. Sex is when you give them *this*." Her fingers curled against Devon's crotch and a laugh jumped out of her.

"And none of these motherfuckers are ever getting that from me, baby." Both of them were laughing now. Tracy's eyes seemed faraway but sincere, and Devon could see this was Tracy's code. It was good to have a code.

And was it that party when she caught Luke? Or the one over the line in New Hampshire? That brick house in pine trees behind an apartment complex where old people lived? Luke didn't even bother to lock the door, and when Devon walked in looking for him, she didn't know what she was seeing at first, Luke standing at the toilet with his pants around his knees holding a hairy pumpkin in both hands, his dick going in and out of it, the pumpkin a plump face and fine brown hair, Megan Monroe.

Devon had yanked the door shut so hard a mirror in the hall shook on its nail. She was pushing through dancing bodies holding Solo cups and smoking joints and cigarettes till she was outside walking in the cold without her coat down the driveway through the pine trees in the dark.

Something hurt and something didn't. His face just before he jerked it toward her, his eyes closed, his mouth half-open, his sickness getting healed and it didn't matter who the doctor was, and that's what hurt. Her power was in every girl, in every girl's open mouth.

Devon crossed her arms. She felt like crying, but she felt free of something, too, boring Luke McDonough and his constant need for her to be just one thing. She knew she'd never loved him, but had she ever even *liked* him?

Ahead was the building of old people's apartments. Every window had curtains over it, the shades pulled, lamplight shining through the cracks. She wanted to keep walking, but her coat was back in the party and so was her ride with Bobby and Trina, and three hours later she was drunk in the backseat of Bobby's car and every time Luke touched her shoulder or knee she'd pull away till he stopped doing it, and then for a few months Luke and Megan Monroe were a couple and maybe he'd texted his friends about what Devon Brandt had done to him whenever he wanted, or maybe, though she doubted it even then, Devon had become beautiful all of a sudden because only fifteen minutes into any party and a handsome boy was talking to her, one of the boys the other boys wanted to be, the LAX boys, the hockey boys, the big smart ones who lifted weights and talked about law school and business school and their bright shining tomorrows, and they always wanted to get her alone, and drunk or straight or half-drunk, Devon would wander down a hallway with one, or out onto a deck with another, or go on a beer run in a car with someone else, and it took a while, maybe a year, maybe more, before it came to her that those first steps with him or him or him were steps into her hope that *this* would be something—no, *this* would—that one's cute half-smile, his eyes on her chin because he was too shy to look up, or that other one's straight white teeth, his smile because he liked whatever it was she'd just said to him, and she would go and it was never any different, the talking going quiet, the hand on her waist, the kiss that didn't lead to more kisses but to what they really wanted. Once or twice, maybe four times, she'd turn and start to walk away, but their voices—so hungry, so insistent, some confused and actually hurt, others with a raised tone, a little dangerous—it was easier to just trade his tongue in her mouth for what was behind his zipper. *It's not even sex. Sex is when you give them* **this.**

But then other girls began to treat her differently. If she walked by a group of them standing at their open lockers, or at the mall huddled outside H&M or Forever 21, or gathered around a keg in a loud basement under blue light, they'd glance over at her as coldly as if she'd just betrayed each one of them. It was like every girl had been sworn to some kind of secret at birth and now Devon Brandt was going around and telling each boy she met just what it was.

But Devon had never felt joined to these other girls in the first place. They had only begun to notice and respect her once all the boys began to notice her too. And these two things just did not go together.

One night in winter. There was ice in the streets, and Christmas was over but lights were still strung around the windows and doors and hedges, most of them unplugged, and Devon was standing with the others under the streetlight on the sidewalk in front of Bobby's house when Belinda Miles ran up and slapped her across the face. "Stay the fuck away from Victor! You hear me?! I'll fucking *kill* you!"

Bobby grabbed her and pulled her back, and Luke was laughing, four or five others too, girls and guys, though Trina was staring at Devon from under the streetlight. She wore a fake fur coat with a fake fur hood, her made-up face inside it all shadow. The next day Devon got a text from her.

People are talking.

So.

U cant do shit with hooked up guys.

I didn't know about Vic.

For real?

He told me they broke up.

It'd been the week between Christmas and New Year's, every night a party, and they were parked in Victor's F-150 behind the beer store in Lafayette Square. Victor sat behind the wheel holding the cash he'd collected from everyone. He was Puerto Rican and had a fake ID and always smelled like a cologne nobody else ever wore, sweet and spicy. It made Devon think of palm trees and swimming pools. He was also quiet and polite, and he sat there telling her that nobody at school was as *bonita* as she was. His truck's windows were fogged up. A car's headlights swept through them, then away. He ran one finger along her cheek.

"What about Belinda?"

"We're all done with that."

Then they were kissing and then he was no longer quiet or polite, his hand on the back of her head, his moans so loud she was embarrassed for him. After, she stayed in the truck while he went inside for the beer. She wiped at her mouth. She wanted something to drink. She wanted to go back to when he was calling her the most *bonita* girl in school, and she wanted to stay there, in that moment, just a little while longer.

Victor dropped two thirty-packs into the snow in the bed of his truck, and he climbed in behind the wheel and started the engine without looking at her.

Devon said, "I need a beer."

"You can wait." And he said it without a smile. No sweet calm in him, just some kind of regret and it was all her fault.

T: You need a boyfriend, D.

Just before winter break, Devon saw a boy walking across the plowed student parking lot under the cold sun. He was holding the handle of a guitar case covered with decals and bumper stickers, and the only one Devon could read was: *Kill Your TV.* He was skinny and wore skinny jeans and a ratty dungaree jacket, his hair longer than hers, and there was something about how he moved through the lot of cars starting up and pulling away like they weren't even there, the way he stepped over the guardrail and walked in his sneakers over frozen snow into the bare woods, his hair, his guitar, the way he could turn his back on them all so easily.

Devon was smoking a Merit up against the brick wall waiting for Trina, who had her own car now, and when she walked up, all shiny hair and tired eyes and breasts in a sweater, Devon said, "Who's that kid?"

She pointed to the boy with the guitar disappearing into the woods. Trina shrugged. "Who cares? Sick Something, I know that. Who'd fucking want to be called *Sick?*"

A buzz against Devon's hip. Old Zeppelin in her head. She leans the vacuum handle against the bureau and wedges her fingers into her front pocket and holds her iEverything close to her sweating face.

Sick: If u say so D.

Like it's still two years ago and she's blowing smoke out the side of her mouth and watching him and his guitar case get lost in the bare trunks and bare branches and all she wants to do is meet that kid.

If u say so D.

He doesn't believe her. She stands there staring at his words. He doesn't believe her, and he doesn't hurt anymore that he doesn't believe her, and she wants to write something, but what? She lifts her thumbs. They hover over the glass like snake heads. A new song, that old man Plant young again and in tight bell-bottoms, his shirt open, his blond hair curly long, and he's singing slow that he's working from seven to eleven every night, so tired there's no blood left in him, and it was Sick who gave her these headphones, Sick who showed her how music all day in her head could save her. Her thumbs drop to the glass, and she's going to type U *don't believe me but u should.* Just that. But her iEverything buzzes in her palm like an egg hatching, and there, in the upper right corner, is a new one she opens, Sick's falling away:

Is this u? Cuz this is me, the man who can't stop seeing your face in his head.

An electric guitar is piercing her and it's all wrong now and she'll fix it in a second, she will, her insides rising up past the gray music for the bright news in her hand, her thumbs going to work.

THE RAIN'S BEEN COMING DOWN for five straight days, and Francis stands at the French doors staring out at it. The ground is saturated. In the center of his yard a brown pool is dimpled with what keeps falling, and he worries about Beth's flowers. What if they drown? That's possible, isn't it? For a plant to get too much of a good thing? His right knee hurts. It always does in weather like this. Ever since the front of his car had cracked the house's foundation and the fire-fighters had to use the Jaws of Life to pry the steering column off his crushed knee. The poor woman inside that house had been baking pies. Thank God he was out for all of it. Beth at home after the hospital, how fortunate he was to have a nurse for a wife all those weeks he lay in bed on his back.

His insurance from the school paid for visiting help, but she wouldn't hear of it. She switched her shifts to overnights so she could be home with him, and how efficient she was. She brought him meals just before he became hungry, his water glass always full, his urinal clean and empty, and when Francis had to use the bedpan she helped to turn him on his side just an inch shy of the pain that could fire up from his new knee and fractured calf bone and pinned ankle till she could wedge the pan under him. She knew to leave without a word, and that first time she cleaned him, his stench in the air, Francis's face had burned. But when she was done she held the bedpan as if it did not hold what it did, and she'd leaned down and kissed his forehead and said, "I've done this more times than you've taught classes, honey."

It was a side of her he'd never quite seen before, skilled warmth tied to total competence in all she did for him. It left him feeling both grateful and unworthy, which increased over the weeks of his convalescence when she just did not do what he feared she ultimately would: shame him for having gotten drunk, for crashing his car, for endangering the lives of whoever could have been on that boulevard or in that house on Thanksgiving Eve. Instead she treated him as if he'd already shamed himself and she didn't have to; she treated him as an injured and afflicted man she did not want to lose.

"I'm too young to be a widow, Francis." Those were her only words of admonishment, and they came that first day in the hospital when he opened his eyes to see his right leg in a sling suspended from a metal frame over his bed, an IV tube taped to his left arm. Beth's eyes were dry, but her face looked soft with a pain she would not show him.

George was there too, his tie loosened above the vest of his three-piece suit. He'd been gaining weight over the years, and his cheeks looked pink and shaved too closely. He held up a thick blue hardcover.

"It's *The Big Book*, knucklehead. Read it."

And Francis did. One horrible story of drunken loss after another. But the only power he needed to surrender himself to was his unabated fear and remorse. There were his eyes opening to that jarring bump over the curb, the looming corner of that house, the splintering pain of his convalescence—no more.

Never.

Ever again.

The week after February vacation, his crutch snug under his arm, he relieved his sub at the school. She was a dutiful and officious young woman less than a year out of college, and she looked disappointed to give him back the reins. He patted her shoulder and told her he'd be more than happy to write her a letter of recommendation. He was more than happy in many ways.

There was the light-shouldered feeling he'd come close to his own execution but had somehow been given a reprieve he did not deserve but would take anyway. He would also take the daily rides to and from school, his driver's license revoked until the following Thanksgiving. Usually it was Beth and occasionally George. For a week or two it was Rita Flaherty or the new young science teacher who drove a Mustang and called him Mr. B. Toward the end of that school year, though, it was his sister-in-law Evelyn who drove him in her own matching Seville.

Those first few mornings and afternoons, sitting beside her in the leather comfort of the passenger seat as Evelyn drove, Francis would chat about whatever came up for he was surprised to find he felt shy around George's wife. For thirty-two years, he would only see her at restaurant dinners or perhaps a wedding or funeral, usually through the smeared prism of his weekend drunks. As Evelyn accelerated up the highway, Francis's crutch on the backseat where she'd laid it, he was twenty-one again, home from the war, living in George's house while Evelyn served him meatloaf and scrutinized him more than once as he played a game with little Charlie or held the baby, and in Evelyn's quiet presence behind the wheel Francis felt caught, though why should he? He *was* caught. Everything was known and he was paying for it dearly. But in the midafternoon light, as she drove and he prattled on about one thing or another, mainly his various students and their varying troubles, he would glance over at his sister-in-law and take her in.

She was five years older than he but looked younger. She'd never been a smoker or a drinker, and except for some looseness around her eyes and under her chin, there'd been few changes in her face over the past three decades. Her hair had just begun to thin, and it was freshly styled and still auburn, the gray either colored or removed, Francis did not know. She wore a skirt and blouse, a silk scarf pinned across one shoulder, one of George's gold gifts around her wrists and hanging from her ears, for rarely did she leave her house looking any different. But what he'd failed to ever notice is that Evelyn *listened* to people. On those rides that spring and a few times that fall, she certainly listened to *him.*

He would just begin to feel he was filling her car with useless noise and she'd say, "Did that girl who wrote the abortion essay ever tell you it was her?" His sister-in-law would have both hands on the wheel, her eyes on the road, her chin raised slightly in a pose of easy alertness, and Francis would nod and say, "No, Evelyn, she never did."

Uttering her name like that had felt more intimate than he'd intended. Francis would quickly fill in the silence after it because he *did* feel closer to Evelyn than he had before.

Only a few years later he stood beside her in Comeau's funeral parlor, his arm around her shoulders as they stared down into the open casket. They were just minutes from the start of calling hours, the place too quiet, George too still, his cheeks too pink, his hands crossed over themselves in a gesture of humility he had never once made in life. Charlie had rested a Red Sox cap near his father's shoulder, and Francis could hear his nephew out in the front room talking loudly to the funeral director, something to do with the board of selectmen, and in Charlie's voice Francis could hear the mild panic of the boy thrust fully from the shadows into the sun, both his hands on the helm of a ship he still was not certain he knew how to sail.

Evelyn was crying so softly her shoulders barely moved. Francis pulled her closer. He handed her a tissue and kissed the top of her head. He loved her. In that moment, he did. His brother's widow, his nephew and niece's mother, his steadfast friend and driver through the year of his redemption; it was his turn to help *her*.

But had he?

No, not really. By then the Sunday dinners at Charlie and Marie's were already fading and becoming more sporadic, and it was Beth who spent some time with Evelyn. Beth who would meet her for coffee or lunch and once invited her over to their house on a Sunday. Such a stark afternoon. Just the three of them quietly eating pork roast and sweet potatoes at the small table, a yard full of dead leaves on the other side of the French doors. Small talk. Beth pouring Evelyn more wine. Without George, it was as if the thick barnacled chain that joined them had sunk to the bottom of the sea and all Francis and Beth could do was watch Evelyn drift away from them over the whitecaps.

She's eighty-six now, living in Brookwood on Whittier Lake. He should call her. No, he should visit. Perhaps this weekend.

Devon's bedroom door opens and then she's standing in the kitchen smiling at him. Her red headphones lie hooked around her neck, but her hair is brushed back, and she's wearing makeup and small silver hoop earrings, her nose stud gone. She looks happier than he's seen her in months.

"You look very pretty, Devy."

"You look sad."

"No, no, it's just my knee."

"You still okay to drive me to work?"

The rain. He offered through her door, and she'd yelled *Thank you!* Then that boy's voice in her machine, like an echo in an empty room. *Is that him?*

Yeah. He was in a war, too.

Francis wanted to hear more. He had never spoken to Devon about any of that. But family talked about family, didn't they? Maybe Charlie had told her about her grandfather and grand-uncle. Yes, that was probably it.

*Devon darlin', do you really wanna leave me and go to **work**?*

You know I don't. I'll text you on my break, okay?

Devon darling. No more Sarah. Francis had turned and walked back down the hallway, his right knee buckling slightly at the kitchen's threshold. The entire week of rain, when she wasn't at work she was in her room talking to that young man on her machine, leaving it and him only for the bathroom or to eat quickly at the table with Francis, forking her macaroni and cheese into her mouth, smiling over at him while she chewed, or gazing out the French doors at some sweet story unfolding in her head. Francis had seen it over and over again, the girl in the corner whose new radiance shines not from the boy who has found her but from the chance to direct all the love that's been pooling inside her and now it's a warm flowing stream and everything her eyes fall upon is beautiful to her, even her great-uncle standing there ashamed of himself; part of him feels she has not earned any of this, just stumbled upon it, and did she just stumble upon filming herself sexually as well? This new judgment of her, he's had it all week. Every time she enters a room or leaves it, he tries not to see but *does* see the blond prostitute kneeling between the young executive's knees, Charlie drunk and laughing it up behind him, his daughter still nascent dust somewhere.

"You okay?"

"Take the car, Devy. I should have put you on my insurance by now anyway."

"Really?"

"Really." He pulls the keys from its hook beside the telephone. Beth's keys hang an inch away, her five-year-old Corolla still sitting in the garage.

Then Devon's arms are around his neck and she kisses him twice on the cheek just beneath his eye. There are the heartbreaking scents of her shampoo and makeup and ironed cotton blouse, and he stands at the living room window and watches her run under the rain to his car, the lights and wipers coming on, his Buick back-

ing slowly and carefully out into the street. He should just give it
to her. No, that's an old man's car. What he should do is give her
Beth's Corolla. Perhaps Monday morning he'll look into the paperwork of doing just that. He could have done it sooner, of course. He
could have put Devon on his insurance policy so she could drive
herself to and from work on weekend nights, but then she wouldn't
need him, would she?

Last night, at their dinner of fish sticks, French fries, and peas,
all frozen dishes he'd heated up in the oven and on the stove, Devy
had squirted ketchup onto her plate and said, "Want me to write that
essay tomorrow?" She asked this lightly, no dread anywhere.

"No, honey, let's take a break for a bit."

"Why?" She was looking at him, chewing. Her hair was getting
longer. She had one strand of it tucked behind her ear, and in her eyes
was that same hungry curiosity she'd had as a child.

"I don't want to force you to do something you don't want to do,
Devy."

"Who says I don't want to do it?"

"You." He smiled. "Last Friday."

"Yeah, I guess."

He reached over and patted her shoulder. "You're a smart young
woman. Go back to school when *you* want to."

She nodded and chewed and looked out the French doors into the
rain. "I'm just kind of surprised. You seemed so into it."

"*You* need to be into it, not me."

Devon shrugged and sipped her water and stood to scrape and
wash her plate. She seemed disappointed and she seemed relieved.
Is that what she's gonna do her whole life? Be somebody's fucking chambermaid?
Charlie's fingers pulling at his napkin, his hunched shoulders. Francis hadn't told Devon he'd met with him. Above the running of the
faucet, he turned his head and said, "Have you heard anything from
your dad?"

"No. Why should I?"

Francis nodded and said nothing, for what was there to say?

Out the living room window rain splatters onto his concrete driveway and the street beyond, its culvert a rushing stream. Another quiet night ahead. The newspaper. The tap and slide of stacking the cards of solitaire on Beth's computer. Maybe tea and some Brahms on the record player. Murderers of time until he climbs behind the wheel of his car and drives the few blocks to The Whaler to pick up his Devy and bring her home. But now he's had a hand in squashing his own joy in that, hasn't he?

As he should. She's eighteen. Old enough to vote for the president. Old enough to be shipped overseas with an M2 carbine she'd only learned how to shoot weeks earlier. That first boy, how the blood sprayed from his startled throat, how his body fell as if it had never held life at all.

This won't do. Francis lowers himself into his chair, his knee aching all the way down. He picks up the phone and holds his glasses to his eyes and punches in 411. There is a taped voice in Spanish. All the countries of the world slipping one into the other. Then, of all things, a woman is speaking directly to him in English. He tells her the city and he tells her the state and then he tells her what he wants, which is the number for Brookwood Retirement Home, please. The one on Whittier Lane.

DEVON SITS IN the booth near the kitchen door folding a stack of linen napkins. The rain is whipping against the windows, and there are only two tables taken on the floor, and Devon hopes Danny will let her leave early. He's already sent Rayna and two waitresses home. Any bussing Dotty can do. She's been waiting tables here since Reagan was president, whenever that was. Danny wouldn't like it, but her iEverything is on the seat beside her and she keeps glancing down at it in case Hollis texts her.

Hollis. His name is like a cool damp cloth over hot skin. It's the title of her favorite book and her favorite movie and her favorite CD. It's what she would call anything good for her.

Last night, the way he jumped when his mother slammed a door. He had on a white T-shirt that made him look smaller, and there were dark whiskers across his chin and throat. He tried to shrug it off, but he looked scared. She said: "Is that what you mean?"

He nodded, his eyes on hers through the screen.

"Were you like that before?"

He shook his head.

"Shouldn't you talk to somebody about it?"

"I'm talking to you, Devon."

The way he said her name. *Devahn*. Like there was so much more to her than there was. That's how he made her feel all day and all night long, that she had a purpose, one that went deeper than hair and skin and spit. This started on Sunday, just as soon as she got home from The Whaler and Skyped him. They began talking deep right away. It was hard not to feel she'd known him in another place and time, maybe another country, like the one he kept talking about, how hot it'd been, how bad it had smelled.

"I can't describe it, Devon. Shit in the rivers. Trash fires. Rotting donkey carcasses. Sheep and dogs. And—you know—"

"What?"

"The dead."

"People?"

"You okay with this?"

"Yeah."

"You sure you okay with this?"

"Yes, Hollis." His name a key to a rusty lock sitting at the bottom of some well inside her. And he kept asking her about her.

"Why'd you quit school? Couldn't take all the bullshit no more?"

"No, I couldn't."

"You're so pretty. I'm sorry, but them boys must've been *all* over you."

"Just one." Her face hot with the lie though she kept seeing Sick, the side of his face as he slept beside her, his short nose and parted lips, the blond down on his cheeks that looked so young and boyish compared to what Hollis had. She said: "Nobody sees you for real there. I got tired of it."

"Say that again." He held his face in his hands. It was like he either really needed to hear something or was praying he wouldn't.

"What?"

"About people seeing you. Say that again."

"Nobody sees you for real?"

He nodded, dropped his hands. She could hear the slap of bare skin on bare skin, and she pictured him in shorts or his underwear. Something opened up behind her abdomen and she felt shy.

"It gets hard to be called a hero when you know you ain't."

She wanted to ask what he meant by that, but it seemed like the wrong question or that asking a question at all seemed wrong, so she just nodded and he changed the subject and started talking about how he couldn't keep a job, that he'd be fine for a while and then he wouldn't. One was pouring concrete for foundations, but the man he worked with, a Mexican, looked too much like a hajji.

"I knew he wasn't, but I just couldn't be around that black hair of his and that brown skin of his under that hot sun. Does that sound bad?"

"No." She wanted to say it sounded honest.

His eyes were narrowed on her like she was some bright light visited upon him.

"I done some bad things over there."

"Everybody's done bad things."

"Not you."

Devon didn't say anything, but she felt a little pissed off and didn't know why till she said, "Don't make me somebody I'm not, okay?"

He nodded. He lit a cigarette and blew out the smoke. She wanted to take the cigarette from his lips with two fingers and put it to hers.

She'd almost felt like that with Sick, but this was different. This was like meeting herself in the skin of a boy.

"You're strong, Devon. You're so damn *strong*."

It's not a word she would have ever used on herself, but hearing it from him she believed it. Or started to anyway.

Danny Sullivan stands at her booth. His hair is wet. So are the shoulders of his black button-down shirt he keeps untucked over his gut like he's twenty years younger than he is. He pushes his glasses up his nose, and she can see he needs to wipe off the lenses.

"You can punch out when you're done with those. You need a ride?"

"No, I have my uncle's car."

"You do?"

"Yeah." She keeps her eyes on the linen she's folding because she just knows he's checking out her breasts.

You're so damn **strong**.

She makes herself glance back up at him. He's not looking at her breasts, he's looking at her working hands. "He and your aunt used to come in here quite a bit. Everybody was shocked when she went."

"Yeah."

"He holding up all right?"

"I think so."

"He's lucky to have you there, kid."

"I guess."

"There's no guessing about it. He *is*, believe me." Danny turns to leave. "Careful driving home, hon."

She thanks him and likes him in that moment, but he also leaves her feeling bad. *He's lucky to have you there, kid.* Because she can feel the end of that up ahead somewhere. It's like driving at night and knowing a car's coming over a rise, even though you haven't seen its lights yet.

Two nights before, Hollis told her about his father's father and how a long time ago he left them all some land and Hollis has always been entitled to his nine acres. Then this morning, Skyping him just as soon as she'd peed and brushed her teeth and hair, he said: "I got that Airstream, Devon. Everything works good on it, too. There's some big old cottonwoods on the brook, and I'm gonna put her there in the shade and fish for my damn supper."

His mother had yelled then, her voice coming through the wall and Devon's screen two thousand miles north. They were like the sounds you remember from a bad dream.

"She yelling at her husband?"

"'Fraid so."

"Why didn't you buy that trailer a long time ago?"

"Had to save up my D-checks."

She just looked at him.

"Disability." He glanced down and away. She almost asked him where he was hurt, but she knew the answer and felt stupid. All that jumpiness. The bad dreams. She'd heard how so many soldiers come back like that. She wanted to help him with it. She did.

Across the floor, a woman laughs. Devon picks up the last napkin and looks over at her sitting with a man, a coffee cup in front of them both, a dessert in the middle of the table they seem to be sharing. It looks like he's telling her a story, and they're wearing matching T-shirts and they look happy.

She stands and pushes her iEverything into her front pants pocket. She finishes folding the last napkin, rests it on the pile with the others, then picks it up to carry to the bussing station, her heart already kicking up as she pictures herself hanging Francis's keys on the hook in the kitchen, giving him a peck on the cheek, rushing into her room to sit on her bed and open her laptop and go back to where she wants to be all the time now. With Hollis Waters, his full name a present he gave her just today. Hollis Waters. It sounds like a real place on a real map. Relaxed and warm and nowhere you'd ever want to leave in a hurry.

FRANCIS IS SITTING at Beth's computer in the dining room researching restaurants. It's what Beth would do. Read reviews and take a virtual tour of the place. For his lunch with Evelyn, he wants some place one step above casual but below formal, and he wants it in town, perhaps on the river where there used to be mills but no longer.

Evelyn's voice has not aged much. If she hadn't told Francis she'd failed her eye test and could no longer drive, he would have forgotten he was talking to an old woman.

"I suppose you'll have to drive *me* this time, Francis."

"That's only fair. I'll pick you up for lunch."

She invited him to eat at Brookwood, but he imagined a dining room full of cheerily dressed widows and a few sputtering men his age or even younger, and it was as if he was suddenly holding one foot over a swirling black whirlpool and he politely insisted on taking her out instead.

The truth is, he has not given this kind of thing enough thought on purpose. Two nights ago on his way to the bathroom at three in the morning, the rain drumming the roof shingles above, his knee had buckled and he'd pitched sideways into his bureau and just missed a fall onto the hardwood floor. Doug Richards, the vice principal for years, fell at seventy-eight and broke his hip and ended up in assisted living and never busted out. Died there two years later staring into his applesauce.

So many stories like that. Too many. But some things you simply do not think about until you must. Those months of convalescence nearly thirty years ago. Beth, his breezy and energetic nurse. Younger than he was, a moderate drinker and never a smoker. It was natural to glimpse her decades later spoon-feeding him in his last hours, Francis Brandt dying at home in his bed with his wife beside him.

Francis taps the enter button a little too hard. He watches a promotional video for a restaurant called The Tap, one that specializes in prime cuts and microbrews, and he likes the tall booths and the green glass sconces in the walls and the pressed tin ceiling above, but he feels mildly guilty. Is it because he's using his wife's computer to find a place to take Evelyn to lunch? He shakes this silliness away like a hovering mosquito and is writing down the number of the restaurant when there comes a knocking on the door.

No one ever knocks at that door. Something dark flutters through Francis's chest, and he pushes himself from the table and stands. He pictures a police officer under the exterior light, Devon hurt, his car turned over in the wet street.

It's Charlie. Under the light, his face is beaded with rain, his collar unbuttoned, his tie loosened, and in his eyes is the unfocused focus of a drunk.

"Sheeome, Uncle?"

Sheeome. For a millisecond, Francis isn't sure of what he's just heard.

"Come in, Charlie."

In the bright kitchen, Francis switches on the burner beneath the water kettle. Charlie stands near the table, his hands at his sides, and even though Francis is taller, he feels slight in his nephew's beefy, drunken presence. "Tea, Charlie?"

"Where's she sleep?"

"Guest room down the hall." Francis is about to say more, that it's good he's here but he should probably come back when he's sober, something like that, but Charlie is already halfway down the hall and Francis is following him.

"Charlie?"

Charlie opens the door and walks into a room that surprises Francis. Devon has left the bathroom light on and it casts itself across the ironing board and unmade bed, clothes strewn around the floor.

"Yep," Charlie says. "Same old, same old." He sits on the edge of Devon's bed and pulls her computer onto his lap and opens it.

"Charlie, we're going back to the kitchen now." Francis steps forward. He's holding out his hand as if to take the fingers of a child. "Come on, Charlie. This is Devon's room."

"Yeah? She paying fucking *rent*, Uncle?" Charlie's eyes are on the screen before him, his face lighted by its glow. He taps keys, waits, then taps a few more. "There we are. Isn't that nice. Take a look, Uncle. See for yourself."

Before Francis can turn and leave, Charlie has pivoted the screen on his lap and there is Devon's lovely face, her eyes closed, her cheek concave as she sucks—the hallway is a dark tunnel Francis cannot get through fast enough, that hot flat light on the pines above those men and boys digging as if their hope itself was digging, then that first shot before that terrible, cracking barrage of denial—Francis hasn't yelled in years, has he ever yelled? For what comes out of him now feels so underused he fears he has only yelled in his dreams, running from Hunt's jeep to stop what Francis's own people had only filmed.

"You hear me, Charlie?! Get out of my goddamned *house!*" Francis has to steady himself with one hand on the table. Down the hallway Charlie moves slowly, unevenly, a blocky figure in a Brooks Brothers shirt and dark tie. Then he's standing in the light of the kitchen and there's the low whine of the water coming to a boil on the stove.

"What's the matter, Uncle? Can't take it?"

"Get out, Charlie."

"Can't take your sweet little Devy doing that? Well try being her *father.*"

Francis's eyes ache. The sides of his head pulse.

"You think you're better than me, Francis? Do you? *I* raised her, *you* didn't. You read her a story once a week, that's all *you* did. And she's living with *you?* Give me a fucking break."

The water is shrieking now and Charlie begins to smile, his eyes dark and on something beyond Francis. He turns to switch off the burner, to do at least that, and there Devon stands in the doorway to the living room, her red headphones resting around her neck, her hair sticking to her scalp, her blouse wet enough Francis can see the white strap of her bra. She nods in the direction of her father. "What are you doing here?"

"I could ask the same of you, couldn't I? What *are* you doing here?

Freeloading off an old man? *Using* people? Is that all you're ever gonna do with your life, Devon? Be a fucking *tramp*."

"Fuck you." Devon turns and what happens next happens as dreams happen, Charlie lunging across the kitchen with the speed a drunk should not have, the thrust of Francis's lower leg, how his foot catches his nephew's ankle and then Charlie's arms and chest and belly slap the living room rug and the front door slams and Charlie lets out a groan, Francis's Buick starting up and pulling away.

There's a twinge in Francis's right knee. He has to lean against the stove.

"You all right, Charlie?"

His nephew rolls onto his side. He's breathing heavily and his shirt is opened. His belly rises and falls, and the hair around his navel is George's hair, George's navel.

"I should kick your ass, Francis."

"Looks to me like you keep kicking your own ass."

Charlie props himself up with one arm. His tie hangs along his shoulder, and his eyes are on the rug under the lamp table. He shakes his head. "Nobody's kicking my ass."

He sounds defeated. Francis allows what he just said to hang in the air. He switches the fire back on under the kettle. "I'm making you some tea."

"I don't want any fucking tea."

"I'm not asking you, Charlie. And if you try to drive away from here I'm calling the cops."

Charlie looks up at him from the floor. His cheeks are flushed, his hair dyed and thinning, but Francis sees the boy he used to be, the one who always seemed to be pushing at invisible walls around him, searching for the one that might actually stop him.

"I fucked up, Uncle. I really fucked up."

"Who doesn't?"

Francis steps over and holds out his hand. Charlie stares at it, measuring whether or not he's being insulted. Then he reaches for it, and Francis braces his knees, ignores the burn in his right, and pulls.

IT'S AFTER TWO when Devon steers back into Francis's driveway. She drove by it once to make sure her father's car was gone, and when she saw it was she could also see the light still on in the kitchen. So was the one over the door, and she pictured her Uncle Francis sitting up waiting for her. She felt bad about that. But it was her father's fault, not hers.

She'd known that was his Lexus as soon as her lights lit it up in the rain, and maybe she'd been too much under the influence of Hollis Waters because she'd felt strong and like someone you might actually respect and so for a few minutes she actually thought her father had come to see how she was doing. That maybe he even missed her.

But how stupid could she be? Did she forget it was a Friday night? Did she forget that was her father's excuse to drink till he could hardly lift his hand to his face anymore?

Tramp.

That's just never going to go away, is it? Those first ten or twenty miles up the highway it had hurt all over again, his judgment of her, his hatred. All the good she'd been trying to do and build—work, save money, quit smoking, keep her room and clothes clean, spend time with Francis and work on her GED, and now Hollis (something beautiful that has come from her only bad habit, her nightly roulette around the world)—it was all swept down a street drain.

But then she jerked on her Dr. Dre's and found something live, one boy white, the other black, and they were shout-singing about being rene*gades*, and Devon hadn't driven on the highway for months and it felt good to be moving fast into her own light up the wet asphalt, the windshield wipers slapping away the rain, and she wanted to slap her father's fucking face because the only thing that was really gone was *him*, and what was she losing anyway? The clacking of his golf cleats across the kitchen floor? Those tiny purple veins that had started to show on his cheeks? His quiet cruelty to her mother? How his eyes passed over her hair and round face and big body like she was an exit off a road he wished he'd never taken? Was Devon going to miss the way he'd started to look at his own daughter as she stood at the kitchen island eating a yogurt? Like something good had shown up in his house that was only supposed to be in other houses, like Amanda Salvi's condo behind the gym off the highway? Was Devon going to miss seeing her father on Salvi's Fuckbook page? Drunk and shirtless under the sun, his arm around her? His stubby fingers inches away from her left breast? Would Devon miss his stack of *Penthouse* magazines on the toilet her mother must feel against her back every time she peed? And would Devon miss her father's spit flying out of his mouth as he condemned her for being everything he was always sniffing after? Just not his own flesh and blood? His own living little girl?

North of Portsmouth, Devon exited the highway and pulled into a Dunkin' Donuts drive-through. In her head, a deep-voiced boy was lying on his prison cot counting his money from memory, thinking about the ride he would own when he got out. *And I know you'll be waitin' fuh me. I know you will.*

The rain had lightened up. Devon pulled off her headphones and leaned out her open window to shout her order into the intercom. Above it was a lighted panel of color photos of bagels with eggs and cheese, and she ordered one and a black coffee with three sugars. The girl at the window was pale and skinny, maybe a year younger than Devon, but as Devon handed her a ten she felt so much older than this girl.

Hollis. He was twenty-seven. Twenty-seven and an ex-soldier and in love with *her.*

"How do you know that?"

"I've been around the world, Devon. I *know.*"

The words came out of her almost on their own. "Me too."

"You just saying that?"

"I never just say anything."

He'd nodded and reached his hand out till it darkened the screen. "I need to touch your face."

Her skin tingled hot and she wanted to say the same thing back.

Hollis said: "Is that all right?"

She'd nodded. A knocking came, Uncle Francis's voice through the door. "It's raining hard, Devy. Need a ride to work?"

The skinny girl in the window handed Devon her coffee and then her bagel in a warm bag, and Devon parked Francis's car and ate quickly, her headphones still around her ears. Hollis told her it'd be a week or more before he got electricity out to his trailer, but it was too far out in the country for the Internet. He'd have to drive into town and park outside the library that had WiFi, sit in his truck and Skype her that way.

And they could talk on the phone.

"But I need to see you, Devon."

"Me too."

"No, I mean *see* you."

"Me too, Hollis." She loved using his name while she was looking at him. It was like sealing an important envelope and dropping it into a mailbox. But it was late and she hadn't even ironed her work clothes yet, and when she told him she had to go he looked a little surprised and hurt. Later, folding linen napkins at the restaurant, Devon wished she hadn't talked about work right after he told her he needed to see her. She *did* want to see him, too. She did.

Francis's front door is unlocked. Devon lets herself in, then turns the deadbolt and thinks of her father as she does it, sees his drunk, mean smile before he laid into her. Francis's living room feels so small to her, his kitchen too. On the table under the light are two empty mugs, a plate of crumpled teabags beside two spoons. At first it's like seeing something impossible, a tiger in your bathtub, a fish swimming in your bed. Francis's bedroom door is open an inch, and there's the urge to step in there and wake him up and ask him if he really sat down and drank tea with Charlie fucking Brandt? But it's clear he did, and now her belly lifts and twists because please tell me my father did not tell Uncle Francis anything about me. Please tell me they talked about any fucking thing else.

Her heart beats the taste of old coffee up into her mouth, and she hits the switch of the overhead light. The dark hallway feels short and narrow. A dull glow comes from under her closed door. Uncle Francis? Is he in her *room*? She pushes the door open and steps inside, but her room looks as she left it, her bed unmade, her shorts and T-shirt she tossed on the floor under the ironing board because she had to dress fast for work. She doesn't remember leaving the bathroom light on. It would be so wrong if her uncle was in there, but he's not. The shower curtain is open, and her mascara, eyeliner, and blush lie on the lid of the toilet tank, her toothbrush and toothpaste behind the faucet on the sink. She lets out a long, shaky breath and wants to Skype Hollis right now, see if he's up like he usually is, and she's stepping toward the door to close it when she sees her laptop. It's not closed on her pillow where she left it. It's on the edge of the bed and it's open, its screen dark and facing her, facing her and the room and her open door like a big text that's just come in and must be opened; it must be opened right now.

It was summer and Devon was eight or nine. They were all at the beach, her mother and father, her Uncle Tony and Aunt Veronica and their three kids, Devon's cousins. The grownups were sitting or lying on a blanket on the sand, talking and laughing, and Devon's mother looked pretty in a maroon bathing suit with a skirt over her hips. Her father and Uncle Tony were drinking from cans of beer. There was a dune behind them and Devon was running up it in the hot sand, her feet burning, the sun in her eyes, and she couldn't see the top but there was tall grass there where she and her cousins were going to hide, and just as she got to the ridge, there came Steve's mean voice, "Not you, Devon." Then his hands pushing against her bare shoulders and she was falling backwards, rolling down that hot dune where she almost hit her head on a piece of wood. There was Steve's laughter in the air, grown-up voices talking as if nothing had just happened to her, the waves smashing and sucking back. She would have to start all over again. But why? So Steve could do it to her again and again?

Her face took up the whole screen and Devon had tapped buttons so hard and fast the image froze and she slammed her laptop shut and flipped it across the mattress. Her father. Her fucking asshole piece-of-shit mean father. His only message to her. His only thought about her now. His two hands pushing her shoulders and watching her fall, and did he even think about how hard she'd been climbing? And did he show this to Uncle *Francis*? The thought was like a coat hanger being pulled through her guts, Francis seeing her do that. *Did* he? Did her father fucking *show* him that?

But why else would he leave it on her screen like that? Facing her door like that? It was a message from both of them. A warning. A punishment.

But not Francis. *Please.* Not her great-uncle who before anyone else had always, always looked at her with kindness, his eyes full of love and respect. With him, she never felt small, only big, only that, and that's why she'd called *him* in the middle of the night last March. Because she knew he would not make her feel worse than she already did. Because she knew he would help her just by being Uncle Francis.

But she can't even look at him now. How can she wake up tomorrow and walk out into that kitchen and see him? His stooped shoulders, his glasses hanging around his neck. The real smile he always has ready for her? She can't. She won't.

For a long time she stands in her room and does nothing. The ceiling feels too low, the walls close. She stares at her upside-down laptop on the other side of her mattress. She walks over and opens it and avoids the screen and taps buttons till it goes dark. She closes it. Bobby Connors. If he hadn't been there, Trina might not have posted what she did, sending it to everyone, including Amanda Salvi who showed her boyfriend, Charlie Brandt.

Big, sweet Bobby just like everyone else. No, *worse*.

Devon had called Bobby from the house phone. He'd had to cover his own phone and tell someone to shut up so he could hear. *Yeah,* he said, *Luke says it's at his house. We're just getting out of practice. Want us to come pick you up?*

Us.

It was late on a Saturday morning, warm for March, but there were still patches of snow on the ground, the sun shining on the bare branches, and it almost made her feel better when Bobby's Sentra pulled up in front of her house. Saturday was her father's sleep-it-off morning. Walking by his Lexus in the driveway, Amanda Salvi's naked picture newly branded into Devon's brain, she felt like kicking a dent in it. She'd almost thrown her father's phone across the room, but instead she left it on the kitchen island where she'd picked it up, left the picture of Amanda on it, too. Her mother was out shopping and if she found it when she came home, well then she fucking found it.

And there they were. Bobby behind the wheel, Luke in the front, Davey Price in the back. She didn't know him well, but he reached across the backseat and opened the door for her. She climbed into the thump of gangsta rap and the smells of shampoo and Axe and Luke's wintergreen gum. Bobby drove off before she'd barely pulled the door shut, and all three boys' hair were wet and Bobby had a Red Sox cap on sideways. She noticed he'd shaved his chin strap. He looked younger but more handsome.

"How's it goin', Dev?" Davey was pouring beer from a can into a Dunkin' Donuts cup, handing it to her. It wasn't even noon yet, but Davey had one of his own between his legs and she took it.

"Bobby, where's Trina?"

"Yeah, *Bobby*," Luke said from the front. "Where's your little *wifey* today?"

"Fuck you, McDonough." Bobby sipped from his own Dunkin's

cup. Luke was laughing and Bobby turned up the music, a kid yelling he's gonna kill anything movin'. Davey's cup touched hers. She
glanced at him and he smiled, his eyebrows raised as if he'd just told
a joke and now was the time to laugh. He drank from his beer and so
she did, too. It was cold and didn't taste bad. She was a little hungover
from the night before. She remembered her cheek against Luke's
shoulder. His arm had been around her, his hand heavy but sweet on
her hip, like maybe he loved her once and didn't want anything bad
to happen to her. He'd had three more girlfriends after her, and she'd
had what she'd had. They were ancient news.

She drank from her beer. She had to squint at the sun shining
through the windows. Bobby gunned his Sentra onto the highway
and he was bopping his head to a new song now, the rap about the
boy who kills his girlfriend for getting pregnant, and Devon wanted
him to switch to something different. Davey Price was talking to her.
She turned to him and had to raise her voice. *"What?"*

"You runnin' track this season?"

She shook her head. That had ended sophomore year when she'd
started smoking Merits because she liked how it killed her appetite
and how good it felt when she was drinking. Thinking this made her
want one, but she'd left them in her coat from last night. Davey was
wearing tight corduroys. She could see how thick his legs were. He
and Bobby lifted weights together in the off-season and Davey was
bigger and he looked good in shorts beside a pool, but something was
wrong with his face. His chin was too short and his eyes were close
together. It made him look stupid and unlucky and a little mean. He
cracked open a vodka nip, poured half into his cup, then dumped the
rest into hers.

"What the fuck, Davey."

"*Hey*, we've been doin' sprints since six this morning. Downtime,
baby." He smiled and drank, and for a while she just sat there holding
her cup, the bare trees whipping by off the side of the highway, Bobby
tapping two fingers against the wheel while the singer sang about

slashing Cindy's throat and stuffing her in his trunk, the bass thumping fast as a panicky heart. Devon just wanted to get her phone and
go back home and call Sick. She was going to borrow her mother's
car later, and the two of them were going to drive to the mall to see a
movie about the future when only children were left alive. Sick loved
any story about a time that wasn't now, even if it was sad. She should
have just taken her father's car to get her iEverything. He wouldn't
be up for another hour, at least, then he'd start his day in the kitchen
in his open robe mixing himself a glass of beer and V8. Like just
the few sips of beer she'd taken were helping her. Already she didn't
feel so dry and rusty, her thoughts jagged, her tongue dull. Each sip
made her feel oiled and a little lighter, and the vodka made it taste
better, and anyway she didn't want to be anywhere near her father's
car, smelling his smell in it, putting her hands on the wheel he put his
own stinky fucking fingers on.

Bobby took the exit ramp too fast. Devon leaned into Davey and
spilled a splash onto his knee, his shoulder smelling like wool and
Axe and boy.

"*Connors*, we're fuckin' losin' our drinks back here, dude. Ease *up*."
He swatted at the wet spot on his corduroys and smiled at her like he
knew she couldn't help herself. There was a story about him sophomore year. Something about an accident when he was a kid, a friend
of his who got really hurt and his parents blamed Davey. Something
about a bow and arrow and the other boy's spleen. Something bad.

Davey tapped her cup and drank. She sipped from hers. They were
passing big houses set back in the trees. In the bare woods there was
more snow on the ground, but up near the houses there was brown
grass and hedges, no dead leaves or pine needles anywhere. The bass
was thumping so fast it was almost one long note, then it was quiet
and still and the singer was rapping softly about watching his car sink
into the river, his baby and their baby inside. Bobby drained his cup
just before he turned into Luke's driveway. There were tall pine trees
on both sides, Luke's white house rising up ahead like good news. His

father's silver Mercedes was parked in one bay of the open garage, and Devon drank down her vodka beer to hide her cup. She said: "Luke, can I have a piece of gum?"

"I'm out, Dev."

Then they were all leaving Bobby's car and walking quietly into the open garage past Luke's father's car, Luke moving by Bobby to unlock the door into the rec room. It always looked different during the day. Like seeing a movie star with no makeup. The wide-screen TV was off, and so was the fish light over the ping-pong table covered now with neat piles of folded laundry. Out the sliding glass doors the lawn was brown, and the boathouse looked small and damp and dark.

Bobby sat in front of the wide-screen with Davey, the controls already in their hands as *Call of Duty* flared up on the screen, grays and greens and then soldiers running and shooting at each other. Luke handed her a hard lemonade and a nip.

"I don't want to party, Luke. Can I just have my phone, please?"

"It's upstairs. What's your rush?" He grabbed the stereo's remote and then a song was playing from freshman year, that blond country singer who whaled on her cheating boyfriend's car with a baseball bat. Luke looked a way she'd only seen him once or twice, and that was after they'd gone swimming in his pool. Instead of the sideways flow he kept across his forehead, his hair was combed back wet. It made his face look bigger and like a grown man's, like his father who was probably upstairs writing checks for bills or something, and Devon didn't like how Luke was smiling at her, as if they were still together and she was special to him because of what she could do, though she'd never told him he was her first.

He drank down half his hard lemonade, poured the nip in, and handed it to her. "Here, Dev."

"Go get my phone, Luke. I have to go."

"Why? You got plans?"

"Yeah, I do."

"What, with that Sick kid? C'mon, Dev, you can do better than that."

The country singer was hitting her angry-happy notes and there was machine-gun fire from the couch, and Devon just wanted some fucking quiet. "Go get my phone, Luke."

Then she was walking across the brown grass down to the water. The ground felt soft under her, her legs hard and jerky, and she knew she was a little drunk, thinking of Amanda Salvi's ass and tits and smiling face. Devon had met her at a party once. She was the older sister of one of Rick Battastini's friends, this loud chick who laughed too much and worked in a law office, and is that how she met Devon's father? Through their work somehow? And why would she want *him*? Did he spend money on her? Did he promise her things the way they all do? Though what boy had ever promised anything to Devon Brandt? She noticed the hard lemonade bottle was in her hand, and she drank from it and stared out at Whittier Lake through the trees. Way on the other side were tiny houses she knew were as big as this one because only rich people lived on this lake, men taking what they want and leaving the scraps to the rest.

"Here, Dev."

She turned and Luke put her iEverything in her hand. His eyes were on her lips, her chin, her throat, and he looked weak the way he used to. She felt strong and dirty. He put his arm around her. She leaned her head against his shoulder. She wanted to tell him that her father was cheating on her mother. She could almost feel the words rising up to her tongue, but she'd never talked to Luke about anything serious before and she wasn't going to start now. Still, it felt good to have his arm around her. It felt good to rest her cheek on his shoulder. She could feel his muscles under his sweatshirt, and it smelled clean.

"'Member that?" He raised two fingers in the direction of the boathouse. She nodded. She was so young then. Just a kid in the dark in the back of a boat.

"Nobody does it like you, Dev."

"That's nice." She meant for that to come out hard, but it came out soft, and she drank from her bottle and he drank from his. She thought of Sick. They'd waited for spring before they did it. He'd told her spring was his favorite season because dead things stopped being dead and so maybe we should do it then, D. It'll be even better that way.

Luke was kissing the top of her head. He turned and lifted her chin and kissed her lips. It was slow and sweet and she could taste his beer and hard lemonade, his stubble against her chin. It was like tripping and falling onto a pile of leaves, surprised at how they can hold you. She pulled away. "I need to go home, Luke."

"Not yet."

"Can you just drive me right now, please?"

"One last time, okay?"

"No." She put her hand on his chest to push him, but she didn't push him.

"Please, Dev. We're graduating soon and then we're all going to college and it won't be the same, ever." That need for her. It was in his voice again and, for the first time, in his words too. Fighting him would take a long time. It would take more care than she had to give it. His tongue in his mouth or that other part of him, both connected to a boy she could care less about really. With Sick she was D., and D. was smart and beautiful and kind, but this was Dev now and soon she would never see this boy again, and it was always over so fast and then she'd be walking away free.

"You gonna fucking drive me home?"

"I will, Dev. I promise, I will." Luke's voice so weak for her as he led her around the boathouse, his palm damp in her hand, his fingers cool. There were birch trees there she hadn't seen before, and he leaned against one and unsnapped and unzipped his jeans and now she didn't want to. She'd have to kneel on the ground that was dirt and pebbles. But Luke's thing was out, hard and straight and looking wrong in the air like that, and he grabbed her sweater and pulled her close, his eyes so hungry and so excited he looked a little scared, and even then she liked this part. She always had. That moment when she was everything and he was nothing.

Just once more and she was gone.

She squatted and drank down her hard lemonade and dropped the empty bottle onto a patch of snow, though she wished she hadn't done that because she would want something to drink soon.

It was taking a while. Her thighs were burning and her jaw ached, and she didn't like how he pulled on her head with two hands because it reminded her of Meghan Monroe in the bathroom. *No one does it like you, Dev.* So she worked harder with her hand to make it end faster and he was pushing into her mouth as if she didn't need to breathe and she was about to pull back when she heard behind her the sound of pebbles under a boot.

"Man, look at her." Price's voice, a wide smile in it, and she jerked back and opened her eyes to see his iEverything pointed at her, the tiny glass eye of his camera. "Davey!"

He was laughing, and Bobby was too, and Luke was quiet, but his fingers were in her hair and he pulled her face back to what she'd just let go of. "*C'mon*, I'm almost *done.*"

"*No.*" She tried to stand but he had her by the hair and with his other hand he was jerking back and forth on himself, and she couldn't breathe and then he let out a groan as warm spurts fell wetly across her cheek and nose and eye, and Davey was laughing as if he'd just scored points in a game, and Luke let go of her hair and she fell back on her hands. "Fucking *ass*holes!"

She turned and scooped a handful of dirty snow and wiped it across her face. She couldn't quite open her left eye, and with the other she saw Bobby up against the boathouse unzipping his jeans and pulling out his hard-on. He stepped toward her with it, and Davey was holding his iEverything close and Devon slapped at it and missed, and then she was up and pushing past Bobby and running across Luke's yard around his house and down the long driveway.

One of them was calling her, calling her name, and it was hard to see out of her eye and she wasn't running straight. The pine trees on both sides of her were so tall and so old, and she ran faster.

FRANCIS LIES IN THE DARK listening to the rain. It's eased up quite bit, just a smattering of it now and then against his window. When Devon came in an hour or so ago, he nearly climbed out of bed and pulled on his robe to greet her, but he couldn't. He kept seeing her concave cheek, and he just could not.

Ditch of the Bodos. It's where he'll store this image of Devy, too. Close a door on it and lock it. Never open it again. Except Francis knows this does not work, that she'll arrive in his dream world that way, a dirty movie of his precious niece for which he only has his nephew to thank. But does he? *See for yourself, Uncle.* Yes, Francis had left her room as quickly as he could have, bad knee and all, but why didn't he close his eyes? Certainly he knew without knowing what Charlie was up to. Surely, he could have looked away and seen only wall, door, hallway. Why did he look? Why this perpetual pull toward darkness? Why?

After Charlie was gone, Francis had walked down the hall and pulled Devon's door closed. Once again he'd been a passive participant in something ugly, and he heard Beth's voice as clearly as if she were standing behind him. *Quit stooping, Francis. You're tall, don't be ashamed of it.* But he was ashamed. Some part of him always had been. And he will not judge this child. He will not.

From the other side of his small house he can hear the muffled strains of her voice through her door and his. She's talking to that boy again. She must be. *He was in a war, too.* So perhaps he is not a boy after all. Perhaps he is a veteran of the recent wars, for every generation seems to get one, doesn't it? The old sending the young to far-off countries to kill other young people.

He will not judge Devy. How *can* he? This man who would drive away from the high school on a lovely October afternoon, the sun high, the dying tree leaves at the height of their beauty, and soon he'd be sipping vodka from a Styrofoam coffee cup while steering north up the highway for home and all the good work he'd done earlier in the day would be tossed into the fire he was building in his own blood and brain: Burn it, burn it all; burn being a good teacher, burn being a good man, burn being a good citizen and following the rules, and burn them especially—burn the rules, these invisible cages around us, for if he's learned nothing in all his years he's learned that, that from our first gasps for air till our last, we simply want to be left alone to do what we want to do when we want to do it, and because this is rarely the case we crave oblivion in any way it presents its dark, sweet self to us. Devy and her closed eyes and concave cheek, how is this any different from Francis pouring one nip then two then three more into his Styrofoam coffee cup, all of which he will stuff into the trash barrel outside the 7-Eleven before floating in for breath mints and bottled water and his smiling return to hearth and home?

"That's all I ever wanted, Uncle. A home for her, you know? A *home*."

"Drink some tea, Charlie."

Charlie did. He raised the cup and sipped loudly, his eyes on his reflection in the French doors. His shoulders were slumped, and he seemed to be staring at a man he used to want to talk to but no longer.

"I think she needs to hear that, Charlie."

"She fuckin' hates me."

"I don't think so."

Charlie held his cup in the air. He sipped again. He lowered it slowly, set it carefully onto its saucer.

"Well maybe *I* fucking hate me."

"Maybe you hate your behavior, nephew."

"What's the difference?"

"Behavior can be changed."

Charlie looked at him, his eyes pink and heavy-lidded. He held his head back accusatorily. "I don't think so."

This wasn't the time for argument. Not now.

"Charlie, I want you to rest on the couch for a while before you drive, okay?"

"Nope. I'm good." Charlie stood and drained his tea as if it was a beer. There was no reasoning with a drunk, and Francis knew he would have to stop him physically, but he'd gotten lucky once and doing it again was out of the question.

"Charlie, if you get behind that wheel, I will call the police."

"Do what you fucking want, Uncle. I'm going home."

Perhaps if Charlie had backed carefully out of the driveway, Francis would have done nothing. But his nephew's car had jerked backwards into the road, its headlights flashing across Francis's neighbor's windows, and then, as if he'd made his point, Charlie drove slowly away. For a long while, it seemed, Francis held the kitchen telephone in his hand. He saw the cracked foundation and splintered corner of that house on the boulevard. He saw his own crushed lower leg hanging in a sling. He saw the stainless steel bedpan in Beth's hands, and there was really no need to see anymore. He put on his glasses and dialed, trying to remember the make of his nephew's sedan, its color, its plates.

It's quiet now. No rain or gusts of wind. In the darkness, Francis can no longer hear Devy's muffled voice either, and he's relieved. His eyes are going, but his ears still seem to work and for this he's grateful. The strains of her voice, they were in the urgently confiding tones close friends use with one another. Or lovers. How is this possible?

But it's time for sleep. Early tomorrow he'll have to call Marie. Find out first if the police did locate and stop Charlie, which they may not have. But for Charlie's sake, Francis can only hope they did. Maybe it was even Jimmy Swansea, and then Francis will offer to do what he can. Charlie will need rides to and from work and—who knows?—perhaps meetings like the ones that saved his father. Like the ones that probably saved his marriage, too. And maybe tomorrow won't be the best day to take Charlie's mother to lunch. But then again, why not? Why not tell Evelyn it was him who did this? Her brother-in-law, Francis William Brandt, who'd taken action and hopefully prevented something catastrophic?

Francis's knee still hurts. He hopes he hasn't injured it, but he also feels more substantial than he has in a long while, his ship righting itself a bit. He sees himself standing before a sea of children not unlike Devon. On their own too soon, their faces a mask he'd like to talk his way into. Perhaps he should put his name in as a substitute. He can do that. One or two days a week, he should. Why not?

He turns on his side and rests his hand on the surface of the cool, empty sheet beside him. That Thursday night in January. He'd gone out for milk for her tea the next morning, that's all, just that, so who was this man who unlocked the door and closed it to the cold and hung up his coat and hat? Who was this man who took off his gloves and pushed them into his coat pockets and carried the milk into the warmth of their living room to find his wife fast asleep? Her reading glasses hung just beneath her nose, and her chin had dropped and what was this on her blue sweater? Oatmeal? No, for he could smell it as he lowered himself to her, and so this man was expecting a high fever, a stomach flu, a wife who would need Pepto-Bismol and help to bed. Not this stillness. Not this absolute quiet. Her hands he grasped falling away like useless objects left behind.

Francis feels sleep begin to cover him like a warm blanket. There is Devy's concave cheek and her closed eyes, Triz smiling up at him in the Tiki light, Beth's damp head leaning against his shoulder as he kisses her hair and lifts a dueling pistol and aims its long barrel at his own nephew who is running, running toward a ditch under an unrelenting sun.

DEVON OPENS HER LAPTOP and Skypes Hollis. It's past two, but he doesn't sleep. He says that's when they come for him, when he's lying on his bed in the quiet dark. He sees them, fathers and uncles, mothers and little kids, all huddled in their night clothes in the dirt.

The screen becomes his face. The lamp with the burned shade is on behind him, and he looks like he's been sleeping. He's clean-shaven and he's wearing a white T-shirt with a rip in it on his left shoulder. She can see his skin.

"Did I wake you?"

"No, honey. You know I don't sleep."

"Can I come see you? Like, really soon?" Her voice sounds young to her, and this makes her feel shy but Hollis is nodding his head, his eyes on her, and it's like what she's just said is a song in the air only he can hear. "In two days I'll be in my Airstream. Can you be here in two days?"

"I think so. I mean, I know so."

"You sure?"

"I have to."

"Good."

"Yeah, good." Devon feels a little scared, and Hollis lights up a cigarette. He's nodding again, smiling at her, blowing smoke through his nose as if it's love and he has so much of it, so much of it to give.

DEVON WALKS SOFTLY down the hallway. She flicks on the light over the kitchen table. On the counter beside the fridge is Francis's blood pressure medication and her GED notebook, and she grabs it, then pulls a pen from the jar of them under the phone. Aunt Beth's car keys hang beside Francis's. Her reading glasses still hang from a magnet on the fridge too, and Devon thinks how he's always been so quiet about missing her. *He's lucky to have you there, kid.* Her face warms. She glances at his bedroom door. It's open a few inches, and she tip-toes quickly across the kitchen and shuts off the light and hurries to her room.

She sits at the small desk she's never sat at before. She turns on the lamp. She pulls out her iEverything and sees it's 2:47 in the morning. The sun will be up soon. She opens the notebook and writes:

Dear Uncle Francis,

   If I could change the

She crosses this out. She slowly rips out the page and balls it up and flicks it at the wall. *Dirty Devon.* Bobby and Luke made that website, but what if tonight only her father logged onto it? What if Francis never saw it? He still knows. Her mean, shit-faced father, how could he not tell him about his tramp? She'd come to live with Francis to start clean. But how can anyone ever be clean with family? Blood is too dirty, dirty with love that can so easily turn to hate.

She writes:

Dear Uncle Francis,

   Thank you for being so good to me. I don't deserve it. Maybe I never did.

                    LOVE,
                    Devy

She reads it, then stands and leaves the notebook open to that page and drops the wadded paper into the trash basket. She carries the iron and ironing board back to the closet, and she folds the ironing board as quietly as she can and leans it under the closet shelf, pushing the iron up there and pulling her duffel bag down. It's the one she used for track meets so long ago, and as she stuffs her underwear and an armful of bras and T-shirts into it, she sees herself running again, running under a hot sun.

She picks her underwear and shorts up off the floor and empties the bureau drawers of her clothes, pushing them all into her bag on the bed. She cleans the bathroom and zips all she needs into a cosmetics case her mother loaned her. It's from Lord & Taylor, and Devon feels like she's stealing it. She shoves it on top of her clothes beside her laptop and cord, and she zips her duffel and carries it to the doorway. Then she makes her bed, pulling the spread as tightly as if she were at The Whaler. Outside her window the sky is still dark, but she knows it won't be for long.

She has almost six thousand dollars in the bank. She'll have to be there as soon as they open. She'll go to the one on River Street because they have a big parking lot down in the back near the flood-wall. It'll be a safe place to leave Aunt Beth's car. Then it's a short walk to the train station in Railroad Square, and she'll text her mother to call Francis and tell him where it is. She'll text her not to worry either.

But you should paint yurself, D. Sick. She'll text him, too. But first she'll sit back in her train seat and put on her Dr. Dre's and pick music that makes her feel free, the car rocking over the bridge rails and the swirling dirty water below, heading south to places she's seen on her screen but only from the insides of rooms in houses on streets in cities she used to think were all the same, but how can they be if Hollis Waters is from one of them?

She pulls the duffel bag over her shoulder. She glances down at her open note to Francis, then she's tiptoeing down his dark hallway and into his kitchen past the door to his bedroom where he sleeps alone. A hollowness opens up in her chest. She promises herself to come back and visit him before it's too late.

It's hard to see. There are only the shadows of things. She feels along the fridge to the wall and the phone, touching first her uncle's keys, then her dead aunt's, a woman Devon can feel judging her from the grave even though she's only borrowing something, not stealing it. She has never stolen anything in her life, and she never will. She steps into the cool, still air of the closed garage and she sees Sick's face. The way he looked at her as she let him in, the only one. His hair hung down and his lips were parted and as he moved inside her his eyes seemed to shine with a sweet sadness, the kind that only comes when you know something good can never, ever last. But you keep going anyway. All you can do is keep going and never quit.

ACKNOWLEDGMENTS

———

I'd like to thank Kourosh Zomorodian for his expertise on the work of a project manager. I'd also like to thank my mother-in-law, Mary Dollas, for her help with bank telling details. And I'm particularly grateful to my daughter, Ariadne, for her help with Facebook and cyberspace, in general.

And here's to my agent Philip Spitzer (and steadfast Lukas and Luc), and to my truly gifted and essential editor, Alane Salierno Mason.